WITHDRAWN

Praise for *Shoot the Bastards* (published in the U.K. as *Dead of Night*)

"…may belong with the darkest of Noir writing, but it is also utterly thrilling, multi-layered, skillfully executed, educational, thought-provoking and ultimately a really satisfying read."

—tripfiction.com

"I have discovered an exciting, new thriller writer and I can't wait to read more."

—alittlebookproblem.co.uk

"…scenes which will make you wince, others that will have you on the edge of your seat, heart pounding."

—jemedsbookreviews.com

"…the tension never ceases in this all action on the edge of your seat story."

—booksfromdusktilldawn.blog

"I was totally gripped by the feisty and determined female protagonist Crystal Nguyen, an undercover journalist investigating corruption and bribery."

—off-the-shelfbooks.blogspot.com

"The action and intrigue come thick and fast throughout the book, which is superbly paced. And it all leads to an explosive climax, which I found hugely satisfying."

—simplysuzereviews.blogspot.com

SHOOT THE BASTARDS

SHOOT THE BASTARDS

A CRYSTAL NGUYEN THRILLER

MICHAEL STANLEY

Poisoned Pen
PRESS

Published by Poisoned Pen Press, an imprint of Sourcebooks
P.O. Box 4410, Naperville, Illinois 60567-4410
(630) 961-3900
sourcebooks.com

Library of Congress Cataloging-in-Publication data is on file with the publisher.

Printed and bound in the United States of America.
SB 10 9 8 7 6 5 4 3 2 1

To the men and women involved in rhino conservation

CAST OF CHARACTERS

Boss Man	Crys Nguyen's name for Chu Nhan, boss of a smuggling gang in Ho Chi Minh City
Chikosi, Bongani	Game guide at Tshukudu; also works with an anti-poaching team in Kruger National Park
Chu Nhan	Boss of a smuggling gang in Ho Chi Minh City; Crys calls him Boss Man
Davidson, Michael	A journalist who investigated rhino poaching and rhino-horn smuggling before Crys
Dinh Van Duong	Official in the Vietnamese Department of Environmental Affairs
Do	Associate of Dinh Van Dong in Ho Chi Minh City

Donald	Associate of Søren Willandsen at End Extinction NGO in Ho Chi Minh City
Goldsmith, Sara	Editor at *National Geographic* magazine
Ho Van Tan	Vietnamese man who survives plane crash in the bush
Joe	Seller of rhino horn in Ho Chi Minh City, who works with the smugglers
Le Van Tham	Seller of rhino horn in Ho Chi Minh City
Mabula, Colonel	Son of Anton Malan
Malan, Anton	Owner of the Tshukudu Nature Reserve, who breeds rhinos and harvests their horns
Malan, Johannes	Son of Anton Malan
Ng	Supplier of rhino horn in Saigon Port
Ngane, Petrus	Night guard at Giyani police station
Nguyen, Crystal	Minnesotan journalist of Vietnamese descent
Phan Van Minh	Translator in Ho Chi Minh City
Pockface	Crys Nguyen's name for a thug from Mozambique involved with the rhino-horn smugglers

van Zyl, Hennie	Leader of an anti-poaching team in the Kruger National Park
Willandsen, Søren	Director of End Extinction NGO in Ho Chi Minh City
Wood, Nigel	Director of the Rhino International NGO in Geneva

Prologue

Michael Davidson wiped the sweat off his face, irritated that his hand was unsteady.

He'd been following the white pickup for almost two hours. He was actually surprised that he hadn't lost it somewhere along the way because he'd had to keep a long way back, as there was very little traffic. But the roads were straight with few major intersections—that had helped. Eventually, near a small town called Giyani, the pickup had turned onto a dirt road. After that he'd been able to drop even further back and just follow the dust train. The dust had stopped at the gate of a smallholding.

He drove slowly past at the entrance. The pickup was nowhere in sight and had probably been driven round the back of the ramshackle house. The entrance was nothing more than a double metal farm gate that you pulled closed by hand, with a cattle grid below it. It was secured with a padlock, but it wasn't much of a barrier.

He was very tempted to call it a day—he'd already connected most of the links in the rhino-horn smuggling chain. But there was still the crucial connection to establish—the one between the local traffickers and the people who would smuggle the horn out of the country to Mozambique. He had to document that.

And if his tipoff was correct, the transfer would happen today. This would be his one and only chance. And if he succeeded, the payoff would be big—both in money and reputation. But these were very nasty men, and they had a lot to lose.

He drove on until he found a driveway where he could pull off and be sure his vehicle wouldn't be seen from the road. Then he grabbed his camera and walked back to the padlocked gate. Perhaps he could just hide near it and photograph who came and went.

But once he reached the gate, the lure of a scoop was too strong to resist. If he merely photographed a vehicle leaving the farm, what would that prove? The chain would not be joined.

Anyway, they wouldn't be expecting anything—he was sure they hadn't noticed him following them. So, it wouldn't be such a huge risk, and there was thick brush around he could hide in if he had to.

He wet his lips and carefully scanned his surroundings. Nothing. Quickly, he clambered over the gate, dropped to the ground and moved off the driveway into the veld. A couple of cattle on the next property raised their heads and looked at him, but there was no other response.

He started to think about ways he could get close to the house. The problem was that the area immediately around it had been cleared. Some optimist had planted scraggy grass, but it had mostly lost the battle with the hard, dry ground. He couldn't see anywhere near the house where he could hide safely.

Then he heard a vehicle approaching.

He was surprised. The pickup had just got there.

Davidson dropped to the ground behind a low bush, thankful for at least a little cover.

He felt the familiar effects of an adrenalin surge. He'd done a stint covering the war in Afghanistan and, while he hadn't enjoyed the danger, there'd been a peculiar exhilaration in knowing that every step you took might be your last. But there also had been fear. And that was what he felt now.

A man came down the driveway and opened the gate for the vehicle that had just arrived. It headed up to the house, and he heard the man following it.

Then the footsteps stopped.

Michael pressed his body into the ground, annoyed with himself for not moving further into the bush. The footsteps started again.

Were they coming closer?

There was a snap of a twig.

Davidson realized the man wasn't on the road anymore and wondered if he should make a run for it.

But the man was close and almost certainly armed. Davidson's heart hammered.

He lay dead still, feeling the stones and grit through his jeans, and realizing that he'd picked up some thorns when he hit the ground. The back of his neck itched with sweat, and something many-legged was crawling on his arm. He forced himself to ignore it.

The man had stopped. Then he heard the sound of a urine stream hitting the dust. He heard a zip being pulled up, and the footsteps resumed up the driveway. He breathed a sigh of relief.

Shortly after, he heard voices and vehicle doors slam, but then it was all quiet again. They'd all gone into the house.

He lifted his head and looked around cautiously, but there was no sign of either vehicle. He decided the main entrance to the building must be on the other side.

He scrambled to his feet and rapidly worked his way further into the bush and round the house, trying to keep low and out of sight of any of the windows. After a few minutes, he could see the door with the pickup and the new vehicle parked in front of it. The problem was that from where he was, he wouldn't be able to see what was happening or take pictures, and if he tried to get much closer, he'd be exposed. He needed elevation.

He spotted a large sausage tree between him and the vehicles.

He'd have preferred to be closer, but then, further away was safer. The tree would have to do.

Hoping that the men were all engaged inside with their transaction and that they hadn't left a lookout, he worked his way forward, keeping the tree between him and the house. There were no sounds except those of the bush—the trill of insects, the harsh cackles of green wood-hoopoes. Reaching the tree, he stood up and realized he'd lucked out. From here he actually had a good view, and from up the tree he'd be able to see the front entrance and the vehicles clearly. He'd just have to climb high enough to be hidden by the large leaves and huge sausage-shaped fruits.

There was a convenient branch not too high off the ground, but it was dead. He'd have to use it to lever himself up, and if it broke it would attract attention. He clenched his teeth and reached up for it, trying to grab smaller side branches at the same time to distribute his weight. He could feel that the dead branch was brittle, felt it protest…felt it crack. But it held long enough for him to lift himself into the canopy. His haste caused some rustling, and the dead branch had made some noise. He held his breath, his heart racing again. There were still only the bush sounds.

He checked his camera and blew some dust particles off the lens. Then he got some pictures of the new vehicle—a beaten-up panel van—including its license plate, which indicated that it was from Mozambique. Just as he suspected. On the side was painted "Maputo Electrical" with a lightning logo.

Then he waited.

It took a while, but at last two men—Asian, by the look of them—emerged from the house, each with a holdall, obviously heavy. One of the white men he'd been following came out after them.

Davidson wondered if the other man was still in the house.

Michael slowly lifted his camera and rested the lens on a branch. It wasn't long before his patience was rewarded in a way he couldn't have dared hope for. To open the back door of the van, one of the men had to drop his holdall—and it wasn't fastened. For a few seconds, Davidson could see into the bag quite clearly through his zoom lens.

It was stuffed with rhino horns.

The man picked up the bag and tossed it into the back of the van, making no attempt to hide it, and his partner did the same.

As Davidson zoomed out to get a wider shot, the missing second white man walked into the viewfinder. He was at the side of the house. Michael froze, his heart thumping. The man was scanning with a pair of binoculars.

In a few moments, he would be focused on the sausage tree.

PART 1

Duluth, Minnesota

Chapter 1

Crys caught Kirsten, the leader, fifty yards before the crest of the hill. At the top, she was five yards ahead. It was all going to hinge on the last downhill.

Float on the downhills, her coach had told her. *Don't force it!*

Her lighter body would work against her. Kirsten was heavier and stronger.

Float! she told herself.

If she could get to the bottom even or slightly ahead, she was confident she was faster on the home stretch.

She concentrated on keeping her body loose.

The first turn was a long arc. She was still ahead as she came out of it. The second was a tester, steep and sharp. The type of turn she'd always struggled with, tightening up and not committing.

She could hear Carl's voice: *Float!*

She struggled to relax her muscles and headed into the turn. Down and around, faster and faster.

At the end of the turn, she was still ahead. Now a long straight. She could sense Kirsten gaining. Then she could see her, edging ahead.

Ahead was the last curve—sharp to the left followed immediately by a tight turn to the right.

Float!
Suddenly, Crys was in the zone. Fatigue and fear drained away. She was on the outside watching herself. Watching herself float through the taxing S-curve. Watching herself ahead by five yards at the bottom. Watching herself cross the finish line ten yards ahead of a struggling Kirsten. Watching herself raise her ski poles in unbridled joy.

———

"And the winner of the 2017 Minnesota Women's Biathlon is… Crystal Nguyen!"

The small, enthusiastic crowd of skiers and spectators whooped and applauded.

As she pushed through the crowd to the podium, Crys was experiencing an almost out-of-body experience. It was as though she was watching herself being patted on the back, relishing the taste of her first major win. Part of her was thrilled, part surprised at the positive reception, and part feeling a bit of an anticlimax after the hundreds of hours of training she'd put in.

As she stood between the two runners-up, holding the trophy above her head, she realized what a strange sight it must be. She, a typical Vietnamese woman—short, black hair, dark olive skin; they, tall, blond women of Nordic descent. She was pretty sure that it was the first time a woman who wasn't white had won such a high-profile race.

The press realized they had a good story, and photographers crowded around, cameras flashing.

"Crys, what's it like to be the first Vietnamese winner?" shouted a reporter in the crowd.

"I don't know what I'm feeling at the moment," she replied with a smile. "But I'm sure it's no different from what other winners feel—elation, satisfaction."

"But don't you feel proud that a Vietnamese can beat the Americans?"

"I don't think about my heritage when I'm skiing. I'm just proud to have won against such tough competition." She indicated the two women next to her. "Being Vietnamese has nothing to do with it."

Let's get this over with, she thought.

"Is there any particular aspect of your training that made the difference?"

Crys nodded and pointed at the back of the crowd. "My wonderful coach, Carl Hansen. Without him, I'd still be on the course." She lifted her hands and applauded in Carl's direction.

———

It was around eight o'clock when Crys opened the front door of her rented home on the outskirts of Duluth. She, Carl, and his wife, had enjoyed a leisurely celebratory dinner at a local restaurant. Now she wanted to savor the day by herself.

She loved the quietness of living on a cul-de-sac, with a forest as a neighbor, loved the fact that hardly anyone used the road in front of her house. No one ever peered in the windows or knocked on the door wanting to borrow a cup of sugar. Better yet, she wasn't asked to the occasional neighborhood get together. To the few people who lived on her road, she was invisible.

She lit the wood stove and sat down in her favorite chair. She had one thing to do before settling in. She picked up her phone. Should she phone? Or should she text? She could feel herself tense up. There was a risk either way. She wanted to phone, to speak to her mother, to tell her of her victory. But if her father heard them speaking…she shuddered at the thought of what he would do. Especially if he was in a bad mood. Which he usually was. It was a big risk. Normally they spoke when he wasn't around, usually when her mother was out shopping and could use a pay phone. They knew he often checked her mother's phone to see who she'd been speaking to.

Crys took a few deep breaths. She so wanted to share her good news and have a good chat. But she'd seen her mother's face after one of her father's tantrums. She couldn't take the chance.

Even a text was risky, even though she'd told her mother how to turn off the notification sound. But it was less risky—her mother could read it later, when alone, then delete it. Reluctantly she started typing.

After she'd pressed SEND, she unrolled her yoga mat on the floor. She needed to stretch and center herself after the excitement of the day. She sat down and slowly twisted into a half lotus, her tired muscles protesting with each stretch. She breathed deeply, closed her eyes, and quietly chanted her mantra: *Úm ma ni bát ni hồng. Úm ma ni bát ni hồng. Úm ma ni bát ni hồng. Úm ma ni bát ni hồng.*

It took some time before she was able to clear her mind of the myriad images of the day: the perfect shooting score, the terrifying final downhill, and the trophy—the trophy she and Carl had worked so hard for. Slowly, she began to relax. Her heart rate slowed, and she tried to open her mind to nothingness.

Half an hour later, she stretched out into the downward dog, holding it for a minute, then ended with a couple of minutes in the corpse pose.

When she stood up, she took her glass of water and sat next to the stove, gazing into the flames.

It had been an almost perfect day—with one exception. Her friend Michael had promised he'd fly in from New York to root for her, but he hadn't appeared.

Michael was a writer for the *New York Times*. They'd become good friends because of their shared interest in the environment, particular endangered species. He'd originally contacted her to talk about a series of articles she'd written for the *Duluth News Tribune* on the plight of gray wolves. After that, they'd emailed each other a lot, chatted on the phone, and met on several occasions at conventions in various parts of the country. They were kindred spirits and became close. He was serious and committed to wildlife, but he was also fun…and good-looking in a craggy sort of a way. He was the sort of man she'd been waiting for, and she could feel herself falling for him. So she'd been thrilled—with just a touch of jealousy—when *National Geographic* had invited him to write an article on rhino-horn smuggling.

While he was traveling in Vietnam and South Africa, they'd kept in touch as usual. He let her know what he'd learned on his trip, and then he'd tease her about the frigid weather in Minnesota. In return, she'd write that she knew the rhino assignment was just a cover for a vacation in the sun. They were both looking forward to getting together at the time of her big race. It would be great to have the support of such a good friend, Crys had told herself.

Then the emails stopped coming.

In his last email, about four weeks earlier, he wrote excitedly that he'd found out about how the rhino-horn embargo was being circumvented in South Africa and was going digging for the final pieces of information he needed for his article. He'd jokingly invited her to his inevitable Pulitzer reception.

Initially, she hadn't been concerned about his lack of contact; it was normal—he was pursuing a difficult story, after all. She understood that. But when she still hadn't heard from him after a couple of weeks, she'd started to worry. For the past ten days she'd been trying to contact him—both by email and by phone on his New York and South African numbers. All to no avail.

Finally, she'd sent an email to *National Geographic* asking whether they knew where he was, but they hadn't replied.

She decided that now she had some free time, she was going get to the bottom of the matter.

———

The next morning, she negotiated an early morning snowfall on the way to her office at the *Duluth News Tribune*. She poured herself a cup of coffee and sat down to plan what she needed to do to find Michael.

She pulled out her cell phone. First, she called Michael's New York numbers—at home and at the *New York Times*, but only reached voicemail messages that indicated he was on assignment overseas. As before, she left messages asking him to call her.

She also tried his South African number; it went to voicemail immediately, suggesting that the phone was turned off. She left a message there too.

She knew that Michael was from Princeton, New Jersey, but he'd told her that he wasn't on speaking terms with his father. That had struck a chord with Crys, who hadn't spoken to her own father for twelve years, since he threw her out of the house for not behaving as he thought an obedient Vietnamese daughter should.

Next, she called directory assistance and was given the numbers of three Davidsons in Princeton. She called the first and asked the man who answered whether he had a son, Michael Davidson.

"Why do you want to know?" he asked. "If you're trying to collect on his debts, you've come to the wrong place."

Crys guessed this wasn't the right Davidson, but it would be rude to just hang up.

"No, nothing like that. I'm looking for a Michael Davidson who is a journalist with the *New York Times*. I must have the wrong number."

"Yeah, that's my son. He's with the *Times*. What's it to you?"

"He and I are good friends and exchange emails quite often. I haven't heard from him for a while and was wondering if he was ill or something," she said, not wanting to worry him about his son being missing in Africa.

"I've no idea where he is. I haven't spoken to him for two years."

"He's on a project overseas and—"

"He's sure to be up to some no good somewhere or other. Probably hiding from the debt collectors."

Crys frowned. This conversation wasn't getting her anywhere.

"Would you have the number of his ex-wife? Maybe she knows something about where he is?"

He gave a sour chuckle. "Sheila? Forget it. She'd love to get her hands on him. He's always behind on his alimony payments, and he owes the doctors and hospital a fortune for his daughter's surgery. Fool didn't have health insurance. Must have got his brains from his mother."

"I'm sorry I disturbed you, Mr. Davidson." Crys was eager now to hang up. She didn't want to listen to any more unpleasant family stories. "Thank you, though."

"Good luck finding him," the man said and rang off.

Crys felt a pang of sadness that he seemed to care so little about his son. Shouldn't he be concerned, no matter what had happened between them in the past? She knew Michael had been married, but was puzzled that he hadn't mentioned a daughter. She wondered if he was scared that telling her would put her off him. Or perhaps whatever had happened to her was too painful to talk about. And whatever his father had said, Crys was pretty sure Michael would be paying off his debts. He just seemed that sort of person.

There was one more call she wanted to make before calling *National Geographic* to follow up on her email.

"Barbara Zygorski," the voice on the other end of the line said.

"Hi, Barb. This is Crys Nguyen. How are you?"

"Well, thanks. It's been a long time."

"Sure has. I wonder if you've heard from Michael recently."

"Not for a while. Probably a month or so. Last I heard he was heading for Mozambique, hot on the trail of some smugglers. What's up?"

"I'm really worried. He's usually so good at dropping a line every day or so. Now it's been four weeks."

"Knowing him, he's probably up to his ears in crocodiles somewhere in the bush. With no internet connection."

"You've been at the *Times* a long time—would you do me a big favor?"

"If I can."

"Could you ask someone in IT to check if Michael has used his email account anytime since I received my last email from him? It was exactly four weeks ago today."

There was silence on the line. Crys decided to wait for a response.

"I don't know…"

"Look, I know it's against policy and all that, but this could help us find him. I'm sure you know someone who won't blab."

Another pause. Then: "Okay, Crys. I'll see what I can do, but I'm not making any promises."

Crys thanked her and hung up.

Finally, she phoned the *National Geographic* office and asked for Sara Goldsmith, the editor who'd offered Michael the rhino assignment.

Crys introduced herself and explained she was calling because she'd not heard back in response to the email she'd sent inquiring about Michael Davidson's whereabouts.

"I do apologize for that," Goldsmith said, "but I've been trying to find out where he is myself. I was waiting to have some definite news before I got in touch with you."

"Do you mean you haven't heard from him either?"

"Well, when he was in Vietnam, and after he headed for South Africa, he'd email me every few days with updates and asking me to keep his notes and photos for safekeeping. Then about a month ago, his emails stopped coming. The last place we know he was at was a rhino farm called Tshukudu Nature Reserve near Kruger National Park. I spoke to them recently, and they said that he had been there, but had then left for Mozambique—something he hadn't told me about. Anyway, we then contacted the South

African police and asked for their help. They took a while to get back to us, and when they did, they said that the only contact they'd had with Michael was in a town called Phalaborwa, where he'd interviewed the police chief about some poachers they'd caught who'd been given stiff prison sentences. They did tell us that South African Immigration had confirmed that Michael went to Mozambique around that time, then returned ten days later. There's no record of him leaving South Africa after that. I insisted that they open a missing person's docket, but I haven't heard back, I'm afraid."

"So, he must still be in South Africa, unless he left illegally— which is unlikely."

"We're worried that something may have happened to him," Goldsmith said. "Smugglers are generally not a pleasant group of characters."

Crys's chest tightened. "Have you contacted his family?"

"As far as I know he's an only child, and he told me his mother died young. I located his father, but he said the two hadn't spoken in years."

"I just spoke to him too. He has no idea where Michael is… and apparently doesn't care."

There was a silence. Cry wondered what could have happened and realized Sara must be doing the same thing.

"You've got to send someone to find him," Crys said at last. "You can't just stop looking."

"We've thought about hiring a private investigator, but nobody who has anything to hide will speak to them. They'll just clam up. We'll be wasting our money and end up knowing no more than we do now. I guess we just have to leave it to the police for the moment."

"But you've got to do something!" Crys protested with a sinking feeling that everyone had washed their hands of Michael.

"So, what do you suggest Ms. Nguyen?"

"I…I don't know…"

When Crys put the phone down, she slumped in her seat. It seemed that Goldsmith had spoken to everyone Michael had had recent contact with, without any success. Michael had truly disappeared.

And no one seemed to care too much about it.

Chapter 2

That evening, Crys couldn't focus on anything. She tried to watch TV—a BBC wildlife documentary—but she couldn't concentrate. Her mind kept wandering to Michael and what could have happened to him. No one went off the radar for a month without letting someone know where they were. But what could they do to find him?

Sara Goldsmith hadn't been optimistic that a private eye would ever get close to the people who had useful information, and she was probably right. Government officials and the police would be open to meeting, and perhaps the farmers that Michael had spoken to would, too, but the people actively involved in poaching almost certainly would stay clear.

So, who was left? That was the question that haunted Crys for most of the evening.

The answer came to her when answers often did—when she was in a yoga position and her mind was clear. She should go herself.

It made perfect sense. She had a strong personal interest: she really liked Michael and their friendship was developing. She had the qualifications: she was a relatively well-known environmental writer with a strong background in investigative journalism. Her general focus of interest was endangered species—and rhinos certainly fit that bill. And she had the time—her last major project had just been published.

All she had to do was convince *National Geographic* to send her to look for him and work on the article.

She untwisted from her half lotus and was so excited by the idea that she nearly forgot to end her session with stretches and a cool down.

When she stood up, she could barely wait until the morning, when she could call Sara Goldsmith and make her suggestion.

———

"Good morning, Ms. Nguyen. I didn't expect to hear from you so soon. Have you heard from Michael?"

"Good morning, Ms. Goldsmith. Unfortunately, I haven't. But I have been stewing over our conversation yesterday and the fact we couldn't come up with a good plan to look for him."

Goldstein didn't respond.

"Okay, so I have a suggestion that I've thought through carefully, which I think would work."

"And that is?"

Crys hesitated, then took the plunge. "I'll go…"

She paused, but again there was silence from the other end of the line. She realized she was going to have to convince Sara.

"I can go under the pretext of writing a story about rhino poaching—just like Michael. If you'll let me see his notes, I should be able to speak to the same people he spoke to and perhaps find out who he thought was involved in his big story."

"Hmm…it's an interesting idea," Goldsmith said at last. "And you're willing to fund yourself?"

Crys took a deep breath. "Actually, I was hoping that you would hire me to finish writing Michael's story."

This time there was a very long pause. Crys wished she'd

worked her way around to the suggestion rather than just throwing it out immediately. But she wasn't good at prevarication.

"I don't know," Goldsmith said eventually, and Crys's heart sank. "I'm worried that Michael may have run afoul of the smugglers—they are *very* nasty, I believe. I wouldn't want the same to happen to you."

"Ms. Goldsmith, I can do the job. I'm an investigative reporter and deal with environmental affairs…."

"I know who you are," Goldsmith interjected. "That's not the issue. I've been very impressed with the reporting you've done on the plight of gray wolves and how poaching disrupts their social groups."

For a moment Crys was taken aback. This was a huge compliment, coming from such a prestigious source. She felt herself blush.

"Thank you," she stammered. "I wouldn't have thought you'd ever have read any of my work."

"Because of who we are and the people who are our customers, we try to keep tabs on everyone who's doing good work in the same areas as us. Your name has popped up a few times, including from Michael, so we've been keeping an eye on what you've been up to. I thought your gray wolf piece in the *Duluth News Tribune* last week was excellent. And it was widely syndicated too."

Crys wasn't sure what to say, so she just repeated a thank you.

"So, what you're suggesting is that *we* send you," Goldsmith continued, "because you'll have a better chance of gaining access because of the *National Geographic* connection. Is that right?"

"Exactly."

There was a silence. And the longer it lasted, the less optimistic Crys became.

"I don't know."

"Please give it some thought, Ms. Goldsmith. We have to do something. This isn't just about the story. Michael may be in serious trouble. We have to find out what has happened to him."

"Give me a call tomorrow. I'll have an answer, but don't get your hopes too high."

———

The next twenty-four hours moved as slowly as the sap from the maple trees next to her house during a spring cold snap. Every time Crys looked at her watch, after what seemed like hours, only minutes had passed.

She slept so badly that she left the house at seven the next morning to ski for an hour. Anything to keep her mind off the clock. She'd had three cups of the *Duluth News Tribune*'s coffee by the time she called Sara Goldsmith again.

"It's Crys Nguyen, Ms. Goldsmith."

"Please, call me Sara…"

"Have you thought about my suggestion?"

"Of course."

Crys waited anxiously for her to continue.

"Are you sure about this, Crys? If Michael ran into trouble researching his story, you could too. It could be extremely dangerous."

"I'm willing to take that risk. And I'll be very careful."

"If I say yes, when could you leave?"

"As soon as I can get organized. Perhaps by tomorrow night. Every day may make a difference to Michael's safety."

"Crys, listen to yourself. You're talking about rescuing him, not finding him. That's a big difference. You aren't qualified to rescue anyone…but, I suppose you are qualified to find someone."

Crys held her breath. Had she overstepped the mark in her enthusiasm?

There was another of Sara's long silences.

"Okay, Crys. I have management permission to hire you to work with Michael on finishing his piece. We'll obviously pick up all expenses, and there's a reasonable stipend if we publish your article."

Crys felt a huge wave of relief. "Thank you, Sara. Thank you. I won't let you down. I promise. Please send Michael's material by overnight. I'll email you the address. And also, please email me the names of anyone you know he spoke to so I can set up meetings with them."

"I'll send the email now, and you'll get the material tomorrow morning. I'll include the remit I gave to Michael. So, you'll know what we asked him to do. Any questions?"

"Not at the moment," Crys replied, her head spinning with excitement.

"There is one other thing: Michael's deadline is six weeks from now. I need you to meet that."

"Six weeks? For the travel and research and writing? Michael had more than twice that."

"If you don't think you can…"

"No, no, of course, I can make it. I was just taken back by how quickly everything was happening. You'll have your article on time."

"And remember, Crys—officially I'm sending you because I need that article. That's your first priority. Understood?"

"Yes."

"If you can find out about Michael, so much the better. But that's not your top priority. And anything you do find out, you report it to the police. Don't put yourself at risk."

———

After she hung up, Crys gave a series of fist pumps. Not only could she look for Michael, but *National Geographic* had just given her a huge professional opportunity. And she'd get to a continent she'd always wanted to visit. After wolves, elephants were her favorite animal, even though she'd never seen a live one. And Africa had the biggest population of them in the world.

There was another huge bonus. She would have to go to Vietnam.

She'd been born there, but when she was a year old, she, her mother and her brother had left for Minnesota, taking advantage of the refugee program. Crys had never been back.

She stood up and walked down the hallway to her boss, Scott Nielsen's, office.

He looked up as she came in. "You look pretty pleased with yourself."

Crys nodded, a huge smile lighting up her face. "*National Geographic* has asked me to be a co-author on an article on rhino poaching! I'll have to go to South Africa."

"That's wonderful! When do you need to leave?"

"Tomorrow!"

"Tomorrow?" Scott gasped. "Why so soon? I've stuff I want you to do."

As she explained what had happened and why she was offered the job, Scott raised his eyebrows. "You never cease to amaze me, Crys. Now you're a one-woman search-and-rescue mission. Okay, you'd better get going, but there's a price for me being so accommodating—a weekly column on what you've been up to in Africa. Okay?"

She nodded. "Of course. It'll be fun to write something more casual than the *Geographic* stuff."

"Drop me an email tonight about the projects you're working on. I'll make sure they're covered."

"Thanks, Scott. I just can't believe this has happened to me."

———

That night Crys was frantic. There was so much to organize.

She started by going online and buying an open ticket to Johannesburg via Atlanta.

It was going to be fifteen hours on the plane. Not her favorite activity.

She then sent off a number of emails to set up appointments in South Africa, to be followed up the next day with calls.

The next morning, she raced around Duluth trying to find clothes more suitable for Africa than Minnesota, and a good, but not-too-expensive, camera.

When she got home, the parcel from Sara was on her doorstep. She grabbed it, made a cup of coffee, and skimmed through Michael's material to find out who he'd spoken to and what he'd learned about rhino poaching and rhino-horn smuggling.

She was immediately drawn into his investigation. He'd met with several government officials and NGOs in Vietnam, as well as some people involved in selling rhino horns and rhino-horn powder. It seemed that either consumption was increasing or supply was decreasing, because several of the people selling rhino horns had complained about a shortage and rising prices.

After that, he'd gone to South Africa. And that's where the trail stopped. There was nothing since he'd emailed her and Sara about being close to a breakthrough on how rhino horn was being smuggled out of that country.

There was no hint of what he had found out or who was involved. It was a mystery.

She put the notes aside with a frown. Now she needed to pack. She could read the material more carefully on the flight to Johannesburg. Perhaps she would find some detail she'd missed

PART 2

South Africa

Chapter 3

Crys wanted to scream. She'd been sitting outside the minister's office at the Department of Environmental Affairs in Pretoria for more than two hours, basically twiddling her thumbs. Instead of interviewing the minister about the future of the rhino population in South Africa, she was struggling to keep awake as jet lag took hold of her body. To make matters worse, she'd heard nothing from Delta about her luggage, which had failed to show up on the carousel at Johannesburg's Oliver Tambo airport the night before.

"Do you think the minister will be available soon?" she asked the minister's secretary for what felt like the hundredth time.

The secretary shrugged. "Dr. Duma said she'd be back by now, but it was the president who wanted to see her. He's a little unpredictable when it comes to time."

"I've flown here all the way from the United States for this appointment," Crys said, trying to keep the annoyance out of her voice.

Organizing the meeting with the minister by phone from Duluth had been difficult enough. Now she didn't think she was going to see the minister at all. Crys forced a smile, trying to keep in the secretary's good books. "What does her schedule look like tomorrow?"

The secretary glanced at her computer screen. "Impossible. She has a meeting at eight. Then a lunch with her counterpart from Mozambique, and in the afternoon, she flies to Switzerland. The best I can do is to take you to Mr. Tolo, the deputy minister. Let me call him and see if he's willing to talk to you."

Crys wasn't happy with the offer, but accepted reluctantly. But she did recognize the deputy minister's name from Michael's notes. The minister had sent Michael to meet with him as well.

A few minutes later, she was shown into Tolo's office. He waved her to a seat and went back to reading a letter.

At last he looked up. "What can I do for you, Miss Nguyen?" He pronounced her name "Naguyen".

Tired and irritable, Crys couldn't stop herself: "It's pronounced like the word 'when'. It's Vietnamese." Seeing his raised eyebrows, Crys tried to adopt a more pleasant tone. "It's very difficult to pronounce, I know. And thank you for agreeing to see me, Mr. Tolo, particularly at such short notice."

Tolo stared at her, impassive, so Crys pulled out her notebook and launched straight into her list of questions.

But he wasn't helpful, and Crys found his answers superficial, even evasive at times.

She told herself to keep calm.

She was frustrated, though, that she had to keep pushing to get answers to her most important questions and began to think that Tolo either didn't know much about the rhino situation, or simply didn't care.

Eventually, he held up his hand. "Miss Nguyen," he said, using the same mangled pronunciation as before, "we appreciate your concern about the rhino population here. But we know what we're doing. We're managing the situation."

"Mr. Tolo, I'm not here to judge," Crys said, "just to gather facts for an article *National Geographic* has asked me to write. Southern Africa lost about fifteen hundred rhinos last year, with over a thousand of those in South Africa itself. How can you say you have the situation under control?"

Tolo sucked in his lower lip. "I didn't say there wasn't a problem. I said we're doing what we can. South Africa is much stricter on these things than most other countries in Africa. And poachers are often shot on sight here—although that's not allowed, or encouraged, of course. We appreciate the support we get from *National Geographic* and the World Wildlife Fund and so on, but we don't need to be told how to run things." The smile he now gave her wasn't exactly warm. "Maybe you should visit your countrymen in Vietnam and tell *them* to stop buying rhino-horn powder. That would be a huge help."

"I'm going there when I've finished here," Crys replied, trying to keep the irritation out of her voice. "And I certainly plan to ask why they're the biggest consumers of rhino-horn powder."

Tolo didn't respond; he just pointedly glanced at his watch.

Crys realized her time with Tolo was running out, so she tried a different approach. "Some experts advocate legalizing trade in horns that have been legally obtained—from rhinos that have died naturally in a national park, for example. What is the South African government's position on that?"

He shook his head as though it was a stupid question. "CITES is the body that regulates international trade in animal and plant products, and they're against that practice. However, as you probably know, it is legal to trade rhino horns here in South Africa, as long as they are not exported. But as there's no local demand, it makes no difference."

"What about sawing off the horns?" Crys asked. "Some private game farms have done that. And they stopped losing rhinos right away."

Tolo sucked his lip again. "Impossible! That may work for a game farm, but in a big national park where there are thousands of rhinos? You have to find them, dart them, and remove the horns. That's very expensive. Tens of thousands of dollars each time. Then they grow back, so you have to do it all again a few years later. Where's the money going to come from?"

Crys wasn't getting anywhere.

"Mr. Tolo, a colleague of mine from *National Geographic*, a Michael Davidson, interviewed you a few months ago. I wonder if you've spoken to him since."

Tolo shook his head. "I remember talking to someone from your magazine, but don't remember his name. But I'm sure I haven't spoken to him since. Why do you ask?"

"We haven't heard from him for a while, and he hasn't returned to the U.S. from South Africa. We're concerned."

Tolo just shrugged. "In that case, I suggest you take it up with the police rather than Environmental Affairs."

"As part of the research for my story," Crys continued, realizing she wasn't going to learn anything about Michael, "I'd like to spend time with one of the anti-poaching units in a national park. I want to see how they operate. Can you arrange that?"

"Impossible! It's too dangerous. It's a war out there, you know. As I told you, some of the patrols shoot to kill. And the poachers shoot back. I can't put you at that kind of risk."

Crys started to explain to him how she could look after herself, but could tell he just saw a young Vietnamese woman who'd only be in the way. She sighed. It wasn't the first time she'd had that problem.

He stood up and, after scrabbling around in a filing cabinet, handed her a thick envelope. "There's lots of background information in here. I'm sure it will answer any other questions you have. Now, I'm afraid I have another appointment."

Crys had nothing to show for her morning except a few notes that added nothing to what Michael had already written.

———

As she left the building, a wave of heat hit her. It was difficult for her to comprehend that just three days before, she was cross-country skiing in Minnesota at twenty degrees Fahrenheit. In Pretoria, it was about ninety-five degrees and sticky.

If she didn't miss Tolo's attitude, she certainly missed his air conditioning.

There was a rush of people on the sidewalk. South Africa's economy may have been shaky, but downtown Pretoria was frenetic. A scruffy man came up to Crys and asked her for money. She shook her head and started to move away, but he followed.

"I'll get you a taxi," he said. Crys shook her head again. It had only taken a few minutes in the cab to get to the department from the hotel, and she was looking forward to the walk back. Fortunately, he wasn't persistent and vanished into the crowds.

As she walked on, however, she had the sensation she was being watched. She spun around just in time to see the man who'd asked her for money. He quickly looked away and pretended to be going in another direction.

She thought he was probably looking for an easy target.

Crys knew more than a little karate. A scrawny pickpocket didn't worry her; but she did hold her briefcase more firmly, and when she reached her hotel was pleased to escape the crowds and the heat.

When she opened the door to her room, Crys was relieved to see her suitcase on the bed. At last, something was going right: Delta had actually come through with its promise to deliver.

Crys went to open it, but as she did, she noticed that both locks were broken. All that was preventing the contents from falling out was the colorful strap she always used—more for identification than for security.

Crys groaned. Her next stop was at Tshukudu Nature Reserve on the border of the Kruger National Park, so she'd have to buy a new suitcase before heading out there.

She flipped the case open.

"What the—?" Crys couldn't believe what she was seeing. Someone had been through her belongings. Her neatly folded clothes had been taken out, scrunched up, and stuffed back in; all her toiletries had been removed from their bag, but not replaced. And the lining of the case had been cut. Someone had been checking to see whether anything was hidden behind it.

She wondered why anyone would do something like that.

It wouldn't be customs—Crys had traveled a lot and knew they were usually halfway decent at repacking suitcases. She pulled out her phone and pressed the number for Delta's baggage services.

After waiting for an age to get through to the right person, Crys was assured that her bag had left the airport in good shape. She frowned as she rang off, staring at her jumbled belongings. Could this have happened after her suitcase arrived at the hotel?

She picked up the room phone, called the concierge and asked if he had taken delivery of the suitcase.

"Yes," he replied, "at about half past two."

"Did you notice if it was in good shape?"

"Yes, it was. Is there a problem?

"Yes, there *is*! It's wrecked—someone's broken it open. And they've been through it. My stuff's all messed up."

"I'll call the police right away, madam."

"No…don't bother." Crys sighed, dropping onto the bed, exhausted. "My insurance will cover the suitcase itself, and I don't think I've lost anything. It'll just be a waste of time to get the police involved. But…" She thought for a moment. "You didn't notice anyone following the porter who delivered the suitcase to my room, did you?

"No, madam."

"Who has access to room keys? Because if the porter delivered it intact, somebody searched it *in* the room."

"No one other than the housekeeping staff has a master key. And also the porter—but he only had it while he was taking it up for you."

"Would it be possible to look at any CCTV you have of the

foyer of the hotel and the passage to my room, please? I'd only need it from the time the suitcase was delivered to you."

There was a silence. Then he answered that he'd check with the manager, but didn't think there would be a problem. He'd let her know the next morning.

Crys thanked the man and hung up.

She was beginning to feel a little spooked—first the man following her and now this. She lay back on the bed, letting the cool draft of stale air from the air conditioning unit flow over her, but her mind was still racing. Her first day in South Africa hadn't been a good one.

Crys decided a little yoga would help her calm down, so she folded a towel on the floor, sat down, and twisted into a half lotus. She breathed deeply, closed her eyes, and started softly chanting her mantra: *Úm ma ni bát ni hồng. Úm ma ni bát ni hồng. Úm ma ni bát ni hồng. Úm ma ni bát ni hồng.*

She slowly began to relax. Her mind focused. Her heart rate slowed, and she tried to open her mind to good thoughts. But images of the vandalized suitcase rattled around her head. *Úm ma ni bát ni hồng. Úm ma ni bát ni hồng.*

After about thirty minutes, Crys brought herself back to the present, uncoiled, and went for a hot shower. She resigned herself that there was nothing more she could do that evening, so prepared for a night of jet-lagged sleep.

As she put her head on the pillow, Crys realized there was a bright spot in all of this. She could use her bad first day as a topic for her special column for the *Duluth News Tribune*.

With that thought in mind, Crys closed her eyes and fell into a troubled sleep.

Chapter 4

When she woke up the next morning, Crys realized it was time to put the bad start to the trip behind her and move on.

She'd contacted the Tshukudu Nature Reserve before she'd left Minnesota, and they'd said she was welcome anytime. It was a private conservancy where they protected rhinos, but also bred them and harvested their horns.

Crys phoned the main number and asked to speak to Johannes Malan, with whom she'd exchanged emails. When he came to the phone, Crys asked if she could take him up on his offer and visit for a few days.

"I'd like to arrive tomorrow, if that's okay?"

"Of course. Take the 11:45 SAA Airlink flight from Oliver Tambo International to Phalaborwa. We'll meet you around one." Crys was intrigued by his accent—flat and rough, with rolled r's. "It's about a two-hour hour drive back to Tshukudu. Call me if there are any problems."

At last a positive response. Crys immediately felt better. Tshukudu was the last place she knew Michael had been. She had high hopes that she'd be able to pick up his trail from there.

Her excitement mounted as she realized that she was soon going to be in the real African bush.

———

With time to spare and a lovely day outside, Crys decided to go for a run. After nearly twenty-four hours of being cramped in planes, her body needed the exercise.

She put on her running clothes and shoes, grabbed her point-and-shoot camera, and walked out of the hotel. What struck Crys immediately was that nearly everyone on the streets was black, from beggars, to street vendors, to men in tailored suits—businessmen or politicians, she guessed, this being the country's capital. It was a huge contrast to Duluth's sea of Scandinavian blond dotted with just a few black faces.

Crys ended up spending as much time taking photographs as she did running. There was color everywhere. She loved the elegant women in their vivid, African dresses and was amazed at the street vendors selling everything from food to intricate toys made from wire—something that wouldn't happen in Duluth.

And then there were the gorgeous trees that had no leaves but were smothered in hundreds of small blue flowers. She'd read that Pretoria was called the jacaranda city and now understood why; almost every street was lined with them. And with what seemed overkill, blue-flowered agapanthus grew below the jacarandas, almost as though they were offspring.

And the birds—they were nothing like the ones she knew in Minnesota. They were of all colors, sizes, and shapes. She spotted one big character with a curved beak and a raucous call, as though it was crying "haaa!" And a little further on, some tiny, iridescent birds that reminded her of hummingbirds were dipping their beaks into the trumpet-like flowers of a roadside plant.

But Crys decided Pretoria wasn't a good running city. The sidewalks were uneven, and the car traffic was heavy, and she could feel the fumes in her throat. So, after about an hour's jogging and sightseeing, she returned to the hotel.

As she walked through the lobby, she stopped at the concierge's desk to ask whether they'd checked the CCTV coverage.

"I am so sorry, Ms. Nguyen. There seems to have been a technical problem. The man who services the cameras didn't push the flash drive in far enough, so nothing has been recorded since yesterday morning. A bad mistake. We're looking into it."

That was convenient, she thought. It was quite a coincidence that the cameras were off at exactly the time someone was breaking into her room. Except, of course, they hadn't broken in. So, they must have had a key.

Crys shook her head and gave the concierge a hard look. He glanced away. He knew she'd seen through his story. But she decided to drop the matter—there wasn't much more she could do about it.

———

From her room, Crys placed a call to Lieutenant Mkazi at the Phalaborwa police station. He had responded to Sara's inquiry about Michael, and Crys wanted to know what progress had been made since then—if any.

When she was eventually put through, she explained who she was and asked what the police had discovered.

"We have been following this up, Ms. Nguyen, but it takes time to track down what has happened to people. Let me say first that we are doing everything we can. But we have a big area here—some of it wild country. We can't search everywhere."

Crys deduced immediately that he had no news.

"We have looked for his rental car, and we have tried to trace his cell phone. Neither has helped. The phone was off for some time in the area of Giyani—that is a small town north of here—but then it moved from there. Of course, we don't know if Mr. Davidson was with it. And then at some point the signal went off permanently. Perhaps the battery went flat. Perhaps it was destroyed. The place where that happened is in the bush. There's nothing there. And at that point the phone was moving. We suspect it was in a vehicle."

"He has two cell numbers—a U.S. one and a South African one. Did you trace them both?"

There was a pause. "Please give me the numbers."

She did, and Mkazi promised to check.

"When the phone went dead, was it in his vehicle?"

"We can't say. The car rental company has tracking devices on their cars, but this one could not be activated. Perhaps it was faulty, but..."

As Crys digested all this, she felt almost nauseated. It didn't sound good. If Michael had broken down somewhere with a flat cell phone or no signal, the car's transponder should still have identified the location.

"And there's been no trace of him?"

"No, that is correct."

No trace...Crys forced herself to ask the next question. "So, what do *you* think happened to him, Lieutenant?"

There was a long silence. Crys thought the man wasn't going to answer her question at all.

But at last he did. "We cannot say. Sometimes people are hijacked. The cars are quickly broken up and the tracking devices disabled. Most times the people are released and they are found. Occasionally not. A month is a long time..."

Crys swallowed. There didn't seem much more to say. She thanked him and disconnected. For a few minutes, she sat dead still, her shoulders slumped, wondering if she was wasting her time and *National Geographic*'s money. But then she realized that nothing had really changed. The police knew nothing more than before. This was all just speculation.

Michael was onto something big. He was on someone's trail. Whatever happened was related to that, not some random hijacking.

She wasn't going to give up hope, but resolved to find out exactly what his big story was. She *was* going to find him.

The next morning, Crys headed out, eager now to be in the African bush, away from the frustrations of the city.

Phalaborwa Airport was unlike anything she'd seen before. It was of African design with long wooden beams and a high thatched roof. Much of it was open to the outside. It would be no good in a Duluth winter, she thought.

Johannes came himself to meet her. He was the stereotype of the white African bush guide—boots, khaki shirt and shorts, and a sunburnt face, a bit spoiled by a scraggly beard. Crys guessed he was in his mid-thirties. He was also a few pounds overweight. Crys had read that South Africans liked their beer, so that was probably the cause.

He took her bag and put it in the back of his truck, then opened the passenger door for her with a smile.

"It's a bit of a drive, I'm afraid, Ms. Nguyen." Crys ignored the mangling of her name. "We've got two thousand hectares to the west of the Kruger National Park. We're part of a big game-conservation area bordering the park. It's mostly private farms running tourism, hunting, and so on…in our case it's rhino conservation."

Two thousand hectares, Crys thought. That was nearly four and a half thousand acres. A big ranch by anyone's standards.

It was not long before they'd left the small town behind and were on their way through the bush. After a few minutes, Johannes pulled over and pointed out a group of antelope not far from the road.

"Those are kudu. One of the biggest antelopes around here."

They were gorgeous creatures: sandy-colored with gentle stripes and huge corkscrew horns. One took fright and ran off, its tail folded back, flashing white.

They drove on, both still smiling at the sight.

"There aren't any other visitors at the lodge right now," said Johannes. "So, you'll eat dinner with my father and me in the main house tonight, if that's okay?"

"That sounds great. Thank you."

After a while, Crys decided to ask about Michael.

"Johannes, a friend of mine from *National Geographic*—his name is Michael Davidson—he visited Tshukudu a month or so ago. Do you remember him?"

Johannes shook his head. "My father told me that someone from your magazine had visited, but I was taking some tourists on a safari at the time, so I never met him. He was also working on rhinos, wasn't he?"

"That's right."

"Are the two of you going to meet up to exchange notes?"

"I hope so, but we've lost track of him. I was hoping you may know where he was headed."

Johannes shook his head. "I don't, but my father may. Ask him over dinner."

It was another two hours of driving through the countryside before they came to an impressive entrance made of stone. The guard lifted the boom and waved them through, onto a road that was little more than a bumpy dirt track through the bush.

As they lurched along, Johannes's radio squawked. He stopped the truck, picked up the mike, and started talking in a language Crys didn't understand.

After Johannes had finished speaking, he asked Crys if she was up for a little detour. "They've found a rhino that's been caught in a snare. I think you'll be interested in how we deal with it."

Crys nodded enthusiastically. "Rhino poachers?" she asked, pulling her notebook from her backpack.

"No—poachers use high-powered rifles. This was probably set for a big antelope like the kudu we saw. Someone wanted it for the meat. The rhino's yanked the snare out of the ground, but it's cut into her foot, so we're going to have to dart her and cut the wire off. You'll be able to watch the whole process."

As they drove on, Crys was already thinking of the copy she could write. She pulled her camera out of her backpack and clipped on a medium-range zoom. This could be an amazing column for the newspaper, she thought.

When they arrived, the rhino was staggering about, and the rangers were keeping their distance. Johannes looked worried. "It's Mary," he said. "She's a fixture around here. They must have darted her already. If she falls badly, she could hurt herself. I'd hate it if anything happened to her."

They watched for a few tense minutes, unable to help, but at last Mary lay down and passed out. But it was another ten minutes before Johannes said it was safe to approach.

"You can touch her."

Crys put out her hand and felt the rough hide and hair. Up close Mary was a really impressive beast, but there was something disturbing to see her lying there, being handled like a domestic animal. Crys stepped back and began to take pictures.

A ranger cut off the snare with wire cutters, and then Johannes examined the wound in Mary's foot.

"It's not deep," he said. "We do have to worry about infection, though, so we'll dose her with antibiotics and put on some antiseptic cream."

One of the rangers adjusted the radio collar she wore like a loose necklace and changed the batteries. Another came up and talked to Johannes, pointing at the horn. Crys leaned down and felt it. It was just a big stump, smooth and hard like polished wood.

"It's grown a bit," Johannes said. "We wouldn't normally harvest it yet, but since she's already out, we may as well cut it back now. They grow back, just like hair—which is exactly what they are. Just keratin."

Crys already knew that, but didn't say so. Instead, she stepped back and watched as a ranger cut the stump of horn down with a fine-toothed hacksaw. It was reduced by less than two inches, yet Johannes carefully weighed the cut-off section and bagged it.

"What's that worth?" Crys asked.

"Here, not that much—about twenty thousand dollars, I'd guess. We can trade horn legally in South Africa now, but there's not much of a market locally, and you can't sell it outside the country."

Crys nodded; this matched what Deputy Minister Tolo had told her.

"On the black market in Vietnam," Johannes continued, "at a hundred and twenty-five thousand U.S. dollars a kilogram, Mary's horn would be worth around half a million dollars if we allowed it to grow to full size." He paused, letting the amount sink in. "The *real* question, though, is what would a poacher get for it here in South Africa? About ten to twenty thousand dollars. And that's more than these people can make in a lifetime."

Once Mary was given the antidote, everyone hurried back to the safety of the vehicles. Pretty soon she lurched to her feet and, if a bit disoriented, looked well enough. She made a mock charge at Johannes's truck—just to make a point, Crys thought—and then headed off into the bush at a trot.

Johannes laughed. "That's my girl! She'll be fine. Let's go and have a cup of coffee and get you settled in."

"Is it dangerous to keep tranquilizing rhinos?" Crys asked as they drove toward the house.

He shook his head. "There's a lot of experience with these drugs these days. We use a tranquilizer called M99—it doesn't really bother them."

"But if you can't sell the horn, what's the point?"

"We're protecting the rhinos. If we don't remove the horn, the poachers will, and leave us a dead rhino."

"But what about the impact on their social structure? Isn't that supposed to be an issue with harvesting horn?"

He shrugged. "They're not like elephants, you know. Elephants use their tusks to help with feeding and all sorts of stuff. And once the tusks are gone, they don't grow back. With rhinos, the horn is just for fighting, and we've found that the biggest bull still becomes dominant without it. And, he's still alive to do it, of course." He spun the steering wheel to avoid a big pothole in the track. "That snare this afternoon was nothing," he went on. "If our rhinos had horns, this place would be an armed camp with the poachers shooting at our game guards as well as the rhinos."

"I really want to meet the anti-poaching teams for myself," Crys said, "but the government people won't help me."

He hesitated, frowning. "You want to visit one of the teams? You'd have to go into the national park for that...I might be able to set that up, though, if you're serious. We know people there."

"You could? That would be great—it's exactly the reason I'm here. To get a real understanding of what's going on." And to find Michael, she added to herself.

"I'm not sure they'd let you go out with one of the patrols, though," he said doubtfully.

She could handle that part herself, Crys thought. She knew she was pretty persuasive.

"When Michael Davidson was here, did he go out with one of the anti-poaching groups?"

Johannes shook his head. "I don't think so. As I said, I was away at the time, but I would have heard if he had."

Crys felt a pang of worry. She wasn't getting any new information about Michael.

They drove in silence for a while, then Crys asked, "So what do you do with the horns you cut off? They must be a target for the poachers too, surely?"

He took a few moments before replying, looking like he was concentrating hard on his driving. "We store them...off-site, somewhere safe..."

When he didn't continue, Crys realized he wasn't going to say anything more on the subject. But she'd been thrilled to meet Mary. And she felt a surge of excitement because it seemed there was a chance she'd be able to join an anti-poaching team.

So far, it had been an excellent day. Except for the lack of information about Michael.

Chapter 5

Johannes and Crys sat on the veranda outside the main house and enjoyed a variety of sandwiches with their coffee, entertaining themselves by throwing crumbs to the iridescent birds Johannes called glossy starlings. The veranda overlooked a small waterhole supplied by a solar-powered pump, and while they ate, a parade of impala came to drink. Crys's face lit up and she couldn't help pulling her camera out and snapping away with abandon. It was a magical moment.

"I can't believe I'm in the African bush at last," she said. "I've dreamed about it for so many years."

"And, of course, you've watched all the *National Geographic* videos and documentaries," Johannes said with a smile.

She nodded. "Aren't they amazing? It's remarkable how the videographers catch some of those amazing moments."

"Thanks to satellite TV, we get the *National Geographic* Channel, and the BBC. I also really liked *Blue Planet* with that oke—what's his name? David...somebody or other."

"Attenborough," Crys chimed in. "He's incredible."

Johannes nodded, and they sat quietly, enjoying the moment.

"Tell me a bit about yourself, Crys. I've never met a Vietnamese lady before."

"What do you want to know?"

"How you got to write for *National Geographic*—that must be a really hard job to get. What you like to do in your free time. That sort of thing."

Talking about herself was not Crys's thing. But, nevertheless, she took in a deep breath and tried to summarize her career as best she could, and then told Johannes all about competing in the biathlon.

"You mean you ski for several miles, then have to shoot a target?"

"Yes—alternating between lying down and standing. Standing is the hardest by far. Your heart is pounding; you're struggling to breathe normally; and your muscles are exhausted. It's very tough to hold the rifle steady."

"That sounds really hard."

"And if you miss the target, you get to ski several hundred more yards for every miss."

Johannes shook his head. "It would be like shooting after playing rugby. I don't think I could do it."

Crys smiled and assured him she thought he would.

Then they lapsed into silence, and Crys soaked in the newness of Africa.

Eventually, Johannes stood up. "Let me show you your accommodation."

She was reluctant to move from this perfect spot, but she stood, too, and they walked toward a string of five chalets.

"Just be careful walking outside at night, and don't go beyond the electric fence. It's a single-strand fence about five feet off the ground. It's designed to keep out the big animals like elephants and buffalo– and the rhinos, of course—but occasionally they break through. We don't have any lions on the property, so you don't have to worry about them."

"Who is she and what does she want?" Johannes's father, Anton, asked in Afrikaans when Johannes returned to the house.

"Her name is Crystal Nguyen," Johannes answered, trying hard to pronounce Crys's name correctly. "She's writing about rhino conservation. And she's a real looker."

"She's Vietnamese?"

Johannes nodded.

"How do we know she's not spying for one of the smuggling gangs?"

"I don't think she is. She phoned last week to arrange a visit and when I heard her name, I had the same thought. So, I called *National Geographic*. Turns out she's fine."

"If it's not a cover…" Anton growled.

"She seems really nice," Johannes said. "Thrilled to be in Africa, in the bush. She's never been before. Was very excited when we saw a few kudu, and nearly wet herself when she touched Mary after we darted her. I don't think we've anything to worry about."

Anton just grunted.

Johannes decided to push his luck and see if his father would help out with his contacts.

"She's keen to visit one of the anti-poaching teams. She wouldn't want to do that if she wasn't on the level. Maybe we could see if Hennie would help?"

"Why should we help her? She'd just be a nuisance."

Johannes wasn't sure that he had a good answer to that. He liked her—her enthusiasm and commitment. He wouldn't mind getting to know her better. None of that would wash with his father, though.

"If she sees what it takes to stop the poachers, she may be more willing to see rhino conservation from our point of view."

"Nothing to do with her being a real looker?"

Johannes laughed. "She's more than that, Dad. She just won a big biathlon competition."

"What's that?"

Johannes explained as well as he could what winning a biathlon entailed. "So, you see, she must be really tough. And she can
shoot."

"With a .22?" Anton scoffed. "That's no more than a pea-
shooter." He paused. "Ag, okay. I'll see what I can do."

———

After unpacking, Crys went outside and settled on her porch.
It was hotter than Pretoria, but there was a freshness to the air,
carrying with it a beautiful scent, which seemed to come from a
nearby tree covered in lemon-colored flowers. She made a mental
note to ask Johannes what it was.

She opened her laptop and navigated to the folder that con-
tained the photos Michael had asked Sara Goldsmith to store.
Starting with the most recent, she flipped through them, paying
closer attention than she had when she looked at them on the
flight over.

Michael was a prolific picture-taker, but he had outdone himself during the short time he'd been at the rhino farm. There were
photos of everything, from the entrance to the farm to the chalets;
from a variety of views of the exterior of the house to shots of the
interior rooms. There were even several of Johannes and an older
man being served by a black man at the dining room table. There
were photos of the game vehicles, the electric fence, various trees,
and, of course, rhinos.

Why there were so many of Tshukudu?

She decided that Michael must have been doing something
similar to her—also writing for his main employer, the *New York
Times*. The good news was that if she missed something, she
would be able to find it in Michael's collection.

When she finished looking at the photos, she worked on her
notes and photos for a while, and since Tshukudu had Wi-Fi,
she was able to catch up on stuff from home. Pretty soon the

afternoon was gone. She took a shower and changed, and headed across to the main lodge for dinner.

Johannes and his father were already in the living room.

The older man stood up and introduced himself as Anton Malan. Crys guessed he was mid-sixties and looked fit.

He shook her hand and kept hold of it. "Please say your name again. I didn't quite catch it." His accent was even rougher than Johannes's.

"Crystal Nguyen. But call me Crys. Everyone does."

"Pleased to meet you, Ms. Nguyen." He pronounced it carefully, then let go of her hand. "Let's sit down. Boku will get you a drink."

Crys walked over to a handsome black man dressed in formal waiter attire and stuck out her hand. "Pleased to meet you, Boku. I'm Crys Nguyen. Please call me Crys."

Boku looked very uncomfortable, but eventually he shook Crys's hand with the weakest handshake possible.

"I'll have an orange juice, please," she said hastily, then turned back to the others, frowning.

"He's not used to being treated like that," Anton said. "He's been one of our servants for fifteen years. We treat them well, but not as equals."

Crys opened her mouth, but then closed it again. She realized she had a lot to learn about this country, which only twenty years earlier had forcibly kept the races apart.

Crys was astonished when they moved through to dinner. It reminded her of old British movies set in the colonies. She'd never encountered anything like it—its formality made her uncomfortable.

They sat at a beautiful table made from a yellow wood, with the white-jacketed Boku waiting on them. When he wasn't serving, he stood quietly in the corner of the room. Johannes and Anton ignored him, except for an occasional thank you.

"You are obviously from the USA, Ms. Nguyen," Anton said. "Whereabouts?"

"Well, actually I was born in Saigon—Ho Chi Minh City now. My family left after the war and settled in Minneapolis in Minnesota. There are a lot of Vietnamese people there." Crys purposefully kept the statement bland, trying to stop any further personal questions. Fortunately, Anton was just making small talk and didn't really want to hear her life story.

"Bit of a change of scene for you here," he went on.

"You have such a beautiful place," Crys said. "And I was so lucky to see them taking the snare off Mary."

"Bloody poachers," Anton growled in reply. "They shoot the bastards in the national park, you know, but we have to use kid gloves or there's no end of trouble."

"They weren't after the rhino, Dad," Johannes interjected. "It was a snare for a kudu."

"They'd take the rhino if they could. Even for the stump of horn that's left." Anton turned to Crys. "Did he tell you what they'd get for a horn?"

She nodded, and then asked: "According to a World Wildlife Fund survey I read, fewer Chinese now believe that rhino horn is a medicine. Will that help, do you think?"

"Nearly fifty percent of Chinese still believe in it, though," Johannes replied. "And that's a lot of people. A *lot* of people."

Anton went on eating for a while, then put his fork down with a clunk. "Surveys are rubbish. People changing their beliefs?" He shook his head. "Look at the locals here. They are trustworthy, good workers, Christians. But they still believe in witchcraft."

Boku cleared away the plates, apparently oblivious to Anton's comments. Crys felt embarrassed for him and wanted to change the subject. In any case, she was really keen to ask Anton about Michael. This was her best chance of discovering something useful, since no one had picked up his trail after Tshukudu. She was almost scared to ask, though. What if he had nothing to add to what he'd told Sara Goldsmith?

"I wanted to ask you about a colleague of mine," she said to

Anton after a pause. "A man called Michael Davidson. He works for the *New York Times.*"

Anton looked up. "Davidson? Yes, he was here about a month ago. Wasn't he also supposed to be investigating the rhino-horn trade or something? For *National Geographic* also, I think."

"That's right. Do you know where he went after he left Tshukudu?"

Anton signaled with his glass for Boku to bring him more wine. "Well, he was here for a few days, then said he was going up to Mozambique. I told him to watch his step. They don't like newspaper reporters over there. I told all this to the police when they contacted me. You know anything more about this, Johannes?"

Johannes shook his head. "Crys already asked me. I was taking a group of tourists on a camping trip when he visited, I guess. Why did the police get involved?"

"He never came back to the States from South Africa," Crys responded. "No one knows where he is. *National Geographic* asked the police to try and trace him."

"Are you a friend of his?" Anton asked, taking a sip of his wine.

Crys nodded. *There's a good chance we'll end up more than friends*, she thought.

"Did the police come up with anything?" Johannes asked.

"Basically, that he did go into Mozambique and returned to South Africa about ten days later. After that, nothing." She paused. "How can someone just vanish and no one knows what's happened to them?" She didn't mention Lieutenant Mkazi's theory of a random hijacking.

Anton shrugged. "We're a long way from anywhere here, you know. If you head into the bush you could lose cell phone signal, break down, I don't know. It could be a long time before you're found."

It all seemed very casual to Crys. People had GPS these days. In the twenty-first century, you didn't just get lost and disappear.

"Didn't he tell *National Geographic* what his plans were?" Johannes asked.

Crys shook her head. "When *National Geographic* asked me to take over this project, they sent me all his notes for the article, but they were all about the interviews he'd done and so on. Nothing about what he was planning next. There is one thing. Michael sent me an email saying he was onto something big—smuggling horns out of South Africa—but I've no idea about the details."

"Something big?" echoed Anton. He sat back, pushing himself away from the table. "Something big can be dangerous…" He stared at Crys as though he didn't like the taste of this conversation very much.

"You think he might have been talking about rhino-horn smugglers?"

Anton signaled to Boku to bring dessert. "Can't say. But those are not good people to mess with."

"How do you think—"

"Look," Anton interrupted. "I told that lady who phoned from your magazine everything I knew about Davidson. Was it worth you coming all the way out here and going through everything all over again?"

"Well, I needed to talk to you about your rhino farming anyway," Crys said, taken aback by Anton's reaction.

"Didn't he have all that in his notes?"

Crys met Anton's eyes without blinking. "Yes, but they were sketchy. And it is better for writers to form their own impressions—you can't write an article like this from someone else's notes. Not if you're a professional."

"Anyway," Johannes soothed, "you're very welcome here."

"Of course," Anton agreed, but he didn't sound as though he meant it.

Crys felt a wave of disappointment. Again, she'd learned nothing more. Michael had been here. He'd asked questions. He'd left for Mozambique and when he came back, he'd disappeared.

And somehow, she seemed to have upset Anton in the process of asking about it.

Boku served the dessert—a sort of filled tart that he said was called *melktert*. "That means milk tart," Johannes chimed in. "It's a traditional Afrikaner farm dish."

Crys took a forkful and liked it immediately. It was smooth and deliciously creamy. After she'd enjoyed a couple more forkfuls, she thought that asking Anton about the business might lighten things up. "I'm interested in your business model," she said to him. "Is it mainly tourists coming to see the rhinos?"

But Anton looked annoyed and gave a sour laugh. "Business model? Let me explain something, Ms. Nguyen. If I want a business model, I have real businesses in Joburg, where I make good money. Here, I don't make money—it costs a fortune to run this place." He paused. "So, you'll want to know why I do it, then. Well, I'll tell you. They're predicting that the white rhino will be extinct in fifty years. But they're wrong. It isn't going to happen, because I'm not going to let it happen. *That's* my business model."

Crys didn't respond and focused on finishing her dessert.

———

After dinner, Johannes walked outside with Crys. The moon was setting, and once they were away from the lights of the house, the stars were incredible—so many more than she saw in the northern hemisphere, and seemingly so close.

"My father's quite passionate," Johannes said at last. "We both are. You can think what you like, but it isn't selling the rhino horn that motivates us."

"But you support legalizing the trade?"

He nodded in the darkness. "It's the only way of replicating our model. Others will start doing the same thing—breeding rhinos. It'll create an industry and provide jobs. And we can flood the market with horn and crash the price, and then poaching will become much less attractive."

"And then you will make money."

He shrugged. "We're stashing away a lot of horn that could be worth something one day. But right now?" He shook his head. "That's not why we're doing this."

They continued to walk, gazing upwards.

Then Johannes said, "The good news is that I've been able to set up a visit for you with one of the anti-poaching teams in Kruger. I know the guy who leads it. The even better news is that they're flying a helicopter in tomorrow afternoon and can pick you up here on the way. You'll fly over the national park. You'll be able to get some super pictures." He smiled broadly. Crys could see he was pretty pleased with himself.

"That's really great, Johannes. Thank you so much. I really appreciate all the trouble you've taken to help me."

"I want you to see what it's really like out there, Crys. What the alternative to our approach is. Once you've seen that side, I hope you'll at least give us the benefit of the doubt when you think about ours."

"You've already done so much for me, Johannes, but can I ask you one more favor? I need some really good rhino pictures to illustrate my article, and your rangers know where to find them. Is there any chance one of them could take me out at dawn tomorrow—just to get some shots?"

"Sure. No problem. In fact, I'll take you myself—I'm always up early."

He stopped and looked up, pointing to a group of stars. "There's Orion, the hunter. You see those three bright stars in a line? That's his belt. And the three small ones are his sword." And if you look at that very bright star—that's Sirius, the brightest star in the sky. That's the eye of Orion's dog."

Crys knew the constellation well, but hadn't seen it with such a backdrop. She gazed in awe at the Milky Way cutting a bright path across the sky.

They didn't have a sky like this in Minnesota.

———

It'd been quite a day, and Crys was really tired, but she felt she was getting somewhere, at least for the article. Johannes had gone back to the house, and she was walking back to her chalet. It was easy to spot—just fifty yards across the lawn, the porch light still on.

Suddenly she stopped in her tracks. There was a light on *inside* her chalet too. She was sure she'd turned them all off. But now she could see it moving around in the room. A flashlight maybe? With a shock, she realized she'd left her travel wallet lying on the dresser. Everything of importance was in it—passport, cards, cash.

"Hey!" Crys shouted, breaking into a run, not thinking about what she was doing, simply worried about her valuables. "Hey!" Then the light went out.

She reached the porch and yanked open the door, but there was no one inside. She dashed into the bathroom and looked out the back door, but there was no sign of anyone. No sound. No flashlight.

Then she went back into the room and checked the dresser. Everything was still there. Even all the cash, as far as she could tell. Had it been moved, though? She wasn't sure. She grabbed the wallet and passport and ran back to the house.

Anton was at the front door having a smoke.

"Someone was in my room," Crys said. "With a flashlight. I saw the light as I came up to the porch, but he was gone when I got there."

Anton stubbed out the cigarette and shouted for Johannes.

"Come inside," he said, as Johannes arrived, asking what the matter was.

A few moments later he headed outside with a powerful flashlight, shouting for the staff.

"Are you sure it wasn't a reflection or something?" Anton asked. "We only have our own people here at night and I trust them all. Although…" He shrugged.

"Could someone else get in here? It's just…" Crys hesitated, but decided to get it off her chest. "It's just, when I was in Pretoria, I…I thought someone was following me. And my suitcase was broken into and searched."

Anton shook his head. "In Pretoria, it was probably the government. They don't like foreign journalists much. They might keep an eye on you there, but they wouldn't follow you out here."

She and Anton sat down in the living room in silence. And a few minutes later Johannes came back inside.

"I've got the trackers looking around," he said, "but they won't see much in the dark. We'll look again in the morning. We'll move you in here for the night."

Anton snapped his fingers. "Fireflies!" he said. "They were out tonight. Maybe you saw them reflected in the glass. Some of them are really bright out here, and there's not much moonlight."

"No, no. I know what fireflies look like," Crys insisted. "It was a flashlight. I'm sure."

But Crys wasn't *sure* that she was sure. Had the light flickered? She started to wonder if it was her imagination after all. An imagination fired up by what had happened in Pretoria.

The two men watched her, seeing her hesitation. Johannes looked concerned; Anton had a small smile.

She'd had enough. "Look, whoever it was is gone. I should've locked the doors when I came for dinner. Stupid of me. And I don't want to move. I'm fine in the chalet. Really."

Johannes looked concerned, but Crys smiled. "Honestly. It's okay."

"All right," he said. "But I'll walk you back, check the place, and make sure everything's locked up properly."

She nodded, grateful.

Once Johannes had seen Crys back, checked the doors and

windows and left, she locked the door, and climbed into bed. She thought she'd fall asleep at once, but that didn't happen. Her mind was up to its usual tricks.

She'd been in South Africa three days and in that time, she'd been followed by a man she'd taken for a pickpocket, someone had trashed her suitcase, and now someone had been going through her chalet while she was stargazing with Johannes.

And then there was Michael. She was doing the same thing Michael had come out here to do. And then he'd disappeared.

It wasn't a prescription for sweet dreams.

Chapter 6

Crys was dressed and showered before dawn, then went and sat on the porch to watch an amazing sunrise. The sun's color was different from what it looked like in Minnesota. Here it was fiery orange. Perhaps it was the sand in the air.

She inhaled deeply through her nose. A South African expat friend of hers in Minneapolis had once told her that Africa had a unique smell. Sitting there, she immediately knew what he meant. She tried to find words to describe it, but couldn't find any to do it justice: earthy, sweet, rich? Each of these words was part of the smell, but not all of it.

She closed her eyes and listened to the calls of unfamiliar birds. Two overpowered the rest. The first was a raucous, repeating call, made by a brown, grouse-like bird with a reddish beak. It was quite tame and jumped onto the porch, presumably to look for crumbs. The other bird was a dove of some sort. Its call sounded something like "my FA-ther, my FA-ther" and went on and on—it could become very irritating if you were trying to sleep in, she thought.

She'd been sitting for only a few minutes when an open Land Rover pulled up, and Johannes jumped out, a big smile on his face.

"Morning," he beamed. "Another beautiful day in paradise. Are you ready to go? The light will be perfect in fifteen minutes or so."

Crys picked up her camera bag and stepped off the porch. Johannes opened the passenger door with a little flourish and closed it behind her as she sat down. She wondered if he did this for all women, or whether he was trying to impress her.

"How long will it take to find some rhinos, do you think?" Crys asked as he climbed in behind the wheel.

"Shouldn't take long, once we're outside the electric fence."

And he was right. They'd only driven for about five minutes beyond the gate before he stopped and pointed into the bush. "There's a big, white-rhino male with no horn. I'll drive until the sun's behind us. That'll give you the best light."

He drove slowly around some bushes, looking for the ideal spot.

"Rhinos are nearly blind, but they can see movement," he said. "That's why, if you're on foot and a rhino charges, you shouldn't run. Just stand still."

Crys looked at him to see if he was joking.

"It's true," he said with a smile. "But it would be nearly impossible to do. They can weigh up to four tons."

She put the zoom lens onto the camera, wondering whether she would be able to outrun a rhino.

"You can't outrun a rhino," he said, as if reading her thoughts. "But it doesn't matter how slow you are, as long as you can run faster than at least one other person." He looked at Crys, serious for a moment, then burst out laughing. "It's okay. You'll be safe. Let's go."

He moved the Land Rover into a gap between two bushes and turned off the engine. The light was glorious, and the various greens of the bushes were rich and saturated with color. The rhino paid no attention, so Crys had plenty of time to snap away with different zoom lengths and exposures.

"Do you have any that still have their horns?"

"*Ja*, there are some we're about to harvest, but we'll have to look for them. I know where they were yesterday, but today..." His voice trailed off as they drove back to the dirt road.

A few minutes later, Johannes pulled off the road and again they were bouncing through the bush.

Suddenly he stopped. "There!" He pointed straight ahead.

Crys peered through the bushes but couldn't see any rhinos. "Where?"

"Straight ahead. Twelve o'clock."

She searched again, then saw them. Three big ones, all with their horns intact.

"Hold on," he whispered.

The Land Rover moved forward, rocked its way over a fallen branch, then stopped about twenty yards from the small group. Again, Crys took dozens of pictures, thankful for digital technology.

Eventually, the light lost its early-morning richness, and they headed back to the lodge for breakfast.

———

Crys and Johannes were the only ones at a table that had more food than they could eat in a week: various fruits, cereals and cold cuts, three different breads, a plate of cheeses, together with orange juice, a pot of tea, and a pot of coffee.

The moment they sat down, Boku appeared. "How would you like your eggs, madam?"

"None for me," Crys replied. "There's more than enough here. Thank you, Boku."

He nodded and asked the same question of Johannes, who just shook his head.

Crys was halfway through a large bowl of fruit salad, when a man appeared in the doorway. Johannes beckoned him into the room, and he whispered something into Johannes's ear. Johannes nodded, thanked the man, and sent him on his way.

"Well, I don't know what to say," he said once the man was gone. "They can't find any tracks out of the ordinary around your chalet."

Crys could almost hear the question tacked on to this—*Did you really see someone?* He didn't ask it, but she began to doubt herself.

They ate in silence for a while. Then, Johannes stood up. "Now, please excuse me. I'd better get to work. The chopper will be here about five o'clock. You should take long pants, a long-sleeved shirt, and hiking boots if you have them. And a dark jersey as well. If you don't have any of that, I'm sure I can find something that would work. Also, make sure you spray yourself with mosquito repellent. There's been an outbreak of malaria not far from here."

"No problem, I have all those things," Crys said, smiling at him over the rim of her cup. "And thanks for the photo op this morning."

He smiled back and left her to finish her coffee.

———

Crys had never been in a helicopter and couldn't wait for five o'clock that evening. At four-thirty she went and sat on the porch of her chalet and started sorting out her photos. Every few minutes, she'd look up into the blue sky in the hopes of seeing a chopper approaching.

She heard it before she saw it—the *wap-wap* of the blades growing louder and louder. A few moments later, it came into sight, and in seconds it was hovering over a concrete slab about a hundred yards from the chalet. It descended slowly and settled down, blowing clouds of sand in all directions.

She picked up her backpack and camera bag and headed toward it. Halfway there, she met up with Johannes and another man.

"Ready for the big adventure?" Johannes asked.

Crys nodded. "Can't wait. And it'll be my first helicopter ride."

"This is Bongani," he said, indicating the man beside him. "He's our senior guide. He accompanies our guests on our safaris. He'll be going with you."

"To keep an eye on me?"

"Absolutely." Johannes's face was serious. "I don't think you really understand what you are getting yourself into. It could be very dangerous, and I don't want a dead journalist on my hands."

"I can look after myself," Crys said firmly.

But then doubt crept in. Michael had been a war correspondent in Afghanistan, and it seemed he couldn't look after himself.

She bit her lip.

Johannes was watching her, seeing her hesitation. "Look, you have no idea," he said, shaking his head. "But Bongani knows the ropes. He works with the anti-poaching teams when he's not busy with us. Hennie's the team leader. Do exactly as he says and remember: this is *not* a picnic. If you find poachers, there'll be shooting, and the bad guys won't stop to check that you're a reporter."

"I'll be careful." Crys made sure her tone was as business-like as his. "I promise."

He patted her on the back. "Time to go."

They walked over to the chopper, where the pilot was standing outside.

The man shook hands with Johannes and nodded at Bongani. They chatted for a few minutes in Afrikaans. Then Johannes turned to Crys.

"Crys, this is Frikkie van der Merwe. Frikkie: Crys Nguyen from Minnesota in the States. She's writing an article on rhino poaching for *National Geographic*."

They shook hands.

"Jump in next to me," said Frikkie. "The others are waiting. It'll only take about fifteen minutes to get there."

———

Crys was so excited she could hardly sit still. The roar of the engine, then the liftoff, the tilt forward, and they were away, climbing to what Frikkie told her was fifteen hundred feet.

"Look over there," he said through the headphones. "Buffalo. Two to three hundred."

From that altitude, it was difficult to identify the dark patch on the ground as a huge herd of animals. It looked more like a ridge of rocks.

"Elephant," he said, a little later, pointing ahead.

There was a small herd clustered around a waterhole. As the helicopter approached they moved away from the water and headed for the bush.

"Scared of the noise," he said.

Crys was in heaven. All her life she'd dreamed of the wildlife in Africa.

This could challenge my love of wolves, she thought.

All too soon, they were descending into a small clearing with a group of tents at one end. As soon as the rotors stopped, a man in camouflage clothes walked over and opened Crys's door.

"Hennie van Zyl." He shook her hand. "You must be Crys."

She nodded. "Thank you so much for letting me join you."

"To tell you the truth, I didn't want you along. It's too dangerous. But Anton can be very persuasive."

"I thought Johannes arranged it," Crys said as she disembarked.

"No. It was his father who called us to ask. We always try to help him out."

She smiled, but wondered why Johannes had told her that he'd made the arrangements.

"Okay, Crys," Hennie continued. "Here's the deal: things may happen out there in the bush tonight. Maybe we'll meet poachers, maybe not. Either way you can write about what we do, but no names and no details we don't approve. If you don't agree, you'll wait at camp and can chat with us when we come back."

Crys didn't like being restricted like that, but she realized she didn't have an option. "Okay, agreed," she said, but wondered what it was he wanted to hide.

He nodded and took her to an area next to the tents. A group of men were lounging around—some smoking, some cleaning their guns. They all looked at her as she walked up. No smiles, no greetings.

"This is the chick that Anton wants us to take tonight," Hennie told them. "Her name's Crys."

"Thanks for letting me tag along, guys. This *chick* is working on a story for *National Geographic* and wants to see all aspects of the war on poaching."

There was no response from the men.

"Crys, have you ever used night-vision glasses?" Hennie asked, breaking the uncomfortable silence.

She shook her head.

"They give us a better chance of seeing anyone out there."

"How do they work?"

He dismissed the question with a wave of his hand. "Not important. Have you ever used a firearm?"

"Yes, many times." She looked him squarely in the face, expecting skepticism.

"What sort?"

"Mainly .22 long-range bolt-action. I compete in biathlons." She wondered if he knew what that was. "But I've also used several other rifles at a range."

"Have you ever been shot at?"

"No. And I want to keep it that way. How often do you encounter poachers on these patrols?"

"No poachers for about a month, but fifteen dead rhinos— shot, then the horns cut off with a reciprocating saw."

"What happens if we run into poachers?" she asked, wanting to know the protocol.

"Try to kill us," one of the men muttered. "Maybe not you. They'd want you for something else—"

"If they spot us," Hennie interrupted, "they'll probably shoot. They don't want to be caught. Some of them even have AK-47s."

She knew Hennie was trying to scare her out of going. But her mind was made up. She *was* going to do this. She felt her adrenalin start pumping.

"You don't use bulletproof vests?" she asked, keeping her tone casual.

"Too cumbersome for the bush." He held up a rifle. "Take this .303. It's also bolt-action. Only has four bullets before you have to reload. Even if you have to shoot, it's unlikely that you'll fire more than once or twice—either he'll be dead or you will. Here are a few more bullets, just in case. I hope you don't have to use it." He dropped them into her hand.

"Here's the safety catch. You release it like this." He demonstrated and then reset it. Then he thrust the rifle into her hand. She thought it felt like a lump of lead compared to her Anschutz biathlon rifle.

"If you shoot any of us, you have to buy the beers."

Finally, there was laughter from the men. Crys realized it was at her expense.

———

There were seven in the group. Crys would go with Hennie, Bongani, and a tracker named Kai—a short man with almost Asian features. Ariko, a National Parks ranger, was leader of the second group. The other two were Sampson and Thabo—both National Parks rangers and trackers.

"We've all been hunting poachers for several years," Hennie said as he made the introductions.

"If it's okay, I'd like to interview them all when we get back," Crys said.

"We'll see what they say," replied Hennie. He didn't sound optimistic.

He called the group together, then pulled out his radio.

"Radio check." He clicked the transmit button. Several radios buzzed. "Okay. Use the radio only when needed—if you see anyone, hear anything, or get shot at. Also, if you find a rhino alive or dead."

Crys didn't have a radio, but everyone else plugged in their earpieces and adjusted them until they were comfortable.

Hennie glanced at Ariko, who nodded. They'd clearly done this many times—except now they had an American journalist along with them. Crys breathed deeply. She didn't want to cause any problems...or get shot.

"Okay, Crys," Hennie said, taking a step toward her and standing slightly too close for her comfort, "last chance. Are you sure you want to do this? You can easily change your mind—stay here and be safe."

Crys wished she could tell him about the one-woman war she'd waged in northern Minnesota against the wolf poachers, and some of the risky things she'd done to thwart them there. Maybe he wouldn't just see her as some *chick* who was in the way. But she told no one about that period of her life, and that wasn't going to change.

"Not doing that. I'm sure I want to go."

"Have you peed?" Hennie asked. "Can't do it out there, you know—attracts lions."

Crys's mouth fell open. But he smiled. "Just kidding. Let's go."

Chapter 7

As Crys walked, all she could see were surreal shapes of trees and bushes and white images of impalas and other animals that she couldn't identify. It was a strange feeling, as though she was half-blind. Fortunately, when she looked at the others in her group, she could make them out clearly—all were obviously human.

She wondered whether the poachers also had night-vision goggles. It was a scary thought. If they did, she and her group would be sitting ducks. And lions and other predators possessed natural night vision. She kept glancing around, scared half to death, but determined not to show it. She had to trust that Hennie knew what he was doing.

Suddenly, Crys heard something behind her. She jerked round. It was only Bongani, closer to her than she'd thought. She took a deep breath and moved on.

It was hard going. Crys struggled to walk quietly because the night-vision glasses didn't show dead branches lying in her path. So, she began to mimic Hennie's steps, trying to put her feet where his had been. Sometimes, they had to work their way between thorn bushes that grabbed their clothing, then wouldn't let go. Once she tripped and had to save herself by grabbing a branch. Hennie swung around but didn't say anything. Crys could sense his irritation.

Progress was slow, but not random. Hennie knew where a ranger flying a microlight patrol had spotted a black rhino earlier in the day. It was close to where the most recent kills had been. He was hoping that the poachers had stayed around to bag another horn—another fat paycheck.

After a long hour, Hennie called a stop by raising his hand and looking back down the line. Crys took a few gulps from her water bottle and chewed on a power bar. Hennie indicated that the group should huddle around him. Shielded from prying eyes, he checked his GPS to make sure they were on track.

"Okay, listen up," he whispered. "We're about half a mile from where I think the rhino is likely to be. We have to be even more careful now. Keep at least ten yards behind the person in front. Bongani, you take up the rear and keep a lookout behind."

Bongani nodded, and Crys felt a surge of adrenalin. She wondered if this was how her father had felt when he was stalking Vietcong. It must have been terrifying doing this day after day, knowing that you wouldn't hear the shot that killed you. She shuddered.

Hennie took off the safety on his rifle and indicated that all of them should do the same. The clicks sounded deafening, even though they tried hard to deaden the sound. He put his finger to his lips—as if they needed telling—then motioned them forward. Crys waited for a few moments to let him get ahead, then followed.

The group moved even more slowly now, often stopping to make sure that the fuzzy images in their goggles were animals, not humans. After twenty minutes, Hennie stopped and pointed to the right. There, through the trees, Crys saw the white silhouette of a rhino. It couldn't be anything else—the shape was unmistakable.

Hennie motioned them together again. And once again spoke in an almost inaudible whisper. Everyone leaned close and, even then, almost had to lip-read. "Kai and me are going around the other side. Bongani and Crys, you stay right here. Ariko is off to the south. Each of you find a big tree and stand right next to it. That'll shield you from view from one side. You'll see the poachers if they come, because they'll have to get close to the rhino to shoot it." He looked at me. "You understand, Crys? No mistakes."

She nodded and took several deep breaths, trying to slow her racing heart. Even with her exploits in northern Minnesota, she'd never put herself in such a dangerous situation before. And she'd never felt so scared.

———

The next hour crept by, and Crys was having a hard time keeping still. What made it worse was that she didn't know what was going on. She couldn't see Bongani, who was hiding behind a tree about twenty yards away. And she didn't know what any of the others were doing. They were all out of sight.

The whole time, she was terrified that a poacher was creeping up on her, and that she could be killed at any moment. She was sure anyone nearby would hear her heart because it was pounding so loudly.

Suddenly a white figure moved out from behind the tree Bongani had chosen. Crys held her breath and took aim with her rifle, praying it was him and not someone else. The figure came toward her. Was it Bongani or a poacher? She couldn't tell.

"Crys," the figure whispered.

Crys let out her breath. It was Bongani. He leaned over and whispered, "Hennie has seen two people moving toward the rhino. He wants us to move around behind them to cut off their retreat."

She nodded and gritted her teeth.

Bongani moved off to the left at a faster pace than they'd used before. Crys struggled to follow his footsteps while keeping an eye out for low branches and glancing back in case someone was coming up from behind.

They'd walked for another fifteen minutes or so, when Bongani stopped and motioned Crys to come up level with him.

"Hennie says the poachers are within range. They're going to shoot them."

"Without warning?" Crys whispered. "Is that legal?" She knew that some of the stuff she'd done in Minnesota wasn't legal either. But none of it involved killing anyone.

Then two shots rang out, the boom of a big-caliber rifle and the crack from a smaller weapon. Crys thought that the bigger was probably Hennie's Remington 80 elephant gun. Then came a fusillade of shots, then another two from the big-caliber.

Then silence.

Bongani put a finger on his earpiece for a moment and listened. Then he whispered, "Hennie thinks there were four in total. Two are down; the others are headed this way. You go behind that mopane bush over there." He pointed over to the left. "I'll find another one. Remember, if you see anyone coming this way, shoot. Don't wait for them to shoot first."

"What if it's Hennie?" Crys whispered nervously.

"It won't be. They've something else to do..."

Before she could ask him what, he'd disappeared. She crawled behind the thick mopane bush and lay down, her heart beating wildly. She wondered what Hennie's group could be doing. Maybe the rhino had been shot and needed attention.

After about ten minutes, a shot rang out. Crys nearly jumped out of her skin. It seemed to have come from right next to her. She looked around but saw nothing. Then another shot, equally close. Then silence.

And more silence.

The blood was pounding in her ears. She didn't know if Bongani had done the shooting or had been shot. She turned her head slowly to look behind her. Nothing. Nobody. She breathed deeply, and soundlessly repeated her mantra to get her heart under control. Eventually it slowed down a bit.

Suddenly, a white image appeared from behind a tree to the right. Crys swung her rifle toward it and sighted.

"Crys. Don't shoot. It's me, Bongani."

It had to be Bongani. A poacher wouldn't know her name. But she kept the rifle aimed at the oncoming figure, just in case. Finally, she lowered it.

"Let's check that the two I shot are dead," he said. "Then we must go to where Hennie is."

Crys stood up and walked out from behind the bush. She was shaking. Ahead, she saw two white figures lying motionless.

"Keep your rifle ready," Bongani said. "If the left one moves, shoot him. I'll watch the one on the right."

They moved slowly toward the two bodies, dodging from one tree to the next. There was no movement. Eventually, they were behind trees only a few yards away. Crys stopped, unable to believe what she'd got herself into.

"Watch the left one carefully, Crys," murmured Bogani.

She aimed at the man, not completely sure what she would do if he did move. Then Bongani ran from behind the tree and kicked a rifle away from the other man's grasp. Then he kicked the man in the stomach. There was no reaction. He repeated the same thing with the man Crys was covering. Same result. Both were either dead or so severely wounded that they couldn't react.

Crys held her breath as Bongani felt each man's pulse.

"Dead," he said, looking in her direction. He picked up the rifles and took all the bullets he could find. "Let's go."

"Are you just going to leave them here?" Crys choked, shocked.

Bongani nodded. "When the hyenas have finished, nobody will even know they were here." He walked on.

For a moment, Crys couldn't move.

He turned to see where she was. "It's better this way. Believe me."

———

Following his GPS, Bongani led them slowly through the bush. Crys suddenly recalled her thought at dinner the previous night that people didn't disappear in the twenty-first century. Maybe she'd been wrong. Maybe what was left of Michael was lying in the bush somewhere being polished off by hyenas. She felt sick.

As they approached the others, they heard a scream, followed by shouting, then another scream. Crys froze.

Ahead, Bongani had lifted his hand. "I think we should wait here."

"Why? What's going on?"

"You don't want to see."

Crys's reporter's instincts kicked in. "Oh, yes I do."

Bongani shrugged. He took off his night goggles and indicated she should too. They walked forward and soon reached Hennie and the others, standing in a circle.

Nearby, a body was lying on the ground. A poacher, surely. Crys assumed he was dead, because no one was paying attention to him. All their eyes were turned to another figure, spread out a couple of yards away.

The man's hands were bound together and tied to a tree. His legs were splayed apart, each foot secured to a bush. He was naked. Hennie had a flashlight pointed at him, and Crys could see a gaping wound in the man's thigh. It looked as though a shot had nearly taken the leg off. She put her hand to her mouth.

Then she saw a flash of a blade. Hennie had a large knife in his hand and was shouting at the man in a language she didn't understand. The man shook his head desperately. But Hennie leaned over him and ran the knife between the man's nipples. Blood welled out of the wound.

Bongani made a choking sound and turned away.

Hennie shouted some more. The man shook his head again. Once more Hennie leaned over him. This time he grabbed the man's ear.

And then, with a sweep of his hand, he cut it off.

Crys couldn't believe what she was seeing. Part of her wanted to run forward. To stop the barbarity. But her feet seemed welded to the ground, and she was unable to turn her eyes away.

Hennie dangled the severed ear in front of the man's face and shouted again. Again, a shake of the head.

This time Hennie took a step back and kicked the man in the side. The man screamed. Hennie grinned. Crys could see his teeth. He said something to the man again. But once more the man shook his head.

I've got to stop this, she thought. But deep in her stomach she knew that she couldn't.

"Okay, you blerry kaffir," Hennie shouted. "Let's see how tough you really are."

And with that he grabbed the man's penis and sliced off the top, as easily as if he were cutting a piece of ripe fruit. The sound that came out of the man's mouth was unlike anything Crys had ever heard: agonized fear.

At last she found her voice. "Hennie. Please!" she shouted.

He ignored her. He asked the man another question, but he shook his head again. And this time Hennie hacked off the rest of the penis and the scrotum. Like a butcher at his chopping block.

"Bastard!" he shouted and kicked the man in the head. Then he turned away.

"Let's go. It's a long way back," he said, as casually as if he was on an evening stroll.

A wave of nausea rose from Crys's belly through her chest. She stumbled a few yards into the scrub and threw up.

Breathing heavily, her mouth burning with stomach acid, she choked back a sob. And then threw up again.

Chapter 8

Hennie and his men sat around the fire, with cups of coffee. Some had a sandwich in hand; others dunked a rusk into their coffee to soften the hard-baked confection. Crys hadn't appeared yet.

"Do you think she'll keep her mouth shut?" Sampson asked.

"Most *National Geographic* reporters are real pros," Hennie replied. "I think she'll keep to what she agreed."

The men stared into the flames.

"I thought she did pretty well," Hennie continued, "considering she's only been in Africa a few days. Most people, men or women, wouldn't have had the balls to do what she did."

"She did what we asked. She's tougher than she looks," Bongani said.

"She must have been shocked out of her skull when you cut off his balls," Ariko said. "Probably never dreamed of anything like that."

Hennie shrugged. "Hard to know what people dream about."

"Wish she would wake up," Sampson growled. "I want to get out of here."

"We'll give her until ten-thirty. If she's not up, I'll wake her," Ariko said.

"No, let me do it," Sampson said, lifting his rifle. "This should be loud enough to get her up."

The men around the fire laughed, imagining what the woman's reaction would be to an elephant gun being fired right outside her tent.

———

Crys opened her eyes and looked at her watch. It was just after ten. She'd only had about five hours' sleep, and they weren't good. Some of the time, images of the man tied to the ground had flashed into her mind, and she'd heard his screams. Other times, she saw hyenas, licking their lips, saliva dripping from their powerful jaws, creeping toward the man. He was struggling, knowing he was going to be eaten.

And sometimes it wasn't the poacher she saw.

Sometimes it was Michael.

She closed her eyes and pulled the pillow over her head, hoping the images would go away. They didn't.

Eventually she dragged herself out of her sleeping bag and unzipped the tent. She saw that the others were sitting around a fire, a blackened kettle balanced on a twisted grate above it.

"Coffee?" Hennie offered.

Crys nodded. "Thanks."

He spooned some instant coffee powder into a tin mug and poured water over it.

"No milk," he said.

"No problem," she mumbled.

"Sugar?"

"Two, please."

After adding the sugar and giving the liquid a stir, he handed Crys the mug. She sat down on a dead tree they'd pulled close to the fire. Like the others, she gazed at the flames.

"Crys, I need to remind you of what you agreed to yesterday.

You can report what you saw, but no names, places, or dates of what happened. Understand?"

She nodded. She had to stick to her word.

"Good. Now, how're you doing?"

Crys didn't answer right away. She didn't really know how she was feeling. Or what she was feeling. Her mind and emotions were in turmoil. Eventually she murmured, "I'm okay." She didn't know what else to say.

"What would you have done?" Hennie asked.

Crys looked around the group. Everyone was staring down into the fire.

She took a breath. "Couldn't you tell them to put their hands up instead of just shooting them?"

"We tried that at the beginning. One of my friends was killed when they opened up with an AK-47. If they see us, they don't hesitate. They shoot to kill. So now we do the same. We shoot the bastards!"

"What about the other man—the one on the ground? Did you have to...?" Crys's voice cracked. She swallowed, trying to stay calm. "Did you have to torture him and leave him to be eaten alive?"

"He was going to die anyway. He was hit badly and was going to bleed to death. And it was too far to carry him."

"You could've tried to stop the blood. You could've got the Land Rover. He might have survived. And...and...." She couldn't stop herself. "You looked as though you were enjoying it!"

"He knew what he was getting into when he signed up as a poacher."

There was a long silence.

"What were you asking him?" Crys said at last.

"I wanted to know where he came from."

"What difference does that make?"

"If we know where he comes from, we can go to his village and encourage the villagers not to cooperate with the men next up the chain."

"You mean kill them like you killed him!" she snapped, her anger rising. "Is that why he didn't say anything? He didn't want his village destroyed. That's what the Americans did in Vietnam—killed innocent villagers to find out where the Vietcong were."

Bongani stood up and walked away.

"And which side were you on, Crys?" Hennie's lips formed a tight, thin line. "The brutal Americans or the brutal Vietcong?"

Crys gripped her mug and drained it.

Eventually she said, "I wasn't born then. My father was in the South Vietnamese army."

"He was lucky to get out," Hennie said.

"He didn't. At least not then." She stared into her empty cup. She didn't want to talk about her family.

"What happened?" Hennie asked, taking a softer tone.

Crys normally avoided answering questions about her family, but with the events of the previous night sharp in her mind, her usual barriers were down. She turned and looked Hennie in the eyes. "The Vietcong put him in prison for thirteen years. My mother got pregnant with me after one of her annual visits, and I was born just before he was released. We were lucky that she wasn't harassed…or worse. She and my brother and I were able to get to the States in 1989. My father was only allowed to join us a couple of years later."

Nobody said a thing. She didn't know what was going through the heads of the men around the fire, but she was thinking of her father. She hadn't spoken to him in more than ten years—since he'd thrown her out of the house for not being a "good Vietnamese girl" and obeying his every wish, for being too American, even though she was raised there. The familiar ache spread from her chest to her throat.

Then Hennie broke into her thoughts. "The problem with you Americans is that you want rhino poaching to stop, but aren't willing to accept what has to be done to accomplish that." He threw a branch onto the fire. "What you really need to do, if you want to stop rhinos being killed, is to put an embargo on all Vietnamese trade. That's where most of the horns go. And you know what for?" He glared at her. "For medicines that don't heal anything and for sniffing at yuppie parties. And it doesn't even give them a high." He threw the dregs of his coffee onto the fire.

"I get it why poachers are willing to take the risk," he continued. "They can earn a lifetime of income from a couple of horns." He pointed to the others sitting around the fire. "But *we're* working at the bottom of the food chain. We don't get anything extra when we catch or kill a poacher, even though our lives are in danger. We do it so rhinos don't disappear from the planet."

He picked up a stone and threw it at the fire. It hit a log and sparks flew up, crackling. "We can only try to stop the poachers— the U.S. has the influence to stop *the trade*. But what does it do? Nothing. Because too many people are making too much money. Or perhaps it's feeling guilty about what it did in Vietnam…"

Crys knew there was some truth in what he said, but couldn't take any more of it—of him; of what she'd seen. Of his justifications. All she could see was the grin on his face as he tortured the naked, mutilated man.

She stood up and headed back to her tent.

"We'll give her a few more minutes to get her shit together," Hennie said. "Then we're off."

Crys turned and glared at him.

———

Crys stayed in her tent until Bongani called out that they were leaving.

"Do I have time to interview the others?" she asked, realizing that she probably had lost the opportunity.

He shook his head. "No, we don't. Anyway, they don't want to talk to you. They think it's bad luck having a woman around."

"Oh, they do, do they? And what do you think?"

He shrugged and looked away. "Come. We need to go."

He led the way through the bush to the helicopter, which was standing in the clearing, its rotor turning slowly. Crys climbed on board and, a minute later, they were airborne and on their way.

She stared out the window on the trip back to the farm, but she saw nothing. She was totally lost in her thoughts. As the chopper touched down, it felt as if it had just lifted off.

Johannes was there to meet them. He offered his hand to help Crys out, but she avoided it and jumped down instead. He hesitated a moment, then thanked Frikkie and nodded to Bongani.

"I'm relieved you're safe," he said as they walked back to the chalets. "How did it go?"

Crys didn't really want to talk about it. "It was very interesting and very frightening," she said. "I'm pleased I went, though."

"Did you run into any poachers?"

She glanced at his serious expression. She suspected that he knew exactly what had happened. That Hennie had radioed him that morning or perhaps even late the previous night.

She nodded. "We did." She took a deep breath. "They killed four."

"Good." Johannes gave a small nod, looking straight ahead. "Perhaps they'll learn the risk isn't worth it."

She didn't respond.

Crys felt his hand on her shoulder. It was only a light touch, but it was unwelcome. "I'm impressed you're willing to go out and see what actually happens on these patrols. Most newspaper people seem to look it up on Google and then file their reports."

She nodded again. His hand dropped away.

"Tomorrow, we have a safari going out," Johannes continued, his voice brighter. "You're welcome to join it. The numbers aren't finalized yet, but there'll probably be about eight guests in two game-viewing vehicles—tourists who want a taste of the wild." Then he smiled wryly. "Perhaps they should have gone out with you last night. That was probably more wild than they've ever dreamed of."

Crys didn't respond to his joke.

"We'll go to an area bordering Kruger. It's private, so we can set up a camp there."

"How long will we be there?"

"Four nights. I'll be the leader. Bongani will be my head ranger and back me up."

Crys was tempted. However, four nights was quite a long delay in her search for Michael—a search that so far seemed to be leading nowhere. And she was still feeling burned by the events of the previous night.

But a reporter had to be careful not to judge—no matter what they'd seen or experienced. It was the only way to gain trust and get to the truth. She forced a smile. "That's great. When do we leave?"

"Straight after breakfast. You'll notice the other chalets will be occupied tonight."

She thanked him and headed back to her quarters as he made his way to the house.

"Dinner's at seven. See you there," he shouted over his shoulder.

She waved to indicate she'd heard, but wasn't sure she'd go. She needed some time to herself.

———

Crys sat on the porch and tried to digest what she'd seen—to make sense of it. But the same kaleidoscope of thoughts and images kept going round and round in her head. Eventually she went to look for Bongani. He'd been on patrols before. Maybe he could help her understand what it was all about. And she also wanted to ask him about Michael.

She found him working on one of the game-viewing vehicles.

"Bongani, I don't know your last name," she said as she approached.

"It's Chikosi."

"Are you busy?"

"I'm just setting up this Land Rover for the trip tomorrow. Can I help you with something?"

"Can I talk to you for a few minutes?"

He hesitated, then nodded. "We can go over there." He pointed to a bench in the shade of a tree with a wide-spreading crown.

"Bongani," she began after they'd sat down, "one of my colleagues from *National Geographic* stayed here about six weeks ago. His name is Michael Davidson. Did you meet him?"

Bongani shook his head. "I saw him but didn't speak to him. He was doing the same as you—writing a story about rhinos."

"Do you know where he went when he left? We've lost track of him."

He just shook his head again and looked down at the ground. "No, I don't. Sorry."

She suppressed a sigh. Every possible avenue to trace Michael seemed to lead to a dead end.

"Another thing," she said after a moment, "you've been on those anti-poaching trips before. Is it always like that?"

"No. Most times we find nothing. Maybe a dead rhino with the horn cut off. Then we try to follow the tracks of the poachers, but they usually get away. They have vehicles not too far away."

"Did you…?" she stopped. Crys wondered if she could ask the difficult questions she had in mind. But she knew she had to. This story wasn't some interest piece. It was important; big. And that meant asking the hard questions. "Did you ever kill someone before?"

Bongani sat stone-faced. Crys thought he wasn't going to answer. "Yes," he said at last. "Just once."

She suddenly realized that last night may have been as hard for him as it had been for her. "What do you feel about it, Bongani? Is it right to torture and kill people to save animals? Is it worth it to fight for them like that? That man we left for the hyenas—"

"He knew what would happen if we caught him." Bongani's words were clipped, hard. "He accepted the danger."

She didn't think she was getting through to him.

"Look, where I live, in northern Minnesota, we have wolves. They're wonderful animals. Smart and beautiful. Poachers hunt them, and they're endangered. I tried to stop the poachers. I sabotaged their snowmobiles, shamed them in the media, and so on, but I never wanted to…to *kill* them. But now I wonder, if there were only a few wolves left, would I be willing to do that?"

Bongani turned to face her. "Crys, you don't understand at all. This isn't about rhinos or wolves or some other animal. It's about money. Poachers take on the job for *money*. They don't care about the animals. Most of them can't get work. They can't make a living, can't support their families. What they get paid for one rhino horn will support their families for several years. Of course, they're willing to take the risk. And you probably would, too, if you were desperate like they are."

Crys wanted to reply, but she was a journalist. If someone begins talking, you let them continue. She waited, and he went on.

"It's not a question of right or wrong. The poachers see it as a matter of survival. Their own."

"I'm confused. Why do you go on anti-poaching patrols if you are so sympathetic to the poachers?"

"For the same reason they poach—I need the money for my family. For my village."

"But that man yesterday. The one on the ground…" She paused to let him speak.

He opened his mouth to respond, but then just shook his head and stood up. "I have to get back to work."

———

When she returned to her chalet, Crys pulled out her laptop and rattled out her first report for the *Duluth News Tribune*.

But when she'd finished, she wondered whether she should send it. She knew what would happen if she did. Some readers would be appalled by the torture. Others would cheer that the poachers had been killed. For them, saving a species was worth the loss of human life.

She closed the lid of her laptop and went out onto the porch. The relentless sun was baking down and the bush was shimmering in the heat. Nothing moved. Even the birds had stopped calling. She sat down and let her mind wander, hoping it would lead her to a decision.

Most of the afternoon had passed before she finally sent her piece. She felt good, finally making the decision to do so—to say what had happened and let people form their own opinions. After all, that was her job.

In the end, Crys did go to dinner. She wanted to learn more about the area they'd be visiting on the trip. And she was hoping it would lead to another piece for the newspaper. At worst, she'd see more of the African bush without being in the firing line of rhino poachers.

During the meal, Crys mentioned that she'd written her first article.

"You didn't mention any names, did you?" Anton asked sharply. "I vouched for you, you know."

"No, I said I wouldn't, so I didn't. I keep my word, Anton. But I did report what happened." She paused, looking from Anton to Johannes. They concentrated on their plates. "Even the torture."

Neither Anton nor Johannes said anything. Their meals seemed to be occupying all their attention. So, it was as she'd guessed; they had heard all about it. And neither looked upset.

Crys finished her dinner in silence and excused herself before dessert.

Man or Beast? It's a War Out There.

Crystal Nguyen, South Africa

There are about 25,000 rhinos left in the world, most of which are in South Africa. In 2016, the country lost over 1,000 of them, mainly white, or square-lipped, rhinos. The reason? Poaching for their horns.

In places like Vietnam and China, powder from rhino horn is thought to cure a variety of ailments, including cancer. Vietnamese yuppies snort the powder to get high. And some think it is a potent aphrodisiac.

So, it is not surprising that people are willing to pay a lot of money to get it. In fact, ounce for ounce, rhino-horn powder is more expensive than gold. A big horn has a street price of around a quarter of a million dollars.

Enter the poachers. With that sort of money around, poverty-stricken Blacks are willing to risk their lives for a payoff of about ten to twenty thousand dollars per horn, an amount that can be more than a lifetime's income.

These poachers put their lives on the line by walking through the game preserves of Africa, where predators like lions abound, to find and kill a rhino. They are armed and dangerous, often carrying AK47 automatic rifles.

And on the other side are the game rangers who want to stop the poaching—to save the species. And they go to great lengths to succeed.

Last night I joined an anti-poaching team in eastern South Africa. We walked for several hours with night-vision glasses to an area where poachers were believed to be. Eventually we found a group of four near an endangered black rhino. The night-vision glasses gave our team an advantage. Three poachers were shot dead. No challenge, no opportunity to surrender.

I was told that the poachers don't hesitate if they see an anti-poaching team. They shoot to kill.

The fourth poacher was then tortured to find out which village he came from, so the rangers could visit it to persuade them not to work with the poaching cartels. After witnessing the torture, I can only imagine what they would have done to the village if the man had talked.

What I witnessed raises the inevitable question: What is more important: the life of a rhino or the life of a human being?

Chapter 9

The next morning, when Crys went to breakfast, there was no sign of Johannes. The eight new guests were already there, helping themselves from the buffet of eggs, bacon, sausage, toast, and a variety of fruit and cereals. One couple greeted her—she recognized them as Midwesterners by their accents. She took some fruit and muesli and a cup of coffee and joined them at their table. There was also a couple with two teenage boys, and another couple who her new friends informed her were English.

There was still no sign of Johannes, so Crys caught Boku as he went past to fill up the coffee urn and asked him if there was a problem.

He nodded. "Yes, but Mr. Malan will come now-now."

Crys frowned, wondering what that meant. She hoped there wasn't some problem with the rhinos.

Finally, Johannes appeared, looking haggard. "Sorry about the delay, everyone. We had a few last-minute issues to sort out, but we can get underway now. So please finish your coffee and get ready. We'll collect your luggage from the chalets, and we'll leave from here in about fifteen minutes."

As the group started to break up, he came over to Crys's table, his face drawn and pale. There was a slight sheen on his cheeks.

"You okay, Crys?"

She nodded. "I am. But what about you? What's the issue? Has something happened?"

"Nothing. I've just had a bad night, and I have a headache this morning. Maybe I'm getting a cold or something. But I'll be fine. See you outside in a few minutes."

Crys nodded, unconvinced, and went to fetch her things.

———

It was a three-hour trip to reach their destination. The group arrived just in time for lunch: two staff members had gone ahead to set up, and food was waiting for them. Nonga, who was in charge of the camp, showed them around.

The camp was set in a grove of large shade trees, and the comfortable two-person tents were spread out under them. In the center was a communal dining area covered by a flysheet, adjoining an outdoor kitchen.

Wherever they walked, there was a continual hum of insects going about their business, and the big trees attracted birds as well as campers.

"That's called a purple turaco," Nonga said, pointing at a large colorful bird with crimson wings. It settled on a branch and made an ugly coughing call.

Crys would have been happy to stay for a month.

Because of the heat, they waited until later in the afternoon to go on their first game drive. The group split between two open vehicles, with Johannes driving one and Bongani the other. The first sighting was some elephants, and the vehicles moved slowly to get close. Crys was both excited and a little nervous in case they charged.

But Johannes assured them the elephants would ignore them because they were used to vehicles. It was a great photo opportunity, and the guests produced cameras of various sizes and snapped away until the huge creatures moved off silently and disappeared.

Later, they came across a pair of mating lions—he, a glorious male with an enormous, dark mane and scars on his face; she, beautiful, sleek and young, in the prime of her life. The two vehicles stopped and watched from a safe distance for over an hour. The lions mated six or seven times. Each lasted what seemed only a few seconds, then both animals took a power nap. Then they did it again. And again. And again. He seemed to enjoy his orgasms, judging by the sound, but she just lay there. The guests shared the inevitable jokes about some humans being exactly the same.

Finally, as the sun was about to set, swelling and reddening as it sank toward the horizon, they spotted a mother jackal with pups, playing outside their den. The pups pounced on and chased each other, tumbling through the dried grass. Crys was charmed.

I want to take one home.

As they headed back to camp, Crys realized the tensions from the night patrol in Kruger had finally drained away. She couldn't wait to head back out the next morning for more wildlife-viewing.

Arriving back at the camp, they found a hardwood fire roaring, and there was the promise of barbecued meat ahead—a *braai*, Johannes called it, rubbing his hands together. He was obviously pleased by how well the afternoon had turned out, but he still didn't look well. When he wasn't talking to the guests and leading the party, his shoulders slumped and his face fell. As they sat around the fire after dinner, he told them to be ready for a six a.m. start, then, to the disappointment of some guests, excused himself.

Crys moved over to where Bongani was sitting on a log and took a place next to him. "Do you think Johannes is all right?" she murmured, not wanting to alarm the others.

Bongani shrugged. "He's sick. Maybe he'll be better tomorrow."

She had plenty of questions she wanted to ask about the animals they'd seen, but Bongani seemed withdrawn—not sick like

Johannes, but preoccupied. Everyone else was chatting and joking and generally having a good time. When she thought about the poachers she'd seen hunted and tortured just two nights before and only about fifty miles away, it all seemed so distant and unreal.

She wondered what the others would say if she told them about it, but she wasn't tempted. She'd keep those thoughts to herself.

She sat watching the flames change colors and shapes, imagining that she could see fire creatures climbing from the logs. It was an opportunity to think over the last five days, her introduction to Africa. If she was honest with herself, she hadn't learned much more than she already knew about rhino poaching, rhino farming, and rhino conservation. But she had learned something invaluable. Her view of how things happened and the workings of the African bush had changed dramatically. Now she understood that here someone could disappear, perhaps never to be found. For example, someone on the trail of "something big."

It was now five weeks since Michael had disappeared. Five weeks with no sign of him, no trace of his vehicle, no message, nothing. She'd talked to Sara about time being important, that every day might affect his safety. One could think like that in the States; the reality of Africa was quite different.

She had to face it. Everything she'd heard pointed to one conclusion: he wasn't still alive. He'd died somewhere out there. Someone had killed him.

She put her head in her hands.

Her first thought was to try to accept it, to move on. To write the very best article about rhinos that she could and dedicate it to him. But then she realized that wasn't enough, not for her and not for Michael. She had to find out what had happened to him, and she had to get to the bottom of the "something big." And, above all, to make sure the people responsible paid for their crimes.

"Are you okay, Crys?" Bongani asked.

She sat up and nodded. "I'm okay. Yes, I'm okay."

———

There was no sign of Johannes the next morning at the brief predawn breakfast. And, as they approached the Land Rovers, Crys saw that Nonga was behind the wheel of Johannes's vehicle.

She put her hand on Bongani's arm as he was climbing into his. "What's going on?" she asked. "Is Johannes really sick?"

He shook his head and climbed into the driver's seat. "He has a bit of fever and doesn't want to make the others sick," he mumbled, not looking at her.

Crys wasn't convinced. She'd only known Johannes a couple of days, but she didn't think he'd miss the drive unless he was really ill.

When they returned to camp before lunch, Crys decided to see for herself how he was feeling. Although it was already quite hot, he was sitting in a canvas chair inside his tent wearing a fleece. He was shivering.

She put her hands on her hips and stared at him. "Malaria?"

He nodded. "I've...I've taken some Coartem. We always keep them with us, in case. I'll be...I'll be fine after a day or so." He seemed to be finding it difficult to concentrate.

"I hope you are. Why did Bongani say you had flu, though?"

"I didn't want to worry the tourists. People...who've not lived in Africa...don't understand. Look, I think...I think...I'd better lie down. It'll break pretty soon, I'm sure. I've had it before. I'll be better by...by dinner, I reckon."

He stood up so shakily, Crys stepped forward to take his arm. He let her lead him to his stretcher, where she eased him down and pulled the blanket over him. He closed his eyes without another word, and immediately fell into a shivering, fitful sleep.

After watching him for a moment, she went to find Bongani.

"We have to get Johannes back to Tshukudu," she said. "He's very sick."

Bongani just looked at her.

"He's got malaria, you know."

Bongani nodded. "I know. Doesn't he have the pills?"

Maybe that was how it worked in this part of the world: if you got sick you took the pills, and you got better. Or you didn't...

But she couldn't accept it.

"Can we contact Anton?"

Bongani shook his head. "We're in the Letaba River valley. We'd have to go up into the hills. There we could get a signal from Giyani and make a call. But that's quite far. And I shouldn't leave the guests."

"Don't you have a satellite phone or something, for emergencies?"

He shook his head again. His face showed concern, but he didn't seem to want to do anything about the situation.

Crys knew it wasn't really her problem, but she was worried. Johannes was desperately sick. They shouldn't just leave him like this.

After lunch she went back to see how he was doing. There was an untouched plate of food next to his bed. He was shaking now, and she could see he was drenched in sweat.

"How are you doing, Johannes?" She put out her hand and touched his shoulder.

At first, she thought he hadn't heard her, but then he opened his eyes and looked at her. The whites seemed slightly discolored. But she couldn't be certain in the dimness of the tent.

"Who are you?" he muttered. "C-c-call M-Marissa." He turned his head away. It seemed to be a huge effort. "G-go away. Just call M-M-Marissa."

There was no one called Marissa at the camp, so she asked him who he meant, but he didn't reply. The short speech seemed to have sapped all his strength.

As Crys left the tent, Bongani was walking toward her.

"He's delirious," she told him. "Do you know someone called Marissa?"

"Marissa? He used to have a girlfriend called that. She was a nurse."

"We've got to get him to a hospital, Bongani. I'm scared he'll develop cerebral malaria if we don't act quickly."

She thought he was going to argue—again giving her some excuse why they shouldn't do anything. But after a moment, he nodded, standing up a little straighter.

"Okay, Nonga will take him to Tshukudu in the *bakkie*. Then Mr. Malan can decide what to do. But then we have only one driver for the game vehicles. Jacob could drive the other one, but…"

"Look, I can drive the second vehicle," Crys said, brushing aside the obstacles. Johannes needed medical attention. "I've driven in worse conditions than this. Dealing with snow and ice at home every winter is much more challenging than a little sand."

———

By the time Nonga had brought the pickup, Johannes seemed to have improved enough to walk to the vehicle—with Bongani and Nonga each supporting an arm. He made no objection other than another request for someone to fetch Marissa. They laid him on the bench seat in the back.

"Nonga will call Tshukudu about an hour before he gets there," Bongani said. "They can send a helicopter from Phalaborwa if he's really bad."

"He *is* really bad, Bongani."

Bongani looked away.

Some of the guests were upset about Johannes leaving and Crys taking over one of the vehicles. She expected Bongani to explain, but he simply promised that Nonga would be back the next day. It was clear that mention of malaria was taboo.

The afternoon game drive went well. Crys handled the vehicle easily—as she knew she would. But she was a bit nervous when they got close to the elephants again, unsure whether she'd know if and when to speed away. What had been exciting when Johannes was driving was scary when she was the one responsible for four guests. But she followed Bongani's lead, and all was well.

As they bumped back to camp across the dried grass, negotiating the patches of scrubby bushes, Crys thought that this would make a great story for the newspaper—game guide for a day.

After dinner, with the guests chatting about all they'd seen and not missing Johannes at all, Bongani called Crys aside. He led her outside the reddish ring of firelight.

"Crys, I'm sorry," he said in a low voice, "but I have to go away from camp tonight. There's a memorial for my cousin. I should've been there all day today, but, of course, I couldn't leave earlier…I must at least be there for a while tonight. To pay my respects. Will you be okay with the guests?"

Crys didn't feel at all comfortable with the idea. "I can't tell you what to do, but I'm not happy about it. What if one of the guests gets into trouble?"

"They'll all be asleep soon."

"I don't think you should go. I don't want to be responsible if something goes wrong."

"Please, Crys. It's very important for me. He and I were very close."

"Where is it? How long would you be gone?"

"His village is about an hour and a half from here."

"An hour and a half!" That meant three hours there and back, plus the time Bongani would spend paying his respects; he'd be away all night. She didn't like it one bit—the group seemed to be losing its leaders rather too quickly. And she knew nothing of what could go wrong in the African bush.

She shook her head, but realized he was going, whether she liked it or not.

"I would really prefer you didn't go. But…"

"I'll be back before six for the morning game drive. Nonga

will be back before lunch, too, so you can go back to being a tourist." He hesitated. "Crys, thank you for helping us out… helping *me* out." It might have been the shadows, but his face displayed a strange tension that made her wonder if something else was going on.

She nodded again, and then he was gone.

Chapter 10

Crys woke up with a jerk, her heart thumping in her chest. For a moment she was confused, wondering what had roused her. Had it been a nightmare? Then she realized it was a voice outside the tent.

"Crys. Crys. Wake up!" The tone was low, urgent.

It took another few seconds before her mind finally caught up and she recognized Bongani's voice.

"Crys. Wake up!"

She fumbled for her flashlight on the floor next to her sleeping bag and turned it on.

"Crys. Are you awake?" Bongani rasped.

"What's the matter?" she asked, sitting up. "It's the middle of the night."

Was one of the guests sick?

"Get dressed," he whispered. "Quickly. There's been a plane crash."

That made no sense to her. "A plane crash?" She had to be dreaming. There wasn't an airstrip anywhere near the camp, was there? "A plane crash?" she repeated.

"Yes. I heard it when I was driving back from my cousin's. It crashed on an old landing strip about three miles from here. I think it…I think it hit an elephant."

Crys gasped. "Hit an elephant?" A plane crashing into an elephant? This was becoming ever more bizarre.

"Get dressed. Please. I need someone to come with me. Someone who can drive. I watched you today. You did a great job." Bongani sounded desperate. She could see his outline faintly on the other side of the tent wall. "I'll fetch the rifle. I may need to shoot it."

"Shoot an elephant?" Crys shook her head, trying hard to get her mind around what was happening.

"I don't think it's dead. The noise was terrible."

She wriggled out of the sleeping bag, dressed quickly, and started to think what they might need. "Get some spotlights and a first-aid kit," she said through the canvas, matching her tone to his—they didn't want to wake the guests. "Someone may be hurt. And get a couple of bottles of water. There should still be some hot water in the thermos. And grab the instant coffee."

As she left the tent, she picked up her sleeping bag. If anyone was in shock, they might need it to warm them.

Outside, she hurried over to the dining area. Bongani was there, loading the stuff into a cardboard box. He had Johannes's Winchester 70 rifle slung over his shoulder.

"The first-aid kit and lights are in the Land Rover," he whispered. "I left it a bit down the track, so I didn't wake the guests."

Crys nodded, beginning to wake up properly. Dealing with panicked tourists was the last thing they needed. Then she paused for a moment. Actually, she was also a tourist. When had that changed?

She started to analyze what had occurred. Something must have gone wrong with the plane. No one in their right mind would try to land in the bush at night, even if it was a full moon. She looked up and saw that in fact it was at least a couple of days until full moon. She glanced at her watch. It was near three in the morning. Why were they flying at that time of night anyway?

She looked around for Bongani, but he was already on his way to the Land Rover. She started to follow him.

The only thing that made sense was that the plane was involved in something illegal. She'd read that a lot of drugs were smuggled into the States from Central America on small planes that flew in so low they were undetectable by radar, dropped their cargo, then left again, still undetected. Those pilots were willing to take the risk of landing at night on unlit dirt strips.

She wondered if something like that was happening here. Maybe they were smuggling ivory...or rhino horn. Or someone was entering or leaving the country illegally.

Whatever it was, she knew she needed to find out, particularly if rhino horn was involved. This might be exactly the lead she'd been looking for.

But as she reached the Land Rover, another question popped into her mind: why was Bongani coming back from his cousin's village so early? He'd said he'd be back just before six. She'd have to ask him when she had a chance.

The Land Rover wasn't new, but the engine had been well looked after. The body, on the other hand, was bashed all over from bumping into trees and bushes as various drivers chased down game. Bongani started the engine before Crys had even closed her door, reversed off the road, and swung it back in the direction he'd come from.

"It took me half an hour to get here from the strip. It's about three miles. The road's pretty bad. Some deep sand here and there. I was worried I'd get stuck." He paused. "Use the spotlight and look out for ellies. They're hard to see, even in a good light. At night everything is gray like them."

Crys nodded and plugged in one of the spotlights, her pulse quick, as adrenalin coursed through her body. The thought of hitting an elephant really frightened her. She'd seen YouTube clips of them flipping over a vehicle with no trouble.

As they lurched through the night, she began to worry about what might be ahead of them. If someone had been hurt in the plane—which was highly likely, given what Bongani had said—it would take hours for an ambulance to arrive from Phalaborwa or Giyani. But as they had no way of notifying a hospital in any case, they'd have to drive the injured there themselves.

They bumped toward the crash site, both thrown around the vehicle, and Bongani wrestling with the steering wheel, shifting into low-range gear when they hit soft sand. It was going to be a slow three miles.

And then they heard it. A terrifying sound—part trumpeting, part an anguished cry. Bongani slammed the brakes, bringing the Land Rover to a stop so they could listen. Crys shivered. The anti-poaching trip had been scary, but this was something else. She was much more scared now. An elephant could weigh six tons. Much more than the Land Rover. And there was likely to be a herd of them ahead. A herd of angry elephants. Her stomach tightened, and she could feel her heart beating faster.

She wondered if it was smart to go on? What if the elephants charged? What if they wanted revenge for their injured friend? She and Bongani would be dead in seconds, flattened into the sand.

She tightened her grip on the spotlight.

She looked over at Bongani; the moonlight was bright enough to show that he was just as worried.

"Maybe we should go for help; or at least wait until it's light," she said. "Can we get hold of the park rangers?"

Bongani shook his head. "Even if we could, it would be several hours before they could get here. We've got to go and see what's happening. Maybe the pilot is injured. Or his passengers."

As much as she disliked it, Crys realized he was right. "How do you think we should do it?" she asked. This was his country—his work—she had to trust him. There was nothing else she could do.

"We won't know until we can see them. We'll be in trouble if they're around the plane. We won't be able to get inside. And getting close to the injured ellie isn't going to be easy. The others will be angry."

Getting close to an injured elephant? This was insane. It was only yesterday that she'd seen her first one. She was definitely a long way from Minnesota.

They moved forward at a crawl now, neither speaking, both staring hard into the dark.

"There!" Bongani pointed over to the left. They could see a number of large shapes moving around. The noise was almost deafening now. The trumpeting was the scariest thing Crys had ever heard. It was indescribable—unlike anything she'd heard before—animal, human or otherwise. Her chest tightened, and she took several deep breaths as she tried to focus.

"And there's the plane." Bongani pointed straight ahead.

The plane lay about two hundred yards from the milling herd. It was right way up, but even at this distance, they could see it was badly damaged.

Crys pointed the powerful beam of the spotlight at the elephants. They immediately turned and stared into the light. They were agitated, ears flapping, trunks up in the air, trying to smell whether the vehicle posed a danger. Behind them Crys could see an elephant on the ground, moving, trying to stand, but not able to. If it'd been clipped by the wing, it probably had broken bones. If the prop had hit it, it could be sliced deeply and bleeding. Either way it was in great pain.

The largest elephant moved toward them. Crys struggled to keep the light steady as Bongani turned the Land Rover in the other direction, in case he had to make a quick getaway. The elephant stopped, lifted its trunk, and sniffed. Then it moved forward again.

"Let's get out of here." Crys whispered as though the elephant could hear her over the noise of the engine. Five tons of elephant coming toward her was more than she could handle.

Bongani shook his head and put the Land Rover in gear but kept the clutch in.

Crys glanced at him. She willed him to get them out of there. But he did nothing.

The elephant stopped again. It was only forty yards away. If it charged, Bongani might not be able to move quickly enough. It sniffed the air again and flapped its ears.

It was a stand-off, and it lasted for a long, drawn-out moment. Then, the elephant turned and moved back to the group. Bongani exhaled, and Crys realized she'd been holding her breath, too. She gasped in a lungful.

"How did you know that it wasn't going to charge?" Crys gasped.

Bongani shrugged. "I didn't, but they generally aren't aggressive unless provoked. It decided we weren't a threat."

Crys swallowed. "Generally aren't aggressive" seemed pretty poor odds to stake their lives on.

"How're we going to get close enough to the injured one?" she asked.

"Hold the light on it. I'll take a look." Bongani grabbed his binoculars from the shelf in front of him.

Crys did her best to keep the light in place, but it was difficult with the elephants milling around in front of their injured family member. Bongani was looking carefully at the downed creature. "I think the prop hit its back legs. I can see…I can see blood and at least one deep wound."

"Do you think it can recover?"

Bongani shook his head. "I'm not sure. It doesn't look like it. And I can tell it's in a lot of pain. We have to put it out of its misery." He put the binoculars down and looked over at Crys.

Crys hated the idea but was impressed by Bongani's commitment to stopping the animal's suffering. "Okay, but how do we get close enough to make sure you can get a clean shot without the others charging?"

He didn't answer immediately, and Crys had an idea.

"Get in the back and let me drive now. I'll do a wide arc to the left and come up directly opposite the elephant's head. That should give you a good shot to the side—from about fifty yards. Will that work?"

For a moment Bongani hesitated. Then, leaving the engine running, he climbed over to the next row of seats. Crys slid over into the driver's seat, put the Land Rover in gear and let out the clutch, making a smooth start. She eased forward, picking her way through the bushes so that they'd come up on the right side of the elephant. Her senses seemed sharpened by the night and the adrenalin. Somehow, her driving was better than it had been during the day.

When she reached the verge of the airstrip, she paused. They were more than a hundred yards away, and she could hear that the herd was very agitated.

"When I get close, I'll turn around," she said. "You can use the back seat as a rest. And if the elephants charge, going forward is a lot easier than reversing."

"Okay. Good idea."

As she moved the vehicle slowly forward, Bongani clambered over the seats to the back row. There, he rested the rifle on the seat-back.

At about seventy yards, the biggest elephant moved toward them again. Crys stopped. This time she didn't have the light on its eyes. It would have a clearer view without the blinding spotlight. She didn't dare move the Land Rover. The only sounds now were the rattle of the diesel engine and the injured elephant groaning. The trumpeting had stopped, and there was something ominous about the quiet.

After a few minutes, Bongani whispered that they should move ahead.

Crys nodded and eased forward again, as slowly as she possibly could. In the headlights she saw the elephant lift its trunk once more. Then it tossed its head and walked away. She relaxed a little.

At about sixty yards, she did a tight circle so they ended up fifty yards from the injured elephant, facing away from it, as they'd planned. She waited, idling the engine.

"Turn the engine off," Bongani said. "I may only have one shot, and I don't want the vibration."

She turned off the ignition. The Land Rover shuddered as the engine cut. She prayed that it would start right up if they needed it to.

"Now turn it on, but don't start it," Bongani whispered. She did as he said, and the fuel pump came on again. That would make starting it easier. She was grateful that Bongani knew what he was doing.

She thought about him for a moment. From working on the anti-poaching squad, to leading a safari, to dealing with an injured elephant, he really was quite impressive. It made her feel a little better.

"Now, shine the spotlight on its head," Bongani said.

Crys reached across to the passenger side and picked up the spotlight. She had to stand up so she could focus the powerful beam on the elephant's head, which was writhing in all directions as the suffering creature struggled. Then she noticed the biggest elephant heading for them again. It wasn't charging, but it was coming, with long determined strides.

"Quick, Bongani. The big elephant's coming for us!"

Bongani took the shot; there was a crack, and he jerked back with the recoil. The big elephant stopped in its tracks, shaking its head. Crys's ears were ringing, but she heard Bongani ask, "Did I get it?"

Holding the light in one hand, she checked with his binoculars. "It's not moving. I think…Yes, I think it's dead. Great shot." She sat down, shaking, her pulse thudding in her ears, but managed to start the engine without stalling it. "Let's get out of here and see if we can get to the plane."

She was determined now to see what was in it.

Chapter 11

Crys had to navigate her way through the long grass in a circle away from the elephants to reach the far side of the plane, but she tried to keep an eye on them as she drove. From that distance, it looked as though they'd formed a ring around the dead one, all facing in, as though they were mourning. Crys had read that they did that but hadn't really believed it. Now she felt her eyes prick with tears and had to blink them away. There was no time for weakness.

They edged up to the plane on the side away from the herd.

"We must keep watch," Bongani said. "You wouldn't believe how quickly they can move."

Crys shone the spotlight over the plane and decided it was a Cessna 210. It was badly damaged. The right wing was bent backwards, probably from hitting the elephant. The prop was twisted, and what looked like dried blood was splattered over the cowling and windshield. The undercarriage was down, but the left wheel had collapsed so the plane was tilted over with the left wing almost touching the sand.

The registration number was C9-773. "Is that a South African registration?" she asked.

Bongani shrugged.

She thought that was strange—you'd think he'd know. Especially as he flew regularly in the helicopter.

She pointed the light at the ground. There were deep ruts in the sand curving toward the plane from where the elephants stood. The plane had probably spun to the right after hitting the huge creature. They were lucky it hadn't flipped.

The right door of the plane was open—the passenger side. She shone the spotlight into the cockpit. There was no one in the passenger seat, but as she raised the beam they saw the pilot. He was slumped over the controls on the far side. And he wasn't moving.

"The pilot's hurt!"

Forgetting the elephants, they both jumped out of the Land Rover and ran to the pilot's door. But no matter how hard they pulled and pushed, they couldn't get it open. Giving that up, they dashed around to the other side, and Crys climbed in, pulled her flashlight from her pocket and shone the beam onto the bent-over figure. The pilot's head was caked with blood. She gritted her teeth and reached out to feel his neck for a pulse.

There was nothing. The man was dead. Her thoughts immediately turned to his family, wherever they were. What would they do without him?

A lump formed in her throat. She felt a need to see his face, to stop her thinking of him just as "the dead man," so she gently lifted his head away from the controls.

And there, right in the middle of his forehead was a hole—made by a small-caliber bullet from the look of it.

Crys's mind spun. She sat back and let his head drop gently onto the control panel. This man hadn't died in the crash landing. He'd been shot dead. And it had to have happened after the crash.

For a moment she couldn't speak. Then she found her voice. "Bongani!" she shouted. "He's been shot."

Bongani didn't reply. She twisted round, but she couldn't see his expression in the darkness.

What was going on with him? Why had he suddenly clammed up?

"Bongani," she said urgently, "didn't you hear me? There's a shooter around. We have to get out of here."

She was about to scramble out, but stopped. She had to see if there was anything—or anyone—in the back of the plane. But all the seats were empty. There were only blood spatters.

She climbed out and went to the cargo hold. She shone her light through the window. Other than bottles of oil and some rope, there was nothing. She turned to Bongani—he looked in shock, unsure what to do.

"Come on, Bongani, get with it! Push the door closed," she said. "We need to stop animals getting to the body. They'll be attracted by the blood."

He closed the door while she shone her light around, looking for anything that could tell them what had happened. Then she saw it: a set of footprints led into the dark toward the other side of the clearing. And next to the tracks was a trail of blood.

"Let's get out of here, Bongani. Whoever shot the pilot is still around, and I don't want to end up like him. We need to get the police."

They returned to the Land Rover, constantly looking over at the elephants, whose rumbles and calls indicated they were still distressed and dangerous. It was only when Crys and Bongani were ready to go that she realized they'd need the location for the police.

"Hold it, Bongani," she said, putting her hand on his arm. "I need to get the co-ords for this mess."

The Land Rover had a Garmin GPS mounted on the dashboard. Bongani had explained it was just for emergencies, and it was hardly ever used since the guides knew the area so well. Crys recognized it as similar to the one she'd used in the Minnesota Boundary Waters. She turned it on and waited impatiently while it booted and picked up satellite signals. Then she found the menu item that showed the coordinates and stored them before turning it off.

"Now they can bring in a chopper, if they want," she said. "Okay, let's go.

———

The drive back gave Crys a chance to think over what had happened. She was sure that the plane was being used for something illegal, but she didn't know what. There were no clues at the crash scene, no sign of contraband goods. She also knew that someone wanted to prevent the pilot telling anyone what had happened. So much so, they had shot him. Crys could feel the itch to know more. She felt it could be a connection to the rhino-horn smugglers.

Just as puzzling as the crash itself, was Bongani's behavior. From being on top of things in putting the injured elephant out of its misery, he'd gone to being almost catatonic—not answering her questions, not reacting to the murder scene. Then she remembered being puzzled about the time he'd returned to the camp. He was back much earlier than he'd said.

"Bongani," she said.

He didn't answer, but just continued to wrestle with the steering wheel.

"Bongani. Talk to me. Why were you back at camp so early? I thought you'd said you'd be back just before six."

It took a while before he answered.

"Everyone was exhausted. Normally, we remember someone the whole night. But everyone was too tired to continue after about one. So, I headed back."

That explained his unexpected return, but not his strange behavior. She was too tired to follow up on that right then. It would have to wait.

It was nearly five by the time they got back to camp, and streaks of red were beginning to appear in the east. Crys felt a wreck.

She hadn't had much sleep, and now her sky-high adrenalin had collapsed back to normal. But there was a lot to think about. The two of them were responsible for the guests.

"Bongani," Crys said as they approached the tents, "we have to contact the police."

He nodded. "We can drive up into the hills once we've sorted out the guests. It's about an hour, but the road's really bad."

That was not what Crys wanted to hear. The track to the nearest hills would take them back close to where the plane had crashed—where a murderer might be hanging out with a gun. That made her think about the bloody trail they'd seen. She realized they didn't know how many people had been on board when the plane crashed. Maybe the blood was from the shooter, who could have been injured in the crash, or maybe it was from another passenger on the plane, who might also be shot or seriously injured. There were hyenas around too: they'd seen a pack of twelve the day before—to say nothing of the mating lions.

With Bongani acting strangely, Crys realized she'd have to take responsibility. She could see only one option for what to do.

"We've got to get the guests out of here," she told Bongani, trying to keep the concern from her voice. "They have to be safe. The best idea is to get them packed up and take them back to Tshukudu. Anton will know what to do then. And the police can contact them there if they need to."

Bongani nodded. "Jacob, the cook, can drive them back," he said. "He knows the ropes, and Mr. Malan might need him. As soon as they leave, we can go back toward Giyani and call Mr. Anton and let him know. And we can call the police from there too."

In a way, Crys was grateful that they hadn't been able to call the police as soon as they'd found the body. Police all over the camp harassing the tourists would have complicated things further. It was better to keep things as simple as possible.

And she'd have time to try to figure out what was going on.

———

They needed to get the guests together and make an announcement. They were going to be upset that their trip was being cut short, but that was the least of the problems.

Bongani found Jacob and asked him to wake the guests and lay out a light breakfast. A few minutes later, Jacob went from tent to tent. As usual, he stopped in front of each tent and played a short tune on a small, handheld xylophone. He called it a dinner gong. It was pleasant to hear, but loud enough to break through a deep sleep.

Twenty minutes later the group had assembled around the breakfast table, helping themselves to something to eat and drink. They were still expecting the morning game drive and chatted quietly about what they might see.

Bongani grabbed some cereal and a coffee and ate quickly. Then he went to the head of the table. "Can I have your attention, please?" he said loudly.

It took a few moments for the group to quiet down.

"I have some bad news. Something happened last night that may put you in some danger. So, you all have to go back to Tshukudu this morning. Jacob will drive you."

Immediately people started talking and asking questions, alarm on their faces.

Bongani held up his hand. "Please, please. Let me explain. Last night, I heard a plane crash in the bush not far from here." There was a buzz from the group. "Of course, that's not a danger. But Crys and I went out, and when we got there, we found the pilot dead." He paused. "Not from the crash, but from a gunshot."

That caused quite a stir.

"There was a passenger on the plane, but he wasn't anywhere to be seen. Our guess is that he shot the pilot and headed into the bush." He looked around at the group. "So, you see why I need to make sure you're not in any danger."

The group was full of questions, but gave Bongani no chance to respond. He looked confused, not knowing which question to answer first.

What was up with him? Crys realized he needed help again.

She jumped up and shouted out, "Listen everyone, we *have* to do what Bongani says. Do you want to stay here and possibly get shot?"

Everyone stopped talking.

"Okay. Let's go," Bongani said firmly, pulling himself together. "Please pack up as quickly as you can. We'll leave the tents here. You'll be settled and safe back at Tshukudu very soon."

———

With the guests grumpy and scared, but safely in the vehicle with Jacob and on their way back to Tshukudu, Bongani and Crys drove back toward the airstrip.

Crys kept a careful lookout as they bumped along. This time she wasn't that concerned about elephants, but if there was an armed murderer around, she very much wanted to see him before he was too close. The rifle was between the two front seats. Loaded. Every time they came to a blind bend, she put her hand on the stock, half expecting to see a man in the middle of the road pointing a gun at them.

After about two miles, Bongani turned off onto a side road that led up into the hills. In reality, it was more like the bed of a river that had rushed down the hill, clearing away the soil and vegetation, leaving rocks and potholes. But after about ten minutes of grinding along in low-range gear, they came to an open spot with a view toward the north. They could make out the airstrip in the distance.

Bongani stopped the Land Rover and switched on his cell phone.

"Ask him how Johannes is doing if you can," Crys said.

He nodded, then after a few seconds he said, "I've got a signal." He punched in a number. Pretty soon he was telling Anton the whole story. It was a broken, frustrating few minutes. They kept getting cut off, and Bongani had to dial again and again, and repeat himself several times. But at last he managed to convey everything that had happened.

He disconnected, shaking his head.

"What did he say?" Crys asked.

"He'll phone the police and get them out here, but that could take several hours. He says we should wait for them at the camp, because they'll want to question us. As soon as they're finished, we must head back to Tshukudu. He said we shouldn't go back to the plane. Too dangerous. And he's already made a plan for the tourists."

"And Johannes?"

"He's doing okay."

"That's good news at least," Crys said, trying to find some relief in the situation. "Let's get back to the camp then, and wait for the police there."

But Bongani shook his head. "I have to try and find that man— the one who's hurt. I can't leave him for the hyenas like…" He broke off, but Crys knew what he was thinking.

Crys didn't like that proposal at all. She thought Anton's instructions made sense. They shouldn't go looking for a murderer, no matter how injured he was. They didn't even know if he was alone. They didn't even know it was a man, for that matter. They knew nothing. As a reporter she was really keen to find out, but as the person tracking down an armed murderer, not so much.

"I don't think you should do that, Bongani. You could get shot. I think we should do what Anton said."

"But there may be other passengers who are alive. They may need help."

Crys felt a sinking feeling in her stomach. "But is that up to us, Bongani?"

Bongani paused, thinking. "Who else have they got?" he said without looking at her. "The police won't be here for hours."

Crys thought it through. What Bongani was saying was true, but it never made sense to risk a life to save another, especially when there was so little information. And the only information they had was that at least one person out there was a murderer.

"Anton said we shouldn't go back there, and I think he's right."

"I have to do this, Crys. I'll drop you off at camp first."

Then it dawned on Crys that Bongani may have a different reason for going back to the plane—one he wasn't willing to share. Perhaps he knew something about the cargo. Perhaps that was what he was after.

Now her curiosity got the better of her fear. She made a quick decision.

"It's too dangerous for you to go alone," she said. "Okay, let's take a look. We'll go together. But we need to be super careful."

"I'm fine by myself."

Did he not want her with him? This made her even more determined. "No, Bongani. I'm coming—it's always better with two."

Bongani hesitated, but then nodded. "Thank you, Crys."

Crys realized that she'd just have to follow Bongani's lead and hope that he knew what he was doing. And hope she didn't become an obstacle to what he wanted to find.

Chapter 12

They drove back down the hill and headed to the airstrip. When they got close and could take a good look around, Bongani stopped, and Crys scanned the area with her binoculars. The dead elephant lay like a gray mound where it had fallen. The rest of the herd wasn't in sight.

There was no sign of any second man.

She focused on the plane and saw the dead pilot's head through the cracked windshield. The passenger seats still seemed empty.

"I can't see a second guy," she whispered to Bongani and passed him the binoculars.

He studied the veld for far longer than she had, pausing occasionally and adjusting the focus wheel.

"Okay," he said eventually. "I'll drive past the plane and stop behind it. It will be hard for him to surprise us if he's inside. If there's no one there, we'll follow the trail."

Crys could feel the adrenalin building up again. Following a murderer through the bush sounded mad.

Bongani put the Land Rover into gear, and they set off through the bushes, keeping well away from the plane. Then he swung the vehicle round behind it, leaving a clear area ahead of them in case they had to make a quick getaway.

They stopped and Bongani took the rifle, gave Crys the tiniest of nods, and climbed out. Crys watched as he walked slowly up to the plane.

"Be careful…" she murmured, even though he couldn't hear her.

When he reached the plane, he stretched his neck and peered through the back window for a moment. Then he waved Crys to come. She slipped out of the Land Rover and covered the ground to the plane in seconds.

Nothing had changed since the previous night, except that now there was a buzz of black flies around the pilot's head, settling and taking off, their hum almost as sickening as the smell of dried blood. They also noticed the distinct smell of decay. Bodies decomposed quickly in the heat of the veld. Crys closed her eyes for a moment.

Opening them, she looked around. "Well, this is all we have to go on," she said, pointing out the footprints and blood trail they'd seen the previous night.

Bongani nodded. "I'll go ahead."

They moved forward slowly. The trail led up toward a stand of trees. Crys examined each one with her binoculars, but saw nobody. Then she hurried after Bongani, not wanting to be separated from him.

When they reached the edge of the strip, the trail turned to the right. They followed it for another couple of hundred yards.

"He's badly hurt," Bongani said, pausing to point at the blood trail. The spots seemed to be more frequent and the footprints dragged.

He raised his eyes. Up ahead there was a rocky outcrop, thrusting up from the surrounding plain.

"Yes, I bet he's there," Crys said. "Maybe there's a cave or something." She looked through her binoculars and scanned the rocks systematically, making sure not to miss anything, but still she saw nothing.

They moved on again slowly, making frequent halts to check ahead.

Suddenly a shot rang out, a *POP-pop* echoing off the rocks.

Bongani dropped to the ground and Crys followed, planting her face in the soil. She spat out sand and grass. Her heart was racing. She couldn't quite get her head around what had happened—she'd never been shot at before.

She crawled on elbows and knees, twigs and sharp grass blades scratching her face, until she was next to Bongani. "I think that's a handgun," she whispered. "That's what it sounded like to me. He'll be lucky to hit us at this distance."

Bongani didn't reply. He lifted his head a few inches…then a few more.

"Do you see him?"

"No."

"He must be behind those thick bushes to the right of the rocks."

Another shot—*POP-pop*—and a sharp thwack nearby that made Crys jerk sideways. The bullet had hit a tree just to her right.

Crys raised her head too. "You'll never hit us at this distance," she shouted. "You've got no chance. Throw out your gun. We can help you."

Silence. Just the whizz and whir of insects.

Bongani looked at her sideways and tipped his chin up. He wanted her to shout again.

"Come out with your hands up or we'll start shooting," she yelled.

Bongani waited a few seconds, then aimed at the rocks close to the bushes and fired. A small puff of dust flew up as it hit the rock. Three bullets left in the magazine.

"Is anyone else with you?" Crys shouted.

Still no reply.

"You've got no chance. Come on out."

Still nothing from the bush.

"The police are on their way. We called them on our way here. They have our co-ordinates. You know what they'll do if you don't come out. They'll pump a million bullets into the bush. There'll be nothing of you left to bury..." She nodded to Bongani, and he fired again. Two bullets left.

Still nothing.

Crys simply couldn't believe she was crouching in South African scrub, trying to negotiate with a murderer. A murderer who had a gun and clearly wanted to kill her. Despite what she'd said, there was every possibility they were in range. Particularly if he was silently creeping up on them. The fatal shot could come at any moment. She was sweating from more than the heat now.

"If you come out now, the police will take you back alive."

They still had bullets, but Crys was worried about another possibility: what if the killer wasn't alone? What if there had been other passengers in the plane, and he was holding one hostage? What if Bongani killed them by mistake?

This had to end, and soon. But Crys had no idea how to break the standoff.

Bongani let off another round into the rock above the bush—another puff of dust sprang into the air. He reloaded—quick, efficient. Back to four bullets.

"Okay...I come." It was a weak voice, not a shout, more a whine. And it was not South African. Crys let out a sigh of relief and glanced across at Bongani. He was stock still, the rifle still ready.

They heard stuttering footsteps approaching, and a crack as the man stood on a dead branch. Then the bush parted, and he hobbled out, his hands raised, one holding the handgun. There was blood on his trousers and in his hair and down the left side of his face.

Crys stood up now, amazed. He was Vietnamese—unmistakably so, from the shape of his face to the tone of his skin. It was the same as hers.

"Throw down the gun," she ordered in Vietnamese. "Now!"

The man dropped it.

"What did you say to him?" Bongani asked.

"He's Vietnamese. I told him to drop the gun."

Bongani looked puzzled by this development. "Oh…" he said. "Get his gun. Be careful."

While Bongani covered her, she cautiously went up to the man, picked up the gun, then backed away to a safe distance.

"Turn around," she said, still keeping her distance.

When he was facing in the other direction, Bongani came to stand beside her. "Search him," he said.

Crys took a breath and approached the man. How did you pat someone down? She'd only seen it done in movies and at the airport. She squared her shoulders, stepped forward and began patting the man's arms, armpits, chest, back, groin. All she found was keys and a wallet in his trousers, and some papers in his shirt pocket.

"Here's something," she said over her shoulder.

She pulled the papers out. There was a passport too. She flipped through it.

"He's from Vietnam. His name is Ho Van Tan." She examined the stamps. "Looks as though he's in and out of Mozambique a whole lot. Okay, let's take him to the plane." She prodded him with the gun.

"Wait," Bongani said.

She turned to him.

"I want to look where he was hiding."

"Why?" she asked.

But without answering, Bongani pushed his way through the bushes in the direction from which the man had emerged. She wondered why he was so keen to see where the man had hidden out.

She had no option but to keep Ho covered and wait for him to return.

And while she did, she was more certain than ever that Bongani was thinking about the plane's cargo.

After what seemed like an age, but could only have been minutes, Bongani reappeared carrying an aluminum briefcase.

"There was no one else there. But I found this."

So, there was cargo—and Bongani knew it. He had to be involved in this in some way. She was sure there would be rhino horn in the case.

"He has keys," Crys said, nodding at Ho. "I felt them in his pocket."

Ho angrily shook his head. "No. No keys."

"He's lying. They're in his right trouser pocket."

To her surprise, Bongani grabbed Ho and jerked his arm behind his back, so violently the man gave a yell of pain. He struggled weakly, and Bongani got the keys from his pocket with little trouble. Crys was shocked—Bongani had previously seemed quite gentle. Perhaps he was showing his true colors. But something puzzled her—if he was working with Ho, wouldn't he have known him? There had been no sign of recognition between them. And why would Ho have shot at them if he'd expected Bongani to rescue him?

When Bongani let go, Ho sank to the ground. He was clearly in bad shape.

Bongani just stood, holding the keys and the briefcase as though that was that.

"We should go back now," he said.

"Don't you want to know what's inside?" she asked, suspicious he didn't want her to know. "Maybe drugs? Or rhino horn?"

Bongani hesitated.

"Open the damn thing," she said. There was no way she was leaving before she knew what was inside.

Bongani looked unwilling. But at last he fiddled with the locks. Crys watched his face carefully to assess his reaction. As he pulled open the lid of the case, his eyes widened and his mouth dropped open. Crys followed his eyes to the contents and gasped.

"Oh, my God."

It was full of money. U.S. greenbacks, all one-hundreds. It was a fortune.

Chapter 13

Half an hour later, Crys was behind the wheel of the Land Rover, driving them back to the camp. Ho was slumped in the seat next to her, apparently exhausted by the walk back to the vehicle. Bongani sat behind him, covering him with the handgun. As they went, Crys tried to get information out of the man, asking questions in Vietnamese about where he'd come from and who the dead pilot was. Ho said nothing. Every now and again, he shook his head. It was as if he were drunk.

Half a million dollars in a briefcase, she thought. It had to be for something big. It could be the connection to Michael she'd been looking for.

"Do you know a Michael Davidson—a reporter from America?" she asked him in Vietnamese. "Tell me now!"

"Don't know any Americans," he replied, shaking his head again, and he refused to say anything else.

Crys felt her frustration building. Every time she felt she was getting closer to finding out something useful about Michael, the rug was pulled from under her. But he could be lying. She would question him again when they reached the camp.

After about ten minutes of rough bumping and bouncing, Ho let out a groan and leaned forward. He put his head on his knees and let his arms hang down. It was clear now he was in a lot of pain. After another minute or so, he let out another weird, strangled groan and seemed to collapse further.

"I hope he doesn't die," Bongani said, leaning forward a little. "The police will want him to talk."

Crys shuddered at the thought of what Ho was in for if the police were anything like the anti-poaching team.

"What were you asking—?" Bongani began, but suddenly Ho sat up. Crys glanced at him…right into the barrel of a gun. She froze, cursing herself for missing a second gun when she'd searched him. It must have been in an ankle holster. She gripped the wheel harder, looked forward at the road.

"Don't move!" Ho yelled at her. Then turned back to Bongani. "Drop gun, or I kill her."

"If you shoot her, I'll kill you," Bongani shouted back, but there was uncertainty in his voice. Crys hoped Ho wouldn't pick it up.

"No problem. I die if police get me anyway. Drop gun. Now!"

Crys was beginning to panic. He was going to kill both of them. They bounced down into a deep rut and up again, Crys almost losing control of the vehicle. She tightened her arms and clenched her hands harder round the wheel.

Her mind raced through her options—none of them seemed good.

Think!

The moment seemed to stretch. The sun seemed suddenly hotter. The air thick and oppressive. She almost couldn't breathe. And then an idea came to her.

"Bongani…" she said carefully, "he's going to kill me. Drop the gun and grab the back of my seat so he can see your hands."

"Then he'll kill both of us!"

"Drop the gun, dammit, and grab the seat."

She hoped he could figure out what she was going to do. She eased her foot onto the accelerator, letting the vehicle speed up, but not too much.

Bongani dropped the gun and, as soon as Crys saw Ho lean backwards to retrieve it, she slammed hard on the brakes. Ho spun forward, lost his gun, and his head slammed onto the metal over the dashboard. He collapsed, sliding down so he was half on the seat and half on the floor. She grabbed the gun and jumped out of the Land Rover. Bongani followed, his eyes wide. He'd figured it out.

"Fuck," he said. "That was clever."

Crys took a deep breath. "I thought that was the end of us."

He opened the passenger door and grabbed Ho, dragging him onto the ground.

There was no movement from the man. He fell into the dust like a rag doll. His arms were twisted and his legs bent awkwardly.

Crys suddenly had an awful feeling. She pushed Bongani aside and felt for Ho's pulse.

There wasn't one.

A wave of panic hit her. Had she killed him? Had she taken someone's life...? She stumbled backwards.

"He's...he's dead." She turned to Bongani. "He's dead. We killed him... *I* killed him."

Bongani just stared.

"What are we going to do?" The panic was rising.

After a moment, Bongani said, "Why don't we take him back to where he was hiding? If someone finds him, they won't be able to tell we did anything."

Crys put both hands on the side of the Land Rover to support herself, shaking her head, trying to think clearly.

"No. It was self-defense. We'll just have to explain it all to the police. I didn't mean to kill him. You saw that. He pulled a gun on us! I was looking into the barrel of a gun. I had to do *something*."

"What about the money?"

She let go of the Land Rover. "The money?" For a moment, she didn't know what Bongani was talking about. In her confusion, she'd forgotten about the briefcase stuffed with dollars.

It came back to her. "We'll give it to the police. It'll be their problem. We'll just tell them exactly what happened."

Bongani shook his head. "You don't know the police here. They'll keep it for themselves. It's a lot of money."

Crys gaped at him. "They can't do that! We know all about it. I'll be writing about it in the paper. They'll have to investigate it properly. And surely they'll be more concerned that two men have died?"

Bongani was shaking his head. "They won't care about the dead men. They'll just want the money. We'll just be in their way."

"We have to turn it in to them! It's not ours. We can't just keep it!"

He stared at her, still shaking his head, lips slightly pursed.

Suddenly Crys guessed exactly what he wanted. "That's it, isn't it Bongani? You want to keep the money yourself!"

"We have to. It's not safe—"

"Don't tell me what to do! It's bad enough I've killed someone. And now you want to turn me into a thief?"

"Crys, I know about this. You don't. This is my country, not yours. The police—"

"It's not right, Bongani. I won't do it!" She was beginning to shout. "And anyway, as soon as you start flashing the money around, everyone will know it was you who stole it."

They stared at each other. A stand-off.

Bongani broke the silence. "It's not the money. I don't want to steal it. I just don't want to be killed by the police!" His voice was angry too now, and he was clenching his fists.

Crys bit her tongue. She wanted to scream at Bongani, tell him that he'd wanted the money all along, that whatever was going on he was part of it. But if she was right about him, that could be extremely dangerous.

"Crys, please," Bongani continued, more quietly. "You don't understand. Last year, a jewelry shop was robbed in Johannesburg. They got away with diamonds and other stones, and a lot of Krugerrands. The police tracked them down to a town called

Hoedspruit, near Phalaborwa, and raided a house belonging to the mother of one of the robbers. *All* the robbers died in the shootout. And the mother and the grandmother, too…The old lady was bedridden. Both women were shot in the head like the pilot. By the police—'for resisting arrest' the police said."

She turned and walked away a few steps. She looked down at the man she'd killed. If the police here were so corrupt, how could she trust that they would understand that she'd acted in self-defense? How could she plead her case?

"And the diamonds and Krugerrands?" she asked, still looking at Ho.

"The police said they never found them."

At last, Crys realized what Bongani was saying: if the two of them weren't around, they wouldn't be telling anyone about the briefcase. She turned back to Bongani. She could feel herself shaking.

"You mean…You must be kidding…They'd really just kill us?"

He nodded but didn't say anything.

Crys couldn't believe the police were really like that in South Africa. Could they be that corrupt?

"There are two of us," she said, "and I'm from the US and a newspaper reporter…They wouldn't dare touch me, would they? There'd be…there'd be an international incident…Something…"

Crys put her hands to her head, as if she were trying to contain the realization that was growing there. The police would use what she'd done against her—so they could keep the money for themselves. It was unbelievable.

Bongani pointed at the briefcase. "That money, Crys, it's for the rhino poaching. Everyone is involved. Do you think they can operate without the police? The police get their share. Always. Think about what Hennie did the other night. Why did he do that, Crys? It's because the police won't do anything. And if anyone speaks up, they disappear. I know these things. I—"

"How do you know that's what the money was for?" There was an accusation in Crys's voice, and she moved toward him.

Bongani hesitated, then took a step back. "It's such a lot of money. The police will want it. They'll kill us. Nobody will know; nobody will find us."

Suddenly Crys thought of Michael again. He'd come to this part of the country, found something big, and vanished. And the police said they'd discovered nothing. But had they looked? Or did they know what had happened to him all along?

She felt way out of her depth. It seemed she was either going to be arrested or dead. She turned away from Bongani and took a few steps down the track. She squatted down on her haunches and put her head in her hands. How had she got into this situation? She didn't mean to kill Ho, and now she might be killed herself...for trying to help. This had to be a dream, a bad nightmare.

She stayed in that position for a couple of minutes, but then, instead of panic, and despite the heat, a kind of chill calm settled on her. There had to be a solution to all this. She stood up and walked back to Bongani.

He was standing watching her calmly, as if he knew she'd come around to his way of thinking eventually.

"What should we do then?" she asked flatly.

"What I said—take him back to those rocks and leave him. But we keep the money."

"The Land Rover tracks, our footprints—we'd never get away with it."

"We'll say we followed the tracks then gave up."

She looked into his eyes. "It won't work, Bongani. There are cartridges we won't be able to find, bullets, DNA, fingerprints."

He was silent for several seconds. "Okay. We bury the money here. We can come back for it later."

She glowered at him.

What if he wanted it all for himself? she asked herself. Then he'd make sure she couldn't come back for it.

But she couldn't read him; his face was impassive.

She had to trust him for the moment—play this by ear. And watch her back too. She had to make a choice. Now.

"All right, all right, we bury it here. But we tell Johannes and Anton *everything* as soon as we're back at Tshukudu. Make it their problem. This is too much for me. I'll get the GPS co-ords so we can find it when we come back."

Then an idea occurred to her—a little insurance policy. She leaned inside the Land Rover and took the briefcase out, opened it, removed a bundle of bills, counted out ten and gave them to Bongani. A thousand U.S. dollars. That would help his family. And hopefully save her too, if he ever decided to say she was the one responsible. She put the rest back.

"I'm sure you can use the money," she said. "Don't tell anyone and be careful how you spend it."

He nodded.

"Okay, let's bury the case."

In saying that, Crys knew she was stirring up a hornet's nest. The police would want it, Bongani would want it. And somebody had lost it and would want it back. She was betting that somebody knew something about Michael.

Bongani nodded again. He quickly unclipped the spade from the side of the Land Rover, walked about thirty yards to the side of the track, and started digging.

It didn't take long in the soft sand to make a hole big enough for the briefcase. Crys threw it in, and Bongani covered it up, smoothing the surface and kicking leaves over it.

Back at the Land Rover, Crys grabbed the GPS and noted the coordinates of the hole. While she did that, Bongani used a dead branch to erase their footprints in the sand, walking backwards toward the vehicle.

"What are we going to do with him?" Bongani asked, pointing at Ho.

"Put him back in the passenger seat. Just make sure he doesn't fall out before we get back to the camp."

Crys helped him lift up the body and dump it into the seat. Bongani closed and locked the Land Rover door, then climbed into the back. He clearly had no intention of riding back to camp sitting next to the corpse.

"Let's get going," Crys said. "We're going to have to persuade the police we didn't murder this man."

Chapter 14

By the time Bongani and Crys reached camp, they had their story straight. The last thing they wanted was each to give the police a different story, so they agreed they'd tell the truth exactly as they remembered it…except for the briefcase. Bongani was sure that mentioning that would put them in danger. So, they'd leave it out altogether. It seemed pretty straightforward, and they didn't see how it could go wrong. At least that's what Crys told herself.

Climbing out of the Land Rover, Crys noticed Bongani flipping through the money she'd given him, looking carefully at a couple of the bills and holding them up to the light.

"You think they're fake?"

He shook his head. "I don't know. There must be half a million dollars in that case. If it's all real, it could feed a village for years."

"That money was for something illegal," she said. "Maybe to buy rhino horn, as you said. Or ivory. Or smuggled diamonds…"

"We can't let the police find this," Bongani said, folding the notes up. "I must hide them." He headed to the kitchen tent and a few moments later came out with a zip-lock bag.

"I'll hide them where no one will find them. Go and start the Land Rover, please."

Puzzled, Crys did as he asked.

Sitting in the driver's seat, the engine turning over, and doing her best not to look at the dead Ho slumped in the passenger's side, she watched as Bongani sealed the bills in the bag and then walked to the edge of camp. Near one of the big, spreading jack-alberry trees, he scooped some sandy earth out with his hand, making a shallow hole, then dropped the bag inside and covered it over.

"Okay, Crys." He beckoned with his dusty hand. "Bring the Land Rover over here and park it with one wheel right over where I've buried the money."

Smart, Crys thought. Someone could search the camp and the Land Rover and never find it. But there was still a pointer to the briefcase: she'd entered the coordinates of where it was buried on the GPS.

Crys decided she'd better hide that too. They couldn't leave anything to chance.

She took the GPS into her tent and started wrapping it in one of her towels. Then she hesitated. She would need a backup of the coordinates in case the GPS died. She switched on her phone, waited impatiently for it to boot up, then chose the contacts menu and added two new names: Katie Latimer and Longley Svenson. She gave Katie's number as +1 612 followed by the last seven digits of the latitude of the money; Longley's she used for the longitude. Then she turned off the GPS, wrapped it up, and asked Bongani to help her hide it.

"Under the wheel on the bonnet of the Land Rover," he said pointing.

"You're pretty good at hiding things."

He nodded, serious. "You have to be, where I come from."

She wasn't sure what he meant by that but decided not to ask.

They'd hardly had anything to eat at breakfast, so Crys made sandwiches, which Bongani washed down with a cold beer, and she with orange juice.

When she'd finished, she felt exhausted. More than anything

she wanted to sleep before the police arrived, even if it were only a power nap.

She hesitated. She and Bongani were the only two in the camp, and if she was right about Bongani's involvement in the smuggling, what was to stop him getting rid of her while she was asleep? He could easily say that Ho had shot her; he could use Ho's handgun.

Then the briefcase of money would be his.

"You must be tired," she said to Bongani. "Go and have a nap while we wait. I'll keep watch for a while."

"Are you sure?"

She nodded, and he walked off to his tent.

She walked over to a tree from which she could keep his tent in sight, then sat down and leaned against it. After a few minutes, her eyelids started to droop. She shook her head. She needed to stay awake.

She thought about what Bongani had said.

Did the South African police really kill people for money? It was hard to believe. But Bongani's story was terrifying—if it was true. Maybe he had made it up…

Her eyes drooped again. She let them stay like that for a few seconds, then shook her head again and slapped her cheeks.

She couldn't figure out how Bongani was involved. He knew what the money was for, but didn't know Ho. And he was obviously scared to be found by the police with the money.

Her head nodded and slumped forward.

———

Crys woke from a deep sleep with a start. Someone was shaking her shoulder.

"Wake up. Wake up."

She opened her eyes and saw a policeman standing over her.

"Hello, Officer," she stammered. "Sorry. I must have drifted off. Didn't have much sleep last night." She shook her head and pointed. "Mr. Chikosi is in that tent."

She stood up. "I'll be back in a minute." She headed for the bush toilet.

When she returned, Bongani was standing near the policeman, rubbing his face.

She saw that the police had arrived in two four-by-four vehicles. One was a closed van—to remove the pilot's body, Crys guessed. They were in for a surprise: there were now two bodies.

The leader of the group was a Sergeant Nkomo. He introduced himself and his men.

Crys ran her hands through her hair to straighten it and beckoned him aside. He frowned but followed her over to the Land Rover. He took a slight step back when he saw Ho.

"This man..." The words stuck in Crys's throat. "This man was in the plane too. He...he tried to shoot me, while we were bringing him back here. I slammed on the brakes and...and he hit the windscreen."

"And that's how he died?" asked Nkomo, scowling.

"Yes," she said, trying to speak clearly. "Yes. That's how he died. I only meant for him to drop his weapon. It was...an accident."

He studied her in angry silence for a moment, then turned to the Land Rover and checked out the body.

"Step over there," he ordered her, pointing toward Bongani.

She did as he said and watched as he moved away toward the trees and made a call on a satellite phone.

He returned after about five minutes, looking a bit calmer.

"Headquarters is sending a detective," he said. "He'll be here tomorrow. Now I have to secure the crime scene and take full statements from everybody." He barked some orders in a local language, and a man headed for one of their vehicles.

"He's going to guard the plane and make sure nobody interferes with it," he explained. "Now, I will take your full statements."

The sergeant led Bongani and Crys into the shade of the dining area, and they spent the next hour giving him their stories. He laboriously wrote them in longhand in a large spiral-bound notebook.

"We will stay here until the detective comes," Nkomo said when it was done. "We have sleeping bags."

"You and your men can use the guest tents," Crys told him in as friendly a manner as she could. "And we have plenty of food and some beer—it was meant for the guests…"

As he walked away, she felt a little less anxious. Nkomo had seemed to accept the story of Ho's death. She hoped she'd been worrying too much.

Chapter 15

It was late the next morning when another police Land Rover arrived. It didn't come from the same direction as the others, but from the airstrip. Crys figured they'd gone there before coming to the camp. Probably the detective wanted to get his head around the crime scene first.

The driver pulled up in the shade of a large mahogany tree, and he and his passenger climbed out. The passenger was obviously the detective—a large, overweight man in plain clothes with damp sweat marks under his arms. He looked hot and tired and not very smart. Crys guessed that the interviews wouldn't take very long.

The detective walked up and looked at Bongani and Crys in turn. Then he said to Crys, "I am Colonel Mabula. You are...?"

"I'm Crystal Nguyen. I'm on a safari from Tshukudu Lodge. And this is Bongani Chikosi, who works for Tshukudu."

Mabula nodded, looking them up and down—a little rudely Crys thought. But then she reminded herself what he must have heard about what had happened.

"Let us get out of the sun," he said at last. "And could we get something cold to drink?"

"May I offer you a beer?" Crys asked, thinking that it would start things off on the right note.

"No, thank you, I'm on duty. Cold water would be fine."

He took over the dining area and, once Crys delivered the water, asked them to wait until he called them. They found what shade they could from the jackalberry tree, while Mabula sat with Nkomo at the table.

———

"Well, sergeant. What do you think?" Colonel Mabula got straight to the point.

"Sir, I took statements from both of them. Here they are." Nkomo handed over his spiral-bound notebook.

Mabula opened it and read both statements carefully.

"I'm pleased you have a good handwriting, Sergeant. I could read most of what you wrote."

"Thank you, sir."

"What's your impression of the two?"

Nkomo took a few moments before answering. "I interviewed them separately, of course, and asked them a lot of questions. Their stories were very much the same."

"Do you think the stories are true? Or did they just agree to say the same lies?"

"I think the stories are true. But they both seemed very nervous."

Mabula took out a handkerchief and wiped his forehead, wishing it wasn't so hot.

"This woman…" He checked the statement again. "Naguwhen, as you've written it here. She is from Vietnam?"

"She is from America, she said. A reporter."

"She is Vietnamese," Mabula said firmly. He knew well how involved the Vietnamese were in rhino-horn poaching. Now this Vietnamese woman had suddenly appeared in the middle of what he believed was a big smuggling operation. And with the man, Chikosi…

This was supposed to be coincidence?

"This man, Ho, who was killed in the vehicle. He is also Vietnamese. Did they say he had anything with him apart from these documents?"

The sergeant shook his head.

"Did you ask them?"

Again, Nkomo shook his head, looking a bit puzzled.

Mabula watched him for a few moments, saying nothing. Then he asked, "Did they do anything or say anything after you'd taken their statements that made you suspicious?"

"No. They were helpful and polite."

Mabula sat for a few minutes, then said, "We'll see. Please ask the woman to come here. While I talk to them, you and your men will search the camp."

Nkomo jumped up, but Mabula stopped him. "Carefully, Sergeant Nkomo—you must search the camp very carefully."

"Yes, sir," Nkomo responded. Then he went to fetch Crys.

———

From under the jackalberry tree, Bongani and Crys watched the two policemen's discussion.

"What are they saying?" Crys murmured to Bongani. But he just shook his head. He couldn't hear.

At last, Nkomo stood up and called Crys over.

She walked to the dining area, her anxiety like a hard ball in her belly.

Once she'd sat down, Mabula fixed her with a stare that seemed to go on forever. "I read your statement," he said eventually, "but I want to hear your story directly from you. Please tell me everything—from the beginning."

Crys started with Bongani waking her up in the middle of the night and went from there. Mabula sat sipping his water and listening to her without comment, until she came to the elephant episode.

"He shot this elephant?" he interrupted. "He had no authority to do that."

"The animal was suffering..."

"This was not your decision. You should have left it for the authorities."

"We needed to get to the plane. We thought the people inside might have been injured, and it wasn't possible with all the elephants around." She decided not to mention wanting to see if there was a connection to Michael. "We assumed we could shoot it if human lives were in danger," she said.

He didn't look convinced, but he waved his hand. "Go on."

"After that I climbed into the plane. There was only the pilot there. He was slumped over the controls, and I thought he was dead. I tried to find a pulse, but I couldn't feel one. So, I lifted his head—"

"Why did you move the body?"

"I wanted to double check he was dead."

"And when you did, you saw that he had been shot?"

"Yes, right in the head."

He considered this for a moment. "Do you have any firearms other than the hunting rifle, Mrs. Nguyen?"

"No, not here."

"Where then?"

"I have some guns at home in Minnesota in the U.S. For target shooting."

"Handguns?"

"No!" she was sweating now. What was he implying? "Are you suggesting *I* shot the pilot?"

"I'm not suggesting anything. Continue with your story..."

He let her summarize the story up till when she and Bongani went back to the plane.

"Why did you do that? Why didn't you just wait for the police?"

"We thought someone else—another man—might be injured. There was blood outside the plane. And there are lions and hyenas…and the elephants…" Crys realized it didn't sound so convincing now, sitting there at the camp.

"Well, you found what you were looking for." Mabula gestured with his head behind her. She knew he meant the Land Rover, and Ho's dead body.

"Actually, he found us."

Crys described how they'd followed Ho's trail, and how he'd shot at them from the rocks. "But we had a rifle, and he only had a handgun. So eventually, well, he gave up."

He nodded and made a couple of notes on his pad. He seemed fine with her story. But his next question shook her. She realized she'd badly underestimated Colonel Mabula.

"What did he have with him?"

"With him?" Crys fiddled with her hair, winding it around her finger. When she realized what she was doing, she held her hands in her lap to prevent them from fidgeting. "Nothing. Just the gun, which he threw down. Actually, he had another gun— which I stupidly missed when I searched him—"

"What did you find when you searched him?" he interrupted.

"His…his passport and…some papers and money. In his wallet. It's still there." Crys was beginning to feel frazzled.

"He had nothing with him of value? There was nothing in the plane?"

She almost blurted out the truth, but she felt something was wrong. Why did he think there was something else to the story? Was he in on it somehow? Was Bongani right—the police had been waiting for the briefcase of money, to take their cut?

She shook her head.

"Mrs. Nguyen—"

"I'm Ms., not Mrs," she interrupted. It was a mistake. She knew he was trying to rattle her, and he was succeeding.

He nodded, one eyebrow raised, and told her to continue. He let her finish the story of the drive back and Ho's attempt to hijack them.

When Crys was done, he looked down at his notes, took a sip of water and glared at her. "I'm looking for a motive here, *Ms.* Nguyen. Two men are dead. We think the first man was shot with the gun you say the second—Mr. Ho—pulled on you. Mr. Ho was beaten to death."

"He wasn't beaten to death. He was hurt in the plane crash and then hit his head on the windshield. I told you what happened."

"My colleagues have examined him." Mabula wasn't looking at her. He seemed to aim his words toward the trees. She knew it was to unnerve her. Then he turned his gaze back at her. "His neck was broken."

She felt like she'd been punched. She hated this. She'd killed the man. But he would have killed them. She was sure of it. "He... he had a gun pointed at me. It was the only thing I could think of doing."

"We may have to open a manslaughter docket. Did you handle the pistol?"

Her prints would be on it. She couldn't lie. "Yes, I picked it up. I didn't want to leave it where the man could reach it! We didn't know he was dead then."

"So, let's look at your story, *Ms.* Nguyen: a plane lands on a bush strip in the middle of the night in the middle of nowhere and crashes into an elephant. This man Ho shoots the pilot— the only person who might get him out of the mess. Perhaps he is angry because it was a bad landing? Do you think so?" He waited until Crys shook her head. "Ho is also injured, but instead of waiting for rescue, he goes off into the night with the wild animals and the angry elephants and two handguns, which won't help him much against them. And where do you think he was hoping to go? Maybe he thought he'd bump into someone to give him a lift to Phalaborwa or Giyani?" He stopped again and stared at her.

Again, Crys thought of Bongani driving back at three in the morning. He'd said he'd been driving past the airstrip. But she couldn't shake the idea that it was more than that, that he'd been working with Ho.

She realized Mabula was still waiting for her response and quickly shook her head.

"But he's lucky," Mabula went on. "You come along to rescue him. So, he shoots at you. Then he gives himself up, but then tries to hijack you."

"That's what happened."

"All this…and he had nothing with him? Nothing of value?"

"No! I keep telling you." She was thinking more and more that Bongani was right: the police cared more about money than dead bodies.

"Ms. Nguyen, you are lying to me. You are in a lot of trouble here. Two men are dead. Murdered. I've checked up on you. You are a newspaper reporter. Maybe you want a big story? A scoop?" His voice grew louder, harder. "Don't play games with me. We can throw you in jail like this." He snapped his fingers close to her face. "Now, do you have anything more to add to your story?"

"No. No," she insisted. "I've told you the truth."

But not the whole truth, she thought.

"Very well, I will speak to Mr. Chikosi now." And Crys was dismissed like a schoolgirl from the principal's office.

She sat down under the jackalberry tree and breathed deeply, trying to calm her nerves. She was sure that Mabula had seen right through her. That he knew she was lying about not finding anything. She wondered if he would charge her with the murder of Ho. And if he did, would she tell him about the money then?

She wondered if it would be better to tell him now? Maybe he'd let them go if he had what he wanted…

She closed her eyes and started softly chanting her mantra.

———

While Mabula questioned Bongani, the other police officers pulled Ho's body from the Land Rover and placed it in a body bag. Then they collected his guns and quietly searched the camp from top to bottom. Crys wondered if you needed a warrant in South Africa to search a bush camp. She didn't know, and she wasn't going to challenge them. She just let them get on with it, watching from her position under the tree, her head still filled with confusing thoughts, and her anxiety on a roller coaster as she worked through various ways this situation could play out.

The police found nothing, though—there was nothing to find without moving the Land Rover. She wondered if they were searching for clues or for money—or even rhino horn....

When Mabula had finished with him, Bongani joined Crys, and they both kept an eye on the police.

At last Mabula walked over to them. He didn't look happy, but it seemed he'd had enough. He probably wanted to spend the night in his own bed.

"I want to see you again in my office in Giyani tomorrow. I'm leaving a man here with you in case you need help." Crys didn't believe for a minute that was the man's real job. "Now, please give me your identification documents."

Crys only had her Minnesota driver's license. She didn't want to part with it but had no choice.

"Where's your passport?" Mabula asked.

"I left it with the Malans at Tshukudu, for safekeeping."

Bongani handed over his identity card, which Mabula scrutinized. Then he pocketed both cards and headed for his vehicle.

"Thank God he's gone," Crys said. "I'm sure he knows we're lying about the money."

"He's bluffing," Bongani replied, appearing remarkably calm. "He just wants us to think that."

She was confused and scared, pulled in different directions. She'd hoped that the plane would yield some information that could be linked to what had happened to Michael, but she'd learned nothing. Instead, she was potentially in serious trouble with the police.

Chapter 16

Bongani and Crys sat under the jackalberry tree, waiting for the other Land Rover to return from Tshukudu with a member of staff who would help them strike camp. Bongani seemed comfortable to sit in silence, but Crys wanted to talk. She wanted to understand him better. There were things they needed to discuss, but she didn't know how to start. Or how much she could trust him.

"You have children, Bongani?" she began.

He smiled. "Yes. Two healthy boys. The one is Tumisang—the first born. He's in grade four now—very clever boy. I hope he'll go to university one day. The other is Tlali. And we also have a girl. Her name is Puleng. It means 'in the rain' because she was born during a big thunderstorm. She brought luck because after the good rains there were good crops." His eyes seemed to look to somewhere distant.

"Does your family live close to Tshukudu? Do you see them often?"

The smile disappeared. "No, only when I have leave. Maybe once a month. They're at my house in Mapata. It's the village where I went that night for the funeral. It takes too long to get there from Tshukudu just for a weekend. It isn't that far, but the roads are bad."

She knew that many people lived that way, but it was sad that he saw his kids so seldom. But then she didn't see her parents either. And her brother only occasionally. She looked at the ground, feeling the pain.

"And you, Crys? Do you have children?"

Crys looked up and laughed. "No. First, you need a husband…"

He looked puzzled. "There must be many men who want to marry you. The men in America must be quite stupid."

She laughed again, more warmly this time. "There are a few. But, maybe I don't want them?"

He nodded. "You're young, so you can wait for one you like, who has some money. But a woman needs a husband and children."

She looked down again. She'd thought that Michael, maybe… but that looked as though it was history now.

At that point, the remaining policeman, a Constable Ngweni, joined them.

Crys tried to strike up a conversation, perhaps because she wanted to give the impression of innocence, perhaps to distract herself from the dark thoughts in her head. But he wasn't talkative and after a few minutes, she gave up.

"Would you like a beer?" she suggested eventually.

"Yes, please."

Crys fetched beers for the two men and a glass of fruit juice for herself, and then they sat in silence, lost in their thoughts.

Eventually, she turned to Bongani. "Surely the others should have arrived by now. Where do you think they are?"

"Maybe the police were talking to them also." He paused, giving Ngweni a sidelong glance. "Anyway, even if they get here this afternoon, it will be too late to go back. We should start a fire, so we can cook some meat."

He stood up and collected an armful of twigs, which he then arranged in a tent-like structure. When it was burning well, he added some small branches. Finally, he dragged over a big log of ironwood and put it on top. They'd used similar logs the night before, which had burned hot for hours. He sat back down, and they all stared into the flames. Silence reigned once more.

As dusk fell, Crys went to the kitchen and wrapped some potatoes in aluminum foil. She returned to the fire and dropped them on the coals. Then, she threw together a salad and grabbed two more beers.

When everything was ready, Bongani cooked the meat, and they all sat round the fire, drinks propped up in the soft sand. It almost felt like a normal evening. But Crys realized she'd done everything mechanically and didn't really have any appetite.

As darkness fell, she heard a birdcall nearby—it sounded like a *prrr*.

"Bongani, do you hear that bird? What is it?"

"That one is an African scops-owl," he said, pointing into the darkness. "It's very small." He held his hands about six inches apart.

"And that one is a nightjar." He pointed in another direction. "It's called fiery-necked. I'm not sure why, because I've never seen any fire on it, or even red on its neck. They say he's calling 'Good Lord deliver us.'"

Crys listened carefully and nodded. It did sound sort of like that. She knew nightjars from the north woods of Minnesota and wondered whether it was of the same family.

Crys looked at Ngweni. His face was blank in the firelight, probably wondering why they were discussing birds, given the events of the past few hours.

When they'd finished eating, the constable said good night and headed to his tent. He'd obviously decided they weren't going to make a run for it, and Crys guessed his instructions didn't include eavesdropping on any conversation Bongani and she might have.

"Mabula give you a hard time?" she asked Bongani.

He shrugged. "Kept asking the same questions, over and over. That's all." He poked at the fire with a stick.

"You seem worried. Want to talk about it?"

He shook his head and gazed at the ground.

She decided to confront him with what had been nagging at her mind for hours. This could be her last opportunity to ask him. Once they were back at Tshukudu, or with the police in Giyani, she might not see him alone again. She looked up at the stars, figuring out how to say it.

She decided to just come out with it. "It's because you were there, isn't it, Bongani? For some reason, you were there when that plane crashed."

He turned to her, his face a picture of astonishment.

"It doesn't take much to figure it out. You said the mourning finished early, but why didn't you sleep there instead of driving back at three a.m.?"

At first, he didn't reply, but she just waited. Most people need to fill a silence, and she thought he probably wanted to get whatever was bothering him off his chest.

"Yes," he said eventually. He turned away from her and looked into the fire again. "Yes, I was there to meet the plane. They told me that all I had to do was drive one of the passengers to a house about an hour away, and he'd give me a thousand U.S. dollars when we got there. It sounded pretty easy. And I really need the money, Crys." He looked at her sideways, his eyebrows raised, questioning.

"Who told you to do it?"

Bongani stared back into the fire. "The people I talk to sometimes."

"What people?"

"Some people in the village. They ask me questions, and sometimes I tell them stuff."

"Stuff? Stuff about what you've seen on the trips maybe? Stuff like that?"

He nodded.

For a moment, she was speechless. He was tipping off poachers! The safari was being used as part of their information

network. Part of her wanted to hit him, but then she thought
of Hennie and his team and what they'd done. She bit down on
her anger.

"Why, Bongani? Surely the Malans would've helped you if
you needed more money. There must have been another way."

"The Malans do lend me money sometimes, but it isn't enough."

"So, you spy for the poachers but then go and shoot and torture
them? Whose side are you on, Bongani?"

"You don't know how poor we are out here, Crys. You live
in America. We have nothing." He shook his head. "My brother
doesn't have a job, and he has three kids; my sister has AIDS; and
I've got my own family. I'm the only one bringing in money for
all those people." He kept his eyes on the flames.

He was supporting all of them on a miserable salary sweet-
ened by tips. No wonder he looked for a little extra by telling his
contact where to look for elephants and rhinos. Especially rhinos.

"So that whole story about the funeral was just a lie to cover
your job for the poachers."

He shook his head. "No, there really was a funeral for my
cousin." His voice dropped. "But...but they had no body to bury."

Suddenly she had a sinking feeling. She knew who Bongani's
cousin was. She remembered how Bongani had walked away
when he saw the man being tortured.

"Oh no, Bongani."

He put his face in his hands, then clutched his head as though
he wanted to squeeze the pain away. "I set it up for him. He had no
work. He begged me. He knew I know the people. I told him no.
It was too dangerous. He would be put in jail, shot, killed, even
tortured. But he insisted. So...so I set it up for him." His body
shook now and his voice broke. "It was his first time."

"You can't blame yourself."

She put a hand out toward him. But he stood up with a jerk,
as if jumping away from her touch. He walked away from the
firelight, toward the trees.

She decided to give him his space and, for want of something to do, went to the kitchen and made coffee for both of them. As she waited for the water to boil, she leaned against the table and thought. Everything that had happened these past few days now began to make sense—it was a tangle of threads, and at the center was a poor man trying to make money for his family. She wondered how Michael fit into it.

When she got back to the fire, Bongani was sitting down again.

"So, what happened with the plane?" she asked as she joined him.

He took the mug from her. "I was waiting there and saw the plane hit that elephant. I thought it was the end of them, but the plane didn't turn over or catch fire. Then it just sat there; there was no sign of anyone. The elephants were going mad. I was scared. So, I decided to come back to camp as though nothing had happened, but on the way, I realized the people in the plane might be badly injured. I had to go back, but I couldn't do it by myself. That's when I woke you."

"You know, that elephant probably saved your life, Bongani. I don't think Ho wanted a ride; I think he wanted a vehicle. You would've had a bullet in your head too—as well as the pilot..."

Bongani got up and threw another log onto the fire.

"Did you tell the colonel any of this?"

He shook his head. "No. Too dangerous."

"Good," she said. "Let's leave it that way."

Crys sipped at her coffee and watched the flames begin to curl round the new log. She couldn't condone what Bongani had done. But now she could understand it. She felt for him and his family and wondered what she would do in his situation. She knew she should tell the Malans about what he'd done— he'd betrayed them, betrayed their trust. But if she did, he'd lose his job at Tshukudu, and maybe worse. And then there'd be no money at all for any of the people he was supporting. And now his cousin's family had lost someone who might have brought in some money. She couldn't make their situation worse. She wouldn't say anything.

Crys closed her eyes. It was one thing to be a reporter—rooting out the real stories, the real reasons for the poaching. It was another to be right in the middle of what was happening.

"Bongani, I have to ask you some more questions."

He shrugged and said nothing.

"I asked you before about Michael Davidson, and you said you saw him at Tshukudu and that was all. But you did speak to him about the poaching, didn't you?"

He nodded. Crys said nothing, waiting.

"He asked me about poaching, and if I knew who the main people were around Phalaborwa or Giyani."

Crys leaned forward, expectant.

"I said I knew a man in my village. But he worked with some other people that I didn't know. White people. They collected the horns from him and paid him. Mr. Davidson was very excited. He said they were the people he wanted to know about." He stopped as though that was all he was going to say.

Crys couldn't contain her impatience. "And?"

"He said he would give me a hundred dollars if I could find out any information that would help him meet them."

"He wanted to meet them?" Crys felt a tingle of excitement. Maybe this was the link she was looking for.

"Yes."

"And did you help him? Did you find out anything?" Crys wanted to shake the information out of him.

"I told him it was very dangerous, that it was better not to mess with these people. But he said he just wanted to talk to them for his article—that it would be okay, that he wouldn't upset them. Or tell them where he got the information.

"When I went home that weekend, I talked to the man at my village—about my cousin…" His voice cracked, and it took a few moments before he continued. "I had to be very careful, but I asked this man and he said these people—he called them 'the Portuguese'—would be driving in a white *bakkie* between Phalaborwa and Giyani on a particular day."

Crys gasped. Had Bongani sent Michael to his death?

She took a deep breath to calm herself.

"A *bakkie*? That's a pickup, right?"

Bongani nodded.

"And what happened?"

"I told Mr. Davidson, and he gave me the money. He said he would follow it up. Then I went on a safari the next day, and I never heard from him again."

"Did you hear what happened to him?"

He shook his head. "But when I went back to the village, the man told me I had to help him with something now. That I owed him a favor because he'd given my cousin a job. And I could make some money as well. I had to meet a plane when I was in the bush..."

Crys was stunned. It all fit together.

"Can you tell me how I can meet these people?"

He turned and stared at her as though she hadn't heard a word he'd said. Crys didn't know what to think. He could tell her, but he wasn't going to.

Dammit, she thought. She was so close, yet so far.

They said nothing for a few minutes while they drank their coffee. As they sat there, she began to realize how arrogant people were in the West. How out of touch they were with the reality on the ground in Africa. All they talked about was the extinction of the rhino—not the abject poverty and desperation of the people. Again, she wondered what she would do if she was in Bongani's boots. She didn't want to answer that question.

She was exhausted, and her eyelids were getting heavy, but there was one more thing she had to do.

"We've got to dig up the cash we took," she said. "We won't be able to in the morning with Ngweni around."

Bongani nodded, and they walked over to the Land Rover. Parking it with the wheel exactly on top of the money didn't seem so clever anymore. There was no way they could start the vehicle—Ngweni would wake up for sure. They would have to push it. Crys climbed in and released the handbrake, then they set to work.

It was hard to move it in the sandy ground. But with a lot of effort, and rocking it back and forth, they rolled it back about eighteen inches. She jumped back into the driver's seat and pulled the brake on again. Then, keeping as quiet as they could, they dug up the cash, shook the sand off it, and hid the bills under the old maps and junk in the glove compartment. The police had searched the Land Rover once. Crys was betting they wouldn't do it again.

After that they headed for bed.

Before she could go to sleep, bad thoughts and images were whirling through her brain. It seemed certain that Michael was dead. And Bongani was involved in helping the poachers and may have sent Michael to his death. But did he have a choice?

And there was the tortured man on the ground in Kruger.

And dead rhinos.

Crys knew she had to calm herself. So, she spent fifteen minutes in a half lotus on the groundsheet, repeating her mantra.

When she eventually lay down, she was sure of one thing: she was going to find out who killed Michael and what had happened to his body.

Chapter 17

Crys woke to the sound of a shot. She sat up on the stretcher with a jerk. It must have been just before dawn because there was a glow coming through the tent's mesh window.

There was an urgent yell. It was Bongani: "Crys! Run!"

Then there was another shout, followed by another report, much louder this time.

She pulled on her jeans and T-shirt as quickly as she could and scrambled out of the tent.

But Bongani's warning was too late. There was a man waiting for her, aiming a sawn-off shotgun at her chest. She froze, half crouching. Then she saw Bongani lying facedown in the sand next to her tent. She stared at his body, then threw herself next to him.

"Bongani!" she cried. "Bongani!

There was no response, no movement.

"Talk to me, dammit, Bongani!"

"Get up or I shoot you!" Crys felt the barrel of the shotgun in her side.

She shook Bongani's arm. Still no movement. She felt for his pulse. It was strong. She looked for blood but found none. They must have knocked him out, not shot him.

"Get up!" The shotgun was against her head now.

The man leaned over, grabbed her by the hair, and yanked her to her feet. Her scalp screamed with pain. He shoved her away.

She looked around. Where was Constable Ngweni? Shouldn't he have been protecting them? Or had he let this man into the camp? Then she remembered the shots that had woken her. They were in really bad trouble.

And it was their own fault for taking Ho's briefcase.

Another man appeared, carrying what she thought was an assault rifle. "Where the money?" he shouted. She didn't recognize the accent.

Part of her head told her she should just tell him where the briefcase was buried. But another part quickly told her no. That would end with a shot to the head. She had to play dumb. That way these men would have to keep them alive.

"What money?" she gasped.

"Where the money?" he asked again. "We make this easy. Give me the money. Then you go."

Crys shook her head, her brain accelerating through excuses to keep him talking. To keep them alive. "We don't have any money. The tourists pay by credit card. We have hardly any cash. Maybe a hundred dollars. You can have it."

He frowned. "Okay," he said slowly.

He took a switchblade from his pocket and opened it. Then he walked right up to her, rifle in his left hand, and leaned over so his face was close to hers. It was covered in pockmarks. She could smell his breath. His eyes were black. Then he looked down at her breasts and used the blade to slice open the front of her T-shirt. She felt a warm line of blood running down her front.

She screamed.

He brought the knife up again.

"Help!" she yelled.

"Nobody hear you."

She knew he was right.

"Please. No, no. Wait!"

He stopped, but he didn't lower the knife.

"Maybe Mr. Ho had money—the man who was killed. He said something about a lot of money...before he died. But he was delirious by then, so we didn't take any notice. He was badly injured. We...we tried to save him."

"What did he say about money?" Pockface demanded.

She had to think quickly. To survive. "Something about the plane. Money in the plane, I think. We didn't believe him."

The man moved the point of the blade to her left nipple and pushed hard enough she could feel the sting.

Playing for time, she blurted out the story of the plane crash and finding Ho. She stammered and repeated herself. Trying to keep him listening. Trying to think what to do.

"Maybe the police took it," she said. "That could be it. They searched the plane. Or maybe they missed it. Maybe it's still there."

Pockface shook his head. "Not there. We look."

Crys heard a groan and looked down. Bongani had come around and was trying to sit up, one hand pressed against his head.

"Bongani," she said. "Are you all right?"

He groaned again and staggered to his feet, standing unsteadily. The man with the shotgun kept him covered.

"Are you okay?" she asked again. She prayed he wouldn't say anything to contradict her.

He nodded. "Didn't hear them coming. Only when I heard the shot"

"Take it easy. Sit down. I was just telling them that we didn't find any money..."

She felt the blade push harder into her nipple.

"But maybe Ho hid it where we found him." She looked from Bongani back to the pockmarked man. "Maybe he didn't want to leave it in the plane. He was trying to get away. That could be it. There were thick bushes there. He could've hidden a packet or something there easily."

"Where you find him?"

She started to describe a route, making it as complicated as possible.

"You show us."

"Bongani, can you find the way back to where Ho was hiding?" she asked.

He nodded.

It was something. They'd bought a bit of time and maybe a chance to improve the odds—if they were really lucky.

———

The plane had crime-scene tape around it—out of place in the middle of nowhere—and the elephant carcass was starting to smell of rotting meat. A group of hyenas was busy with it. They looked up with bloody faces, but they didn't leave their meal.

There was a police Land Rover pulled up nearby, but no sign of the policeman left to guard the plane. Crys was sure he was dead, given that these thugs had already searched it.

She drove up to the plane, and they all got out, Pockface still with the assault rifle and the other man with the shotgun. Crys poked around the plane pretending to look for tracks, trying all the while to think of a plan. But right at that moment she had nothing, not even a hint of an idea.

"He went that way," she said eventually, pointing at the trail of blood.

"Go," said Pockface, pointing with the gun.

Crys led, Pockface behind her, with Bongani and the other thug bringing up the rear.

Crys moved slowly, head down. She was in no hurry, but she was worried their captors would soon run out of patience. She had no idea what she'd do when that happened.

But then she saw some tracks—they were fresh and covered the blood trail, then headed into the bush. She stopped, trying to hide her confusion. She wanted to keep this find to herself—stay a step ahead of her captors.

"Bongani, is that the way he went?" she asked.

"Yes. Up to the right."

She walked on a few paces.

"He went off somewhere here," she said. "He was up in that thick brush." She pointed. "That's right, isn't it, Bongani?"

"You said he was bad hurt?" Pockface said, suspicious.

She shrugged.

"Okay. You go." He waved the rifle toward the trees.

Just then Crys heard a branch snap, not far away. She was right about the tracks being fresh. The elephants were nearby. But going after them was a huge risk. If this was the same group that had been here when the plane crashed, they might still be pretty spooked.

She didn't know how their captors would behave, and she didn't know how the elephants would react. But what other option did they have?

Crys looked over her shoulder at Bongani. His face was impassive.

One of the trees moved slightly. She headed straight for it, thankful they were downwind.

When they reached the trees, she thought she'd mistaken the distance to the herd. All was quiet. Maybe too quiet.

"Here?" said Pockface. "Ho was here?"

His loud voice was all it took. There was trumpeting, and one of the elephants burst out of the bush toward them to investigate. Pockface gave a yell and pointed the rifle in the direction of the elephant. Crys screamed and hurled herself at him. There was a loud chatter right next to her as he let off a short burst. The elephant took off, and Pockface, surprised and winded, stared after it for a moment. That was long enough for Crys to kick him as hard as she could in the balls. So hard, she nearly fell.

He screamed and bent over, clutching himself, and she kneed

him in his face. He collapsed on top of the rifle, and she kicked him in the head. He groaned and writhed on the ground.

Twisting around, Crys saw Bongani grappling with the second man. He'd reacted the moment she had and was now holding the man's gun hand away from him with one hand and hitting him in the face with the other. Then he smashed the gun hand against a tree trunk. The guy screamed, and the shotgun flew into the bush. Crys was already running back toward the path.

"Run, Bongani!" she yelled. "Run!"

She didn't look back but could hear Bongani's footsteps catching her up. There was shouting from behind him. Pockface and his friend were on their way. Their only chance was to reach the Land Rover before they were caught.

It seemed to take forever to get there. Crys's chest was burning, her legs desperate to move faster. But they had a good lead. She jumped in the driver's side and turned the key. Miraculously, the old vehicle started at once. Bongani was grappling with the door handle on the passenger side.

"You stop! I kill you!" Pockface was at the edge of the airstrip, about thirty yards away, the assault rifle leveled at Bongani.

"Get in!" Crys yelled. "Bongani, get in!"

He didn't hesitate. He swung himself into the Land Rover just as it started moving.

"Get down," Crys said, hunching herself low over the wheel.

Sure enough, the windscreen shattered and glass flew all over the Land Rover, and she felt a sharp pain in her shoulder. She accelerated and spun the steering wheel. There was another burst of gunfire and the banging of bullets hitting the vehicle's side.

The Land Rover hit a log, and they nearly flew out. But she kept going, wrestling with the steering wheel to avoid trees and bushes.

After a few minutes of frenzied driving, she was sure they were out of range and slowed down a little, breathing heavily.

"*Eish*!" Bongani said. "You okay, Crys? There's blood on your shoulder."

"I'm fine." It was stinging badly, but she could move the arm. It was just a flesh wound.

"Head up that way," Bongani said, pointing to a track through the trees.

"They'll come after us in the police Land Rover—the one left at the airstrip," she said, adrenalin pumping through her brain, making her think, drive, and fight the pain, all at the same time. "We have a head start, but it isn't much." She put her foot down again and they lurched and bumped along the track.

"Why didn't he shoot me?" Bongani shouted over the noise of the engine. "Why didn't he shoot me when I was getting into the Land Rover? He had the gun right on me."

"That gun could cut someone in half at twice the distance. He must want us alive. That's the only explanation."

She changed to low-range gear to negotiate some deep sand.

"Are you okay?" Bongani asked. "Do you want me to drive now?"

She shook her head. "No time to change. They'll be after us." She managed somehow to bring them out of a rut and they accelerated again.

"Who are they? Where are they from?" Crys said. "I didn't recognize his accent."

"Portuguese, from Mozambique. Many of them help run smuggling operations here for the Vietnamese gangs."

It was starting to make sense. Michael had said he was onto something big, and Anton had pointed out that it was dangerous. If Michael had become mixed up with people like the ones chasing them right now, that could explain his disappearance.

"Were they the people you told Michael to follow?"

Bongani shrugged. "It's possible. But I don't know any of them."

Crys wondered once again how much he really knew.

"Go left here," Bongani instructed. They had come to a fork in the track. "It's a shortcut. I'll tell you where to go."

She swung off in the direction he said.

"It will be harder for them to follow us now," said Bongani. "There are game-viewing tracks everywhere here." He clutched one of the roof supports as they bumped along the dirt track.

She could see what he meant. The track ahead was covered in tire marks and there were side routes branching off every now and again.

"I think Ho wanted the money for himself," she said at last. "Maybe he wanted to buy rhino horn for himself. All he needed was a vehicle."

Bongani nodded. He'd come to the same conclusion.

"Bongani," Crys said after a long pause, "after what's just happened, I agree with you: we can't tell Mabula about the money. I don't trust him—I wouldn't be surprised if he's working with this gang. How else could the Portuguese have known about the crash so quickly? And known to come to the camp? It had to be the police who told him."

Bongani nodded.

"And if we tell the police about the money, there's no way they'll let us go. We've got to stick to our story."

Bongani nodded again, and they drove on in silence for a few minutes.

"Do you think we should be going to talk to Mabula? He could lock us up if we don't tell him..."

"We must see him," Bongani, said. "If we don't, where will we hide? He'll have every road watched, and it will be much worse for us. We must go and talk to him. But not mention the briefcase."

A few minutes later, Crys saw that at last they'd reached one of the dirt district roads. She sighed with relief.

"Giyani is only an hour away," Bongani said.

She relaxed just a notch. But the pain in her shoulder was worse now.

Chapter 18

Crys kept checking the side mirrors all the way to Giyani even though she was pretty sure they'd lost the thugs. The only way they could follow was with the police vehicle, and she doubted they'd drive into town in that, even if they were in cahoots with Mabula.

Crys knew she'd been pretty stupid about the money. She should have realized that once Ho disappeared, someone was going to come looking for him. Even so, they'd found out surprisingly quickly. Mabula and his team were up to their necks in this. She was sure of it. And now they were heading to the police station where he was based. But what other option did they have? Once again, she wished she was writing about this corruption in an article, not caught in the middle of the action.

Crys thought about the amount of money in the briefcase—she guessed it had to be half a million dollars, at least. And it was being carried by a Vietnamese man. With Vietnam the biggest market for rhino horn, Bongani had to be right that the money was connected to poaching. But that amount of money wasn't to pay off a handful of poachers; they were so poor, a few thousand dollars would be enough. There had to be something much bigger at stake.

She started thinking about the stocks of rhino horn Johannes had talked about—the ones the national parks and private farmers held. Legal, but locked down. They had enormous value to the rhino-horn trade but were impossible to export. Half a million dollars could buy a lot of that...if the buyer could find a way to get it out of the country.

She wondered if that was what Michael was after—how the smugglers did that.

She chewed at her lips, trying to ignore the pain in her shoulder. This could be a huge scoop. But who could she tell? She was in no position now to continue her reporting. She had to concentrate on survival.

When they reached the outskirts of Giyani, Bongani said, "You need this." He pulled off his shirt and gave it to her.

She'd forgotten about her slashed and bloody T-shirt, hanging open over her breasts. She pulled over and tried to take her shirt off, but the blood had set on her back, and it was painful when it tugged at the wound. So, she just pulled Bongani's shirt over hers.

She thanked Bongani, touched by his consideration.

He nodded, accepting her thanks. "What about the money?" he asked.

She'd forgotten all about the money hidden in the glove compartment. They couldn't leave it in the open Land Rover, even if it was parked outside a police station. And there was a good chance the police would impound the vehicle anyway.

"Give it to me. They won't search us again, and if they do, I can say it was my expenses money, and I grabbed it when I left my tent." She stuffed the money into her pants pocket, pulling at her scab again in the process.

The police station wasn't hard to find. It was on the main road, and Giyani wasn't that big. She stopped outside, and they went in, causing quite a stir. They made an odd couple: Crys wearing a dirty shirt, obviously too big for her, with smears of blood here and there, and Bongani with no shirt at all, just khaki shorts.

"We've been attacked and assaulted," Crys told the constable at the reception desk, trying to sound helpless and exhausted. "I need to see a doctor. And…and I think some policemen have been murdered."

When she said that, the man looked shocked, but he kept his cool and yelled to someone to get hold of Colonel Mabula, and then called another man to take her to a doctor.

The clinic was only a few blocks away, and a doctor saw her immediately. He gave her a local anesthetic, then stripped off the T-shirt. Once the pain had dulled, he started digging around in her back. She winced.

"What happened?" he asked as he worked.

"Someone shot at us."

"Well, you were lucky. The bullet only grazed your shoulder. Otherwise you'd be in ICU."

He taped a dressing over the wound.

"I've given you a shot for the pain, and I'll get you some pain-killers and antibiotics to take with you. Take the whole course. We want to be on the safe side. And you'll need that dressing changed in a couple of days."

She thanked him, put on Bongani's shirt, and left. The police-man who'd brought her there was waiting outside, talking on his cell phone. He seemed less friendly as he drove her back to the station than he had on the way to the clinic. And in the police station, the constable at reception ignored her when she walked back in.

Somehow in the past half hour, her status had changed. A knot of anxiety formed in her belly. Was Colonel Mabula the reason for the officers' new attitude? Had he already found out about the money?

———

She waited and waited, and no one would answer her questions about what was happening. What was more, she didn't know where Bongani was. The longer she waited, the more worried she became. To make things worse, she was also feeling woozy— from the painkillers and antibiotics, she guessed. She tried to concentrate—she knew she needed to be wide awake when Mabula questioned her.

Eventually a constable took her to an interrogation room. Mabula was waiting. He waved her to a chair, and the constable stood by the door as if she was likely to make a run for it. Then Mabula made her go through every detail of what had happened since he'd left them the day before, recording it on an ancient tape recorder. She assumed he'd heard it all from Bongani already, and that he was looking for discrepancies. Sometimes he would go back over points in the story before letting her go on. Once he stopped her while he changed the tape. When she came to the part about the elephants, he made a sarcastic comment about how she always seemed to be involved with them, but heard her out. At last he appeared satisfied.

"Ms. Nguyen," he said. "I think you are responsible for the death of two of my policemen. This is all because you refused to tell me the truth last time. The men who tried to kill you were probably Portuguese criminals from Mozambique. Some of them work with men like the Vietnamese man you killed—"

"By accident…" she said hastily.

Mabula waved her interjection away with his fat hand. "If I know these people, they're sure to keep trying."

He waited for this to sink in. He was right, she knew. Pockface and his partner would go on looking for them for as long as they thought the two of them knew where the money was.

"Now…" Mabula spread out his hands "…you must tell me the *real* story."

She looked into his round face. Yes, she thought. Then he'll tell Pockface so he can get his cut. And Bongani and I will still be killed.

A wave of fear and anxiety spread through her body. She felt the sudden need to lie down and sleep.

"Look, I've told you everything," she said. "I'm tired, and I've been hurt. I need a shower and some sleep. I want to leave now. Where's Mr. Chikosi?"

Mabula took his time before replying. "Ms. Nguyen, you're under investigation for a homicide that you admit you committed, and you're a material witness to three murders. You aren't going anywhere." He shook his head slowly.

"I'm an American journalist here on an assignment! You know that. If you won't let me leave, I want a lawyer."

"That is possible…when you start cooperating." He gave her a cold smile.

"I *am* cooperating!"

He looked at her in silence for a moment, then stood up and signaled to the constable. "Take her fingerprints and get some photos. Then put her in a holding cell."

"What? No! Why do you need my fingerprints?"

"We need to know who touched what at the crime scene."

"And why are you holding me? Am I under arrest?"

"No. Not yet. I'm…" He seemed to consider what to say. "I'm keeping you here for your own protection. If your story's true, your Portuguese friends are out there wanting to kill you. And we can't have that, can we, Ms. Nguyen?"

She didn't respond. She clearly had no choice.

As he walked out of the room, he turned back to her. "I'm going back out to your camp to see for myself what happened there last night. We'll talk again when I get back. In the meantime, you can think about how long you want to stay in the jail here."

Her heart sank. She felt completely powerless.

———

A constable took her fingerprints and some mugshots.

"Valuables, please," he said.

"All I've got are my car keys. We were attacked in the middle of the night. I didn't have a chance to pick anything up."

He didn't react, simply putting the keys in a bag and zipping it up. He wrote out a receipt and handed it to her. Had he searched her, she would have been in trouble. She still had the money in her pocket.

He took her to a small holding cell, maybe ten feet by ten feet. It was basic. There was a cracked washbasin and a toilet with no seat. There was a small window with grimy glass, secured with burglar bars, and under it was a metal cot with tattered bedding that looked as though it had never been washed. And a wooden chair with a broken back. A naked bulb hung from the ceiling, out of reach. The room was hot, and it stank.

The constable left, locking the door behind him. She opened the window a bit, which let a little air come in and some stuffiness out. Then she used the toilet and washed as well as she could. Next, she pulled the blanket onto the floor and beat out the mattress, grateful that at least nothing alive came out. She noticed that a spring had come through the mattress and torn it—a good place to hide the money before she was searched, she thought. The way things were going, she would need the money later. She kept her back to the door to hide what she was doing and stuffed the money into the mattress. She put the blanket on top and lay down to rest.

Crys's mind was churning. What was she going to do? Perhaps the best was just to wait it out and say nothing. Hopefully the Malans were already looking for them, and after a few days, Mabula would have to let them go.

She wondered if he could charge her with anything. The image of the dead Ho slumped in the Land Rover wouldn't leave her mind's eye.

She rolled over, trying to find a less uncomfortable spot on the mattress.

She was also worried about Bongani. Maybe she was protected

for the moment as an American journalist, but what about him? If they were treating her like this, they may be beating him up.

She realized she was kidding herself. If Mabula was crooked, then he wouldn't play by the rules. Maybe he was already cutting a deal with Pockface to hand her over. The wound on her chest started to sting, reminding her of what Pockface would do.

As much as she tried, she couldn't see a way out of her predicament.

Once again, she wished they'd never gone looking for Ho; wished they'd never found the money. But there was no point in looking backwards. She needed a plan. But, at the moment, she had nothing.

She rolled over again.

She must have eventually fallen into an exhausted asleep because the next thing she heard was the door opening. A stocky, overweight policeman came in with a tray of food.

"Dinner," he said.

"What is it?"

He looked at her, apparently surprised by the question. "The white stuff, we call *pap*. It's a dried porridge. The rest is a meat sauce."

She pulled the plate toward her and began to eat. Despite her fear and anxiety, her body was desperate for sustenance. The last hours had drained it completely.

"Where do you come from?"

She looked up and realized the guard was still there. "America," she said, swallowing. The food was quite tasty, even though the texture was a little strange. "Are you a guard?" she asked, thinking that he might give her some information.

"I'm the night guard here."

"Is Colonel Mabula still here?"

He shook his head. "At night, there's only me. I handle reception, too, from midnight."

She tried a smile, but her face ached. She must have bruised it. She looked at the guard's name badge: Petrus Ngane. "Is my friend Bongani Chikosi here too, Constable Ngane?"

"Yes, he's in the other wing."

"Can I get a message to him?"

Petrus shook his head. "It's not allowed. Prisoners can't talk to each other."

"But I'm not a prisoner!"

He shrugged.

"Well, can I make a phone call? My friends will be worried."

He shook his head again. "Not unless the colonel says so. And he's not here…"

"But I haven't done anything! I was shot—you can see my shoulder's bandaged—and Colonel Mabula is holding me for my own safety." She hoped that was true.

For a few seconds Petrus was silent. Then he said, "Okay, maybe I can help…if…if you have money." Then, without waiting for a reply, he picked up the tray and carried it out, locking the door behind him.

She stared at the back of the door.

It was pretty clear how things worked here.

———

She'd been so stressed over the past few days that she resigned herself to her situation and managed to sleep—although it was plagued by dreams of knives, guns, and pockmarked faces. She was woken at dawn by the light forcing its way through the grimy window.

She washed as best she could, then took a hundred-dollar bill from her stash in the mattress, folded it into her pocket and waited for Petrus.

When he arrived, he had a bowl of the same dry porridge she'd had the day before. There was no milk or sugar or even salt to go with it, but he did put down a mug of black tea.

"You must be happy to be going home now," Crys said. "I wish I was doing that too."

"I'm sure they'll let you go soon," he said, though he didn't sound convinced.

She shook her head. "I'm not so sure."

She pulled the hundred-dollar bill from her pocket and held it out. Petrus's eyes widened, and he put his hand out automatically.

"When you come in tonight, could you tell Mr. Chikosi I'm okay?" she said. "He'll be glad to know. And can you buy me some food? Some candy or cookies or something?"

He nodded and took the money.

"Thank you," she said attempting a smile. "You're the only one around here who's helpful. The others..." She shrugged her shoulders, and then winced at the pain.

Petrus said he'd see her later and hurried out, locking the door.

She was slightly encouraged. At least he had accepted the hundred dollars.

Almost as soon as Petrus had left, a constable came in and told her Mabula wanted to see her.

This time, instead of going to the interrogation room, she went back past reception and into the colonel's office. It was a mess, the desk cluttered and stacks of files on the floor. Mabula told her to sit, then dismissed the constable.

"My men were killed in cold blood," he began. "Constable Mombo was mown down with an AK-47 at the plane crash, and Constable Ngweni was blasted in the back at close range with a shotgun at the camp."

"That's what I was afraid of," she said. "I'm sorry."

"Oh, you're sorry, are you? Really?"

She didn't answer.

"We traced the plane and the pilot," Mabula went on. "They must have flown in illegally from Mozambique. But we found no trace of the men you described. They seem to have vanished..."

"You're not suggesting we made them up?"

"No. They exist all right; we already know that. And they won't stop until they get what they want. You're lucky we're holding you here, where you are safe." The way he said it, though, tapping his desk with a fat finger, she felt anything but safe. For a moment she wondered again whether it would just be easier to tell him about the money. But Bongani's words kept ringing in her head. If she told him, what would stop him from killing her in a cell—or having her taken out into the bush to do it?

She wondered if Michael had ended up that way.

She was beginning to believe that was exactly what had happened to him.

"Look, Ms. Nguyen, we know what this is all about. There's a lot of money involved—illegal money used for smuggling. We can catch these criminals. But we must have that money."

"What sort of smuggling?" she asked.

Mabula sat back. "I'll ask the questions here. Now, *where is the money?*"

"I've told you, I don't know anything about any money."

"Ms. Nguyen, don't play games with me. You're in very serious trouble." He leaned back and assumed an almost satisfied expression. "Mr. Chikosi has already told me you have the money…"

His manner didn't fool her. She knew he was bluffing. If Bongani had broken down and told him, Mabula wouldn't be bothering with her. Or was he just testing her? She didn't reply.

He sat staring at her.

At last she couldn't stand it any longer. "Don't you think we would've given those men the money if we had it? That's all they wanted. They were going to beat us up to get it!"

He thought about this for a moment. At last he said: "No, I think you're too smart for that. I think you realized that they'd kill you both once they had the money. So, you denied any knowledge of it—to keep yourselves alive…"

Perhaps she'd underestimated Mabula once more. He'd hit on

exactly what they had done. She couldn't think of any reply. She was trapped—so she just shrugged.

Suddenly he leaned forward. "It's very important that we catch these people and get the money—this evidence—very quickly." He rattled out his words. "There could, perhaps, be a reward…" He sat back again.

"Reward?" she asked, genuinely confused.

"Half the money. We split it."

She wasn't tempted for a second. It had to be a trap. No policeman would make an offer like that. And if he was crooked, why would he settle for half if he could have the whole lot?

"I don't know what you're talking about. How many times do I have to tell you, I know nothing about any money?"

"Very well, Ms. Nguyen. I must remind you that you have admitted to killing a man under very suspicious circumstances. If you knew about the money, it would be a very convenient way of getting rid of the one man who could testify that you had it."

"He had a gun on us!" she protested. This was going exactly the way Bongani had said it would.

"So you say."

He was about to add something else, but his phone rang.

He picked it up and said something in the local language, and then switched to English. "Yes. Colonel Mabula speaking."

She could only hear one side of the conversation but guessed pretty soon who'd called.

"No, I'm afraid I can't give you any information…Yes, but this is a multiple murder investigation, and we are not ready to share any information about it.…You are not listening. I won't comment on who we're holding here at the moment. You can phone again tomorrow and—"

"I demand to talk to Mr. Malan!" Crys shouted out, hoping the caller would hear her.

Mabula slammed the receiver down at once and glared at her for a long moment without saying a word.

Then he picked up the phone again and held it out to her, but as she reached for it, he pulled it back and said, "You can make the call as soon as you tell me the truth."

"Dammit, Colonel. I've done nothing. You can't keep holding me." She sat back and glared back at him.

"Very well. You'll be held here on suspicion of murder until you decide to cooperate. I suggest you give it some careful thought. Things can get *very* unpleasant for you here. Do you understand?"

She said nothing.

He jumped up and leaned forward over the desk, shouting in her face. "I asked you if you understand!" She could feel flecks of saliva landing on her cheeks.

She closed her eyes and nodded.

After a moment he sat back down. "Very well, then," he said, completely calm once more. "I'll see you tomorrow."

She was led back to her cell, worried and exasperated.

But as they passed reception, she heard a commotion at the desk. She looked up to see a white man arguing with the constable.

She recognized his voice and accent at once. And she was one hundred percent sure that if he turned to look at her, she would see that his face was scarred with pockmarks.

She grabbed the arm of the constable escorting her. "Take me back to the colonel," she hissed. "Right now. I'll tell him what he wants to know."

Chapter 19

As they entered Mabula's office, the constable started to say something, but Crys interrupted him.

"He's here! The man who attacked us. And shot your men. He's at the front desk talking to the constable!"

"What? Here in the police station? Is this some sort of trick?"

But Mabula didn't wait for her reply. He was already on his feet heading for the door. "You wait here," he said. "Mtembo, stay with her."

For the first time, Crys felt a ray of hope. If Pockface was working with Mabula, he wouldn't be at reception. He would be in Mabula's office already, surely. Maybe she was wrong about their connection.

But her hope soon chilled. If Pockface was here, he knew she was too. She was terrified that he'd find a way to get to her.

Crys paced around Mabula's office waiting for him to return. But the minutes dragged on, and there was no sign of the colonel. Mtembo was guarding the door so she couldn't get out.

Her fears started up again. How could Pockface be in the police station arguing with a policeman, when he'd murdered his colleagues and stolen their vehicle? He must have known that she and Bongani would have given a description of him. Was he that brazen? Perhaps he didn't care; perhaps they were all in the same racket…

When Mabula did come back, he went straight to his desk and sat down. "Take her back to the cell," he said.

"What do you mean?" Crys asked, shocked. "Did you arrest him?"

"I spoke to the constable. There *was* a white man here. He was reporting a cell-phone theft. The constable showed me the report."

"No, that's wrong. I'm certain it was the right man. He had the same accent. Did you ask the constable about his face?"

"Thank you for teaching me my job, Ms. Nguyen. He didn't notice anything special about the man's face. Now leave—I have work to do."

"No, I'm sure—"

But before she could finish, the constable took her arm and pulled her away.

When she'd been locked in the cell once more, Crys tried to think it through. Had she made a stupid mistake? She couldn't remember what the man had been saying—she'd concentrated on his accent, not the words. Was it possible that seeing a white man—so unusual here—and hearing the accent had made her jump to the wrong conclusion?

Or was she right to be suspicious of Mabula? As she'd concluded before, if he was working with the Portuguese thugs, that would explain how they'd known so quickly where the plane had crashed. But what was Pockface doing in the police station, then? Certainly, Mabula had been surprised, even angry, and he'd gone off at once to investigate. How could she tell if Mabula had been spun a story about the cell phone, or if he was only upset because Pockface hadn't bothered to keep out of sight?

The one thing Crys was quite certain about was that Pockface hadn't been in the police station to report a stolen cell phone. So, it came down to one thing: how certain was she that the man was Pockface?

Crys turned it over and over in her head. If Bongani was right about police corruption, then Mabula would keep them alive just as long as it took him to get his hands on the money.

There was no option. She had to get out before that happened. Once she was free, she'd be able to reach the Malans and the international press, and then they'd be able to help Bongani.

There was only one problem: she had to escape from a cell in the middle of a building swarming with police.

———

Crys had done a lot of thinking by the time Petrus came in with her supper that evening. He handed her a plastic bag with some chocolate, a packet of ginger biscuits, a Coca-Cola, and a pretzel-shaped pastry soaked in syrup. That would've left him a lot of change out of a hundred dollars, but he didn't offer it.

"Can you stay here while I eat?" Crys asked, forcing a smile. "I could do with a little company."

He nodded at her and readily sat down on the bed. Perhaps he was hoping for another hundred-dollar bill. That was exactly what she wanted him to think.

"Have my friends from the lodge been in touch? They must be wondering where I am…"

"A white man did come asking about you earlier."

Her heart jumped. "Can you describe him? Was he Afrikaans? An older or a younger man?" She guessed it had to be Anton. Johannes would still be too sick to travel.

He shook his head. "No. Not Afrikaans. And his face had lots of little scars. Maybe he was sick one time."

Crys nearly coughed up the mouthful of food she'd just swallowed. She had no doubts left now. It *had* been Pockface at reception, and someone had lied about the cell-phone theft report—probably Mabula himself.

Pockface was looking for her.

It looked like Petrus was the only chance she had. She hoped he had a price she could afford out of what was stuffed inside the bed.

"Look Petrus, I have to get out of here. I'm not a criminal. The colonel is only holding me because he needs someone to blame for the deaths of his policemen. I swear to God I didn't kill them. He hasn't charged me with anything—you can look at your records. And what's he done to catch their killers? Nothing."

Petrus looked at her impassively.

"You said maybe you could help me."

He didn't answer for what seemed like forever. Then he shook his head. "It's too dangerous."

"I can pay. I have cash. More U.S. dollars..."

"How much?" he said almost instantly. Crys felt a tingle of excitement. He'd nibbled at the bait.

She hesitated. "Here? About a thousand dollars."

She could see he was tempted.

"You've got to help me, Petrus. You can have the money. All of it. If you don't, I'll never get out of here. And I've done nothing wrong!"

"Where's the money? Show me."

She shook her head. "I have it. That's all that matters."

Petrus picked up the tray and headed for the door without another word.

When he was gone, Crys thought about what an idiot she'd been. He'd go straight to Mabula and tell him everything. Then they'd search her cell, take the money, and charge her with attempting to bribe a policeman, on top of everything else. Her last option would be snatched away from her.

Crys had a bad night, tossing and sweating in the heat. She dozed, then woke up seized by panic—like someone had their hands around her throat, pushing tighter and tighter. She didn't know what to do; she didn't know who to trust. She wished she'd just given Mabula the damned briefcase of money when he was at the camp. She wished she'd never spoken to Petrus. She wished she'd never come to Africa.

———

In the morning, Crys was lying on her bed, staring at the cracked, stained ceiling, in complete despair when Petrus unlocked the door.

He was carrying a tray with the usual *pap,* and she saw that he'd brought her a jam donut too. She stared at it for a moment, as if she'd never see such a thing before. Then she looked up at him. He was leaning toward her.

"I want that money," he said so quietly she almost didn't hear him.

He's bitten, Crys thought, energy shooting through her body and making her sit up straight. She'd have to play it carefully.

She shook her head. "Only when I get out of here."

He stared at her for a few moments. Was he going to insist on the money in advance? It seemed to take him ages to decide.

At last he spoke. "You must be ready tonight. I'll tell you what to do when I bring your supper. But I must have the money before I let you out."

———

Around eleven that morning, Mabula summoned Crys again.

"I'm not going to say another word without a lawyer," she said as she walked in, not giving him a chance to speak.

His mouth formed a cold smile. "Only when you tell me where the money is."

"And I need to see the doctor again, to change my dressing."

He shook his head. "First tell me where the money is. I know you know."

She didn't respond. It was chilling being faced with the truth like this.

"You know you're making it hard on your friend Bongani. Tell me where the money is, and you both can go. No charges, no problems."

She just looked at him and didn't say a word. She worried that if she did open her mouth, she would give him what he wanted, and then she'd lose whatever advantage she had...and may never see the light of day again.

He waited for a moment and then slammed his hand on the desk so hard that it shook. Crys managed not to flinch. "Tomorrow," he shouted. "Then you will tell me. One way or the other, you will tell me. Take her away."

———

As darkness fell outside, and the filthy little square of window dimmed, Crys waited impatiently for Petrus. She kept checking her watch, and soon she became convinced that something had happened to prevent him coming—something that involved Mabula and Pockface.

But at last he arrived with the tray.

"Where have you been?" she asked. "I didn't think you were coming."

"It's the normal time." He frowned at her.

She bit her lip. She needed to get a hold on herself.

"Now listen," he began. "You must be ready at four o'clock in the morning. I'll let you go. Outside the station, go right down the street until you reach Shimati Road. You can get a minibus taxi there. I'll say you screamed, and when I came, you tricked me and locked me in."

"Won't you be in trouble?" It seemed far too easy.

He shrugged. "I want half the money now."

She shook her head. "You'll get it all when you let me go. Otherwise you won't do it..."

They stared at each other for a moment. Who would be the first to blink?

"Okay," Petrus said. "Four o'clock."

He must need the money as much as Bongani, she thought, and wondered how many people he was looking after.

After he'd gone, Crys sat and thought. This was the last chance to change her mind. As of then, she'd done nothing wrong except lie about the money. Even Ho's death was an accident. She had a witness in Bongani, and there was plenty of evidence to show Ho was an armed and dangerous criminal—who'd already killed the pilot before he turned the gun on her.

But by morning, if she went through with her plan, she'd be a fugitive, guilty of assaulting a policeman and escaping from custody. Mabula would come after her with everything he had. And at the same time, she'd need to keep away from Pockface, who was somewhere out there, waiting for his chance to grab her.

Crys was also worried about Petrus. She'd seen that he always wore a gun. How was she supposed to get it away from him? For her escape to look convincing, she'd have to take it. And he'd never let her do that.

In fact, what if Petrus had no intention of letting her go once he had the money? The gun would be his way of keeping her quiet—maybe permanently. She couldn't trust anyone. Everything she did came with a big risk.

Crys was tempted to call the whole thing off, but now that she knew that Pockface had actually been in the police station, she realized she had no choice. Locked up there, she was a sitting duck.

She would just have to make Petrus's unlikely story work—in her own way—a version of his plan that he wasn't going to like.

Before Crys went to bed, she laid the blanket on the floor and tried to twist into a half lotus. She succeeded, but barely. Her body was very tense, and her shoulder still hurt. She breathed deeply, closed her eyes, and began saying her mantra. *Úm ma ni bát ni hồng...*

Slowly her body relaxed, and her mind rid itself of some of

its stress. Eventually, she tried to get some rest, but she needed to be up before Petrus came to wake her, and she was nervous of oversleeping. She tossed and turned, wondering if she should go through with her plan, but she knew there was really no option. She had to.

She slept, but lightly, and only for a few hours, and she was wide-awake at half past three.

She ripped the already tattered sheet into strips and laid them out on the bed. Then she dug the money out of the mattress and waited.

———

On the dot of four, Crys heard Petrus fiddling with the door bolt.

She had the cash in her hand, and as he walked in, she held it out. He stepped forward eagerly to take it and, as soon as he was close enough, she did what she'd done to Pockface. She kicked him in the balls as hard as she could. As he doubled over, crying out in pain, she kneed him in the face, and he collapsed to the ground. Crys pulled his gun out of its holster.

"Roll on your stomach," she said, holding the gun to his head.

"Fuck. What you doing? Not the plan!"

"Do it!" She prodded him with the gun, and at last he obeyed. "Put your hands behind your back."

She put a foot on his neck, grabbed one arm, and tied the end of a sheet strip to it. She tied the other end to the other arm. It wasn't very secure, but it would hold him for a while.

"Tell me where Bongani Chikosi is," she ordered.

Petrus didn't answer.

She put the gun to his head again. "Where is he?"

"In the other section," he whined. "Left from reception. Second cell."

She took the second strip and stuffed it in his mouth, keeping it in place by tying the third around his head.

Finally, she took his keys off their chain and his cell phone from his pocket. She left five hundred dollars on the table—that would take some explaining when they rescued him—and closed and locked the cell door.

Crys leaned against the door for a moment, her heart racing. She'd just assaulted a police officer—she could hear him struggling and groaning in the cell behind her. She could be putting herself at even more risk than she was already. But elation pulsed through her too. She'd got the better of Petrus, and she was free.

She ran to reception, stepping as lightly and quietly as she could. Then she took the corridor to the left. Petrus had told the truth—the whole station was deserted at night. After a couple of wrong turns, she found the other cells. She looked through the peephole of the second, but it was too dark to tell who was in it.

Crys tapped on the door. "Bongani," she whispered as loud as she dared. She didn't want any other prisoners to hear. "Wake up. It's Crys."

She heard a movement from the back of the cell. Then footsteps on the floor. "Crys? What are you doing here?"

Crys fiddled with the keys until she found the right one and opened the door.

"We've got to get out of here. Mabula is working with Pockface. I saw him here in the police station."

"Mabula…the Portuguese guy…" Bongani was confused. "How did you escape?"

"I'll tell you later. We need to find our stuff."

"You go. I have to stay."

"Are you mad? Mabula wants that money. He'll lock you away forever. If he lets you live."

"I can't go. He's got nothing to hold me on right now. But if I break out, he'll have the whole country looking for me. He'll go after my family."

"Bongani. What are you thinking? It was you who said that

Mabula would kill for the money. Do you think he's just going to let you sit in jail, safe and sound? Next thing, your wife will be in the next cell. Then your kids. Until you tell him. We've got to get away from him."

It took a few moments for Bongani to decide. Crys understood that he was torn between the same bad options she had wrestled with.

"Okay. I pray it's the right thing to do," he said at last.

Crys grabbed his arm and pulled him along. They'd lost too much time already. Petrus might spit out the gag and start shouting any minute.

Back at reception, they searched around for their ID documents and the Land Rover keys, but had no luck. Then they tried Mabula's office, but all the drawers were locked.

"Do you know Mr. Malan's cell number?" Crys asked.

Bongani nodded and punched in the number for her on Mabula's desk phone. She reached Anton's voicemail—unsurprising at four-thirty in the morning—and left him a message explaining what had happened and that they'd contact him again later.

"Crys, you'd better dump the gun," Bongani said when she'd finished. "It's too dangerous to keep it."

Crys hesitated. It could be useful, but Bongani was right—with it, they'd not just be escapees, they'd be armed fugitives. She left the gun along with Petrus's keys on the desk.

"Okay. You know this town. Where should we go?"

"Do you have any money?"

Crys nodded.

"The minibus taxi rank. I know where it is. We have to get out of Giyani. Then we can phone Mr. Malan again. He'll help us."

Making sure there was no one outside the main door of the station, they slipped out and headed through the gate onto the street. It was still dark outside, just the odd street lamp and the moon lighting the way.

Bongani was already on the street, and Crys was closing the

gate after herself, when she was grabbed from behind. A rough hand was placed over her mouth.

"Don't make noise, or I hurt you bad." Then the man took his hand away and twisted Crys around roughly so that she was looking into his scarred face.

He must have seen her shock because he laughed. "Your friend, Petrus. My friend too..."

Chapter 20

Keeping his gun thrust hard against her head, Pockface dragged Crys, struggling, toward a white pickup. Even in her desperate state, she made a connection. Bongani had sent Michael to follow a white *bakkie*. Could it be the same one?

The thought chilled her to the bone.

When they reached the vehicle, Bongani was already there, held with a gun to his head too, by the man who'd been with Pockface at the camp.

Bongani and Crys looked at each other for a moment before pillowcases were pulled over their heads and they were shoved onto the back seat. She felt Pockface climb in next to her.

"No noise," he hissed and jammed the gun in her ribs. Crys winced.

She was struggling to breathe and her heart was racing. Why had she trusted Petrus? She should have guessed he would take bribes from others if he took one from her. She couldn't see her way out of this. All options were blocked, and she'd dragged Bongani with her as well.

As they drove, she tried to steady her breathing. If she drew in too deep a breath, the cloth of the pillowcase covered her mouth, and she felt like she was suffocating. She tried to retreat to the calm place she went during her meditation. But the gun in her side and the rocking of the car made it impossible.

After about ten minutes, they stopped. She guessed it must be on the outskirts of Giyani or maybe a bit further. There was no noise and no light.

She heard Pockface open the door and get out of the car. Then he grabbed her arm and pulled her after him. She could hear the other man dealing with Bongani. She tripped and fell, wrenching her arm, her chin hitting the ground with a sickening jolt that made her teeth slam together.

"Get up!" Pockface yanked on her arm. A shaft of pain shot through her shoulder. She staggered to her feet, and he pulled at her again.

A few moments later, the pillowcase was ripped from her head.

They were inside now. There was a light bulb that blinded her, preventing her from seeing anything else. She screwed up her eyes against the light. Pockface's accomplice grabbed her arm and tied a rope to her wrist. Then he pulled it behind her back and grabbed the other one. Again, pain lanced through her shoulder, and she closed her eyes.

When she opened them, she saw Pockface pull the pillow-case off Bongani's head. Like an uncaged cat, Bongani burst into action, lashing out and knocking the gun from Pockface's hand and smashing his fist into his face. Pockface yelled, and his accomplice let Crys go, darting over to Pockface's aid.

Crys tried to run, but he was too fast for her. Instead of helping Pockface, he turned and grabbed her sore shoulder. She screamed in agony. The man stuck the gun to her head.

"You stop or she dies!" he yelled at Bongani.

She struggled, but he held her tightly

At this, Bongani gave up, and Pockface grabbed his gun from the floor. His cheek was bleeding, but he was smiling. Taking his time, he stood square in front of Bongani and punched him in the stomach so hard he doubled over. Then hit him hard on the side of the head with the gun. Bongani collapsed, and Pockface kicked him in the stomach and then in the head.

"Stop it! Leave him alone!" Crys screamed.

Bongani wasn't moving now. Pockface kicked him again, then stepped back and wiped the blood off his face.

"Fucker! I need him now, but kill later." He added something in Portuguese to the other man, who yanked Crys's arms behind her and tied her wrists tightly.

Pockface approached her, patted her down and pulled Petrus's cell phone from her pocket. He dropped it onto the floor and stamped on it several times until it was in small pieces.

Crys looked around. They were in a small room with two wooden chairs and a bed pushed against the wall. The only window had heavy curtains. She guessed it was barred. This wasn't a bedroom. It was a cell.

"Sit!" Pockface pushed her toward one of the chairs.

As she sat down, he pulled her arms back so her hands were behind the back of the chair. Her shoulder throbbed.

Finally, he tied her feet together and to the chair. She wasn't going anywhere. This was so much worse than the police cell. She was sure now she was going to be tortured. The pain in her shoulder seemed to travel into her head, and she couldn't focus on anything else.

They dragged Bongani to another chair and tied him up too. He slumped forward.

Was he dead? She couldn't tell. And she could soon be dead too. The realization helped clear her mind, holding off the agony for a second.

"Where the money?" Pockface pushed the gun into her forehead.

She shrank from it. "I don't know about any money."

He slapped her across the face. She was so dazed she almost didn't feel the pain.

"Where did you hide money?"

She shook her head. "The man from Vietnam must have

hidden it, like I told you," Crys said, her words slurred now. "It must be near the plane."

He slapped her again. Harder this time. She slumped sideways. "Tell me!"

"I can't tell you what I don't know," she shouted hoarsely, bracing for another slap.

Instead, he took a couple of steps back and aimed his gun at her head. "I kill you if you don't tell. Then I make the fucker tell anyway."

Her head was swimming as she tried to think what she should do. If he really thought she knew, he wouldn't shoot her. He'd beat her up until she told him. But if she told him and he found the money, he couldn't afford to let them live.

Crys knew—as she'd known all along—that they couldn't tell anyone where the money was.

She shook her head. "Please...I don't know..." Her face was wet. She wasn't sure whether it was tears or blood. She wished more than ever that they'd left the damned briefcase in the bush where it could be found. "Please...please don't shoot."

"I count to three, then shoot."

"I don't know. Please."

"One..."

With an effort Crys focused on his face. All she saw was anger. "Two..."

"I...DON'T...KNOW..." she screamed.

"Three."

And he fired. The sound was deafening in the small room. But she was alive. He'd missed.

She looked at him. All she could see was him laughing, but she couldn't hear a sound, and there was no humor in his eyes. At last her ears began to clear and she heard him say, "Good joke. No use to me if you dead right now."

She collapsed into her restraints. She'd gambled right. He couldn't kill them.

The two men walked to the door. Then one turned.

She raised her head.

"Later, not so easy," Pockface said before they went out and locked the door.

———

Crys struggled to free her hands, but she only managed to make things worse. The pain in her shoulder had become excruciating and, with her hands tied, she couldn't find a position that relieved it. And her wrists were burning from the chafing of the rope.

After a while, she gave up. She was there to stay. She breathed deeply, unable to focus on anything but pain.

There was a groan, and then a weak call: "Crys?"

She roused herself. "Bongani... are you okay?"

"Everything hurts, but I think so."

"Bongani, I'm so sorry. This is all my fault. I should've left you at the police station like you wanted."

"I decided for myself..." There was a long pause. Then he spoke again. "We have to get out of here somehow."

"Our only hope is Mabula, and that's a long shot. If he's in cahoots with Pockface, he'll think he's been double-crossed. And if he's not... Either way, he'll do everything he can to get us back...to get his share of the money."

She saw Bongani nodding; his head looked heavy. "I think we're still in Giyani, but if you're right, it will take the police time to find us. And I don't think we have that much time."

It was true. They were soon going to find out how far Pockface and his accomplice would be willing to go to get the money, or whether their frustration would get the better of them.

"We're going to have to tell them," Bongani said.

She sat up now, staring at him in surprise. "They'll kill us as soon as we do! It'll be like pulling the trigger ourselves."

"I don't think so. Maybe they'll take us back to the camp with them—or at least one of us. That buys some time for Mabula to find us. And maybe we'll get lucky again—like with the ellies."

She didn't think that would work twice. And if they gave them the GPS, they might just kill them at once. She didn't know what to do. The situation seemed hopeless.

———

Time passed slowly—Crys guessed it was about an hour, but it could have been less, it could have been more. The pain in her body was almost unbearable. She must have fallen into unconsciousness, because every now and again, she came round, roused by the sound of a phone ringing, followed by muffled, shouted conversations. She couldn't make out any words, but she could tell that it was Pockface yelling at someone.

At last the door opened, and he strode in. His face was flushed, and he was waving his gun around as though he didn't know who to shoot first. But he ignored Bongani and said to Crys, "Boss very angry. Wants me to break every bone till you tell us where money is."

"I can't tell you what I don't know," she croaked.

"Doesn't matter. Must do what he says."

"Don't touch her!" Bongani yelled.

Pockface smiled. "Maybe the fucker likes you, hey?" He leaned over and ran his hand over her face, making her pull away. "You tell me now, pretty girl."

When she didn't reply, he walked behind her and grabbed one of her wrists. She clenched her fingers as tightly as she could. He pried her little finger open and bent it back. She writhed and struggled but had no leverage. He bent it further.

Then there was a crack. And agony so intense it erased all the other pain.

Úm ma ni bát ni hồng. Úm ma ni bát ni hồng. Úm ma ni bát ni hồng. Úm ma ni bát ni hồng.

This time Crys shouted her mantra. And Bongani was screaming for Pockface to stop. His voice seemed to come from a long
way away.

Then Pockface was in front of her again, slapping her hard
across the face, over and over. "You have many bones. I give you
five minutes to change your mind. If no answer, I break them one
by one. Very painful. I will enjoy." He headed for the door. "You
beautiful woman today. Tomorrow not so beautiful."

The door slammed, and Crys heard the key turn in the lock.
She clenched her teeth to fight the searing pain. It didn't help. She
realized that tears were streaming down her face. She was sobbing
uncontrollably. They weren't going to make it out of this alive.

———

"We have to tell him, Crys," Bongani was saying. "I'll tell him.
I can't watch him hurt you like that. If we tell him, we may get
some more time."

She couldn't think straight. If they told Pockface where the
money was, he'd kill them. If they didn't, he'd break her bones
one by one. She let out a big sob. Maybe Bongani was right.
They should tell Pockface and hope the end was quick. It was
their only choice.

But another part of her mind fought that idea. She didn't want
to die. Somehow, she had to buy some more time. Somehow, she
had to survive.

The door opened and Pockface walked back in.

With difficulty she held her head up and said, "I'll tell you
where the money is. I'll take you to it. But you must promise to
let us go. We won't tell anyone."

He looked at her and laughed his loud, mocking laugh. "You
funny."

She heard a ringtone. Pockface pulled a phone out of his
pocket and glanced at the screen.

He put it to his ear. "Good news. She tell me where money is." He smirked into her face. "I go now to get it."

He listened for a few moments, then turned away and walked to the window.

"Not next Sunday," he said, looking serious now. "Sunday after. Need eight men."

He listened again. She could hear a tinny voice, but she couldn't make out what it was saying.

"Three," said Pockface. "Yes, three. And more money. Same." He nodded as he listened. "Okay. See you soon." He disconnected, pocketed the phone, and turned to Crys.

"Good you decide to tell. So, where is it?"

"It's in the bush near the plane. I can't tell you exactly because all the trees look the same. I have to find the GPS. The coordinates are in there. Then I can take you."

"Where is GPS?"

"I left it in our Land Rover. We parked outside the police station, but maybe they moved it."

"Many Land Rovers in Giyani. How I know which one?"

The effort to explain almost felt too much. But she had to say, now that she'd started. "It has Tshukudu Game Reserve on the side. Take off the spare wheel on the hood. The GPS is wrapped in a towel inside."

"Where in GPS?"

For a second her mind went blank. She couldn't think. She wanted to give up, pass out…

"Tell me!" Pockface's voice was a shout, and he took a step toward her.

"When you turn on the GPS, go…go to the main menu. You… you might have to wait for it to…to triangulate. Then choose the option that says…W-Waypoints. Then…"

Pockface lost patience. "Too hard. We fetch GPS and bring it here. Then you show us. Better be there."

He turned and walked out, shouting something in Portuguese.

———

Crys must have passed out after that, because the next thing she knew, both men were back in the room, Pockface carrying the GPS. She had no idea how long it had taken them to find the Land Rover.

He untied her good hand and gave her the GPS.

"It's much easier if we show you where the briefcase is buried," she croaked. "It'll be hard to find, even with the GPS. It'll only tell you the rough location, you need to know the exact spot. You'll be digging for hours otherwise…"

She could see he was thinking about it. He called for his accomplice to come to the room, and they spoke for a few minutes in Portuguese. By the way they were pointing at her, she thought they were deciding whether they should take her along and leave Bongani behind.

Eventually, Pockface shook his head and turned back to her. "Too dangerous. Police look for you. Show me on GPS."

Even in her daze she sat up a little. So that meant Pockface and Mabula weren't in league together…or Pockface was trying to get all the money for himself…

"Show me…" Pockface repeated, slowly, putting his face close to hers.

What was the best thing to do? She turned the GPS on, trying to think hard how she could fool Pockface. He was watching her closely, though, so he could see everything she was doing.

"I have to wait for the GPS to pick up the satellites…" she said, hoping he believed her. It was unnecessary for the information she needed—but it gave her a little extra time to think.

If she gave him the correct position, he'd end up with the money, then come back and kill them. If she gave him the wrong position, he'd come back, and who knew what he'd do before he killed them?

She shuddered. What could she do?

Think, she admonished herself. *Think!*

She could give him the wrong location. That would buy them time. She'd already said the coordinates were a rough location and he'd need them to show the exact spot. Maybe when he came back, they could persuade him to let them show him where the money was. That would be a couple of extra hours.

When the GPS locked onto her position, Crys flipped to the main menu and selected Waypoints. There were eight showing. She selected the last one and deleted it, hoping against hope that Pockface didn't understand what she was doing. He didn't react. Crys breathed steadily, trying not to show her relief. Then she highlighted the last one, which she thought was the location of the camp, and handed the GPS to Pockface.

"We buried the money on the track from the plane to the camp," she said weakly. "On the left side, about ten paces in. You'll need something to dig with. It's not deep. It's in a silver briefcase."

Pockface took the GPS and said something to the accomplice, then they left and Crys heard the door lock.

A few minutes later she heard a vehicle start and drive away. Then silence.

She looked up and saw Bongani staring at her.

They had four or five hours before they found out what their fate was going to be.

Chapter 21

"We've got to get out of here, Bongani. I sent them to the wrong place. I deleted the co-ords of the briefcase and showed them the co-ords of the camp."

"That was clever." Bongani sounded in as much pain as Crys.

"Pockface will be furious when he can't find the money." She allowed herself a grim laugh. "We only have a few hours…then he'll be back."

They both fell silent for a moment. Crys was straining her mind to work out of her next step, and was sure Bongani was doing the same.

"I'm going to try to work my chair up to yours," he said at last. "Maybe I can untie your hands."

He rocked his chair from side to side and slowly made progress toward her. He groaned with the effort, and once he nearly tipped over. Crys gasped. He'd never get the chair up again.

After what seemed like forever, he got his chair back to back with Crys's and reached for her wrists. But he couldn't see what he was doing, and twice he grabbed at her broken finger. She screamed the first time. The second she bit her lip. When he did find the knot, he fiddled with it for at least ten minutes, but it was very tight, and he couldn't apply much force with his hands tied together.

Eventually, he stopped. "I'll try again in a few minutes. My fingers hurt too much right now, but I *will* get it loose."

Crys didn't think so. She could feel that the knot was just as tight as before.

"We need a plan for when they come back," she said.

"Hard to plan without knowing what they're going to do. Maybe I can say that I can find the place without the GPS. Then they'll take us both."

Crys wondered what would happen then. Probably a bullet to the head. And she'd deleted the waypoint. If Bongani couldn't find the right spot, they'd be grateful for a bullet each by the time the thugs had finished with them.

"I can't think of a better idea. Maybe we'll get a chance… somehow."

Crys felt him start on the knot again, but he made no progress.

"It won't come loose," he said at last. She could hear his desperation. "My family…what will they do without me?" The last word caught in his throat.

"The Malans will look after them. I'm sure they will." Crys tried to keep her voice calm, reassuring.

He was quiet for a few minutes. Then he said, "The whole village helped to get me to bush school so that I could become a game guide, get a real job. There aren't many jobs out here, but I worked hard, and learned English well. I wanted to help the village as they helped me. But the money doesn't go far."

Crys realized he was talking about why he'd become involved with the rhino poachers—about how he'd got into this position.

"I understand…" She hesitated. "You said I come from America and don't know what it's like to be poor, but my father and mother came there as refugees. We didn't have much—nothing, actually. But we had the Vietnamese community, and they helped us. People do that. They help. They don't expect a reward."

"I suppose so." He paused again. "How did your father escape from Vietnam?"

"They put my father in prison for thirteen years after the war. When he was released, my mother and my brother and me, we took advantage of the refugee program and went to America. My father followed a couple of years later because he would never have been allowed to get a job in Vietnam. They got rid of the people they didn't like that way. And my father wasn't anyone important—just a soldier who fought in the war."

"My father was a miner. He died in a gold-mine accident when I was young. You were lucky to have a good father."

She shook her head, forgetting he couldn't see her. "He's bitter, Bongani. He likes nothing about America. My mother and I had to do everything exactly the way it would be done in Vietnam. And he beats my mother..." She felt her throat tightening around her words. "I had to get away from them in the end. I used to go to the woods to be with the wild animals. They were my real friends. Not humans. I suppose my trust in human beings was damaged..."

"What happened in the end?"

"My father threw me out of the house for disobeying him. He told my mother he'd kill her if she met with me. And I believe that he would. So, I've made sure I've stayed away. To protect her."

"Why did he throw you out?"

She didn't answer for a while.

"Sorry, Crys, you don't have to tell me."

"No, it's okay: he saw me holding hands with a boy from high school. A white boy. In his world, it was up to him to tell me who I could see and who I couldn't, and then only if he and my mother were present. No physical contact until after marriage... marriage to the person of his choice." She took a deep breath. "I had disobeyed him. Committed the cardinal sin."

Neither of them spoke for a while.

"I don't miss him, you know," she said at last. "But I miss my mother so much. I thought I would get used to the pain in my heart, but I feel it as much now as I did then."

After a while, he said, "You're right. You were also poor. And you had no family, so maybe you were poorer than me."

Crys felt tears running down her face. She had no hands to sweep them away, so she had no choice but to let them flow as she realized she probably wouldn't see her mother again, and that things would never be right with her father.

As she tried to pull herself out of her sadness, she heard the sound of a vehicle outside.

She sat up straighter.

She hadn't expected them back so soon. Her stomach twisted and she felt nauseous. Bongani was desperately working on the knot again, scratching and tugging, but Crys knew it was hopeless.

Then she heard another vehicle. And another. Doors slammed and voices shouted. This was more than just Pockface and his accomplice. What was going on?

There was a long, drawn-out silence. Crys held her breath.

Then a banging. "Police. Open up."

"We're in here!" Crys tried to shout, but it was more like a croak, her throat was so dry. Bongani yelled in his own language.

"Police," came the order again. "Open up."

Silence.

Then a loud bang, followed by shouts and heavy footsteps—big boots. A few moments later there was a loud thud—the door shuddered, and Crys could feel the floor vibrating. Then another thump, and it flew open. Two men in helmets and bulletproof vests burst in and scanned the room for opposition, guns at the ready. Both Bongani and Crys froze, not saying a word.

"Clear," one shouted and ran over to them. "You okay?"

Crys nodded.

He untied her arms. She screamed when he caught her finger with the rope. Then he untied her legs. She tried to stand but collapsed back on the chair. She leaned forward, breathing heavily, as he untied Bongani.

When she looked up again, she saw Colonel Mabula walking in, also wearing helmet and vest.

He stopped in front of her. "Who did this?" His tone was hard, his face set.

"The Portuguese man I told you about…" She could barely talk. "The one at the police station…"

He turned to one of the men. "Get some water for them." He looked back at her. "How did he get you?"

It was payback time for Petrus's double cross.

"Your guard, Petrus, let me out, and they were waiting," she rasped. "They must have paid him to do it."

"Where are they? And how many?"

"We gave them my GPS. They went to get the money." She saw his eyes widen. "There were only two that we saw. In a white pickup truck. I think they'll be back soon."

He put his hands on his hips. "So, you did have the money after all."

She shook her head, thinking quickly. "I gave him my GPS and showed him some coordinates—for the camp. There is no money. I did it to buy us some time. You've saved us, Colonel. Thank you…Thank you…God knows what they would have done to us when they couldn't find the money. They've already broken my finger…" With an effort she held it up; it was crooked and swollen.

One of the men walked in and handed them each a glass of water. Crys took a mouthful and swirled it slowly around her mouth, trying to moisten every dry nook and cranny. The best wine in the world couldn't have tasted better. She downed the whole thing. Slowly, her mouth returned to normal. She held her glass out for more.

"You come with me," Mabula said. "Meanwhile, we'll set up a little surprise for your friends."

He helped her stand. Bongani managed on his own.

"What did they do to you?" Mabula asked him.

"Just hit me a few times."

"You'll both need to see a doctor, then we'll decide what to do with you. Everywhere you go, there's trouble, Ms. Nguyen."

The man returned with more water. She thankfully drained it again.

They walked slowly outside to a police cruiser, each step jarring her body.

"How did you find us?" Crys asked, shading her eyes from the strong sunlight.

"You took Petrus's cell phone, right?"

She nodded.

"We put an urgent request to Telkom to trace it. They told us that whoever had it, stopped here."

"But they destroyed the phone when we got here. Pockface smashed it."

"Not a problem. It was working when you arrived. That's all they needed."

Mabula opened the back door of his vehicle for her, and she climbed in—gingerly holding her damaged hand with the other. Bongani followed.

"It's a good thing you left his sidearm at the station," Mabula said through the open door. "We could have shot you when we found you…then asked questions later." He glared at both of them. Then he turned to one of his men. "Okay, Sergeant, hide all the vehicles and yourselves, and leave two men inside. I want those bastards alive."

Crys frowned. Had they got Mabula wrong? Was he on their side? She couldn't afford to take the chance.

The man nodded. "You heard the colonel," he shouted. "Get going."

Finally, Mabula slipped into the driver's seat of the cruiser. He turned and stared at Crys. "What are we going to do with you?" he said, then turned with an exaggerated shake of the head and started the engine.

Chapter 22

Bongani and Crys were taken to the hospital under guard. Bongani had only suffered bruises, so he returned to the police station before her. But Crys was there awhile.

The doctor gave her a local anesthetic, put her dislocated finger back into place, and strapped it up. At last there was some relief from the pain. She felt her body relax, exhausted from the tension. He checked her shoulder and pronounced that it would heal in due course. After that a constable escorted her back to the police station.

She had a sinking feeling at the thought of returning to her cell.

She was pretty sure now that Mabula wasn't working with Pockface, but that didn't mean he wasn't after the money for himself. She needed to tread very carefully.

But they didn't take her to a cell; she was taken straight to Mabula's office.

"Sit!" He pointed to a chair without looking at her, focusing on something he was writing.

He made her wait then finally looked up. "You're lucky to be here—a fortunate mix of technology and stupidity. You're lucky our technical people in Pretoria were able to trace you so quickly."

She nodded.

"Now tell me what happened."

For the next half hour, she related the exact sequence of events, from the time Pockface had grabbed her to when Mabula's men had burst into the room where they were being held. At the end of it, he checked his notes.

"You say they were speaking Portuguese?"

"I think so, yes."

"But one of them spoke English on the phone?"

"Yes."

"Could you hear what the person he was talking to was saying?"

"I tried to hear, but no."

"Tell me again what the man said on the phone in English."

She repeated what she remembered.

"What do you think it means?"

She shook her head. "I would guess they're planning something in two weeks. It sounds as though there may be ten of them."

"Did they say anything else to suggest what it could be about?"

"No, but Ho was Vietnamese. From my research, I know that Vietnam illegally imports a lot of elephant ivory and rhino horns. So, it could be one of those they were discussing."

"With ten men?"

"Maybe to shoot a herd of elephants," she suggested. "That would take a few men, I'd think."

"Or a lot of rhinos?"

"I don't think so. Rhinos don't usually move about in herds and they're much harder to find than elephants. I think they're planning something that will happen all at once."

"But all this is just you speculating, Ms. Nguyen. No one actually mentioned rhinos or elephants or anything else? Please think about it carefully."

She took a few moments to think through everything again. Eventually, she shook her head.

Mabula stared at her for a few moments. "I don't know what you are up to, but everywhere you go, something bad happens."

Crys started to respond, but he held up his hand. "And then there's the situation with Constable Ngane. You assaulted a policeman and broke out of jail."

Her heart sank. This was what she'd been dreading. She could almost hear the cell door slamming behind her. "But—"

"Do you deny it?"

"No. But I was scared for my life. I'd seen Pockface in the building, and I knew he was after me. And you didn't believe me. I had to get out of here. And I was proved right, because your Constable Ngane had set me up. Pockface had bribed him to let me out right into his arms. It's Ngane you should be arresting, not me."

"I'll certainly be dealing with him. And when I get to the bottom of what happened, you may find yourself back in your cell."

She felt a ray of hope. That sounded like she wasn't going back to the cell—at least not right away.

And then he asked her the last thing she had expected.

"Do you know a man called Michael Davidson?" he said.

"The reporter from the *New York Times*?" Crys replied, unable to conceal the surprise in her voice.

He nodded.

"Yes...yes. I know him very well. He also came out here for *National Geographic* to write about the rhino poaching and horn smuggling, and then..."

Crys's voice tapered off as her brain kicked in. Why was he asking her this? Could he be behind Michael's disappearance? Did he want to find out if she'd discovered anything?

She'd have to be so careful.

"...then he went missing. No one's heard from him for more than a month."

Mabula nodded. "When was the last time you had contact with him?"

"I had an email from him about a month or so ago—he said he was at Tshukudu Game Reserve."

"Well, he left there and after a couple of days went into

Mozambique for just over a week. The police there think he
was talking to rhino-horn smugglers in Maputo—he was seen
with a group of Vietnamese men at a local restaurant they use.
Our guess is that he was getting information for his story. Then
he came back to South Africa, and after that he disappeared.
No trace of him."

At first Crys felt it was safest not to show too much interest, but
now, faced with an opportunity to find out more—perhaps finally
to discover something important—she simply couldn't resist.

"I thought the Phalaborwa police were looking into it? They
told *National Geographic* that they hadn't found out anything. So
how come you're asking me?"

Mabula held her gaze for a while; she wondered what he was
thinking. Then he opened a file on his desk and passed her what
looked like the top of a cereal box.

A shock went through Crys's whole body. She couldn't stop
herself gasping.

There was a message written on the cardboard, and she immediately recognized Michael's distinctive handwriting. It said:
Been held prisoner here for weeks. Help me! This boy
will show you where I am. Michael Davidson. National
Geographic.

Oh my God, she thought. He's alive! He's being held prisoner,
but he's alive!

Crys realized her face had broken into a broad smile.

Mabula was watching her quizzically.

"He's alive," she said. "We'd just about given up hope."

"Well, he was alive when he wrote the note. But if they didn't
kill him immediately, they probably need him for something—
whoever they are. So, yes, I think this means there's a good chance
he's still alive."

"When did you get this? Who is this boy? Can he tell you
where Michael is? I—"

Mabula held up a hand to stop the flood of questions. "We

received it a day ago. But it wasn't brought to us by a boy. A lady found it on a bench in Makosha—that's a suburb north of here—and fortunately decided it might be important and took it to the police there. They recognized the name from our missing-persons" list."

"It's genuine. I recognize the handwriting. You must do something…"

Mabula nodded. "We're working on the assumption that Davidson's alive, and that he's somewhere in this area. We're trying to use our contacts to find out more."

"Colonel, I'm sure I know who has him. It has to be Pockface! Michael was trying to trace those people. He must've found them, and now they've grabbed him. You should search the house—"

"There's no one at the house," Mabula interrupted. "The Portuguese haven't returned yet, but when we have them, we'll certainly interrogate them about your friend. And a lot of other stuff." He paused and stared at her. "How do you know he was looking for the Portuguese gang?"

Crys realized she'd painted herself into a corner. She couldn't lie about this—it was too important. But she also couldn't betray Bongani's trust. She had to speak to him first. She decided it was best to stretch the truth one more time.

"Someone at Tshukudu mentioned that he was talking about it."

Mabula gave her a long stare, and she felt her face flush. She realized he knew she wasn't telling the whole truth.

After a few moments, he opened the top drawer of his desk and pulled out a large envelope.

"I don't know what's going on. The plane crash looks to me like a smuggling operation gone wrong, but we couldn't find any goods being smuggled, and we couldn't find any money to pay for goods. So, I think someone stole whatever was on that plane."

He paused. Crys kept quiet and still, wondering if that was an accusation. "Normally, we'd pick up rumors on the street about a big project, but it's been dead quiet. It's all very strange..." He paused again, looking at her suspiciously. "Now we have the Davidson situation. I'd be amazed if they weren't connected somehow. Are you *sure* you don't have anything else to tell me? It could help us find your friend."

Once again, she'd underestimated Mabula. Maybe she'd been totally wrong about him. But the money wouldn't help him find Michael, and she still had to get out of here...

As if he'd heard her thoughts, Mabula slid the envelope over to her. "Here's your driver's license and your cell phone. I can't hold you any longer, but I don't want you to leave the country until we've sorted out what's happening. You're to call me every morning to tell me where you are. Understood? I believe you still have work to do for your article, so that shouldn't be a problem for you, should it?"

She picked up the envelope, weak with relief. But her mind raced. Was he really letting her go, or was it another trick? Maybe he'd be watching her, hoping she'd lead him to the money. She couldn't care. She was getting out of there!

Now she needed a plan about what to do. If Pockface was still at large, Crys was sure he'd be looking for her, and he'd guess that she'd return to Tshukudu—in the Tshukudu Land Rover. She had to have a different plan.

"Could I please use your phone?" she asked. "And do you have the number for Tshukudu?"

A few moments later she was talking to Johannes.

"Crys!" Johannes cried. "At last. Where are you? Are you all right? We've been so worried."

"I'm okay now...I'm at the police station in Giyani, but I'm being released. I need you to do me a favor, please. I can't come back to Tshukudu. Can you meet me in Phalaborwa in three hours? I'll explain everything when I see you. Can you suggest a good hotel there? And can you please bring all my stuff from the chalet? I hope that's okay."

"The Bushveld Hotel is fine. I'll make a booking, and I'll stay over too. It's too far to go there and back today. And I need to make sure you're safe."

Crys smiled at his concern as she rang off.

She turned back to Mabula. "So, you'll have heard—I can't go back to Tshukudu or use their vehicle. The Portuguese know I was staying there, so that's the first place they'll look, if you don't catch them. Is there a car rental in town?"

Mabula took a scrap of paper and wrote down a name and location. "Where will you go?"

Crys hadn't thought that far. She just wanted to get away from Pockface and Mabula. "As you said, I have my story to write. Maybe I'll head back to Pretoria. I still need to talk to the minister."

Mabula nodded. "Chikosi has the keys to the Land Rover. He can take it back."

"And me? Can I really go?" Crys asked. She could hardly believe it.

"Yes. But don't forget to contact me—every day. I will find out what really happened out there, and if you're involved..." He widened his eyes and leaned back. Then, with a flick of his hand dismissed her.

Crys stood up. "Please let me know if you learn anything about Michael."

He nodded without a word.

She left his office, wondering what had caused his change of attitude. He'd been abrupt, but almost friendly. Could it be the connection with Michael? It was all so complicated.

Changes like that made her nervous.

———

As she walked out of the police station, she saw the Land Rover parked on the opposite side of the street. Bongani was leaning against the side, waiting for her. He looked as exhausted as she felt.

"Crys," he said, spotting her. "Are you okay?"

"Yes, the doctor fixed my finger. It was dislocated, not broken, and he's given me painkillers. And you?"

"Just a few bruises. I'll be okay."

"Bongani, Mabula has a note from Michael. It says he's being held prisoner, but they have no idea where. They need to follow his trail. You need to tell them what you told me about the connection with the white men and the white pickup. His life's at stake now."

Bongani's eyes widened. He shook his head and for a moment he didn't reply. "I can't do that, Crys. It will get back to the poachers that I identified them to the police. They'll go after my family. And they can link me to the plane. And the money. I'll never get away from Mabula…"

Crys was shaking her head. "I've worked it all out, Bongani. Instead of telling Mabula that you got the information for Michael, just tell Mabula that Michael told you that he was trying to trace the men and that he had a contact in your village. Say that he asked you if you knew the man and you told him you didn't. Then you're in the clear but the police have the information they have to have."

Bongani's face fell. "It won't work Crys. They'll know the information came from me…"

"Tell Mabula to be careful nothing about you comes out. He can protect you then."

"Protect me? You're mad. He's a *skelm*, that one. Don't trust him. He knows there must be money and wants it for himself. He'll force me to tell—"

"Maybe we're wrong about Mabula. Maybe he *is* honest. After all, he's let us go. Maybe now we should just tell him about the money and get it all over with."

Bongani shook his head firmly. "No. I know the police here. *None* of them are honest."

Crys thought for a moment. The money was one thing, but Michael's life was quite another.

"I'm sorry Bongani. These men will kill Michael. I know it. We must find him first. If you won't tell Mabula, I have to. But it will look much better if you do it."

Bongani frowned; his mouth was set. Suddenly Crys remembered him manhandling Ho and their argument about the money. She took a step back from him.

But when he spoke, he sounded resigned, not aggressive. "All right. I'll do what you said. Will you wait for me here? Then we can get back to Tshukudu and tell the Malans what happened."

Crys shook her head. "I don't think either of us should go back there right now. The police haven't caught the Portuguese thugs yet, and they know we're from there. Take the Land Rover and park it somewhere out of sight, and then lay low for a few days. I'm going to meet Johannes in Phalaborwa, and I'll explain to him why you're not going back yet."

He lowered his voice. "What about the money?"

She watched his face carefully as she said, "I'll tell the Malans about it. Then it's not our problem anymore."

He nodded. "Maybe that's best." Again, he sounded resigned.

She wondered if he was giving in too easily?

Crys dug around in a trouser pocket and pulled out a hundred-dollar bill, balling it in her hand so prying eyes wouldn't see. "Take this," she said handing it to him. "I don't have much left and will need the rest."

Bongani nodded, and quickly put it in his own pocket. Then he looked at her with a sad smile. "Well, goodbye, Crys. I hope they find your friend."

"Goodbye, Bongani…We've shared a lot, haven't we?"

"We have, Crys, yes." He turned away and headed back into the police station, his shoulders slumped.

Crys hoped they would meet again. He'd become a friend. Even if he did help poachers.

"You again," Mabula said, looking up from his desk as Bongani was brought into his office. "What do you want now?"

"Crys told me you need information on Davidson. I have something."

Mabula's eyebrows lifted in surprise. This was a new development. Chikosi actually volunteering information. He bit back a sarcastic response to that effect and waited.

"He spoke to me at Tshukudu. He said he was trying to get in contact with some white men involved in the rhino-horn smuggling. He said they drove a white *bakkie*. He wanted to meet them." He paused. "And when the Portuguese men grabbed us last night, they were driving a white *bakkie*. Maybe it's the same men… Mr. Davidson asked me if I knew anything about them."

So, it was Chikosi that Nguyen had heard this from, Mabula thought. No doubt she'd told him to come back with this story.

"And did you?" he asked.

Bongani hesitated. "No, I know nothing. I told him he must be very careful with people like that." His eyes dropped from Mabula to his desk.

Mabula slammed his hand on his desk, making Bongani start. One of his untidy piles of folders collapsed. "I'm sick of being lied to, Chikosi! I know all about you. I know you help the poachers. I know you took the money from the plane. *You* told Davidson how to contact these people, didn't you? You have the contacts to find them, don't you?"

"I know nothing…"

"DON'T LIE TO ME! Who told you about the white men? About the *bakkie*?"

"It was Davidson…"

Mabula was sure that wasn't true. Chikosi knew more. Probably Nguyen knew more. And he was sure both of them knew where the money for the smuggling was. He felt it all slipping through his fingers. Time was running out. Not only for Davidson.

"Let me tell you something, Chikosi. If Davidson dies and you have information you haven't given me, you're an accomplice to his murder. We'll add that to your list of crimes. You'll *never* get out of jail. Your family will starve. Think about it."

"Can I go now?"

"Get out!"

When he'd left, Mabula carefully restacked his files, hands shaking with anger. Two of his men were dead. It looked like the Portuguese had got wind of what had happened at the house— they should have been back by now. The money was still missing. And everyone lied to him.

He slammed the desk again.

Chapter 23

It was late afternoon by the time Crys reached Phalaborwa. She bought some clothes, then checked in at the Bushveld Hotel, where she found Johannes had booked her in as promised. The receptionist took in her filthy clothes with a very dubious look—especially when she said she didn't have her credit card with her, but she accepted the hundred-dollar bill.

As soon as she reached her room, she called reception and asked to be connected to Johannes's room. He answered immediately.

She gave him her room number, and they agreed to meet in half an hour. She wanted a long shower first, to wash away the past few days. As she stood under the hot water feeling her muscles soften and stretch, she knew that it would take a lot more, and take a lot longer, to get rid of the memories of what she'd experienced.

By the time she heard a knock on the door, Crys felt a little better. She still ached all over, but she was clean and safe...for the moment. She opened the door and was surprised to see both Johannes and his father standing there.

"Come on in," she said, with a smile.

"We've spent the last few days trying to find you," Johannes said, dumping her suitcase on the bed. "We've been really worried."

"Let's order some drinks," Crys said. "How are you feeling now?"

"Much better, thanks. I was discharged after two days but was still pretty sick for the rest of the week. I'm only just up and about. But what about you, Crys? You look like you've been in the wars." He pointed at her bandaged hand.

"A lot has happened since you left camp, Johannes. It's a long story…" She paused, thinking about how to start. "And there's stuff you need to know, too."

"You've scared the shit out of us," Anton said sternly. "We didn't know what had happened to you." Crys felt like she was being told off.

"There is some good news," she said, changing the subject. "At least, I hope it's good. Michael Davidson is alive. The police found a note from him, asking for help. They don't know where he is, though."

"That is good news!" Johannes said. "When someone disappears for—what is it? Four weeks now since he came back from Mozambique?—that's usually the end of them."

"My guess is that he's being held by the same thugs who came after me and Bongani."

That produced a spate of questions, and Crys realized she'd have to start at the beginning. Once the drinks had been delivered, they all settled down on the balcony overlooking a small garden, and she told them the whole long story—starting from when Bongani woke her with the news of the plane crash. As she spoke, she couldn't quite believe all this had happened to her in such a short time. Her reporter's brain kicked in—it was as though she was describing events in which someone else had been involved.

When she got to capturing Ho, Anton interrupted. "This man, did he have anything with him? I mean…there must have been some point to the plane trying to land there in the middle of the night."

Something about the way he asked the question seemed odd. This was almost exactly the same as Mabula's first reaction. Although she had been intending to, Crys's instincts told her not to mention the money to the Malans after all. And by now she'd learned to take her instincts seriously.

She shook her head, keeping her face expressionless. "Nothing."

She waited for him to press her further, but he didn't, so she took up the story from when Ho had tried to hijack them and finished when Mabula had let her go earlier in the day. She said nothing about Bongani's involvement in the smuggling, so with that and keeping the briefcase of money secret, she was lying yet again. She didn't like it—these men had been good to her. But what could she do?

"There is one other thing," she said, after she'd answered their numerous questions. "When I was being held captive this morning..." She hesitated. "It seems so long ago. Anyway, I overheard part of a conversation between the Portuguese man who was in charge—I call him Pockface—and whoever was on the other end of the line. I know the other person wasn't Portuguese because Pockface spoke in English."

"What were they talking about?" Johannes asked.

"I'm not sure, but I think they were talking about a big operation that's connected somehow with the man on that plane. He mentioned Sunday two weeks from today. And that he needed eight men and more money. And when he mentioned money, he said 'same.' Mabula believed there was money on the plane, but he couldn't find it. I'm sure he held us at the police station for so long because he thought we knew something about it. Maybe Pockface wanted that *same* amount of money again."

"So that means there *was* money on the plane," Anton said a little too hastily, she thought. "In that case, what happened to it?"

She studied his face before replying. Once more she'd need to be careful.

"Well, Pockface certainly believed that. Maybe Ho buried it somewhere..." She turned her mouth down and shrugged, feigning ignorance.

"From what you say Ho was in pretty bad shape," said Anton.

"So, he can't have hidden it that well. Most probably it was to finance the operation. Likely they were going to buy some rhino horns from the poachers. Did he say anything else?"

"Yes. He repeated the word 'three' a couple of times."

"Three?" Johannes asked.

She nodded. "I thought maybe they could be after three rhino-horn stockpiles or something like that."

"It's probably something in Mozambique, like bribing three officials or buying three consignments of horns," Anton said shaking his head and flicking his hand dismissively. "Anyway, it has nothing to do with us, so we've nothing to worry about." He stood up, seeming keen to go. "I'm sure you need a good night's sleep. See you in the morning."

After they'd left, Crys thought about the conversation and was puzzled by Anton's seeming lack of interest in what she'd overheard. She wasn't convinced by his performance.

And why would he think that it would take eight men to bribe three officials or buy three consignments of horns?

———

Crys was glad to have her cell phone and computer back, and she spent the evening responding to messages and sending emails. There was one text message from Sara Goldsmith asking how things were going, pointing out that she hadn't had an update for some time and that the deadline was getting nearer. After a little thought, Crys decided she should call Sara to report on everything that had happened.

"Crys! I was starting to get worried about you," Sara said.

"I'm sorry, Sara. It's a very long story, but I'll try to give you the brief version."

Even that brief version took twenty minutes, not least because of Sara's questions and exclamations of horror and disbelief. But at last Crys could get to the point of the call.

"Sara, I'm not really sure what I should do now. If Michael is somewhere around here, I'd like to go on looking for him, but I'm not sure what I can really do. And I've completed what I wanted to achieve here as far as the rhino article is concerned."

She was taken aback by Sara's immediate and adamant reply.

"No way do you go on looking for him! We had this out before. You aren't qualified to rescue him; the police are and they're on the job at last. You've absolutely done what you can. And we need that article. Work on that. You should follow up in Pretoria too. Didn't you have an appointment with the minister scheduled?"

Crys had forgotten all about that.

"Actually, I would be more comfortable if you didn't stay in South Africa much longer. These maniacs are still after you, for God's sake! There's a CITES meeting coming up too…maybe you should go to Geneva. And you need to get a feel for the trade in Vietnam yourself…" Sara seemed to be falling over herself to get Crys out of South Africa.

Geneva. Vietnam. It was very tempting. But Michael would need her support if he was found. *When* he was found, she corrected herself.

"Sara, thank you for your concern and, yes, I would like to follow up with CITES and in Vietnam. But at least for now I think I should stay in South Africa. I'll go up to Pretoria tomorrow. I think I should get out of this area, but I can come back at once when they find Michael. Would that be okay?"

"That's fine. As long as you promise me that you'll get away from where these Portuguese thugs are operating and *not* try to rescue Michael *yourself*. Otherwise, our arrangement is over. I'm not having two of my journalists in danger."

Crys gave her word, feeling guilty that she was so relieved to be getting away from this area. She'd had enough of danger in South Africa. If there was any way she could help Michael, she'd do it like a shot, whatever the risk. But with the police actively working on it, she had to admit that she'd probably just be in the way.

She thanked Sara and disconnected. She'd fly to Pretoria as soon as she could.

———

The next morning, Crys managed to find a seat on the second of two afternoon flights to Johannesburg. It meant hanging around for about five hours, so she took the opportunity to drive into Kruger National Park before she returned her rental car.

It was a good decision. Mabula had told her that morning that the police hadn't caught the Portuguese—they'd never returned to the house. She was immediately reminded of Sara's warning, and worried that Pockface would come looking for her in Phalaborwa since it was the closest airport to Giyani. She figured going into Kruger would keep her invisible. And, driving around by herself would be very therapeutic. She could just enjoy what the iconic game preserve had to offer. No pressure for once.

It ended up even better than she expected. The entrance gate was just on the outskirts of the town. She stopped and bought a day pass and even a couple of small souvenirs—beautifully carved salad servers in an almost black wood and a couple of matching miniature rhinos. Within a mile of the gate, she saw a small herd of elephants feeding on the mopane trees. Then she followed a side road to a waterhole where you could walk to a blind to view the animals. While she was there impalas, kudu, and zebras came down to drink.

As she drove on she came to a group of giraffes feeding on acacia trees, and was particularly intrigued by how they took leaves off between the thorns with their long tongues. She closed down the part of her mind that was dealing with the traumatic events of the past few days and simply observed. Best of all was a pack of wild dogs, something she'd never seen before, except on television. All had different markings, splotches of brown, white, yellow, and black, but they all shared white tips to their tails.

What beautiful animals, she thought. Perhaps her karma was changing for the better.

Eventually, Crys headed back to the airport and returned the car. She checked in, keeping a lookout for anything unusual, but the crowd of tourists heading back to Johannesburg made her feel pretty safe.

When the plane took off, she relaxed a little, and as it climbed over the Drakensberg escarpment, which seemed to rise almost vertically from the *lowveld* plain, a great jagged wall of grays and greens, she finally allowed herself to think about what had happened over the past week.

She closed her eyes and repeated a silent mantra: *Úm ma ni bát ni hồng…*

When she opened her eyes, she knew the way forward. It was time to get back to her writing. Whatever Pockface was up to was not her problem. But she'd keep close tabs on what the police were doing to find Michael. Perhaps she could even put on a bit of pressure in Pretoria.

She thought through her priorities. Getting a handle on her professional work made her feel safe and in control. The first item was to write the second article for the Duluth newspaper. It was going to be a sizzler. Second, she still needed to meet the minister in Pretoria. Then she'd be able to write the South African section of the article. After that, it would depend on Michael.

As the plane started its descent, she closed her eyes and rested. Once in the terminal, she picked up her suitcase and walked through the automatic doors. A quick walk to the Gautrain station, and she'd be in Pretoria in less than half an hour.

But just as Crys was about to go up the escalator, someone grabbed her arm.

"No noise," said a male voice with a thick accent. "You come."

She swung around and saw the pockmarked face close to hers. She was so shocked, she screamed and managed to jerk herself loose.

"Help! Help me!"

She dropped her suitcase and started to run, but he grabbed her again.

She swung her briefcase at him, hitting him in the face.

"Help!" she screamed again and ran up the escalator, a few steps ahead of him. Halfway up was a man with a cart laden with suitcases. She pushed past him, grabbed the top case, and threw it at Pockface, who was only a couple of yards behind. She turned and fled up the steps, still screaming for help.

When she reached the top, Crys glanced back. Pockface was wrestling with the man with the cart. Then he broke loose and started after her again. She sprinted in the direction of the Gautrain, trying to spot some security personnel.

Then, out of nowhere, two policemen appeared and grabbed Pockface as he reached the top of the escalator.

Crys didn't stop.

Fuck! she thought. How did he find me?

She kept running, awash with adrenalin, but her body failing as the trials of the past few days caught up with her.

Her mind was exhausted too. She'd had enough, and she knew now what she had to do. She forced herself to run on until she reached International Departures. There she scanned the departure board—Lufthansa was the next international flight out.

She looked around for the desk, pulling out her cash. She still had enough for a ticket. She didn't care about her suitcase; it could stay in South Africa. Most important was that she had her briefcase with her notes, camera, and computer.

There were still free seats, and she was able to get through security and immigration in record time. Once she was through, she called the Giyani police station and asked for Mabula. He wasn't there so she left a message for him. Then she chose a seat with a wall behind it and people around her, keeping a look out in case Pockface had escaped and was on her trail.

Fuck Pockface, she thought. Fuck Mabula. I'm getting out of the fucking country.

PART 3

Geneva, Switzerland

Chapter 24

As the plane descended toward Geneva, Crys stared down at the gorgeous city, surrounded by snowcapped mountains and hugging the edge of the long, silvery lake. She let out a long sigh of relief.

She thanked God she was out of South Africa.

This was a far cry from the heat, humidity, and danger she'd just left. As much as she loved the wilderness, there was something very comforting about arriving at this ancient and conservative European city.

She bought some warm clothes at the airport, then headed directly to the reasonably priced hotel she'd chosen during her layover in Frankfurt that was near downtown and the Rhône River. She'd managed to sleep quite well on the plane, so, once she'd checked in, she was planning to get to work on her phone, setting up appointments for the next few days.

She had just had a shower and was thinking about what to do about the suitcase she'd left in South Africa, when her phone rang. It was Mabula, and he wasn't happy when she told him where she was.

"I told you not to leave the country without my permission!" he said angrily.

"Pockface was waiting for me in Johannesburg. If it wasn't for two policemen who grabbed him, who knows where I'd be. I was in danger in South Africa, so I took the first flight out. I had no choice, Colonel."

There was no response.

"Did you get my message?" she asked. "Did you arrest him?"

"That's why I'm calling you," he said more calmly. "By the time I contacted the airport police, they'd let him go with a warning. He said it was just a domestic argument."

"So, he's still looking for me. Leaving the country was clearly the right decision, don't you think?" She couldn't keep the patronizing tone out of her voice. "And I did try to speak to you."

Again Mabula didn't reply.

"Have you made any progress finding my friend Michael?" she asked.

"We searched the house where you were held from top to bottom. There was no sign of Davidson. That puzzles me. I would've thought they'd have taken you to the same place they were holding him. It seems as though they must have several locations."

Crys sat down on the bed, despondent. "And what about the note?

"I've got my men going house to house around the area where the note was found. They're showing everyone his photograph, asking if they've seen him or other foreigners living in the area. It's a predominantly black neighborhood so we should pick up some information soon."

"But nothing yet? It's been several days."

"We're also trying to find the boy mentioned in the note. We think he may do deliveries. Perhaps that's how Davidson made contact with him. But so far, no luck. And I have a man speaking to all our informers, trying to find out where the information came from that led Davidson to make contact with the men with the white *bakkie*. I'm still not convinced Chikosi is telling us everything he knows."

Crys relaxed a bit. At least the police seemed to be working hard on finding Michael—certainly doing more than she could have done.

"Thanks, Colonel," she said. "I hope you turn up something soon. Please let me know if you do. Have a good day."

She lay back on the bed and wondered if she'd ever see Michael again.

———

After a few minutes, Crys sat up and started setting up appointments for the next day. Michael had planned to visit Geneva after his South African trip, so there were no notes for her to use. This would give her new and important material for the *National Geographic* story.

The Convention on International Trade in Endangered Species of Wild Fauna and Flora—known as CITES—had a big meeting coming up, but were able to arrange for her to see some people the next morning, including a brief meeting with the secretary general. And Rhino International, a high-profile NGO, said their director, Mr. Nigel Wood, could meet her after her meetings at CITES.

Making calls, arranging interviews, and jotting down notes while sitting safely at a hotel desk, Crys started to feel she was returning to normal. It was certainly better than fearing for her life in the bush, though her pain was a constant reminder of what had happened.

When she'd finished, she walked over to the window and enjoyed the view of a white peak of a mountain rising above the rooftops. She tried to focus on the present, but her mind insisted on taking her back to Africa. She kept returning to Pockface. What was all that money for? Who was he speaking to on the phone, and what were they planning? And why was he holding Michael?

So many questions and, as usual, few answers.

The Malans had no idea what the money was for, and Mabula

had asked her for her opinion. On the spur of the moment, she'd suggested an operation involving elephants, and the more she thought about it, the more it made sense. That would explain the number of people Pockface wanted. Herds of elephants meant a lot of ivory. And the more she thought about that, the more upset she became. She'd seen gory pictures of the animals after they'd been shot and the tusks removed—blood and huge carcasses everywhere. Was that what Pockface was after? An elephant killing field?

She couldn't let that happen and she was sure it wasn't too late to do something. But it would take someone in conservation with a lot of clout. Someone who would be taken seriously. Crys realized that her best bet was the secretary general of CITES, whom she was seeing the next day. She didn't like the idea of using her meeting—arranged around her *National Geographic* credentials—to try to enlist his support, but she realized that's what she had to do, even if it meant violating protocol.

And then there was Michael—probably alive in South Africa— being looked for by the police. But who knew what shape he was in.

In truth, Crys really wanted to be there looking for him. But Sara was right, there was little she could do, and the article deadline was now only four weeks away. Crys gasped at the thought.

Only four weeks to write a *National Geographic* article!

———

The next morning, she was met at CITES by a charming Japanese gentleman who described himself as the head of Knowledge Management and Outreach services and, by the time he'd shown her around, she was lugging enough documentation to keep her busy for a week.

The secretary general was her final stop. Her guide introduced them, bowed slightly, and left the office to return to his real job.

The secretary general, Dr. Helmholtz, was a carefully polite man, German-speaking, but with meticulous English. Crys explained about her article on rhinos for *National Geographic*, and he nodded frequently in agreement with what she said. He answered her questions and tried to be helpful, but it was clear that he saw rhinos as only a small part of his problem.

"You must understand, Ms. Nguyen," he said, folding his arms, "CITES deals with an enormous number of problems. We coordinate the control of trade in a huge variety of species, from elephants to stag beetles. That does not allow us time to focus on any one group of animals—even one as important as rhinos. Tigers are probably even more endangered right now than the white rhino. Pangolins are headed for extinction, and most people do not even know what they are." He shook his head in disbelief at such ignorance.

"But aren't tigers, rhinos, and pangolins all part of the same problem?" Crys asked. "People believe they have all sorts of miraculous properties and are willing to pay money for that—a lot of money."

This seemed to strike a chord with him. "Exactly right!" he said. "That is why we need to see this in context. It is a human problem, not an animal problem. I am not saying the solution is the same for each species. But, perhaps, the *problem* is. *That* is how we must think about it." He certainly sounded convincing to Crys.

"So, what is your policy as far as trade in rhino horn is concerned?" she asked ready to take notes.

"Well, of course, CITES does not set policy. We implement the policy as set by the signatory countries—in this case, no trade. So that is our policy: no trade." He glanced at her pad, as if he expected her to write the two words down.

"But do you think that's correct?"

He hesitated over that. "As a matter of fact, I do. But that is my personal opinion."

"What about South Africa's decision last year to allow free trade within the country?"

"I refer you to our press release on the subject," he said looking down at his desk. "I do not wish to add to that."

Crys had read the CITES press release. It amounted to very little, and she guessed that Helmholtz thought so, too.

Crys realized she wasn't going to have much more of his time, so she launched into a quick summary of her trip to South Africa.

He heard her out with encouraging nods, but she saw him glance at his watch and then at his computer screen. At the end he said, "Ms. Nguyen, I am truly shocked by your experience in South Africa." But his body language and his words didn't match. "It just shows how dangerous the situation can be," he continued, "and how important it is to control these poachers." He checked his watch again.

"Exactly," she responded. "And I believe from what I overheard that something major is about to happen there. I don't see how they could kill a lot of rhinos at once, but elephants move in big herds. It could be a plan to shoot several herds of elephants for ivory."

"I trust this has all been reported to the relevant authorities, and that they will take the appropriate action."

"That's where you can help, Dr. Helmholtz." Crys paused and leaned forward a little. "I really don't think the authorities are taking this seriously enough."

"How could I help?" He gave a puzzled smile.

"CITES could make sure that the authorities in South Africa act on this."

The secretary general took a few moments to respond. "Ms. Nguyen, I think you may have a misunderstanding about CITES. We are not an enforcement organization. If you have reported the matter to the South African police, that should be enough. But I will give you the name of the person in the Department of Environmental Affairs there, who could liaise with them." He swivelled his chair toward his computer, brought up his contacts, and neatly wrote down a name and number on a Post-it note.

"Thank you, I'll certainly do that, Dr. Helmholtz, but I don't think it will make any difference, and there's not much time— less than two weeks. I need *your* help. You are a very senior figure here with contacts at senior levels. People will listen to you. I'm only a journalist."

Helmholtz looked at her with pursed lips and a small frown, and Crys knew she'd lost him.

"A journalist looking for an even bigger story than the one you already have, perhaps?" he asked in the same polite tone he'd used throughout the interview. Then he rose and came around the desk to shake hands. "Anything my staff can do to help you with your rhino article—contacts, information, et cetera—please feel free to call on us. We greatly appreciate the support of organizations like *National Geographic*."

Crys realized he'd only listened to her because of *National Geographic*. As a reporter from the *Duluth News Tribune*, she wouldn't have reached his office at all.

Now he thought she was just another reporter trying to create a big story.

She couldn't believe that no one cared that animals were about to be slaughtered.

Chapter 25

After lunch, Crys crossed the river to Rond-Point de Rive, where Rhino International had its offices. She was greeted by the receptionist, who showed her to the director's office. Nigel Wood was a very different character from Dr. Helmholtz. He jumped up from behind his desk with a broad smile and shook her hand vigorously. He was a tall man, a little older than her, conservatively dressed in an expensive-looking suit, with a discreet hint of aftershave.

"Welcome to Geneva, Ms. Nguyen. I'm so pleased you could visit us." He was clearly English, but to her surprise, pronounced her name perfectly.

"It's kind of you to see me at such short notice, Mr. Wood, but I needed to fit in Geneva before I go on to Vietnam. I know you must be busy with the big CITES meeting at the end of the month."

"You're on your way to Vietnam? Well, there is a lot on here at the moment, but I certainly appreciate the opportunity to give you our position for your article." He offered her coffee and indicated a seat at his office conference table.

As she had with Helmholtz, Crys explained her project for *National Geographic* and asked about Rhino International's approach to rhino conservation. Wood confirmed what she'd read on its website. Rhino International supported a total ban on all sales and movement of rhino horn.

"There is nearly a total worldwide ban on rhino horn now, Mr. Wood," she responded. "Yet the poachers are winning. The rhino breeders claim that removing the horns from rhinos and then selling them on an open market would drive prices right down and remove the incentive to poach."

He was silent for a few moments, never taking his penetrating, bright-blue eyes off her face.

Eventually, he said, "It isn't the solution, you know. I'll give you a copy of the report we've prepared on exactly this issue. There's no case where legalizing a banned substance has reduced demand. Take marijuana, for example. Where it's been legalized, consumption has increased. The difference between that and rhinos is that you can pretty well supply any demand for marijuana. You just grow more. That isn't the case with rhinos. The horn grows too slowly, and the population grows too slowly."

"What about artificial rhino horn? Some of it is indistinguishable from the real thing, even at microscopic level. Couldn't that change the picture altogether?"

He shook his head vigorously. "The whole thing is based on mystique. Consumers won't settle for imitations."

"So, what's your answer, then? We're not winning the war on the poachers—I saw that myself in South Africa. And it's at a huge cost—in terms of money and people."

"Education. That's the thing." He thumped the desk. "The trick is working with the youngsters, focusing both on the ineffectiveness of rhino horn, and on the awful consequence of rhino extinction. Then the kids talk to their parents. And it's working. It's like the fur trade. That was destroyed because it became socially unacceptable to wear them. We can do the same thing with rhino horn."

"But what can you really achieve that way?" Crys asked. "How can you reach that huge number of kids?"

"Through social media. Facebook, YouTube, WeChat, and so on. Fun ads with cute, animated rhinos, and competitions, et cetera. A lot of kids *do* engage. It *is* working." He paused, shook his head, and then said, "I'm sorry. Perhaps I get a bit too intense about this. Rhinos are very special: the last male Northern White rhino just died, and the Asian ones are just about gone. Maybe there *are* new ideas we need to consider. Meanwhile, we *have* to protect the rhinos we still have. That's my mission here: making sure CITES doesn't throw in the towel and allow trade."

Crys sympathized with Wood's commitment, even if she wasn't yet convinced by his strategy. She was about to ask more about the education initiatives, when he suddenly switched the subject.

"Tell me about what you learned while you were in South Africa." He leaned back in his chair to listen. "I'm sure that will lead to more things we can discuss."

Her first reaction was to ignore his request and keep control of the interview. But Wood's passion appealed to her, and he might also have useful contacts. She hadn't given up on trying to save the elephants, so she gave him a summary of her time in Africa, starting with Tshukudu.

As well as being a good talker, he was an attentive and patient listener, just adding the occasional comment or question. However, when she told him about the plane crash and the subsequent attack by Pockface, he sat forward, concentrating on every word she said.

"Dreadful!" he exclaimed with a deep frown. "You were lucky you weren't killed. Did the police catch the thugs who attacked you? Did they find the money they were looking for?"

"Not as far as I know," she replied quickly. "And it got worse. I was held by the police, but one of the guards let me escape from my cell. It was a setup, though; the Portuguese men were waiting for me. They still thought there'd been money on the plane and that I knew where it was and started to torture me—started off by dislocating my finger." She held up her hand. "I think they would've killed me if the police hadn't got there in time."

Wood leaned back, shaking his head. "What an *awful* experience. I can't believe you're so calm about it!"

"It's behind me." She shrugged. "There's one other thing, though, and I think it's important. While they were holding me, I overheard a phone conversation." She summarized Pockface's call.

Wood held up a hand to stop her, and then asked her to repeat the exact words she'd heard.

"As far as I can remember, he said, 'Not next Sunday. Sunday after. Need eight men,' and then he listened for a moment. I couldn't hear the other person. Then he replied, 'Three. Yes, three. And more money. Same.'"

Wood looked shocked and muttered, "Sunday week? That soon? And three..." He scratched his head. Then he asked, "Did the police have any explanation for what this was all about?"

"Well, everyone seemed to believe there was a lot of money involved."

"But what was it for? Did they say?"

"The police colonel thought it might be for some sort of smuggling. But he didn't really know. He even asked for my opinion."

"Did he, indeed?"

"I guessed that with all those men, and a lot of money, they could be setting up a big elephant operation. I'm hoping you can help stop it. I don't trust the police in Giyani. That's why I escaped. We need to bring outside pressure to bear on the police and nature conservation authorities there, so that they take action and take it quickly."

Wood took his time before replying, rubbing his brow, and frowning. Crys's shoulders slumped. Despite his words, it was going to be the same as with CITES. Not his problem.

"Did the Portuguese men ever mention elephants or say anything that would link with elephants?" he asked at last.

Crys shook her head.

"I think you're wrong about the elephant connection. Look, I'll tell you something—our people in Vietnam have picked up rumors of something big happening in South Africa soon. It's very possible you've stumbled on the same thing." He fixed her with his bright-blue eyes again. "If so, it is big, and it's directed at rhinos, not elephants. We thought it would be in the next few months, but if we're talking about the same operation, it's more like days."

"You have people in Vietnam?"

"The workers in the education programs. They keep their eyes and ears open."

Crys still wasn't sure rhinos made sense. They weren't in big herds like elephants. But it didn't really matter, as long as Rhino International would take it up.

"Well," she said, "if my experience in South Africa helps you get the attention you need, I'm really glad. Please keep me in the picture—it will be an important story. You'll need to get the police and nature conservation to act very quickly. I hope what I've told you helps."

But Wood was shaking his head. "I wish it did. Unfortunately, you've only got a few overheard scraps to add to the rumors from Vietnam, and there's no obvious connection at this point." He frowned, and Crys's heart sank.

"Look," he went on, "one of the senior people from the Department of Environmental Affairs in Vietnam is here for the CITES meeting—his name's Dinh. We must ask him whether he's heard these rumors and, if he has, he may have some ideas of how this all fits together. He's an important person and may be able to give you some connections to follow up in Vietnam for your article. Would you be able to meet him tomorrow if I can set it up?"

Crys didn't hesitate. Wood struck her as the sort of man who wasn't easily brushed off. If Rhino International would get behind this—driven by Wood's enthusiasm—they might save a lot of animals. And it could be a really big news story too.

"Just let me know when and where," she said, smiling.

———

Crys had just settled down to write up the notes from her interviews, when her phone rang. It was Barbara Zygorski of the *New York Times*. She sat up, hoping for something useful.

"Hi Crys, I had to pull in a few favors to get to Michael's emails, but I eventually got there. Sorry for the delay, but I had to be very discreet."

"Fantastic. Thanks so much. Was there anything after the date I gave you?"

"There was, and it's pretty strange."

Crys picked up a pen and grabbed a sheet of the hotel stationery.

"I think Michael must have two mailboxes in his mail program and by mistake used his *Times* one to send an email instead of his personal one. That's easy to do. And, of course, the reply came back to his *Times* inbox, and he replied. So, there were only three emails: two out and one in."

Crys could hardly contain herself. "What did they say?"

"They're all very short. The first one had just one word— 'Agreed'—with a question mark."

"Agreed?" Crys asked. "Nothing else?"

"No. That's it. The second was a reply. It said, 'We agree. Ten thousand dollars.'"

"It sounds as though they're trying to close some deal or other."

"True. And the third—Michael's reply—seems to be a counter offer. It says, 'Ten thousand dollars now; ten thousand dollars when you have the information.' That's it."

Crys thought for a few moments. It sounded as though he was offering to sell them something—probably to get inside a smuggling gang.

"Who was Michael talking to?"

"There is no name, just an email address. It is duong731a@vn.yahoo.com."

"Yes!" she said out loud. She could contact someone who had

been in touch with Michael more recently than anyone else she knew. She copied it down, checking with Barbara that she had it correct.

"When were the emails sent?" Crys asked.

"All on the same day—five days after you received your last one. And there's one more thing: Michael's emails were sent from South Africa, and the duong731a one was sent from Ho Chi Min City in Vietnam."

Barbara then asked if Crys had any updates as to Michael's whereabouts, and Crys filled her in with the little news she had.

"But it seems he may still be alive," Barbara exclaimed. "That's great news."

"Let's hope it's true."

As soon as she put the phone down, Crys wrote a short email to duong731a@vn.yahoo.com inquiring whether the recipient knew where Michael was. She took a deep breath and pressed SEND, wondering if she'd get a reply and whether she should have written it in Vietnamese too.

Then she sent an email to Mabula, giving him the information about the emails and asking him to see if his Vietnamese counterparts could trace the sender.

Even though she thought there was a snowball's chance in hell she'd hear from him, she had to give it a try.

Chapter 26

Wood called Crys the next morning and invited her for drinks at his apartment that evening. Dinh would join them at five. It was astonishing to her. Things seemed so much easier in Geneva than in South Africa. Here, rhinos were saved over drinks.

She spent most of the day pulling together her notes on rhino poaching. She wanted to include some of what had happened to her but needed to clear that with Sara first. She decided to wait to ask until she had a good amount of the article written.

She was also able to squeeze in an hour's stroll along the water's edge, and she couldn't imagine a more beautiful place to do it.

When it came time to go to Wood's apartment, she decided to continue enjoying the fine weather and walked. When she reached it, she found an attractive building with well-tended gardens. The apartment was on the eighth floor and faced the river and the city. She was impressed. She doubted a rhino NGO would pay for this; Wood had to have his own means.

He greeted Crys at the door and asked her to call him Nigel, making a joke about British formality.

"And people call me Crys," she said with a smile. He took her arm and walked her to the living room.

Dinh, the Vietnamese government official, was already there.

He was dressed casually in jeans, a leather jacket, and a cream shirt with a garish tie loosened around the neck. Nigel introduced them, and Crys extended her hand, Western style. Dinh hesitated momentarily at this un-Vietnamese greeting, then took her hand and shook it.

While Nigel went to fetch drinks, Dinh chatted to Crys in Vietnamese, asking about her family and when they'd left Vietnam. She replied that she'd left as a child and hadn't been back, and that she was looking forward to her upcoming trip. He nodded a few times but didn't push for more details, apparently understanding that the period after the war was best left undisturbed.

When Nigel returned, Dinh switched back to English and told him, "Ms. Nguyen speaks very good Vietnamese. If a little rusty." He gave Crys what she thought was a rather condescending smile.

"I've briefed Dinh on your experiences, Crys," Nigel said before she could respond. "I think he needs to tell us what he knows."

Dinh nodded. "Of course. It's not much. Really only one thing. A man came to see me about a month ago. He said he had important information about a big operation in South Africa. Many rhino. This year. He said he had the details."

"Why did he approach you?" Crys asked, her reporter's hat firmly on now.

"He knows I'm with the Department of Environmental Affairs. He thought I'd pay well for the information. He wanted five thousand U.S. dollars—a lot of money in Vietnam. I told him he must explain how he got the information and show me some proof. He said his brother works with the smugglers, and he'd heard about it from them." He shook his head. "I thought it was probably a scam—fake news, as your president would say." He gave the condescending smile again. "I told him he must come back with his brother and some proof of what was planned, then I would give him the money." He paused. "I never saw him again."

"So, you were probably right about it being a scam."

"That's what I thought. But then I saw this..." He dug in an inside pocket of his jacket and produced a folded newspaper cutting, which he passed to Crys.

She unfolded it. It was a short article from a Vietnamese newspaper. At the top were photographs of two similar-looking young Vietnamese men, both smiling for the camera. Dinh looked at her expectantly, a small smile on his face.

He doesn't think I can read it, she thought.

She was irritated, and although she was sure Nigel had heard the story before, she read it aloud anyway, just to make a point.

It was quite short. The two men had been shot to death in an alley in the Saigon Port area. The men were brothers; the one on the left was known to be involved with rhino-horn smuggling. The police believed this might be the reason for the hit. The other man had no record. The police were asking the public for information.

"The one on the right is the man who came to see me," Dinh said when she was finished.

"Did you report it to the police?" Crys asked.

"Of course. They wrote it all down. But nothing happened. The smugglers have a lot of friends, a lot of money." Dinh sipped his drink. "Of course, I was intrigued and investigated, but I couldn't find out anything more. No one was willing to talk to me. Nor to the police. People disappear in Vietnam. One day they don't come home, and that's it. The police go through the motions. Sometimes they never even find the bodies. It's not good."

He let that sink in for a few moments. Nigel got up, went to the window and stood with his back to them, looking out at the lights of the city.

Dinh continued. "Suppose the man's story was true, I thought. Where would you find a group of rhinos like that?"

"On a rhino-breeding farm," Crys said at once. "Like the one I visited. But the horns would be cut off."

"Yes, but I discovered there are some small private and state reserves where that's not the case. Mainly along the east of South Africa. Maybe they would shoot from helicopters with people on the ground to cut off the horns. But then I was doubtful. You would need a lot of men and a lot of money. On the other hand, that could tie in with your story, couldn't it, Ms. Nguyen?"

"So, when Nigel told you my story, it all seemed to fit together."

"Crys," Nigel said, turning back to the others, "do you know what a hit like this could fetch? Say twenty horns? Up to five million dollars on the street. And a small game reserve's rhinos wiped out."

She looked at both men, thinking the whole idea farfetched. Attack a game reserve? Wipe out rhinos from the air? In addition to a lot of money and men, you'd need to be crazy. "They'd call in the army. They'd never get away with it."

"It could be a guerrilla strike from Mozambique," Nigel replied, striding around the room. "The shooters could fly in from there, and the poachers with the horns would fade into the bush as they always do. It could be done in a few hours. Then they would disappear back to Mozambique and—"

"But that would cause an international incident!" Crys interrupted. This was a nightmare, and, in spite of her doubts, Crys was caught up in it. "The two of you must take it to the highest levels. Now you have both pieces of the story, surely they'll take it seriously."

Nigel dropped back into his chair, shaking his head. "You heard what Dinh said about Vietnam. The police there aren't interested in what happens on their doorstep, let alone something that may happen halfway around the world. We'll get our information to the South Africans, but we don't have enough details to get them to act. Perhaps they'll be on alert and manage to catch some of the poachers, but then it will be too late. The rhinos will be dead."

"Perhaps Ms. Nguyen could write it all up for the newspapers and get public attention that way," Dinh suggested. "Use the power of the press." He raised his eyebrows at her.

"But what evidence does she have?" Nigel objected. "A Vietnamese man at a plane crash in South Africa—who is now dead. Another in Ho Chi Min City, who tries to sell a story—who is *also* now dead. No known connection between them, and no clear connection with rhino-horn smuggling."

Crys knew he was right. No one would publish a story like that.

She turned to Dinh. "I believe you've met a colleague of mine," she said. "Michael Davidson."

Dinh frowned. "I have, indeed," he said. "He visited me about a month or so ago. If I remember correctly, he was researching a story on rhinos, just as you are."

"He's in South Africa at the moment, but no one has heard from him for about five weeks. We're all worried because the last we heard he was trying to contact a gang of smugglers."

"A gang of smugglers?" Dinh asked, frowning. "Do you know anything about them?"

Crys shook her head. "Not really. It seems he was trying to negotiate something with someone in Vietnam—we found some emails on his *New York Times* email account..."

Dinh interrupted. "What sort of thing?"

"It looks as though they were haggling over price."

"If you give me the email address, I can have one of my IT people try and trace it."

"That would be fantastic. Thank you." She asked Nigel for some paper, scribbled down the email address and gave it to Dinh.

"Also, from an email he sent to me," she continued, "it seems that some Portuguese from Mozambique are involved."

"Some of the big smuggling gangs are based in Mozambique," Nigel said. "Nasty people!"

"We were beginning to think he was dead, but then he managed to get a note out of where he's being held. The police have it and are going house to house trying to find him."

"They have a note from him?" Dinh seemed surprised. "What did it say?"

"That he was being held against his will and wanted to be rescued."

"How did he get it out?"

"Apparently he gave it to a young boy who was meant to lead the police back. But he never gave it to the police. It was found on a bench by a woman who turned it in."

"Where do they think he is?" Dinh asked.

"Near Giyani—that's where Pockface was holding me. It's quite rural."

"It could take weeks to find him in an area like that," Nigel exclaimed. "And why are they keeping him prisoner?"

Crys shrugged. "Maybe he'd found out about this big thing we've been talking about, and they can't afford to let him blow the whistle on it."

"You'd think people like that would just kill him..." Nigel's voice trailed off as he realized what effect his words could have on Crys.

There was an uncomfortable silence.

Dinh finished his drink and stood up. "Well, I must take my leave."

"Before you go," Crys said, "Michael said in his notes that you were able to set him up with some interviews in Vietnam with people dealing in rhino horns."

Dinh nodded.

"I'd appreciate it if you could set up the same meetings for me."

He nodded and switched to Vietnamese. "It was excellent to meet you, Ms. Nguyen. Here is my card. Please contact me about your arrangements in Ho Chi Min City. It will be my honor to offer what help I can." Crys couldn't tell whether his smile was genuine.

They shook hands and Crys thanked him.

"I'll see you out," Nigel said.

He ushered Dinh into the corridor, and they spoke there quietly for a few moments.

When Nigel returned, he headed toward the kitchen. "You can't leave Switzerland without having a fondue," he told Crys. "If you cut up the bread into cubes, I'll deal with the rest. It'll be ready in a few minutes, and then we can talk about how Dinh's story fits with yours, and what we can do about it."

Crys hesitated, she wanted to keep the meeting professional. On the other hand, a fondue sounded fun and Nigel seemed keen to pursue the poaching issue despite his misgivings.

Nigel poured himself another glass of wine and topped up her orange juice.

Soon they were dipping the bread cubes in the rich cheese sauce, and fishing for the ones that got away. As they ate, Nigel talked about himself—growing up in a posh part of London and going to an English public school, and his eventual rebellion against those conservative values.

"I'm sure you can't imagine me as an angry young man," he said with a hearty laugh. "But I was. Eventually I decided to stop protesting about things like climate change and animal extinctions and actually try to *do* something about them. I'm sure you feel that way, too." He rescued a cube of cheese-covered bread from the pot and took it off his fondue fork.

"I do," Crys said. "After high school, I moved to Duluth in northern Minnesota for college because they gave me a scholarship for cross-country skiing. But they gave me a lot more; they gave me the chance to be by myself, skiing for hours and hours through the Northwoods. Or running in the summer."

"You must have had some wonderful experiences there."

Crys nodded. "One day, in my sophomore year, I saw a gray wolf looking at me from behind a tree. It was—I still don't know quite how to describe it—it was like...magic. Then, it seemed like he was there every time I skied. In my mind, he became my friend. My only friend. The only one who didn't make demands of me. He actually reminded me of myself." She took a deep breath. "Wolves are very social creatures, you know. They live in very tight groups and depend on each other. But this wolf was different, it seemed. A loner with no group." She shrugged. "I even gave him a name—Alfie."

"Alfie?"

Crys nodded, grinning. "I know it sounds weird, but it comes from the Norwegian for wolf, which is spelled u-l-v. I thought it was pronounced 'ulf,' so I changed it to the diminutive 'Ulfie.' Someone I skied with thought I was mispronouncing the name Alfie, so that's what it became."

"Fair enough!" Nigel smiled and speared another bread cube.

"Of course, I didn't see him over the summer, but he was there the next winter. I knew it was him because one ear was torn. Then, one day, halfway through the winter, he wasn't in his usual place. I skied over to his tree and..." Crys took a deep breath. "He was there. Dead. He'd been caught in a trap. It looked as though he had dragged the trap toward where he always saw me. At least, that's what I thought. I convinced myself he was trying to get to where I could see him, so I could help him."

She stopped and glanced at Nigel. He seemed to be taking her seriously, so she went on. "I made a commitment over his body that I would always do everything I could for wolves."

They sat in silence for a few moments.

"That's why I became a journalist," she continued, "writing about the environment and conservation and so on."

Crys was surprised she'd said so much, but it felt good to tell someone all this—especially after South Africa. It helped remind her of why she was so committed to what she was doing—saving animals, one at a time.

Nigel was looking at her with his intense eyes, but she couldn't read his expression. "Have you had enough to eat?" he said after a moment.

———

They adjourned to the living room, and Nigel brought coffee and Swiss chocolates. He sat next to Crys on the couch facing the view, but not too close. Then it was back to business.

"Crys, I've been thinking about what Dinh said," he began. "This operation in South Africa—it must be big. Think about the money it would take. Nothing personal, but they wouldn't have wasted all that time and effort on you for, say, ten thousand dollars. That's peanuts in this business. My guess is it's more like ten times that. For the risk of bringing in their own people as well, they must be expecting to get at least ten horns."

Crys didn't say anything, but she turned it over in her mind. His estimate of the money was off by a factor of at least five. That could mean fifty rhinos. And Pockface had said "three." Was it possible they would target three game reserves at once? It seemed hugely ambitious—mad, even.

"We just don't have enough to go on," Nigel continued, helping himself to a chocolate. "We have a possible date. And that's only ten days from now. But we have nothing but guesses at what and where. Maybe the two stories aren't related at all. Maybe the Portuguese are after elephants, and the Vietnamese are after rhinos. But we can't afford to ignore it and lose more rhinos. And if Dinh's right, and the plan is to hit one of the game reserves, there will be people there, too, and they won't hesitate to kill them if they get in the way. We *must* have more information. But there's no one in Vietnam who can get it for us." He frowned.

"What about your people there?"

He shook his head. "They're picking up nothing. It's all quiet. Too quiet. We need someone these people don't know."

Suddenly Crys realized where this was going, and she felt her heart sink.

"You want *me* to do it?" she asked, her coffee cup halfway to her mouth.

"You're going there in two days anyway. It's all part of the trip you've planned already. And you're a journalist. It's the perfect cover for asking questions, sticking your nose into things."

"No way, Nigel! I was lucky to get out of South Africa with my life. Now you want me to go *looking* for the people responsible for this?" She held up her injured hand. "And being a journalist isn't a cover, it's my *job*! I'm a reporter, not a spy. I can't go around asking questions in confidence and then leaking the information."

"What about the commitment to conservation you were telling me about?" he said, putting his hand on her arm. "If we're right, these people are intending to massacre twenty rhinos and murder a few conservation people on the side."

"Right now I'm more concerned about them murdering me!"

"Look," he went on, in a quieter tone. "I'm only asking you to keep your ears open and speak to the right people. Don't you need to interview the smugglers and people who sell rhino horn anyway? Isn't that crucial for your article? I haven't thought it through, but maybe you can pretend to be in the market for horn yourself to sell to rich Vietnamese people in the U.S. Pretend that your *National Geographic* article is partly a cover for that. It will make a fantastic story afterwards...."

Crys shook her head. "Dinh said people disappear and no one ever finds your body."

He took his time replying. "Look, I can't pretend it won't be dangerous, but asking questions just for your article could be too. These aren't good people. They'd think twice about assaulting a foreign journalist, though."

She laughed ruefully. "That didn't seem to bother Pockface and his sidekick."

"You're right, Crys. You have your article to write, and that's really important. Getting the inside story of what's going on out there to the public. All I'm asking is that you try to pick up information and feed it back to us while you're doing that. Let Dinh set you up with a few contacts. We'll do the rest."

Crys said nothing and stared out at the lights of the city.

"And you might come up with some information about your friend Davidson," Nigel added. "These may be the very people he was emailing."

She realized that was a possibility.

"There's so little time. What can I possibly find out in a week? I can't pretend I'm a local. I may look Vietnamese, I can talk Vietnamese, but I'll be a foreigner there. No one's going to tell me anything about a plan to attack a game reserve in Africa."

"Don't underestimate yourself. With Dinh's contacts there, and your nose for news, we've got a decent chance of coming up with something. That's if you're willing to try..."

Crys had a sinking feeling. Nigel wanted her to trade in Pockface for a gang of Vietnamese smugglers. It was the last thing she wanted to do, but how could she turn her back on the rhinos and a chance of helping Michael?

Nigel didn't say anything more, just watched her with an earnest expression as she wrestled with the decision.

"All right," she said finally letting out a big sigh. "Tell me how we're going to set this up."

PART 4

Vietnam

Chapter 27

Flying from Geneva to Ho Chi Minh City was like so many flights in the era of hubs. Crys flew for six hours or so to Dubai, where she spent more than three hours in the middle of the night, parked in a café. This was followed by another seven-hour flight to Ho Chi Minh.

She spent most of the time worrying about what was ahead. Digging out information for her *National Geographic* article was one thing. Deliberately sticking her nose into the affairs of dangerous people was another. Sometimes she was tempted to just stick to writing her article and forget about the rest. But she had a strong intuition that Michael's "something big" started with his connection with the mysterious duong731a@vn.yahoo.com in Vietnam, and she needed to get to the bottom of that.

Only she and Bongani knew the truth of how much money had arrived in Africa, and where it was buried. And she was haunted by the size of the project it might be paying for. Her instincts told her that the money was somehow connected to Michael's search for the smugglers. It was up to her to find the connection.

Also, it was the first time she'd been back to her city of birth, which had been called Saigon at that time. What was it going to be like? she wondered. She remembered nothing about the place and had only seen photos of the house where she'd spent her first year.

Her emotions were in turmoil as she wondered whether she would feel Vietnamese or American.

———

Dinh had told her someone would meet her at the airport and take her to her hotel. He was also arranging a translator for her meetings. They'd decided that only Nigel and Dinh would know she spoke decent Vietnamese. It was Crys's idea; she'd suggested this deceit to Nigel on the off-chance she would pick up something useful in conversations not meant for her. She was hoping the locals would see her as an American journalist and not as a Vietnamese spy.

A Mr. Do, who described himself as one of Dinh's colleagues, met her in the arrivals hall. She nearly greeted him in Vietnamese but stopped herself and behaved as a full-on American. She needed to stay in character.

"You come with me," he said. "I take you to hotel."

They walked through the oppressive heat and humidity to his car, an old Renault with a nasty knocking sound from the engine and no discernible air conditioning. If it was this hot and humid in winter, she thought, what was it like in summer?

On the road to the hotel, Do gave a running commentary of what they were passing. Crys was amazed that he could avoid the thousands of scooters and motorbikes and talk at the same time, but he negotiated them casually, sometimes taking his eyes off the road to point out a feature of the city.

"Vietnam much changed since war. Ho Chi Min City now modern city. Like New York. And country also modern," he told her. "New buildings, many jobs. People earning money. All Vietnamese working for good future. Want country to be good for our children."

"What do Vietnamese think of Americans today? It's been forty years since the war."

"We happy to welcome Americans. Bring money and happy faces."

What a different attitude from the States, she thought. Many Americans were still bitter about the war, and she'd endured a lot of racism over the years for being Vietnamese.

"I don't understand something, Mr. Do," she said. "If the country is modern, why do people still believe rhino horn can heal sick people? We know it doesn't work."

"Old men don't change. Still believe it powerful medicine. Young men use powder to show off lots of money."

It was a simple explanation, but it was the most convincing she'd heard so far.

———

After Crys had checked into the hotel, Do said, "You tired. Should rest."

Crys could feel the jet lag sneaking up, making her body droop and her energy fade. "Well, yes. And I could do with something to eat," she responded. "I'm seeing an NGO tomorrow morning. Are there any other plans set up for me yet?"

"After lunch tomorrow, I take you to a shop sells rhino horn and elephant ivory, and many more things. Ten-minute walk from here. Meet you at two. Okay?"

She nodded. "Will they help me meet their sources—the people who sell the horns to them?"

He shrugged. "Depends."

"Can you or Mr. Dinh arrange some other meetings too? Mr. Dinh has a list of people I need to see. Maybe I could also interview people from customs and the police?"

"Will try."

"And a translator?"

"Will come with me tomorrow." He looked at his watch. "Must leave now. See you tomorrow."

With that he gave a small bow and headed for the door.

———

Crys hadn't slept well on the flights from Geneva, so was determined to get a good night's sleep. She showered, had a light meal in the hotel, then prepared for bed. After fifteen minutes of stretching, she decided to check her email to see if there was a reply from the mysterious Vietnamese address. There wasn't.

I may as well try again. Maybe they hadn't understood English.

Crys wrote another short email to duong731a@vn.yahoo. com, this time in both English and Vietnamese. She asked for a reply whether or not they knew where Michael was. But when she pressed SEND, it was with less hope than with the first one.

A few seconds later, her computer beeped. An email had arrived.

Oh no! Her email had bounced: "Recipient not known at this server."

Crys hit the desk with her fist.

"Damn!" she said out loud. Her first email must have spooked them.

Then she took a deep breath. Even if the email address had been canceled, maybe Dinh or Mabula could still trace it.

But when she climbed into bed, she had to admit to herself that the email address was likely a dead end.

———

Crys's first meeting was with End Extinction—Michael had visited them too. She didn't expect to learn anything new, but couldn't miss an opportunity to ask about him. Its director, Søren Willandsen from Denmark, spoke impeccable English with only the slightest of accents. His assistant, Donald, didn't say anything, so she wasn't sure how good his English was.

"Mr. Willandsen," she began, "I'm very interested in your views on the trade in rhino horn, but I believe you've already met my colleague Michael Davidson. I have his notes so maybe that will save us some time."

"I remember him very well," Willandsen responded. "Interesting man. He wasn't after the usual stuff, though. He wanted help to meet the kingpins in the trade here. I told him I couldn't assist him with that and advised him not to dig too deeply or he'd end up in big trouble."

"Do you know what he did after that?"

"No. We had a short discussion about our approach to saving the rhino and he left. I didn't hear from him again."

Grasping at straws, Crys showed him the email address, but he didn't recognize it. She sighed inwardly. Another dead end.

They turned to rhino issues. Like Rhino International, End Extinction was in support of a total ban on rhino-horn trade.

"I know it's not working now," Willandsen said, "but we believe that allowing trade would accelerate the extinction of the animals. It may be a case of the devil we know…but we can't take the chance that broadening the availability of rhino horn will increase demand. If that happened, the game will be over."

Crys told him that her research had turned up several rumors of a big operation against rhinos in South Africa in the near future.

"We hear rumors like that all the time, but so far, the way rhinos are poached hasn't changed much. Locals on the ground get paid more than they've ever dreamed of to shoot one, maybe two, animals at a time. We don't think that's going to change."

"I hope not," she responded. "It would be awful if there was a mass slaughter."

He shook his head. "I don't see how that could happen." He paused. "Who else have you spoken to about your project?"

"I got very little useful information from the South African authorities. The minister didn't show for her appointment with me and her stand-in wasn't very helpful. I've also met with anti-poachers and rhino breeders in South Africa, as well as the police, and an NGO like yours in Geneva."

"Oh, yes? Which one?"

"Rhino International."

"Ah, yes. Nigel Wood. We know of him." Willandsen rose to his feet and extended his hand, but there was no smile on his face. "Thank you for visiting us, Ms. Nguyen. Good luck with your research. I look forward to reading your article."

As Crys walked out, she wondered what she'd said that had shut Willandsen down so suddenly. Maybe he and Wood were competitors. But why would two organizations that wanted the same thing be in competition?

As far as she was concerned, nothing in the whole business made sense.

———

By the time she reached her hotel, after pushing through the bustle of people, she was sweating profusely. It was a far cry from the weather in Duluth. And even more humid than she'd experienced in South Africa.

She realized that it had been a while since she'd meditated, and she had plenty of time before her next appointment. So, she laid some towels on the floor and did a series of warm-up stretches. Then she twisted into a half lotus, breathed deeply, closed her eyes and started her mantra.

She began relaxing, and her heart rate slowed.

Úm ma ni bát ni hồng…

She banished all negative thoughts from her head and prepared herself for entering the lion's den.

———

At two she met the translator in the lobby—a short man with oiled hair combed straight back. He introduced himself as Phan Van Minh.

"Where's Mr. Do?" she asked.

"He's not coming. The owner of the shop does not like him because he works for the government. He thinks it will be bad for your interview."

That sounded reasonable. Crys didn't want to start at a disadvantage.

"Is the shop owner expecting me?"

"Yes. The Department of Intercultural Affairs made the appointment."

Crys wondered who they were. Dinh must have been behind the arrangement.

"Okay," she said. "Let's go."

It was a short walk from the hotel, down several back alleys that seemed to get narrower the farther they went. Eventually they stopped in front of a small shop displaying all sorts of dried seeds, pods, and leaves in the window. The shop had no name that Crys could see.

Phan pushed open the door, which rang a bell attached to the frame. They walked into a poorly lit room, filled with all sort of aromas, some sweet, some sour, some appealing, and some that made Crys want to hold her nose. There were hundreds of jars on the shelves, filled with who knew what—it was too dim to see. And below the shelves were banks of small drawers, all wooden with little metal handles glinting in the half-light.

A door creaked open at the back and a man walked in, much younger than Crys had expected. He was taller than most Vietnamese and slender too.

"You are the reporter for the *National Geographic* magazine?" he asked her in Vietnamese. Prepared for this, she looked at Phan to translate.

"He welcomes you," Phan said.

"What is his name, please?"

Phan asked the man and turned back to her after he replied. "His name is Le Van Tham."

Crys recognized the name at once. This was one of the men Michael had visited. She decided to keep that to herself for the moment. Perhaps he would raise it himself.

She held out her hand. "Mr. Le, I'm very glad to meet you."

He hesitated, then shook her hand as Phan translated.

Le indicated that they should follow him into a back room, where there was a small table and four chairs. Phan invited them to sit and asked if they would like some tea.

A few minutes later, the three of them were seated with steaming cups of green tea in front of them.

"Before we start, please ask Mr. Le if I can take his photograph."

Phan translated, and Le nodded.

Crys took out her camera and took several pictures.

"*Cam o'n*," she said, purposefully getting the tones wrong. "Thank you."

Le smiled.

"Mr. Phan, please ask him how long he's been in the business of selling rhino horn."

Phan translated and the answer came back: "Four years."

They continued like this for nearly an hour, interrupted on a couple of occasions by Le needing to attend to a customer or getting up to refill the teacups. Overall, Crys was impressed with the translator: he didn't give her questions or Le's answers any slant.

She learned that Le bought his stock from a man located in the Saigon Port area—hardly surprising since it was well known that most horns came from Africa by boat. That agreed with what he'd told Michael. She also found out that he sold both powdered horn and whole horns, more of the former because it was a lot cheaper.

"How much do you sell a whole horn for?"

When the answer came back, it was one hundred and fifty thousand U.S. dollars per kilogram.

"That is very expensive," she said, thinking of what the South African poachers hoped to make.

When Phan translated, Le shook his head.

"He says it is the best price in Ho Chi Minh City," Phan told her.

"And how much does he pay for it?"

Phan and Le talked for a moment, then Phan told her that it was usually around sixty thousand dollars a kilogram.

"Good profit," she said.

Phan translated. Le smiled.

"Are you worried that your business may result in rhinos going extinct someday?"

After Phan translated, Le frowned and shook his head. His reply depressed her.

"Mr. Le says that saving rhinos is not his business. If rhinos disappear, he'll sell something else."

"And your supplier," she asked. "Can he sell you all that you need?"

The two men had a discussion, most of which was about the difference in availability of powder versus whole horn. Powered horn was freely available and usually mixed with ground up water buffalo horn, but whole horns were in short supply. They also talked about whether it was a good idea for her to know there was a shortage. Crys waited patiently for the answer. It was a good test of Phan's reliability.

"Tell her that it is easy to get horns," Le eventually told Phan in Vietnamese. Phan frowned, then turned to Crys.

"He says it is easy to get powdered horns—usually fake with mostly water buffalo horn—but harder to get whole horns."

Le smiled and nodded.

They chatted for another five minutes or so as she asked questions about Le's clientele. Who were they? How old? Did they really believe in the power of the horn? Crys could have written the answers without asking. The buyers were those Do had told her about—older people with money, who believed in what the horn could do for them, and young people flaunting their money, who didn't care about what the horn could do, apart from showing they could afford it—often mixing it with Viagra or cocaine, depending on the occasion.

Eventually Crys ran out of questions—except an important one.

"Mr. Le, do you remember meeting a man named Michael Davidson? He's my colleague."

Le's eyebrows rose when she mentioned the name, but when he heard the translation he smiled and nodded. He had met Michael, he said, and had a similar discussion, and then hadn't seen him again.

She showed him the email address and again his eyebrows shot up, but he shook his head vehemently. He turned to Phan and said, "It is one of the addresses the boss uses! How did she get—?"

"You are mistaken! Look again," Phan interrupted. Le met Phan's eyes and glanced at the email address again.

"Oh, yes, I see. It is not the address I thought. I have never seen this one before."

Phan turned to Crys. "He first thought he knew it but it was a mistake. He says he's never seen it before."

She was sure Phan had just shut Le up! But she didn't know why.

"Please ask him to look again," Crys said firmly. "I think he did recognize it."

Phan complied, but Le obviously knew what was happening now. He explained that it was hard to tell with email addresses that were just a mixture of letters and numbers. It was definitely not the one he'd first thought it was.

Crys was frustrated, but she couldn't see how she could take it further at that moment. She stood up, thanked Le, and asked if she could take some photos of his shop. When Phan translated, Le nodded.

She took about a dozen pictures and thanked Le again in what she hoped he thought was her only Vietnamese phrase. He smiled and bowed slightly.

"Mr. Phan," she said turning to the translator, "please ask him how I can contact his supplier."

When Phan turned back to her, he said, "He will let me know."

She thanked Le again and walked out. As she held the door open, waiting for Phan, she strained to hear what they were saying.

"Is she legitimate?" Le said.

"Of course," Phan replied, sounding irritated. They checked her out with *National Geographic.*" He noticed Crys watching them and moved quickly to join her.

As they retraced their steps to the hotel, they passed a little coffee shop with a few outdoor tables. At one of them was a face Crys recognized—Donald, from End Extinction. As their eyes met, he gave a nod of recognition, but no smile, then returned to reading his newspaper.

A coincidence? Or yet another man keeping track of what she was doing?

Chapter 28

Crys enjoyed a delicious dinner at a small, backstreet restaurant that seated only about a dozen patrons. She soaked in the atmosphere, the tempting aromas, and general hubbub of people enjoying each other's company. She felt strangely at home, surrounded by people like herself. No one stared at her as though she was out of place as sometimes happened in American restaurants. No one made rude comments that she was meant to overhear.

The shrimp *goi cuan* was both lovely to look at and delicious. She'd always loved seeing the pink shrimp surrounded with greens through the translucent spring-roll wrap. And she couldn't resist a *pho* with pork and extra ginger, just the way her mother's cousin prepared it at her little restaurant in Duluth. It was exquisite. She even chatted to the waitress, letting down her guard and speaking her language. Eventually she dragged herself away and headed back to the hotel.

When she reached her room, she settled down to catch up on her notes and to write another article for the Duluth newspaper. As she went through the information, she realized that so far her visit had added nothing to what she needed to know for her *National Geographic* article. She'd also picked up no information of value for Nigel and nothing to help find Michael.

As if he were reading her mind, at that moment Nigel phoned.

"Crys. It's Nigel. How did things go today?" he asked eagerly.

She filled him in on what had happened and told him she'd learned nothing useful to him.

"Don't worry about that. Just keep doing your job and keep your eyes and ears open."

"There is one thing, though. Phan, the translator Dinh arranged for me, behaved very strangely at the meeting today. He actually seemed to persuade Mr. Le to change his mind about something. I'm quite uncomfortable about it."

"Strange. What was the question?"

Crys told him the story about the email address.

Nigel took a moment to respond. "I'll have a word with Dinh about it."

"Also, I asked Phan to try and set up a meeting with a wholesaler—preferably the one Michael saw," she said, sitting back on the bed. "Is there anything you can do to help?"

"Already taken care of. I spoke to Dinh. Phan will be at your hotel at half past eight."

She was impressed with Nigel's ability to make things happen. Perhaps he was just that type of guy. After all, he'd persuaded her to spy for him, against her better judgment.

Crys told him about how comfortable she felt in Ho Chi Minh City on some occasions, such as the casual dinner she'd just enjoyed, and how uncomfortable she felt on others. Nigel said the CITES meeting was going well, but his real focus was her work. They chatted a bit longer, then hung up. Crys was ready for a good night's sleep, but the reporter side of her brain was mulling over all that had happened at Mr. Le's shop. She wondered if she'd missed something. It had all seemed so upfront, except for the issue of the email address. She made a mental note to visit Le again on her own and ask him privately. She would leave it for the time being because she'd have to speak to him in Vietnamese.

———

Do was waiting for her in the lobby when she went down for breakfast.

"Have eleven o'clock appointment for you in Saigon Port with wholesaler. He is the man Mr. Le tell you about. Mr. Ng. You take taxi with Mr. Phan. I have other work to do."

"Thank you," she responded. "What time should we leave?"

"In twenty minutes."

"But it's not even nine now."

"Port is more than thirty miles away. Bad traffic. Also, Mr. Dinh says you must visit another shop this afternoon. Will arrange for four o'clock. Okay?"

Crys nodded. She had the feeling she was on some kind of tour—being pushed from one sight to another. This was very different from her usual carefully thought through legwork.

———

Phan was waiting when Crys had finished a quick breakfast.

"We should go," he said as soon as he saw her. "It takes a long time to get there." He hustled Crys into the taxi, seating her in the back and joining the driver in front. Crys was distracted by the thousands of scooters, modern and old buildings cheek by jowl, and by the people scurrying here and there, going about their business. Phan stared straight ahead and chatted to the driver.

Crys struggled to keep a straight face as she overheard their conversation. Phan was obviously nervous about the meeting, telling the driver how to avoid the traffic and to take shortcuts. Sometimes he referred to "the important American" being late when they became stuck in a traffic jam. On the whole, the driver just ignored him.

But they arrived in time and the meeting went smoothly until

Crys asked about availability of horn. As with Le the previous day, Ng seemed to want to hide the shortage.

Crys tried to keep a blank expression while being surprised that such a simple question was taking so long to answer.

"Mr. Ng sometimes has difficulty to get the amount he wants, but it isn't too bad—" Phan began, but Ng interrupted and spoke directly to Crys.

When he had finished, Crys looked at Phan. Phan swallowed and then said, "He says it is more difficult to get horns now in Africa. And they're killing the men that get the horns. It's a good thing, because prices are going up, and he makes more profit."

"Tell him that I've heard rumors about a big operation next week in South Africa to kill a lot of rhinos. That a lot of money is involved. Ask him if he's heard anything like that."

Phan repeated this to Ng in Vietnamese. He shook his head and replied.

"He says he has not heard anything," Phan translated.

Crys then asked if Ng could arrange for her to meet the men who supplied him, and when Phan translated he shook his head and made a short remark.

Phan said, "He doesn't know his supplier because everything is done with computers. He's never met the people with the horns."

"Please send them a message and explain who I am and why I would like to meet," Crys replied.

Phan asked Ng if this was possible, but Ng refused. This was private, he said. Phan asked him again, but he was adamant. Eventually he turned to Crys and said that Ng wouldn't do that.

Finally, Crys asked about Michael. Ng remembered meeting him but had no helpful information. And, although she watched him very carefully, she could detect no reaction when she asked him about the email address.

She gave up, disheartened, and soon afterwards they started the trek back to the hotel.

———

When Crys returned to her room, she saw she had a voicemail. She picked up the phone and listened. It was from Nigel.

"This afternoon's meeting is important because the dealer is affiliated to a different cartel from the first one. We think they might be the ones who are organizing the raid in South Africa. I'll phone again tonight."

Crys was beginning to feel pressured. She was getting useful information for her article, but nothing that might help them discover what was planned in South Africa or what had happened to Michael. She was beginning to wonder whether she'd be better off making her own contacts or just sticking to the ones Michael had made.

She met Phan at a quarter to four, and he led the way through the maze of back streets to the next appointment, which was with a local man who called himself Joe. When she asked if that was his real name, he laughed and said it was. "My father was in South Vietnamese army. Friends with GI Joe. So, he called me that." He didn't offer his family name.

His English was good enough that they didn't need Phan to interpret.

Crys went through her usual list of questions and received pretty much the same responses about price and clientele as she had in her previous interviews, but Joe said there was no problem obtaining rhino horn, as long as one was willing to pay the asking price. Crys glanced at Phan, but he didn't seem to be paying any attention. However, when Crys mentioned the potential raid in South Africa, Joe looked startled and switched to speaking in Vietnamese to Phan.

"Where did she find out about this?" he demanded. He glared at Crys as Phan translated.

"There was a rumor in South Africa when I was there," she answered after Phan had finishing speaking.

"Who told you?" He was beginning to sound aggressive. Crys finally felt she was getting somewhere—rattling someone's cage.

"The police there had heard rumors," she replied.

"What do you know?"

"All they told me was there was a story going around about a big rhino kill. Many rhinos. They didn't know any more than that. It was just a rumor."

Joe stared at her as though he didn't believe her answer. Suddenly she realized that if he was involved with the South African operation, then a story may have reached him from South Africa that a Vietnamese woman journalist had stolen a briefcase of money. Now it wouldn't be too hard for him to figure out the connection.

"You must go now," he said curtly. "I know nothing about anything in South Africa."

"Thank you for your time," she said, backing toward the door, hoping that he'd let them go.

"Which hotel you stay at?"

Crys looked at him inquisitively, wondering why he wanted to know that.

But she told him—he could find out from Phan anyway—and he nodded.

"Goodbye," he said, turned his back on them and went through a door into the back of his shop.

"Let's go," she said to Phan. He nodded, looking relieved, and led the way out into the heat and humidity.

Crys was excited that she was finally onto something now. Her question about South Africa had clearly struck a chord.

"How can I find out more about Joe?" she asked Phan as they negotiated the crowded street outside. "I think he knows things I can use in my article."

"Not a good idea," he replied flatly. "He was not happy with you."

"Because I asked about South Africa?"

He nodded.

She realized she'd made a mistake leaving when Joe had told them to. She'd known this was going to be tough, maybe dangerous, and she'd turned tail as soon as he'd looked threatening.

She stopped and turned back. This was the first lead she had to the upcoming raid. She had to speak to Joe again, right away, before he had a chance to link her to the money in South Africa.

Phan's eyebrows shot up. "Where are you going?"

"I'm going back to speak to Joe again. He knows more than he's telling me. I need to find out what that is."

He shook his head vehemently. "No. You mustn't do that! It's not a good idea. He was angry!"

"That's *why* we need to go back."

Phan grabbed her arm. "Don't go back. It is dangerous. He didn't like your questions. People disappear in Vietnam, and I'm responsible for you."

But she ignored his pleas, pulled her arm away and pushed on through the narrow streets, back to the shop. Phan followed hard on her heels, keeping up a constant stream of appeals for her to change my mind.

But she was determined to find out what Joe knew.

When she reached the door of Joe's shop, she stopped, took a deep breath, and tried to open the door. It was locked. She banged on it. No answer. She banged again. Nothing. She looked for a phone number on display, but there wasn't one.

"How did you contact him?" she asked Phan, who was standing a few yards behind her, his face flushed and sweaty.

"I didn't arrange the meeting," he replied. "I was just told to get you here at four o'clock. You must ask Dinh. I think he arranged it. We must go now."

She banged on the door again. "Joe," she called out, "please open the door. I have something important to talk to you about."

There was no sound from within. Crys realized it was useless and, frustrated, she gave up, to Phan's obvious relief.

"Dammit!" she said out loud. Her first real lead and she'd blown it by giving up too soon.

"Yes, yes," Phan said, with a forced smile. "We go now. I take you back to your hotel." He set off firmly.

By the time she walked into the hotel lobby, though, Crys knew what she had to do. First, contact Dinh and Nigel to see what they could tell her about Joe. Second, go back to Joe's the next day and surprise him. He wouldn't expect her to come back. And third, contact the U.S. Embassy, tell them who she was, where she was staying, and what she was doing. If something happened to her, she wanted them to come looking. She'd learned her lesson in South Africa.

———

Her call to Dinh wasn't helpful. He confirmed that Joe was thought to work with a different cartel from Mr. Le, but that he knew nothing else about him. He was just trying to arrange a broad set of contacts for her.

Nigel, on the other hand, was excited at the reaction that her talk with Joe had elicited.

"You're obviously onto something," he said. "You should definitely go back to see if you can get more information. But be careful. These are nasty people."

As if she didn't know that...

Next, she phoned the U.S. Embassy and was surprised that someone answered her after-hours call and was even willing to take her details. When the woman, who was obviously Vietnamese, heard what she was researching, she also cautioned Crys to be careful.

"It's a business that involves lots of money and plenty of influential people, Ms. Nguyen," she said. "That's not a good combination to get involved with."

The more people told her that, the more Crys knew she was heading in the right direction. And the more nervous she became.

It was still too early for dinner, so she took a cold shower, followed by half an hour of yoga. By the time she'd finished, her body felt much better. It was not used to days of relative inactivity. Normally, she skied or ran every other day, but on this trip, she'd done very little exercise.

She took the opportunity to call Mabula. He'd promised to let her know if there were any developments with the search for Michael, but she preferred to keep checking with him herself. And, in fact, he did have some news—both good and not so good.

"I think we got close," he told her. "We spread our house-to-house search to the small holdings around Giyani. There are lots of them, but we had a break. One person told us about a group of Asian men who were using a nearby property. There are Chinese people settling here—same as everywhere in Africa—but not that many, and it seemed worth investigating. Anyway, when we went in it was deserted, but there were signs of someone being held there and of a very hasty departure—food left in the fridge, bedding unmade, even some clothes lying around. We're going over it with forensics. Hopefully, we'll turn something up."

Crys was silent. Were they that close? Michael whisked away just before he was found…

At last she asked, "Do you think they were tipped off?"

"Looks like it. But don't worry. We're close now. They know we're after them. We'll find him."

"Yes, thank you, Colonel."

But she worried that if they were on the run, they might not keep Michael alive.

She needed something to take her mind off the hollow feeling in her chest, so she caught up on her notes, backed up everything she had to a thumb drive and also to the cloud, even though the connection was slow. She definitely didn't want to lose any of the material she had for her article.

It was after eight by the time she walked out of the hotel in search of dinner.

She'd seen an appealing little restaurant a couple of blocks back, so she decided to call it a day and enjoy a quiet meal. As she turned to walk back, she stopped. Donald from End Extinction was standing at the corner of the street, watching her. That was twice now that she'd seen him. No way was that a coincidence.

She walked quickly toward him, her anger rising.

"What's going on, Donald? You're following me!"

He nodded. "Mr. Willandsen told me to follow you. He was afraid you'd get into trouble here, running around stirring up the rhino-horn people."

"He what?" Crys was really angry now.

She was about to tell him to get lost and leave her alone, but she bit it off. She couldn't trust Phan after the experience with Mr. Le; Nigel was on another continent; and Michael hadn't been able to take care of himself. With a sinking feeling, she realized she needed all the help she could get—probably a lot more than one man following her at a distance. But it was something, someone who'd know where she was and what had happened to her if she suddenly vanished the way Michael had.

She had to trust someone in Ho Chi Minh City, and she didn't have many options.

"I see," she said. "Well, okay. Can we talk?"

Chapter 29

Crys didn't sleep well. Her brain was racing. She switched between worries about Michael and how his situation might now actually be worse, and how she could persuade Joe to open up. So far, he was her only lead, so he was the one she had to break.

And now she had a new worry: could she trust Donald? She'd told him what she was doing, and why she thought Joe was her best hope. He hadn't been enthusiastic, but at least he'd promised to help as much as he could. He'd have to keep in the background since it was known that he worked for End Extinction.

Her body was uncomfortable too—the air conditioner was barely working and no match for the hot, humid air that clung to everything. She was bathed in sweat.

Around six she climbed out of bed and took a long, cool shower. Then she called reception to order a cab. Her plan was to go and see the house where she spent her first year of life. She had no memory of it, only mental pictures created by the stories told by her parents. She hoped that actually seeing it would trigger memories and so deepen her connection to this country. She had a flutter of excitement in her chest as she set off. She had no idea of what to expect.

The house was closer to the city center than she'd imagined—it took only twenty minutes to get there. The driver pulled up at the address she'd written on a piece of paper for him and pointed at the building. She took a deep breath and asked him to wait while she walked around. He started to object in Vietnamese, but she shrugged and indicated that she didn't understand. He muttered, and then nodded, but pointed at the meter.

The house that was her first home was a typical Vietnamese tube house—very narrow and very deep. It was one of about ten on the block; Americans would call them townhouses, for want of a better word. All of them were set back from the paved road by about six feet, giving each a minute front garden. Her house had a frangipani tree, giving off a sweet scent, some orchids, and two scooters. The building looked well-kept and was painted an ochre color. She stood on the road for a few moments, hoping that some memories might well up. But it clearly wasn't to be.

Crys took out her phone and took several photos of the house and the surroundings. Then she returned to the cab, disappointed. She'd hoped to have an emotional attachment to the house, but there was nothing. It was just another house.

The driver looked slightly baffled as she got back into the taxi, but he didn't say anything, and they headed back to the hotel. Crys felt oddly empty and a little sad.

———

After a breakfast of chicken *pho* followed by a strawberry-avocado smoothie, she headed out at once to Joe's. Donald was already there, relaxing at a sidewalk café, drinking a cup of the turgid local coffee. As they'd agreed the night before, they didn't greet each other.

Again, Joe's shop was closed, but this time Crys wasn't going to give up, however long it took. So, she sat down at a different coffee shop just down the road, determined to wait him out.

It was over an hour before she spotted him in front of his shop, unlocking the two big padlocks that secured the pull-down shutters. She waited until he'd opened the door and had gone inside, then paid for her coffees and jogged toward the shop.

"Joe," she called as she walked into the multi-scented gloom. "It's Crystal Nguyen."

Joe pushed through a door at the back. Even in the dimness, she could see he wasn't happy.

"I have nothing for you. Please go."

This time she stood her ground. "Please help me. I need to find out about what's going to happen in South Africa. It will be a big story for me."

Joe frowned and shook his head, speaking through clenched teeth.

"I know nothing. You go now."

"Nobody needs to know you gave me the information. I won't use your name."

He shook his head. "People here know everything. Go." He walked toward her pointing at the door. "Go!" he ordered, raising his voice.

Just then his phone rang. He hesitated, trying to decide whether to answer or to finish getting rid of her. Habit won—he answered.

Crys pretended to look at the bottles on the shelves.

"I can't talk now," Joe said in Vietnamese walking to the back of the shop. "The journalist is back, asking about South Africa."

He listened to the response. "No. Of course I haven't told her anything. She knows nothing. She thinks the plan is to kill a lot of rhinos." He clearly didn't suspect that Crys could understand Vietnamese.

He listened again. "I can't do that. I have two big customers coming this morning. If I'm not here, they'll go somewhere else." He started pacing around the small shop. "Yes. Yes. All right. Right away."

He hung up and turned to her. "You must go. Now. I have a meeting I must go to." He herded her to the door.

"Can I come back and talk to you?"

"No. I have nothing more to say. Goodbye." He pushed her out of the door.

There was nothing she could do. She left, but she was determined that this wasn't the last time she would talk to him. And she'd learned one piece of information—it sounded as though the plan didn't involve a big kill of rhinos. That was good.

As she walked along the street, she wondered what she should do. The phone call was clearly something to do with her—or with something she'd be interested in. When she reached the café where Donald was waiting, she sat down opposite him and related what had happened.

"It sounds as though he needs to go somewhere soon. Let's just wait and see what happens," he responded. "I'll keep an eye on the shop."

Sure enough, after a few minutes he saw Joe locking up. "When he was on the phone, was there any clue as to where he'd go?"

Crys shook her head. "We'll have to follow him."

"That's pretty dangerous. He won't be pleased if he catches us."

"This is my only good lead, Donald. Everything else led to a dead end."

Donald gave up the argument. Crys was already moving off after Joe.

For the next fifteen minutes, they hurried to keep up as Joe rushed through the labyrinth of streets and alleys. Soon Crys had no idea where she was or where they were headed, but Donald seemed to know, and that made her feel better. The longer they walked, the fewer shops there were, and she realized they'd entered an industrial area.

Now, there were almost no other people about. She felt her adrenalin level increasing. This was becoming more risky. It was harder and harder to ensure Joe wouldn't see them if he looked back. They hid behind corners of buildings until he either turned down another road or was far enough away he wouldn't recognize them. Crys was both scared she would lose him and scared he would see her. Sweat trickled down her face as she scampered from one hiding place to the next, feeling faintly self-conscious. She wasn't trained to do this; if anyone was watching her, they'd know she had to be tailing someone. Donald wasn't any better.

Eventually Joe turned down a road and, by the time they'd reached the corner, he was nowhere to be seen.

Given the pace he'd been walking, Crys figured that he could have reached any three of the six buildings on the street, but there was no indication of which he'd gone into. She pulled back, out of sight from any of the buildings, and signaled Donald to join her.

"He's gone into one of the buildings. What can we do now?"

Donald shook his head. We can't go door to door. He'd recognize us at once. I think our best bet is to wait at each end of the street. Then when he comes out we can pick him up again."

"But it's important to know who he's talking to. This may be our only chance to discover what the South African plan actually is."

Donald shook his head again and started walking to the far end of the street, keeping his head down so that his face was as hidden as possible.

Crys felt a wave of frustration. She was sure that eventually Joe would emerge from one of the buildings and head back to his shop. All they would know was that he'd met someone here to talk about something. But Donald was right; they didn't have any other option.

After a short while, Donald reached the end of the road, and took cover in a doorway. Almost immediately after that, Crys heard a door slam shut. Peeking around the corner she saw three men she didn't recognize walking up the street toward her. She immediately walked away from them. That way, by the time they reached where she'd been hiding, she'd be halfway down the block. Hopefully, they would think she was just visiting one of the other warehouses in the area.

She didn't look back.

But as she reached the next cross street, two more men came around the corner, just ahead of her. As she stepped aside to let them pass, she realized that one of them was Joe.

He stopped, looking at her, his face a mixture of surprise and anger. She froze for a second, staring into his eyes.

She realized she was in trouble and spun round to run, but in a flash, he reached out and grabbed her arm. "Come with us," he said. His grip tightened on her arm till it hurt.

She tried to shake loose, but he was strong. He just clenched her harder—until she thought her bones would crack.

"Let me go!" she cried, struggling.

"I told you I had nothing more to tell you." He started dragging her along. "Now you've made my boss mad. He wants to meet you. And you're not going to like that."

She saw that the other three men were now close. "Help me!" she shouted trying again to shake loose from Joe's grip.

"Please help me," she begged.

The three men stopped.

One of them laughed. "So, this is the stupid American," he said in Vietnamese.

With a lunge, she finally wrenched herself out of Joe's grasp and tried to bolt away. But there was nowhere to go, and she ran right into the arms of one of the other men.

"I'd like to take her home," he said holding her arms to her sides, his hot breath against her face. "I can teach her a few things."

She struggled some more, her fear skyrocketing.

Joe grabbed her left arm while the other man held the right and they yanked her along toward one of the warehouses. The pain in her shoulder was excruciating.

She could hear them joking with each other in Vietnamese about what they'd like to do with her. It was all she could do not to show she understood. Pain lanced through her shoulder. She stopped struggling. There was no point. She could only hope that Donald had heard her screams.

———

She was pushed into a chair in front of an old metal desk. The chair opposite her was empty.

Then they waited. The five men stood behind her chatting to each other. None of the talk was about rhinos or South Africa or even about her. It was typical men's talk—football and, surprisingly, women's volleyball. But even that was predictable—the discussion focused less on the game and more about how the players would be in bed. She gripped the sides of the chair. How could she get away? The men were between her and the door.

Suddenly, the talk stopped, and a male voice greeted the men. They responded respectfully. Then, a nondescript, middle-aged man walked around the desk and sat down behind it. He stared at her for several seconds before speaking.

"You cause me big problem," he said in heavily accented English. "You steal money in South Africa. Now you try to find out about our rhinos."

"How did—?" Crys began.

He opened a drawer, took out a piece of paper, and slid it across the desk toward her. She leaned forward and picked it up—it was a photo of her, tied to a chair. The chair where Pockface had held her. She didn't remember him taking the photograph, but then she looked almost unconscious in the picture.

"Hurt?" asked the man, smiling and pointing at her fingers, which were still strapped together.

She couldn't speak.

"We hurt you much more…" He wasn't smiling now.

"You are wrong, Mr…?" He didn't finish her sentence. "I didn't steal any money from anyone."

He ignored that. "What you do here now?" He glared at her. "I think you make Ho tell you about me."

She shook her head. "Ho was dying. He didn't say anything." She turned in the chair and pointed at Joe. "I followed him."

Nobody said a word, but the man behind the desk didn't look at all pleased by that news. She looked back at him and tried to sound calm and matter-of-fact, but her hands felt clammy and her pulse was racing.

"I'm writing a story for *National Geographic* about the killing of rhinos and the smuggling of rhino horns. That's why I was in South Africa. That's why I'm here now. I want to speak to everyone involved so people get an accurate picture of what's happening."

"Why you follow Joe?"

"I asked him about an operation to kill lots of rhinos in South Africa. He wouldn't answer me. That's why I followed him. I want to know more about it. It's the whole point of my job."

"Who told you about South Africa?"

"The police in South Africa said they'd heard some rumors."

"Police very stupid in South Africa. Too difficult to kill many animals. I think you force Ho Van Tan to tell you what money was for before you kill him. He tell you this stupid story to confuse you. He was carrying money for us. He dead now. You kill and steal money!"

She shook her head. This was even worse than she'd feared. "I think Ho was stealing your money. He killed the pilot of the plane. Shot him in the head." The words were tumbling out. "Then he tried to shoot me. But he was injured." Desperation popped an idea into her mind. "He died in the Land Rover I was driving to take him to hospital." The story was close enough to the truth.

The man frowned. "Ho not steal money. Trusted partner."

"You can believe what you like, but I think he decided to steal from you and hide the money. He didn't have any money when I found him."

The man stared at her for what felt like an age. "No. I think you don't tell the truth. You know where money is. You tell us now or you not happy."

"I can't tell you what I don't know. I'm just a journalist..."

The man stood up. "We find out if you know." He nodded at the men behind me.

She was grabbed by the arms—again wrenching her sore shoulder—and pulled up from the chair. Then they pushed her through a side door into a large room that was obviously a warehouse.

The boss man walked up to her and stuck his face right in front of hers. "I give you fifteen minutes to change your mind. If you don't tell me where the money is, you will see what we do to people who try to steal from us. Not nice."

He turned to Joe and spoke to him in Vietnamese. "You showed her the way here. If she doesn't tell me where the money is, you will make her talk."

Joe nodded with a smile. "Thank you, Chủ Nhân."

Crys suppressed a shudder, convinced still that she shouldn't let them know she understood.

"But if she still doesn't tell me, you are to blame for this problem." Joe's face fell.

With that the man walked out, and the others followed, leaving Crys to try to find a way out of the mess she'd gotten herself into.

———

She stood in the middle of the empty room, desperate to find a way out but at a loss for what to do. There was another door at the opposite end of the room, so she ran over to it and turned the handle, but, of course, it was locked. She looked around. The only windows were too high to reach. They were near the top of one wall, and the ceiling was about thirty feet above her.

With no escape route, she looked for something she could use as a weapon. The only furniture in the room was a metal chair and an old desk with a lamp with a naked bulb. Apart from that there were only some empty cardboard boxes with *MANGOES* printed on the outside.

And her cell phone was in her backpack, which one of the men had ripped from her when they'd dragged her into the building. It was sitting on the boss man's desk.

The situation looked hopeless. She shook her head, wondering why she hadn't learned her lesson in South Africa.

She searched the room again in case she'd missed something. The only thing she found, behind the mango boxes, was an old can of paint and a bottle of what smelt like paraffin with barely any liquid left in it.

She'd just sat down at the desk when the boss man's door opened, and he walked in.

"Get up."

He held a camera in front of her—her camera. It showed a photograph of her translator.

"Who is this?"

"My translator, Mr. Phan Van Minh."

"How did you find him?"

"Someone from the Department of Intercultural Affairs sent him. He must work for them."

He swiped through a few photos, then stopped. "And this?"

"He's the first dealer I spoke to. Mr. Le Van Minh. The department arranged my meeting with him too. And I think he arranged for me to speak to his supplier in Saigon Port—Mr. Ng."

The boss man swiped some more. "This him?"

I nodded.

"And how do you know about Joe?"

"Look, everything I'm doing here has been arranged by the Department of Intercultural Affairs. I don't know how they chose the people I should meet. I said I wanted to meet different people—dealers, suppliers, importers, people who use rhino horn. Everyone associated with the trade. I assume it's a legitimate government agency."

He stared at her for a few moments. "Why no photo of Joe?" he said at last.

"He told me to leave when I asked him if he'd heard about an operation to kill lots of rhinos in South Africa."

He stared at her again and shook his head in disbelief. Then he looked at his watch. "Five minutes more, then Joe have some fun."

He turned and walked out, and she heard the key turn in the lock.

So, they definitely weren't going to kill animals in South Africa. But they were obviously planning something. Perhaps they were going after horn or tusk stockpiles.

But there was nothing she could do about it. There was no one she could alert.

In the meantime, she had a more pressing problem. How was she going to stop Joe from beating the life out of her?

Chapter 30

By the time Joe walked in, she had come up with a plan, although it wasn't very solid.

"Please don't hurt me," she pleaded. "I'll tell your boss where the money is."

"You tell me, then I tell him."

She shook her head. "I'll only tell him."

He hesitated, chewing his lip, clearly thinking of the consequences for him if she said nothing. He left the room and returned a few moments later with the boss man.

"You have bad men working for you," she said.

The boss man frowned.

"The police put me in jail after Ho died, but your friends from Mozambique bribed a guard to let me out. You know they broke my finger." She held up her hand. "And that's when I told them where the money was buried. I didn't want them to hurt me more. So, they must have the money now. But I didn't see it because the police came while they were gone and set me free."

"They say they not find money. You give wrong place."

"They would say that, wouldn't they? They wanted to steal the money from you. I heard them say so. I gave them the right location. They would've killed me if it was wrong! I think they were working with Ho. Going to steal your money and divide it."

The boss man stared at her for a long time. She held her breath. She knew the story was credible. Everyone involved in this business was violent and out for themselves. If they could betray each other, they would.

At last the boss man turned to Joe and said in Vietnamese, "Get food and water for one week. Then lock all the doors. We need to leave now. We'll talk to her when we get back from South Africa. We can get to the bottom of this story when we meet up with the Portuguese men."

Relief washed over Crys, and she started to breathe again. At least she'd bought some time. But now she was a prisoner... again. Her only hope was that Donald would find her. He must know she was somewhere nearby.

About an hour later, she heard doors banging and a car start up and drive away. She was alone. She had a week to try to figure something out. And she'd learned another important piece of information—the big hit was about to happen—probably on Sunday, just as Pockface had said.

But, again, there was nothing she could do about it, nobody she could tell. And if she didn't find a way out of her predicament, she'd be in very big trouble at the end of that week.

———

She gave it about fifteen minutes, hoping all the men had left, then she started shouting as loudly as she could in English and in Vietnamese.

"Help! Help me, please!" She shouted at the two doors; she shouted at all four walls; she shouted at the ceiling.

There was no response.

Nor could she hear any voices.

She walked around again, shouting as loudly as she could.

To no avail. Her heart sank. It seemed Donald had lost her. Or maybe they'd caught him too.

This was getting her nowhere. She decided to conserve her energy and shout for help again about the time people would be leaving work—around five o'clock, still several hours away.

She'd be crazy with fear if she was here for a week. The thought chilled her to the core. She had to find a way out.

She closed her eyes and breathed slowly for a few minutes, then started to search every inch of the room for something that could help her to escape.

But other than the mango boxes, ten in number, the can of paint, and the paraffin, there was nothing. And she was going to have to use one or more of the boxes as a toilet, a pretty disgusting thought.

For food, they'd left her cans of vegetables and cans of fruit, together with ten liters of water in a large, plastic container. There was also a can opener and a single spoon. They weren't going to help her get out of there.

She decided the best thing she could do was to center herself, so she took one of the boxes, separated the glued ends, and created a rudimentary rug on which she could meditate. For the next half hour or so, she stretched and quietly chanted her mantra.

When she'd finished, she opened a can of beans and wolfed it down. Ten minutes later, she'd eaten the whole lot and started on a can of peaches. They were too sweet, but satisfied her hunger. Food out of the way, she settled down to think through her predicament.

There had to be a way to escape...

————

Her first plan was to try to reach the windows high on the wall by stacking the mango boxes on top of each other. She tried standing on one, but it collapsed immediately. In that form, it wasn't going to work. Knowing triangles made strong structures, she then tried making triangular trusses from the boxes. She could form the triangles, but had nothing to keep them in place, so they also collapsed immediately. She gave up—the boxes weren't going to be of much use.

She looked around and the windows caught her attention. She wondered if people walked past them. Maybe she could let them know she was inside.

She decided to try and throw some cans through the windows. She didn't know whether anyone would see them, but she had to give it a go.

Crys took a can of peaches and used the can opener to scratch the Vietnamese word for help on both ends. If someone picked it up, she hoped they'd look up and see the broken window. She also hoped they'd see her call for help and act on it.

When she was finished, she threw the can at the windows, but missed, and it fell back. It took her three more tries before the can broke the glass and disappeared. She could only wait and hope.

At five o'clock, Crys repeated her shouting routine, but again there was no response. Worse than that, she heard no voices of people heading home. She was beginning to think she was completely isolated.

She took another can, marked it, and threw it through another window. The glass shattered the first time, and she heard the can clatter to the ground outside. She waited, counting the minutes, but again she heard nothing.

When another hour passed with no response and no sounds from outside, she decided that the windows couldn't overlook an outside road—that all her efforts had been in vain.

She sat and stared at the broken window, her mind frozen. She had nothing to work with.

What else she could do?

—

As she was about to eat another can of vegetables, an idea came to her. If she started a fire, maybe someone would notice and come to investigate.

Her first thought was to short out the power point, but she abandoned that immediately. It would just trip the circuit breaker—that was exactly what they were for. Then she thought about the reading lamp and had an idea.

It seemed farfetched and she almost discarded it at once. But she had nothing to lose. She grabbed the flattened mango box she'd been using as a mat and cut out the thinnest strips of cardboard she could with the can opener. Then she pulled off some slightly larger pieces. She took an empty can and stuffed it full of the strips with the thinnest on top.

Now came the tricky part. She went over to the desk and checked that the desk light actually worked. Next, she unscrewed the bulb and tapped it gently with one of the cans. After a couple of hits, the glass broke. She peered inside and smiled when she saw that the filament was still intact—just what she'd hoped.

She screwed the bulb back into the lamp. Then she poured some of the liquid left in the paraffin bottle into the bulb until it just covered the filament.

Shielding her eyes and mouthing a silent prayer, she flipped the switch.

"Yes!" she said out loud.

The paraffin was burning, and she felt the first glimmer of hope.

Carefully, she fed a few cardboard strips into the flames until she had a little bonfire going. Then she held the can full of strips over the fire until it burst into flames. When it was burning well, she threw it at one of the broken windows, but missed, and the burning strips fell all over the floor.

She told herself to keep trying. The plan was good.

She opened another can, making sure the lid remained fixed to the can. She threw out the contents and built up another little fire, closing the lid far enough to prevent the strips from falling out.

She threw the can at the window and this time she succeeded. Now all she could do was wonder what was on the other side. Would someone notice? Would it set light to something, which would attract attention? She was back to waiting.

Nothing happened for what seemed like forever. She couldn't sit still and paced the room, wondering if she should throw another fire can through a different window.

And then, she smelled smoke. Something was burning.

Perhaps her luck had finally turned. Surely a fire would attract somebody's attention. It had better, because she'd run out of ideas…

Another few minutes passed, and smoke started coming in through the broken windows. Whatever was outside had started to burn fiercely. With every second, the smoke grew thicker and drifted inside in bigger clouds. It smelled toxic, choking. Crys hadn't thought about that possibility.

She realized she had to get out of there, and quickly.

She walked around the room shouting as loudly as she could— through both doors and up at the windows, but still there was no response.

The smoke continued to pour in, and she started to cough uncontrollably. Her lungs began to hurt and it was hard to shout, so she beat on the doors with one of the cans. No response. She was terrified now that the whole place would burn down.

She tried not to think of how that would feel…

She was taking shallow breaths through her nose, but the smoke was getting worse.

She lay on the floor in front of the door to boss man's office and started to suck air from the gap at the bottom. It was a little better. But the room was getting hotter and hotter.

She was beginning to panic.

Suddenly she was deafened by a fire alarm. It was so loud she had to hold her ears.

She jumped up and tried to shout again, but the smoke was too much, and she was drowned out by the alarm. She collapsed to the floor and sucked at the tiny draught of fresh air coming under the door.

Úm ma ni bát ni hồng. Úm ma ni bát ni hồng.

She concentrated on slowing her metabolism by breathing slowly and shallowly. She needed to keep calm…

And then she heard sirens. Soon there would be people around the building. It took all her discipline not to jump up again. She knew she had to preserve her strength and wait.

Only when the sirens had stopped and the alarm was silenced, and she could hear voices above the crackle of the flames outside, did she start shouting and banging on the door to the boss man's office with her can.

"Help me," she screamed in Vietnamese. "Here. Here. Help!"

There was no response, and she was struggling to breath.

"Help!" she choked. "Help me, please."

Her head was swimming, and she could hardly breathe at all now.

Bang, bang, bang. Her thuds were slow and weak against the door.

Then she could hear voices in the office. "Over there," someone shouted.

The door handle rattled. "It's locked."

She managed a final bang but everything was going black. Her eyelids were heavy. It felt like she was drowning.

"Break it down! Quick!" The voices seemed far away.

There was a crash against the door. Then another and another. She dragged herself away from it and the small source of air she had left. Then the door burst open. She opened her eyes to see a figure standing above her.

"Here," he shouted. "A woman." She heard him ask in Vietnamese if she was okay. His voice seemed to come from miles away.

She raised her head and nodded weakly. "*Cảm ơn. Cảm ơn,*"

she managed, no longer caring who knew she could speak the language.

"We need to get out," he said and grabbed her injured arm. She gasped, sucked in a lungful of smoke, then doubled over coughing. He pulled her through the door.

As they went through the boss man's office, she spotted her bag on the desk — her camera and cell phone were there too.

"My stuff..." she gasped, pointing. "There..."

The man grabbed her bag and threw in the phone and camera.

Out on the street, she sank to her knees, shaking, and gasping for breath. The outside air seemed like cool water.

"Are you all right?" she heard a man ask in English.

She managed to raise her head to look at him.

It was Donald.

"What...what took you so long...?" she rasped.

"I'll tell you later. We need to get out of here. Can you walk?"

She nodded. "I...I think so..."

He helped her to her feet. "Okay. Lean on me."

Then he put his arm around her shoulders, grabbed her backpack and began to lead her away, back along the street she had originally come down several hours earlier. When they reached the corner, she turned and looked back at the flames engulfing the building.

"Come on," he said. "We must keep moving. We're still in danger here."

———

An hour later, Crys was sitting in Søren Willandsen's office at End Extinction, a glass of water in her hand and a blanket around her shoulders. The stink of smoke was everywhere. She was saturated with it.

"How did you know I was in that building?" she asked Donald. Her voice was scratchy, but she no longer felt dizzy.

"I didn't," he replied. "I lost you when those men took you. So I walked around, hoping I would see you leave. But I didn't."

"Didn't you see Joe, the shopkeeper, leave with several other men?" she asked swallowing more water.

"No. I couldn't be everywhere; I must have missed them."

"And then the fire?"

"When the building went up in flames, I was nearby. I watched the firemen. Then I heard one of them shouting that there was a woman trapped inside. I had to check whether it was you."

"Thank you. I guess I'm lucky the fire alarm worked and the fire department is efficient."

"You see why we were following you now," Søren said. "And you led us to people we didn't know. Did you learn any more about the rumors you told us about?"

Crys looked at him. He hadn't asked how she was. He'd simply watched as Donald took care of her.

They held each other's gaze for a moment. Crys recalled how he'd told her a few days earlier not to trust anyone, and she decided to take him at his word.

"No. Joe seemed upset when I asked him about it. That's when he booted me out of the shop and we followed him. But they spotted me and thought I was spying—which I was, I guess. That's why they locked me up. There was a man in charge, but I don't know his name. And four or five others. All Vietnamese."

"And they didn't say anything about South Africa or a big operation?"

She shook her head. She wasn't going to share what she'd heard—not yet, anyhow.

"That's too bad," Søren said. "You went through a lot and didn't get anything in return."

Crys just nodded.

"What are you going to do now?" he asked.

"I'm getting out of here. Maybe go home. It'll be safer writing my article there than here or in South Africa. I just want to be a journalist again."

Søren stood up. "Well, I look forward to reading your piece when it comes out," he said. "But, if you hear anything more, please let us know."

"Of course," she lied.

———

Donald wanted to accompany her back to her hotel, but she refused. She wanted to move quickly. She remembered that she'd told Joe where she was staying and definitely didn't want to meet him again. So, back in her room, she showered the smoke out of her hair and off her skin, dumped her ruined clothes, then packed up her things and checked out as quickly as possible.

She jumped into the first cab at the hotel entrance, then had the driver drop her off several miles away, around the corner from another hotel. She dashed inside, looking up and down the street, terrified that Joe or his colleagues were following her, but she saw nothing.

Fortunately, the hotel wasn't full, so she checked in and immediately called Nigel in Geneva.

He was shocked by the story of what had happened.

"You're lucky to get out alive."

"I *was* lucky. I thought I was going to suffocate or be burned to death."

He quizzed her some more about her experience, and then asked, "Did you pick up any useful information?"

"Two things," she replied. "First, in a passing comment, the boss man said it was too difficult to kill a lot of rhinos. Joe said pretty much the same thing earlier. So, I think they must have something else planned. My guess is they're going to attack and steal a stockpile of horns somewhere. Or maybe three stockpiles…"

"That makes complete sense," Nigel said. "It's probably Kruger itself. There are several stockpiles there from rhinos that have died naturally. There must be hundreds of horns in those…" He paused, and Crys wondered what he was thinking. "And the second thing?" he asked.

"When they locked me in that room, the boss man told one of his men to get me food and water for a week. Then he said they would deal with me when they returned from South Africa. So, whatever is happening is going to happen in the next few days. That ties up with what I overheard from Pockface too. It's all pointing in the same direction."

"I need to tell Dinh all this. Perhaps he can help from the Vietnam side. We have to move quickly…"

Nigel was quiet for a few more moments.

"This is very helpful, Crys," he said in a business-like tone. "Thank you. I think I can take it from here. I'll go to South Africa myself, contact the South African authorities, and see if I can persuade them to set up ambushes at all of their storage sites in Kruger. That should surprise your friends."

Crys lay back on the bed. At last someone was taking action. It made all her trials and tribulations worth it. "Great idea," she said. "We'll have to leave tomorrow if we want to be there when it all goes down."

"You can't come, Crys. If anyone spots you—your Portuguese friends or your new friends from Vietnam—they'll abort the operation."

Crys sat up again. She had to go back to South Africa. She had to find out how this all linked with Michael. She hadn't been nearly killed for nothing… "But—"

"No buts, Crys," Nigel interrupted. "We can't afford for this to go wrong. Either come here to Geneva and wait for me to return, or go back to Duluth and write your story. I'll arrange for my receptionist to take you to my flat if you want to use it."

Crys stood up. "Dammit, Nigel. It's my story! I haven't come all this way to sit quietly and wait!"

"Crys, I'm telling you, you'll only get in the way."

Crys was ready to explode, but she ground her teeth instead. She could tell this was going nowhere. She wasn't going to change his mind.

"Okay, Nigel," she said. "I understand. I'll think about where to go. Thanks for the Geneva offer."

"Good decision. I'll see you in a week."

"That's what you think!" she said when he hung up.

———

Crys's blood was boiling. She threw the phone onto the bed. There was no way she was going to stay away from South Africa with everything that was happening. There was no way she was going to hang around in Geneva and write her story. What was going to happen in South Africa was her story, and she was going to write it. And she was going to find out the truth about Michael, whatever it took. She didn't need Nigel or his damned permission.

She retrieved the phone and called a local travel agent, asking to be put on the first flight to Johannesburg.

"There's an Emirates flight this evening at 11:55, arriving at 16:30 tomorrow, local time," the agent told her.

She looked at her watch. She had time to pack, check out, and have dinner, and still be at the airport two hours before takeoff.

"I'll take it," she said. "I'll check in at the airport."

Her adrenalin was flowing again. She was going back to Africa and perhaps the biggest story of her life.

PART 5

South Africa

Chapter 31

As soon as Crys had checked into the airport hotel in Johannesburg, she phoned Tshukudu. There was no time to lose. If she and Nigel were right, the strike on the rhino-horn storage facilities was only forty-eight hours away.

She wanted to tell the Malans what was going on, and, if possible, get their help. She also hoped to find out whether Johannes had any information about where the stockpiles might be because she wanted to be there when it all went down.

She was relieved that it was Johannes who answered—she found him easier to speak to than Anton, who always seemed a bit abrupt and offhand. Somehow, she'd rubbed him the wrong way when they'd first met.

"Johannes, it's Crys."

"Crys. Where are you? What's going on? You just disappeared...I was worried. The police said you'd left the country without permission."

"I've just flown into Johannesburg from Ho Chi Min City. There's lots to tell."

For the next ten minutes she recounted what had happened after she left South Africa. It was only when she'd finished that Johannes spoke.

"Honest, Crys, you know how to get yourself into trouble."

She couldn't deny that. "True, but right now the important thing is what's about to happen here."

"What you're saying is that you think this Vietnamese gang is going to attack rhino-horn storage facilities, probably in Kruger?"

"Yes, exactly. But it's just a guess, based on various things I heard. I'm pretty confident that the target is rhino horns, not live rhinos. That's essentially what the boss man who held me said. I'm less confident that the facilities are in Kruger, though. But logically you would think it has the most horns, given its size, right?"

It was a few moments before he answered. She wanted to squeeze it out of him.

"You could be onto something, Crys. We do know that they hold a lot of horn in stockpiles there. My father knows more about it than I do. He's been in this area a long time and has a lot of friends, but I don't think he knows where the sites are. And if he does, he doesn't tell anyone. And certainly not me." He paused, and Crys wondered what he was thinking. "But he did tell me there are three main stores."

Crys felt a thrill of excitement.

"Three is exactly the number Pockface said—three. So, they could be going to attack the sites simultaneously."

Now Crys was more confident than ever that Kruger was the target. Was this what Michael had discovered?

"Do the people there know about what you've just told me?" Johannes asked.

"I assume so. When I spoke to Nigel Wood yesterday from Vietnam, that's what he was going to do as soon as we hung up—contact the authorities and tell them Kruger was the likely location. Then he was going to fly to South Africa right away."

"Why would he come here?"

It was a good question. "I guess he felt he would have more influence if he presented the evidence in person. Who would he have to speak to?"

"The minister, the police, National Parks. The top people are all likely to be in Pretoria." He paused. "I'm surprised you didn't join him there."

Crys didn't feel like telling him that Nigel had brushed her off because she was no longer useful to him. Because she'd be in the way…

"I have to be where the action will be," she said instead. "I'm staying at the airport so I can make an early start tomorrow—once I've decided where to go, that is. And I need to speak to Colonel Mabula to find out if he's learned anything about Michael."

There was silence from Johannes's end. Cry wanted to reach through the phone and shake him.

"Are there any other possible targets?" she asked. "Tshukudu, for example? Private stashes of horns that would be worth attacking?"

"I don't think so," he said cautiously. "We keep our horns in a bank vault in Phalaborwa. Whenever we have a few, we either take them there or have an armed courier do it for us. Most of the farmers do that, so there aren't many horns at the farms. It wouldn't be worth the effort or risk going after them."

"Then I have to be in Kruger," she said. "I just have to decide where. Can you help me find out where these stores are?"

Johannes scoffed. "Are you joking? No one's going to tell you that, Crys. People don't just go and visit them. And anyway, if there is an attack, it will probably be late at night."

For a moment, she wondered if he did know, but wasn't telling her.

"So, how would the attackers get there?" she asked.

"If they know where to go, it wouldn't be too hard. They could just check in as day visitors and then hide out somewhere. Then late at night they'd hit the stockpiles, blow them open or whatever it takes."

"How would they get away?"

"Fly a plane into an old bush airstrip. Or maybe a helicopter.

But Kruger's huge, Crys, and it borders Mozambique. Once they're out of South Africa, you haven't a snowball's chance in hell of catching them."

She rubbed her forehead as she mulled that over, wishing she wasn't so tired. She seemed to be jet-lagged the whole time.

"At least one of the stores will be near Skukuza camp, won't it?" she asked. "That's where the park headquarters is, right?"

"Yes, I guess that makes sense."

"Would your father know? Or one of your friends in Kruger, like that Hennie van Zyl guy from the anti-poaching squad?"

"I can ask, but nobody's going to tell me anything." Johannes sounded reluctant. She didn't want to push him too hard, but he was really her only chance. And she'd come so far…

"Look, Johannes, it's not just for my story. I'm pretty sure now that these people are behind Michael's disappearance. I'm worried that if I'm right, they need to keep him alive until this hit. Maybe they need him to be involved somehow. After that, who knows?"

"What do you mean?"

"He said he was onto something big. We discovered an email address he used to communicate with the smugglers. I'm quite sure one of the traders in rhino horn I spoke to recognized it when I showed it to him. And I know that he was looking for the Portuguese men. It can't be a coincidence. He was following the same trail I have, just from a different starting point."

"So, you think he found the Portuguese smugglers? And they're holding him?"

"Yes. Or they found him…" She hesitated. She hated to make this personal, but felt she had no other option. "Please ask your contacts, and phone or text me if you find something useful. Will you do that? For me?"

It took him so long to reply, she thought he'd hung up.

"Okay, okay," he mumbled eventually. "But don't get your hopes up."

———

Crys paced around the room. Her conversation with Johannes was useful—it had focused her thoughts and convinced her of what she'd already suspected—but she still didn't have any details. She was sure something dramatic was about to happen but had no idea what it was or where it was going to take place.

Her next priority was to check with Mabula to see if he'd discovered anything about Michael. She was beginning to lose hope, though. She was nervous now that each call might be the one that would bring the final bad news. She took a deep breath and dialed his number. There was no answer, and she was forwarded to his answering machine: *This is Colonel Mabula. Please leave a message at the tone. Thank you.*

"Colonel Mabula, this is Crys Nguyen. Do you have any news? Please call me urgently. I have some important information."

She hung up, wondering what Mabula would do with her information. Would he use it for good or for bad? Only time would tell.

In any case, she had to decide quickly where she was going the next morning, so she jumped on the internet and browsed, hoping to find some hint that would set her on the right trail.

She found no speculation about any unusual poaching activity in Kruger or on any of the surrounding game farms. There were a few reports of a rhino or two being poached in different parts of the country, but no indication of anything big coming up.

So, without any added information, Skukuza it would have to be.

She opened the South African Airways website and tried to reserve the direct flight to Skukuza for the following morning. But it was fully booked. She tried the early-afternoon flight instead and found it was fully booked as well.

Damn! she thought. Kruger must be a popular destination.

However, there were flights available to Nelspruit, just outside

Kruger and a short drive from Skukuza, so that was a possibility for her. She'd need a car in Kruger anyway.

Next, she checked the National Parks website to see what accommodation was available. There was nothing in Skukuza, not even campsites, nor at any other camps in the park. In desperation, she tried to see whether day passes were available. They weren't. Again, all sold out.

Crys leaned back from her computer. What was going on? It was highly unlikely that every bed and campsite in a park the size of New Jersey could be sold out.

Maybe Nigel had convinced the South African authorities that there was a real threat against their stockpiles. It would make sense to close the park down as much as they could. They certainly wouldn't want tourists caught in any crossfire. But it seemed she was locked out of the park too.

With nothing else to do, she drew a bath and settled in to soak and think through her options. None of them were really appealing, but eventually she decided going to Phalaborwa was the best of a bad bunch. At least from there she could try to talk her way into Kruger and, if that failed, go up to Tshukudu and see if Johannes and Anton could help.

When she returned to the internet, she reserved a seat on the 11:45 flight to Phalaborwa—there was no trouble with availability there, at least. It would arrive just before one o'clock in the afternoon.

She called Johannes again.

"There's is definitely something going on," she told him. "All accommodations and all day passes for Kruger are sold out for the whole weekend."

"That's impossible! They never run out over the whole park."

"That's what I thought. Nigel Wood must have been able to persuade the right people that the threat is real, or, at least, a strong possibility. But they wouldn't want to make it public, so they're just saying everything is fully booked. It's a clever strategy if they want to keep people away."

"Not you, though, I'm guessing…"

She couldn't help smiling. "Am I that obvious? You're right, I really need you to help me get into the park. This is *my* story. I can't lose out on it."

"Crys, I'll make some calls in the morning, but as I said before, don't get your hopes up. If they've decided no one's going in, they mean it."

"I'm going to fly to Phalaborwa, then make a decision what to do when I get there. If I can get into Kruger, I'll go. Otherwise, is it okay for me to come up to Tshukudu?"

"Of course. You're always welcome here. Let's talk before you check in. Around ten-thirty or so."

———

Crys wondered what Nigel was doing in Pretoria and was angry he wasn't sharing information with her. She'd done all the work to get them to this point. She'd even risked her life—more than once. The more she thought about it, the more furious she became.

But if she wanted to know what was happening in Pretoria, there was only one way to deal with the situation. She had to swallow her pride and call him.

She did, and there was no reply. Her call was forwarded to Rhino International's answering machine in Geneva. She left a message asking that Nigel call her in South Africa as soon as possible.

With no options left, she decided to call it a day. She slipped into bed, turned out the light, and was asleep almost immediately.

Chapter 32

As the small prop jet came in to land at Phalaborwa, she was surprised to find that she was excited to be back—even after everything that had happened to her there.

It had to be the Africa sickness. The one that crept under your skin when you visited the continent for the first time, then itched until you went back again. And every visit made the itch more intense.

Someone had told her that story many years ago, but she thought it was just enthusiasm and had never believed it. Now she had to admit that she did, because just ten days ago all she wanted was to get out of this country.

Johannes was there to meet her and suggested they have a snack at the small airport café.

"Okay, I've been doing all I can—I've called everyone I know," he said. "No one is willing to let you into the park. They all think it's dangerous, and that you'd probably get in the way. A couple said they'd be willing to talk to you afterwards—if anything does happen. Most people seem to think it's probably a false alarm, though."

Crys frowned, feeling a wave of something between frustration and despair. "Thanks, Johannes. I know it's not your fault. But

I'm a reporter. I've gone through hell for this and have provided information that could be really important. And now I'm being shut out."

Johannes shrugged. "I can't do anything more. I would if I could. You know that, I hope."

She nodded. "Well, take me to the park gate. Please. I'll try to talk my way in."

"If you want. But you won't get in. They're only letting in people with legitimate, prior reservations, and I'm told they're checking the IDs of everyone in each vehicle. You'd be turned back in an instant. You're better off coming to Tshukudu. Next week you'll be able to talk to people in the park, as well as the police."

Crys felt helpless. Slowly the realization hit her that, in spite of everything, she wasn't going to Kruger. She simply had to accept it.

"Okay," she said with a sigh. "Let's go."

———

As they drove to Tshukudu, Crys asked Johannes if he'd heard anything from Mabula while she was overseas.

"Not Mabula himself," he replied, keeping a sharp lookout for potholes, "but one of his detectives visited Tshukudu asking about you. And he kept asking about money they insisted was on the plane. Of course, I didn't know anything about any money, but he gave poor old Bongani a hard time."

"Mabula kept pushing me on that one too. And the Portuguese also believed there was money on the plane and that I'd stolen it. To say nothing of the gang in Vietnam."

"The detective asked a whole lot more questions about Michael Davidson, too. It was strange. Apparently, he'd been looking for the Portuguese people, trying to meet up with them. I suppose he wanted to interview them." Johannes shook his head. "I'd go to a lot of trouble to avoid them myself."

He turned off the main road onto the dirt track leading to Tshukudu.

"My father was really angry that the detective had come to Tshukudu at all. One minute he accused him of being on the payroll of the poachers. The next, the man was a corrupt policeman who had stolen the missing money himself. He was upset about the story of the Portuguese too—asking why the detective thought we'd know about it. Frankly, I didn't understand what Dad was on about since we didn't know anything about it at all. He's getting crankier the older he gets..."

They drove in silence for a while, but Johannes was frowning. Clearly, he was struggling with something.

"Between you and me, Crys," he said finally, "the truth is my father's having problems. *We're* having problems. That's what's making him cranky. The economy in South Africa is tanking. Dad's businesses are taking a pounding. We're sitting on a fortune of rhino horn we can't sell—thanks to CITES and your NGO friends—and we're running out of cash. It's got to the point where we may have to sell Tshukudu, and there are some very shady characters ready to buy it just for the rhinos, so they can sell hunting contracts to their Vietnamese clients. No one else is interested."

"No..." Crys was shocked. She'd realized that the rhino farm was a passion rather than a business, but she'd thought Anton was so wealthy that nothing could really affect them.

Johannes glanced at her face. "Look," he added hastily, apparently deciding he'd said too much, "I'm sorry I mentioned it. It's not your problem. It's all off the record, right?"

"Of course."

"You promise you won't mention that I said anything to you? You won't write it in your article?" He looked over at her anxiously.

"I promise."

———

As they approached Tshukudu, Crys realized she hadn't asked Johannes about Bongani. She felt a stab of guilt. They'd been through a lot together.

"I assume Bongani's gone to Kruger with the anti-poaching unit," she said.

Johannes shook his head. "They wanted him, and he was willing to go, but I need him at the farm at the moment. You'll see him when we get there."

Crys wondered whether he'd gone back to where they'd left the money. She wondered if it was still buried, or whether he'd helped himself to it. At that moment, she really didn't care.

Just as they drove through the Tshukudu gate, Crys's phone rang. A glance told her it was Mabula.

"Colonel Mabula. Thank you for calling back."

"Where are you?" he snapped without greeting her.

"Back in South Africa. I arrived back from Vietnam yesterday afternoon. Do you have any news of Michael?"

"Not directly. But we think we're getting very close to the Portuguese gang now. And I'll bet that means we're close to Davidson too. I can't say more than that right now, but I'm optimistic. I'll let you know as soon as something breaks."

Crys sighed. It would have been wonderful if Michael had been safe. Now he was still caught up in whatever Pockface was planning on Sunday. And she still didn't know where Mabula stood in all this.

"That does sound hopeful. I'll certainly be thrilled when those thugs are behind bars." She paused. "I do have some information that you need to know."

"About the thing that's supposed to happen tomorrow, I suppose?"

"Yes. How did you know?"

"The head of a Swiss-based NGO has been whipping up the authorities—"

"Nigel Wood?"

"Yes. Apparently, they're convinced he's onto something. I guessed you must be the reporter he said had helped him. I should have known you'd be sticking your nose in there too." He sounded exasperated.

"I did some snooping around for him when I was in Ho Chi Min City. He had some information that seemed to fit what I'd found out here—the stuff I told you I'd picked up from the Portuguese who kidnapped me."

"Yes, but he's got more than that, apparently. Enough to get the deputy minister excited. He's really bashed a wasp nest."

Damn Nigel, she thought. He must have known that when I'd phoned him in Geneva. She wondered what the additional information was. Apparently, it was important enough to convince the authorities that Kruger was the target.

"Where are you right now?" Mabula asked.

"Just arriving at Tshukudu."

"I want you to stay there. I still need to resolve the issue of the money."

"Colonel, I've told you—"

"I know what you told me," he interrupted, raising his voice. "If Johannes Malan is with you, please put him on the line."

She handed the phone to Johannes.

He listened to what Mabula had to say. "Yes," he said and listened again. "Yes. Yes. I will."

He hung up and gave Crys her phone back.

"What was that all about?" she asked.

"He just wants me to keep you out of any more trouble."

"And are you going to?" she asked, challenging him to say he would.

He shook his head and gave a resigned smile. "As if I could."

She laughed, and after a moment she asked, "Do you trust him—Mabula?"

Johannes shrugged. "You never know who to trust these days."

———

When they arrived at the house, Johannes pointed out which chalet Crys was to use, then went off about his business.

She settled in, feeling strangely at home. Perhaps her case of Africa sickness was severe, she thought.

Once she'd unpacked, she sat on the bed and tried to reach Nigel again. This time she reached his assistant in Geneva, who told her that Nigel was not contactable in South Africa; he'd left Pretoria, but he planned to check in every day. Crys asked him to leave Nigel a message to call her, that it was very urgent.

As she disconnected, there was a light knock at the door, and she heard Bongani's voice say, "Crys, can I talk to you?"

She jumped up and pulled open the door. "Bongani! I'm so glad to see you." She gave him a big hug—something very unusual for her. She even surprised herself. And she certainly surprised Bongani. He wasn't sure whether to reciprocate. His hands touched her back only very briefly.

"Please sit down," she offered.

But he shook his head. "Crys, I think you must leave here." He looked very serious.

She was taken aback by his abruptness. They'd gone through a lot together, and here he was talking to her as if she was a stranger.

"Well, I was hoping to go to Kruger, actually, but I can't get in."

"Not Kruger, it's too dangerous there. Here, too."

"Dangerous here? At Tshukudu?"

"You know I was helping the poachers, Crys," he said. "Not anymore. But I know those people. The big boss, he will hurt my family unless I help him, so I just pretend. What is going to happen in Kruger is very big. But there are other things going on. Things I don't know. Mr. Anton is very upset, very worried. Something's going on here too. You should go back to Phalaborwa till next week."

Crys frowned. Did he know that Anton had severe business problems?

She started to ask about Kruger, but he held up a hand and cut her short. "I can't say any more. I need to go. Please listen to me, Crys." And he turned and left without another word.

She stared after him through the open door and wondered what was going on.

It wasn't like Bongani at all. They'd formed a strong relationship in the few days they'd spent together. Why was he now so cold? Did he know something more that he wasn't saying? He was clearly very scared. It was almost as if someone had warned him off speaking to her...

She walked out onto the porch, more frustrated than angry. Because, besides giving her the cold shoulder, Bongani had also confirmed that the action was going to happen in Kruger. But there was no way she could get there. Yet he'd suggested it was dangerous at Tshukudu too.

She went in search of Johannes.

He wasn't at the house, but Boku told her he was working on his Land Rover in the garage. She walked over to the crude structure that housed all the farm's vehicles. The walls were made from poles, about an inch thick and ten feet tall. Apparently, security wasn't a problem. The roof was thatch, with a lightning conductor rising high above it.

She walked in through the entrance and looked around, and spotted Johannes carrying a toolbox. He saw the look on her face, put down the toolbox and wiped his hands on his jeans.

"Hi, Crys. Anything wrong?" he asked.

"Johannes, I've been thinking. Suppose this attack isn't just restricted to Kruger. Suppose they're planning to hit some of the private farms, too."

"You're not thinking about Tshukudu, are you?" He frowned. "There'd be no point. I told you—we don't keep stock here. If they wanted our horns, they'd go after the bank in Phalaborwa."

"But suppose they don't know that?"

That made him pause. He rubbed his chin. "Have you heard something that suggests that?"

She shook her head. "Pockface said three, and there are three Kruger targets. That can't be coincidence. But still, how well prepared are you?"

"Well, we're really more concerned about attacks on the rhinos. But they all have radio chips and no horns. Anyone stealing them would have to wait at least a year to get any value, and we'd track them down by then. As far as the house is concerned, it's set up to withstand theft…but not an armed attack. But we do have emergency communication with neighboring farms. They could contact the police to send a helicopter with armed men if necessary."

But what if they're all tied up in Kruger? she wondered.

She toyed with the idea of suggesting that, but instead asked, "Do you have any guests here at the moment?"

"Only you, and this evening some guy is visiting from an NGO. Investigating options, fact-finding, he said." He shrugged. "He'll be like all the others, of course. An expert on everything, never seen a wild rhino, and telling us why what we're doing is all wrong. But we can't afford to alienate these people. I hope my father isn't rude to him."

Dinner tonight could be entertaining, she thought.

"Look, I have to replace these spark plugs. The engine's been running unevenly. I'll see you at dinner. Okay?"

Crys nodded and headed back to her chalet. The best thing she could do was to start work on her article.

———

Before she reached the chalet, her phone rang. It was Nigel.

She took a deep breath to compose herself. It wouldn't help to be rude to him—much as she would have enjoyed that.

"Nigel!" she said, brightly. "Thanks for calling me back. Look, I'm working on my article and I need to ask you a few quick questions."

"Where are you?"

"Pretoria," she lied. "I decided it was the best place to work, and then I'd be in a position to interview people next week about whatever happens tomorrow."

He was quiet for a few moments. "Makes sense, I suppose. Just don't go to Kruger. This thing is big and could blow up."

"That's what I need to know. I heard from Mabula that you have some new evidence that has convinced the deputy minister. I thought it would take a bazooka to get his attention."

"It's something Dinh discovered in Vietnam. I can't go into the details now; they want it kept very quiet."

He seemed to have forgotten that everything would be very quiet but for her.

She bit back an angry retort. It wouldn't help to alienate him.

"I'm back in Pretoria next week," he said, "and we can get together. I promise I'll fill you in on everything. Take care." And just like that, the line went dead.

Crys shoved her cell phone into her pocket and clenched her fists. He'd hung up on her. If he'd been within reach she would have hit him. And she was none the wiser about his so-called convincing evidence. She tried redialing the number, but when it diverted to Geneva, she hung up.

She recalled what Søren Willandsen had said: *Trust no one in this business.*

What did she actually know about Nigel and Rhino International? For that matter why had she lied to him about where she was? Her instinct had been to keep him in the dark, just as he was doing to her. As she continued back to her chalet, she realized the more she knew Nigel, the less she really liked him.

She needed to meditate for a while, and then write. And perhaps fit in a nap. She simply had to accept the frustration of waiting for Sunday without being able to do anything.

Chapter 33

When Crys arrived for evening drinks before dinner, she found the new visitor already relaxing with the Malans, enjoying a gin and tonic. She stopped in her tracks in the middle of the room when she saw him.

He jumped up immediately and extended his hand. "Ah, you must be Crystal Nguyen, the *National Geographic* writer. Such a pleasure to meet you. Johannes and Anton have just been telling me about you. I'm Søren Willandsen, I run an NGO, End Extinction, in Vietnam. We do a lot of work in rhino conservation. I hear you're interested in it, too. I'm sure we'll have a lot to discuss."

Crys was so astonished that for a moment she didn't let go of his hand. But he shook his head slightly, and she got the message.

"Mr. Willandsen, is it? Nice to meet you, too."

Anton waved her to a seat and asked what she wanted to drink. He was a little abrupt—the visit from Søren had put his back up, as Johannes had predicted.

"Why don't you tell me how come you're back here," Anton said as he handed her an orange juice.

Crys started with Geneva. His reaction to her comments on CITES and Rhino International was a derisive snort. However, he seemed much more interested in the Vietnam episode and approved of the way she'd escaped.

"Set fire to the whole damned lot of them, did you? Pity those bastards weren't caught in it," was his verdict.

"I'm certain they headed to South Africa," Crys said. "And I'm pretty sure they are interested in the Kruger National Park. What do you think?"

"Me? How should I know?"

Johannes looked away, embarrassed by Anton's rudeness.

"I doubt it's Kruger, though," Anton went on. "The stockpiles there are super-secret; no one knows where they are. And don't put anything about them in your article." He waved a finger at her. "If there's anything in this at all, I'd guess they'd be hitting a bank vault somewhere."

Crys was surprised by his next question. "Can you describe this boss man?"

She tried, but nothing about him had struck her as memorable. "One of the men called him Chủ Nhân—but that just means boss in Vietnamese," she said.

Anton's eyebrows rose as he opened his mouth to say something. He hesitated and then said, "So, Vietnamese obviously, but nothing special about him."

Søren chipped in. "Mr. Wood from Rhino International is pushing the Kruger angle very strongly. He alerted all the rhino NGOs, asking for their support with the South African authorities."

Anton waved a hand at Søren, batting away the idea. "Waste of time. If it happens, it'll be a bank hit. There's a big vault in Phalaborwa. We've got a lot of our stock there. Now that would be a real target."

"We'd be in big trouble if that happens," Johannes commented. "Our insurance wouldn't cover that!"

Anton laughed. "You're buying all this, are you, Johannes? The young lady here has absolutely no evidence that anything is going to happen except for her interpretation of a few snippets of conversations she overheard."

Crys bristled. "Nigel Wood has more evidence. That's why he's come out here."

"And what evidence is that?" Anton's voice was mocking.

"I don't know," she admitted.

Anton gave another snort.

"There *is* the business of the three stockpiles in Kruger," Johannes put in.

Anton glared at him. "Who said anything about three stockpiles? If you know anything, you keep it to yourself unless you want it all over *National Geographic.*" Turning back to Crys, he added: "As for this Wood character, his new evidence is so good he didn't even bother to tell you about it?" He paused to let that sink in. "It's a bit like those end-of-the-world predictions we keep hearing. For my money, on Monday morning, the world will still be here, and so will our rhino horn." He climbed to his feet. "Come on, let's go in to dinner. I'm hungry." And without waiting for them to finish their drinks, he strode out of the room.

—

After dinner and once they'd finished their coffee, Johannes offered to walk them back to their chalets.

Søren immediately said, "Thank you, but don't worry. Crys and I will walk back together. We are near each other."

Johannes frowned, but let them go. Crys didn't object. It was exactly what she'd been going to say. She wanted to speak to Søren, to find out why he'd wanted to keep their previous contact secret.

They walked slowly across the lawn. Crys turned and saw Johannes watching from the veranda. She gave him a wave and he turned away.

As soon as they were out of earshot, Søren said, "Actually, I wanted a chance to talk to you alone."

"What's going on?" Crys murmured. "Why didn't you want them to know we'd met in Vietnam?"

"Look, I know all about Tshukudu. They do good work here breeding rhinos, but we've been worried about horns leaking from farms like this into the Asian market ever since South Africa allowed trade. There have been some rumors…"

"That Johannes and Anton are black-market rhino-horn traders?" He nodded.

It seemed impossible, but by this time, nothing shocked Crys. "So why did you want to talk to me?"

"Two reasons. The first is to discover exactly what you found out in Vietnam. Nigel Wood has used that to get everything focused on Kruger this weekend. You weren't honest when you told me after the fire that you hadn't come up with anything, were you?"

"You're the one who told me to trust no one," Crys said pointedly.

He nodded. "That brings me to the second point. We do undercover work to help with enforcement. That was another reason Donald was following you in Ho Chi Minh City."

"I thought you were more interested in what I was doing than in my safety. But the way it worked out, I can't complain…"

He nodded. "Anyway, we've been investigating Rhino International, and there are a number of suspicious things about it. We can't find out where they get their money. Most NGOs are happy to advertise their funding sources, but not Rhino International. Then there is Wood himself. Did he give you the story about the upper-class background and rebelling to become an ecological activist?"

Crys stopped in her tracks. "He did. Exactly that."

Søren took her arm and moved on. "Well, we've looked into it. We can't find any trace of that background—no public-school records, no wealthy Wood families with a son called Nigel. There are plenty of Nigel Woods to choose from, but none of them fit."

"What are you saying?"

"I mean Nigel Wood's background is fiction. He may have legitimate reasons for making up a new background, but what we see is that Rhino International has no obvious source of funding, and a director who isn't who he says he is. That worries us—a lot. I think it should worry you too."

It certainly did.

Then the reporter in Crys kicked in.

"You'd better come to my chalet," she said.

———

They sat on the veranda of Crys's bungalow, protected from insects by the fly screen. From time to time something large would be attracted by the light, bash into the net and bounce back into the night. An orchestra of cicadas played in the background.

Søren went through everything he knew about Nigel Wood and Rhino International. It wasn't just the lack of transparency and Nigel's fake background. There were things that couldn't be explained—smugglers getting wind of enforcement operations and staff members with shadowy connections. Crys didn't like the sound of it at all and was feeling very uncomfortable about how easily she'd accepted what Nigel had told her.

"But what's the point of Rhino International, if it's not legitimate?" she asked. "Just to find out what the anti-smuggling people are doing?"

Søren shook his head. "Smugglers don't want legal trade any more than we do, because that would depress prices. If Rhino International is in league with the smugglers, its role would be to pressure CITES to keep it that way."

"So, the good guys and the bad guys want the same thing?"

"As bizarre as it sounds, that's right."

Crys sighed in disbelief. But she had to admit that it did make sense.

"Crys, we need to think about some worst-case scenarios here," Søren continued. "If Wood isn't legitimate, what is he doing here? I can see him passing on the information you obtained to the South Africans, but why come himself? Frankly, I think the reaction here is too strong for the snatches you overheard. He's presented some other evidence, and he got it *very* quickly. Too quickly, I would say."

"You think he made it up?" She frowned. "If he did, that could be a disaster for Rhino International. If nothing happens tomorrow, he will look a total idiot."

"Well, he could blame it on you."

She bridled. "If he did, I'd go public with what I know. He'd still lose credibility."

Søren said nothing for a few moments. Then he asked, "Suppose he wants everything focussed on Kruger, why is that? What could he gain?"

"Perhaps opportunity. The chance to do something else in South Africa while people's attention is elsewhere. Maybe blow up rhino-horn stocks or something like that." It made him sound like a mad environmentalist with a James Bond script. She shook her head. "No, that's nonsense."

"Or he could be planning a rhino-horn heist of his own…"

It all sounded totally farfetched to Crys. She frowned and folded her arms. "He's had very little time to set up anything like that."

Søren nodded. "Of course, we may be quite wrong. He may simply be desperate to stop the poachers getting a huge stock of horn and more resources, even if he has to invent some of the evidence. Maybe Rhino International is entirely aboveboard, and all the things they've been doing are part of a plan to infiltrate, to learn more. That could still be the answer."

Crys shook her head. This was all too much—Søren spying on the Malans under the cover of rhino conservation; Nigel infiltrating the poachers. "But surely NGOs don't behave like that!"

Søren sighed. "Let me give you some background on this

business, Crys. From the inside…from my fifteen years as some-one in the know."

———

Crys didn't sleep well, what with jet lag and her mind churning with all that was going on. Eventually, she couldn't take tossing and turning any longer and got up, made some instant coffee, and went and sat on the porch. The air was crisp and the Milky Way spectacular. In any other circumstances, she would be in heaven. However, whatever was happening in Kruger was going down today; she didn't know who to trust; and she was no closer to finding Michael. Instead, she was sitting at Tshukudu doing nothing.

Her head was full of what Søren had told her. They'd talked late into the night, and she'd learned a great deal about the politics of CITES and the associated NGOs, as well as about the rhino-horn underworld. She was astonished at the layers of intrigue around what seemed to be the straightforward missions of the NGOs: the jostling for influence, the backstabbing, the never-ending quest for funds, and even what verged on blackmail.

And apparently it wasn't much different in the rhino-horn trade itself. Gangs fighting each other for ascendancy, groups trying to muscle into every aspect of the business, from the poach-ing, to the shipping, to the selling, to protection. Even the North Koreans were involved, with their embassies being engaged in the smuggling to obtain hard currency.

The major difference between the official and unofficial partici-pants was that the unofficial ones didn't hesitate to kill anyone that got in the way. She knew that was true. She'd come close to death at their hands three times in the past few weeks. And Michael? She forced her mind away from that thought and concentrated on Nigel.

If he wasn't who he said he was, then who was he? And what

was his real motivation? She had helped him without knowing either and now felt very uncomfortable about it. On the other hand, everything negative had come from Søren. The fact was that Nigel had managed to get the South African authorities to act to protect Kruger—a huge plus. And what was Søren doing here anyway? Was it coincidence or did he have some agenda of his own that he hadn't shared with her?

She didn't know which of the two NGO directors she could trust. If either.

Soon it was dawn—the Milky Way gradually faded as the sky turned pale and then brightened, and the air was filled with the sound of birds welcoming a new day.

She could barely wait to hear if there was any news, so, around seven, she headed to the main house for cereal and more coffee on the veranda. However, no one was about, so she made herself comfortable and tried to relax.

After a while, she heard a voice coming from one of the upstairs bedrooms that overlooked the veranda. She guessed the windows were open to catch the cool of the night. Suddenly, the voice got louder, and she realized it was Anton. She sat very still, straining to hear.

"That wasn't the deal! You promised me the money *in advance*." There was silence for a few seconds, and she realized Anton must be speaking to someone on the phone. "That's not my problem! I have everything set up…"

Then his voice dropped, and she couldn't make out what he was saying. It seemed odd to be having a business discussion at seven on a Sunday morning, but maybe his financial problems were even more urgent than Johannes had suggested. Crys shrugged it off.

A short while later, Johannes walked onto the veranda, greeted her, and helped himself to coffee. His face looked drawn. Crys hoped he wasn't coming down with malaria again.

"Have you heard anything from Kruger?" she asked.

"No. Nothing. And there's nothing on the TV either." He sat down opposite her. "And nobody has tried to get to our rhinos. I hope it's all a hoax."

Crys didn't know what to think. Part of her hoped that nothing would happen—that it was all rumor and speculation, and that the rhinos would be safe, the horns stocks secure, but the journalist in her wanted to be at the center of a huge story, with good guys and bad guys, and conflict.

———

Søren came to breakfast around nine. He looked cheerful enough, but he didn't say much. It was as though the discussion of the previous night had never happened. Crys decided he'd make a very good poker player. She was sure Johannes had no idea they knew each other before the previous evening. He ate some fruit and then excused himself, saying he had calls to make.

Anton didn't show up for breakfast. Johannes said he wasn't feeling well and would eat in his bedroom.

Then Johannes left to do some work, and Bongani was nowhere to be seen.

Crys was left alone.

She headed back to her chalet and tried to write but found it impossible—her mind was everywhere except on the story.

At lunch, Crys was the only one who showed up. Even Boku, once he'd taken her drink order, disappeared into the kitchen. It was an eerie feeling—as though she was being avoided.

She checked the TV, flipping through a number of channels, but there was nothing of interest, so she returned to the chalet and again tried to write, again without much success.

She wondered if Mabula had caught Pockface and found Michael. He'd promised to let her know, but that was a day ago. She tried to call him, but it went to voicemail. She couldn't decide whether that was good news or bad.

Every hour or so, she went online and checked the South African news websites, the National Parks site, and even CNN and the BBC. There was absolutely nothing. Either nothing had happened or there was a stranglehold on information.

She went outside and kicked the ground in frustration.

Chapter 34

Everyone gathered for drinks and supper at around seven. It was a buffet because it was Sunday and the staff were off.

Anton appeared and without greeting anyone poured himself a brandy and Coke. Johannes and Søren had red wine, and Crys stuck to her usual orange juice. They helped themselves to food and then settled at the table.

Anton downed his drink and went to fetch another. He returned with the bottles. It seemed he intended to make a night of it.

"I tried to call Hennie in Kruger around lunch, but it just cut to voicemail," Johannes said. "I asked him to call back if he had a chance. But I've heard nothing all day."

"I spoke to Colonel Mabula this morning," Søren commented. "He seems to be taking all this very seriously."

"Only as long as there's something in it for him," Anton sneered. "They're all the same—on the take."

Crys wondered what Søren had talked to Mabula about but decided not to ask in front of the others. Had Michael featured in their conversation?

"You remember Mary, the rhino whose foot was caught in the snare?" Johannes asked her. "Her foot's completely healed. I spotted her when I was working on the fences this morning and had a good look with my binocs."

"Until the next poacher gets to her," Anton said bitterly. He looked at Søren. "Thanks to you people. If you left us alone to farm our rhinos and sell the horn, they would be safe."

"I'm sorry," Søren responded, "but I have to disagree. That would just grow the demand for horn."

"Yes, that's your take on it. Meanwhile, we go broke." Anton thumped his glass on the table. "You can come to the auction when we sell our rhinos to the highest bidder to be slaughtered."

"Dad," interjected Johannes quietly, "Mr. Willandsen is our guest. Everyone has the right to an opinion, even if we don't agree with it."

"That's what you think, is it? Everyone has a right to an opinion, hey? Well, let them put *their* money on the table. Then I'll listen to their opinions."

At that moment the phone rang, and Johannes jumped up to answer it. The rest of them went on eating in an uncomfortable silence, anxious to hear if it was news from Kruger. Anton threw his cutlery on his unfinished plate, poured himself a brandy—no Coke this time –and tossed it down.

After a couple of minutes, Johannes came back. "That was Hennie. He says all the camps are locked down, the perimeters patrolled, and they've checked that all the tourists are safely inside. They found a few stragglers who'd been delayed by elephants and so on, but everyone's accounted for now. If anything happens, they're ready for it."

Anton said something in Afrikaans and laughed loudly. He was well on his way to being very drunk. Johannes ignored him. Crys wondered if this was normal.

"It seems Wood warned them of a possible terror attack, Crys," Johannes said to her. "They're taking it very seriously. I hope... actually, I don't know what I hope."

Crys understood what he meant, yet she did want something

to happen. She wanted the boss man and his thugs to be caught, no one hurt in Kruger, and, yes, a great story. But from what Søren had told her, she realized it wouldn't make any difference. If the boss man's cartel was gone, another group would take its place. Pretty soon it would be business as usual.

She looked round the table, wondering about the people sitting there.

Was Anton selling his horn on the black market to keep Tshukudu going?

If so, did Johannes know? And Søren? He had her followed in Vietnam to find out what she'd learned.

Why did he do that?

Then there was Nigel. He'd come across as totally dedicated—until he had the information he wanted. Then he'd dropped her. Now she had no idea what his real objective was. As for Mabula, she still didn't know if she could trust him, or if his only interest was in getting his hands on the money. But he was Michael's only chance. She felt the familiar ache in her chest.

"There's ice cream in the freezer," Johannes said, interrupting her reverie. "I'll fetch it."

Crys shook her head. "I think jet lag's hitting me, and I want to check the internet in case anything's happening. I'll see you all in the morning."

"I'll walk with you," Johannes offered.

"Don't worry. I'm fine. I don't want to interrupt your dinner."

She headed back to her chalet and immediately searched the internet, but again found nothing. She tried calling Nigel on the off chance he'd answer, but once again it went straight to voicemail in Geneva. She'd run out of options to get information; there was nothing she could do but wait.

She decided on an early night and set the alarm on her phone for five a.m. Hopefully, there would be some news by then if anything had happened during the night.

———

Crys woke suddenly. The room was in complete darkness, no hint of dawn yet. Her first thought was that jet lag was the culprit—making her wake in the dead of night, but she knew that was wrong. Something had definitely woken her.

Then she heard what sounded like raised voices some way off, followed by a sound like a door slamming.

She checked her watch. It was just after four a.m. She pulled back the curtains and saw lights on in the main house.

What could be happening at this time of night? she wondered.

She pulled on her clothes as quickly as she could, and as she did, she heard another shout. Now she was sure something wasn't right. She turned off the lights and went to investigate.

As she walked toward the house, possible scenarios ran through her mind. Maybe Anton had drunk enough to end up fighting with Johannes? But at four in the morning? She stopped under a tree. This was probably none of her business; maybe she should go back to bed.

But something compelled her to keep going—the feeling that something was badly wrong.

She heard a noise behind her and swung round.

It was Søren.

"Thank heaven, it's you," she whispered. "You gave me a fright."

"I heard noises up at the house," he said softly. "And there are vehicles up there."

She'd noticed that as well—there were two vehicles parked outside the house. They hadn't been there when she'd walked back to her chalet after supper.

"Let's take a look," she said pressing on.

He didn't follow immediately, but then he nodded. "Let's see if we can spot anything from the outside. But be careful. Something isn't right about this."

So, he felt it, too.

"I'll go to the left, and you go right," she suggested. "We'll meet on the other side of the house."

He looked alarmed. "We're not police—or the army."

"What else can we do? If something bad is happening, we don't want to just stumble in…"

He nodded but didn't seem happy about it.

They moved quietly toward the house.

Crys pointed at the security lights and guided Søren out of their range. Even in the dark she could see the fear on his face. She wondered if hers showed the same.

They reached the two vehicles, and now they were close, they could see that they didn't have the characteristic Tshukudu rhino logos. Were they visitors from a neighboring farm? Unlikely at four in the morning.

She swallowed and her adrenalin started to pump.

Then she moved round to the left side of the house and indicated Søren should go to the right.

When she reached the corner of the building, she could see light from the living room spilling into the garden; apparently the curtains had been left open. She crept around the corner, hugging the wall.

She could hear a murmur of voices from inside but couldn't make out any words.

Then there was a shout from the other side of the house. Crys jumped, then froze, her heart pounding. Was it Søren? Was he in trouble? She waited, but everything had gone quiet. The voices had stopped.

After a few moments, she edged up to the open living room window. Her pulse was racing as she peeked in.

The first thing she saw was two men holding assault rifles. One man had his back to the wall opposite the door. The other was covering two men in the center of the room. One was spread-eagled on the floor. He was lying facedown, but she could see it was Johannes. Near him, Anton was also on the floor, clutching his stomach. A third man was standing over him, talking to him. As she watched, he kicked out, and Anton screamed.

When the man straightened up, she saw he was Asian.

Then, with a sickening shock, she recognized him. It was Dinh—the government official from Ho Chi Minh City.

Then it struck her. Dinh wasn't trying to stop the smuggling! He was with one of the gangs. And she'd kept feeding him information.

She moved forward a little so she could see the whole room. On the right, against the wall, was another body.

Crys stifled a cry. Held her hand to her mouth.

Michael!

She was sure it was him. And he was either dead or unconscious—a pool of blood around his head. She simply couldn't believe it. She pulled back a little, her mind reeling.

She clamped her hand tighter to her mouth. She was trembling. What was he doing here?

But before she could think about what it could mean, a door burst open, and three more men came into the living room. One was Søren. He was being pushed—almost thrown—into the room by a man who also had an automatic weapon. And behind him was Bongani, with what looked like an old bolt-action rifle.

She gasped again. Bongani was working with Dinh.

Slowly, Crys edged back from the window, not knowing what to think. She'd found Michael but didn't know whether he was dead or alive. And as for the other two, Søren wouldn't give her away, but Bongani knew she was somewhere on the farm, and they would come looking. She had to hide, and she had to get help.

She had to get her cell phone, but it was back in her chalet— the first place they would look for her.

She worked her way back to the chalet using the trees scattered about the compound as cover. She moved quickly, looking about, but there was no sign of anyone following her. Then she heard another scream.

Who was it? she wondered. Was it Anton or Johannes? Søren? Michael?

When Crys reached her chalet, she worked her way around it. She couldn't see in because the lights were off, and she couldn't hear anything. She eased open the door and slipped inside. She stood dead still, listening and letting her eyes adjust to the darkness.

Suddenly there was a flash of light. She jumped and almost yelled out, but then she realized it was her phone, silently indicating an email. Gratefully, she grabbed it and slipped out of the door.

Crys still needed somewhere to hide, somewhere she could use the phone. She couldn't think of anything better than another chalet, so she went to the one farthest from the house, hoping it would be the last they would search. She stepped inside, locked the door behind her, and made sure the curtains were closed.

Then she sat on the floor against the wall and scrolled straight to Mabula's cell phone number and called it. Her heart was in her mouth. What would she do if he didn't answer? He was her only hope. But he answered immediately.

"Colonel Mabula."

"Colonel," she whispered. "It's Crys Nguyen. Tshukudu's being attacked. There are armed men here, and they have the Malans. And Michael's here also, on the floor. I don't know whether he's alive or not. We need help right away!"

"Slow down. Give me the details."

She took a breath and told him what she'd seen.

"Do you have any idea who the attackers are?" he responded.

"Yes. Yes, I do. Bongani Chikosi is with them. And the leader is a Vietnamese man I recognize. His name is Dinh. He's with the Vietnamese Department of Environmental Affairs and knows Nigel Wood at Rhino International."

"*Din?* What sort of name is that?"

"It's Vietnamese. He's from Ho Chi Minh City." She sat up and parted the curtains slightly with her finger but saw nothing.

"And he works with Nigel Wood?" said Mabula. There was a brief pause. "Does that mean Wood's involved too? I'll have him picked up for questioning." There was a silence on the line. "I'll grab some men here and leave at once. But it'll take me more than an hour to get there."

"But we need help now! I don't think these men are going to leave anyone alive."

"Yes, I understand, but all the police helicopters were seconded to Kruger. I'll try and get one back here, but things are chaotic there right now. If that doesn't work, we'll have to drive."

"That could be too late."

"Where are you?"

"I'm in one of the chalets. I'm sure they'll come looking for me. Bongani knows I'm here." She couldn't keep the desperation out of her voice. She checked through the curtains again. Still nothing.

"Now listen. You must get out of there," Mabula said. "Go into the bush. Then climb a tree—it's safer, and searchers never look up. Don't risk getting caught. I'll be there with my men as soon as I can."

"Okay."

"Get going. Now. We'll see each other later, I'm sure."

She hoped he was right.

She turned the phone off; she couldn't risk the screen lighting up. She needed a few seconds to get control of herself, so she closed her eyes, breathed deeply, and repeated her mantra five or six times. She needed to be calm when she decided what to do.

After that, she thought through her options.

The most sensible was to do what Mabula said—head for the safety of the bush. But that meant abandoning Michael. The thought made her dizzy. Her heart gave her no choice.

She needed to help him. And the others too.

She unlocked the door, slipped into the darkness, and headed back toward the house.

Chapter 35

Crys had no idea what she was going to do. They had assault rifles, and she didn't even have her .22 target rifle. The best she could do was to pick up one of the stones that formed the border of a flower bed—bigger than a baseball, but smaller than a melon. It was a bit unwieldy for her, but better than nothing.

She kept looking out for people searching for her, but she saw and heard no one. That worried her. Was she walking into a trap?

As she moved closer to the back of the house, she heard shouting. She couldn't make out the words, only the anger. That was followed by a cry of pain. Then more shouting. More pain. She couldn't tell who it was.

Then everything went quiet. Somehow that was more ominous. Had they killed someone? She prayed it wasn't Michael.

Crys looked around, then moved up to the wall of the house, her heart thumping. She'd just reached the front corner, when there was another shout, followed by a string of shots. That had to be the assault rifle.

There was another shout, followed by what sounded like an argument.

She slipped around the corner, up to the open living room window where she'd been before, and peeked around.

Johannes and Anton were still on the floor, and so was Søren now. Michael's position hadn't changed. Crys's heart constricted. There was no way of knowing if he was still alive.

Dinh's three men were looking on, guns at the ready. Bongani was close to the window, watching the proceedings, rifle in hand, and Dinh was pointing his automatic rifle at Anton. She was so close she could hear what he was saying. She held her breath.

"I know you have many horns here. You open the safe now or you'll be very sorry!"

He kicked Anton in the head. There was no reaction.

"Leave him alone!" Johannes shouted. "Our horns are in Phalaborwa, at a bank." Dinh turned and kicked him too. Johannes groaned in pain.

"You know nothing!" Dinh shouted. "Your father brought all the horns here for his Portuguese friends. They are all here."

"That's not true!" Johannes protested, trying to sit up.

Dinh pointed his rifle toward Johannes and let off a burst that hit the floor just next to Johannes's head.

"You keep quiet. Your father must give me the combination of the safe."

"If you kill him, he won't be able to tell you." It was Søren. "And none of us know it."

Dinh didn't say anything for a few moments. "Get water. Give it to him," he said eventually, pointing at Anton.

One of his men left the room.

Then Dinh turned toward Bongani and pointed his rifle at him. Crys jerked her head away from the window, hoping he hadn't seen her.

"You think I am stupid, hey? I know you work here, and you work for the Portuguese man."

Crys heard Bongani's voice. "No, boss. Nobody tells me anything. I let you in because I hoped you would give me a little money. My family has no food. But I don't know where Mr. Malan has anything."

She felt sick.

"We will see who you work for," Dinh said. "When the old man wakes up, if he doesn't tell me, you will shoot his son. If he still doesn't tell me, you will shoot the other man. That will prove you are my man."

She peeked again. Dinh was now looking at one of his men trying to revive Anton. The man poured water over Anton's head and tried to make him drink. There was no reaction.

"You've killed him, you bastard!" Johannes shouted and started to stand up.

Dinh sprayed another burst next to him. "Lie down, or I will shoot you."

Johannes collapsed.

Crys pulled back again, desperately trying to think what she could do. Her stone was no use at all—she needed a gun. She had no idea where the Malans kept theirs, and the gun cabinet was probably locked anyway.

She wondered if she could lure one of the men outside and disarm him. She decided that wasn't a good idea—the chances of success were close to zero.

The safe way was to wait for Mabula, but almost certainly that was going to be too late for the men in the house. Maybe for Michael, it was already too late. She choked back a sob.

Then it struck her that Bongani wasn't with Dinh and his men. He'd helped them, but from what Dinh had said, he was dispensable. And she could see from his body language that he was upset after what Dinh had said to him. She realized then that Bongani was her only chance—it was a huge risk, but better than nothing. But how could she get his attention?

She could distract Dinh and his men by throwing her rock through the window of another room. But then they'd know someone was outside. She had no chance against assault rifles. She needed a firearm herself. Perhaps she could use fire again—as she had in Vietnam. But she'd have the same problem if she set a chalet on fire. Or one of their vehicles. She'd be dead meat without a weapon.

Her best bet seemed to be to try to attract Bongani's attention from the window. Bongani was the closest to it, so maybe she could whisper to him or tap lightly on the windowpane. She wondered which would get the message across that it was her outside but cause the least reaction inside.

She took a few deep breaths to calm her nerves. And a few more. Then she moved forward.

She peered around the window. Everyone was watching the man trying to revive Anton. She tapped the window lightly. No reaction from Bongani. She tapped again, a bit harder, hoping he'd hear. Still nothing. Now she was worried that one of the others would hear. She tapped again, harder still.

This time Bongani looked around.

She moved so he could see her face and put her finger to her lips. Then pulled back. She was worried he may raise the alarm.

She held her breath, half expecting Dinh's men to come running outside. She didn't hear anything.

She peeked around the window again. Bongani had moved closer, blocking Dinh's view.

It was all the indication she needed.

"Bongani," she whispered, "nod your head if you can hear me."

Bongani barely moved his head, but it was a nod. She was sure.

"I'm going to throw a rock through the kitchen window." She saw his head move again, almost imperceptibly.

"Run to investigate, then try to escape through the front door. I'll wait there. Bring the rifle."

Another tiny movement of his head.

"I'm going."

Another nod.

Crys slid along the walls of the house to the back, where the kitchen was, and picked up another rock. Her heart was pounding, her body tense. This was it.

She took a few paces back and threw one rock as hard as she could at the biggest pane of glass.

There was a crash and the sound of falling shards.

As Crys ran around the house to the front door, she could hear shouts from inside. As she reached the porch, the front door opened and Bongani started to run out.

There was a burst of automatic fire, and Bongani crashed to the ground. His rifle slid from his hand. Crys grabbed it and ran into the darkness. As soon as she reached one of the trees, she hid behind it and looked back.

No one was following. Yet.

She started to sob. Bongani was her friend and trusted her, and now he was dead because of her.

But what else could she have done? she asked herself.

She wiped the tears from her face and then checked the rifle. It was the same as she'd been given on the poacher hunt. A .303 bolt action. She checked that the safety was off and tried to remember how many bullets it held. Was it four in total, or four in the magazine and one in the breech? Damn! She couldn't remember. Better to assume four in total. Not enough...Now what should she do?

She took a few deep breaths to try to calm herself and assessed the situation. Dinh now knew there was someone outside. He could find out who by coercing Johannes. She wondered what his reaction would be when he found out it was her. If he was a typical, traditional Vietnamese man, he'd probably discount her abilities. That was good. It gave her an advantage. Almost certainly, he'd send one of his men to find her. And she was pretty certain he'd enjoy hurting her. Maybe that would stop his men from just killing her if they found her. Also good. Another advantage.

He had also probably written off Bongani. If she was lucky, he wouldn't go looking for the rifle. If he did, though, he'd know she was armed. She wanted to go and help Bongani, to see if he was alive. But she didn't dare do that if she wanted any chance of rescuing the others—of saving Michael. She just had to hope Bongani would survive.

Mabula was probably still forty minutes or so away, so he wasn't going to be of any help. And she didn't know where the Malans' emergency network was to alert the neighbors. So, no help there.

What was Dinh going to do to his hostages? If Anton didn't recover, she was sure he'd kill them all and leave. But even if Anton opened the safe and gave him the horns—if there actually were some—Dinh would take them and then still kill everyone. He was in too deep to leave any witnesses.

So, her first priority had to be Dinh. If she took him out, there was a chance the others would run. Hopefully. That was a lot easier to think about than to actually achieve.

As she was trying to decide what to do, she glanced back at the house. There were no lights on now. Dinh wasn't taking any chances of her picking him off from the outside. He wanted her to go into the house, where he would have a huge advantage.

She definitely wasn't doing that!

———

For what seemed like an hour, but probably was no longer than five or ten minutes, Crys did nothing other than peek around the tree.

She'd heard nothing from the house and seen no one moving outside it. She was sure, though, that Dinh had stationed someone in a strategic position to spot her if she tried to get close. Could she flush that man out and take care of him without exposing herself? Running anywhere was out of the question because of the firepower he would have. It didn't take a marksman to neutralize someone when using an assault rifle.

She had to tempt him out of hiding so she could see him and not the other way around. Then Crys remembered what Mabula had said: "Climb a tree—searchers never look up." If she could lure him close to her tree, maybe she could shoot him before he shot her.

She looked up. The tree was reasonably big, but it had a lot of leaves, which would make seeing him difficult. She took a breath and moved to the next tree, keeping low to the ground. This tree was much better. The leaves were thick and started higher up. And it looked as though she could climb to the lower branches quite easily.

Now to get the man's attention.

She was about to reveal her position. Crys hesitated. She'd been in real peril these last few days, but usually by accident. Now she was calling danger to her.

Am I mad? she thought. And immediately the image of Michael came to her, the blood around his head. And she knew why she was doing this.

Again, she was tempted to follow Mabula's instructions. But finally, she steeled herself, squared her shoulders and took a big breath of African night air.

"Throw down your gun," she shouted. "You are surrounded. You'll die if you don't."

As she hoped, the answer was a burst of firing in her general direction. She aimed where she thought the man was and fired a single shot.

Three bullets left.

She wondered if he realized she was alone.

Another burst of fire answered her shot.

She climbed the tree until she was about fifteen feet up. It was harder than she'd expected because of her injured hand, and her sore shoulder didn't help. But once she was up, she could see the ground in all directions for about thirty yards. If he came into the circle...

"You okay, Lee?" The shout came from the direction of the house.

"No problem," came the response. Then silence.

Crys sat and waited. At first, she felt like the cat, patiently waiting for the mouse to come and play. But as the minutes ticked by, she started feeling more like the mouse. Where was he? Was he watching this tree? Was it safe to get down? Could he see her?

Then she heard a scuffle. Barely a noise in the night, but definitely human. Her heart beat faster, but her senses sharpened and her fear evaporated. She became totally focused. She heard the noise again. She sensed it came from her left. Better than the right for shooting. Crys shifted the rifle close to her shoulder. And waited. Calm. Ready.

She had to do something, because if Mabula didn't arrive soon, it would be all over. She could never match their firepower.

Somehow, she had to get the man to show himself without giving herself away, halfway up the tree.

She took her shoes off and lifted the rifle into shooting position. She could only hope he would react with a spray of bullets when she dropped them.

She took a breath and threw them out of the tree. She heard them hit the ground. Almost immediately there was a burst of fire from a tree nearby. She aimed at the muzzle flashes and fired.

The firing stopped. All she could hear were groans.

Crys slipped down the tree as quietly as she could and moved away, keeping her tree between her and the man. She hoped there were no thorns on the ground.

"You okay, Lee?" The same shout from the house. This time there was no reply.

"Lee, you okay?"

She guessed it would take them a few minutes to decide what to do. She made use of that time by making a wide arc, ending up behind the tree where the man had been. He was still groaning.

When Crys reached the tree, she could just make out the shape of someone on the ground on the other side. She thought she saw the rifle lying a few yards away. Or was it a branch? She wasn't sure.

She had to find out. And she hoped she didn't have to use another bullet.

"Throw your gun away and roll onto your stomach," she said from behind the tree.

No gunfire, but no response. Only groaning.

She stepped out, pointing her rifle at the body on the ground. It was curled in a ball, still groaning. She picked up his rifle and found her shoes. One down, but there were still three heavily armed men in the house.

Crys took a deep breath and started to think about what to do next.

Chapter 36

Crys looked back at the house. Now there was light in one window—upstairs. She thought it was the one where she'd overheard Anton talking about some deal the previous morning.

She had to assume that one of Dinh's men was either outside, lying in wait for her to show herself, or was covering the entrances to the house. As far as she could remember there were three of those: the front door—the one Bongani had tried to come out of; the kitchen door, next to the window she'd broken; and a side door off the sitting room onto the porch. Her guess was that they were all locked, and the kitchen and side doors barricaded. That left only one door to guard. It was the most likely scenario since the two vehicles were parked close to the front of the house.

Crys took a look at the rifle she'd grabbed. How did it work?

She assumed that when she pulled the trigger, it would shoot for as long as she kept it pulled. She had no idea what the recoil was like. Was it strong? Would it push her back? Would she be able to control it? Would the gun even hold its aim or just spray bullets in the general direction it was pointed? And were there even any bullets left in the magazine?

The man had fired three bursts, but she didn't know what that meant. If she decided to use it, she would have to be ready for it to be empty. There were so many variables. But she'd come this far. She wouldn't back out now.

She crept closer to the house, hugging the trees wherever possible. She stopped when she was close enough to see in the upstairs window—about forty or fifty yards away. There was nothing to see, but she could hear voices. Angry voices. She was too far away to hear what they were saying.

She wondered if that's where Anton had his horns and money—in the upstairs room. Maybe there was a safe up there, and Dinh was trying to get Anton to open it—if Anton was alive that was.

Crys longed to turn on her phone to see how much longer it was likely to be before Mabula arrived, but she didn't dare. Any glimmer of light would be enough to attract the attention of anyone hidden outside the house. Maybe even from inside the house—someone looking through a darkened window. She couldn't give up the slightest advantage. She just had to hope Mabula was getting close.

Until he arrived, her best option was to keep shaking things up, keep distracting Dinh and his men, as she had already. If she could keep their focus on her, perhaps Michael and the others might—just might—be able to escape.

She leaned the .303 against the tree and moved slowly about fifteen or twenty yards away. Then she placed the stock of the assault rifle firmly against her shoulder, just as she would her little .22 back home. She aimed it at the lighted window and pulled the trigger for about one second. Crys was deafened and thrown backwards. She immediately dropped to the ground and scuttled back to her tree. There was no response. No return fire. She looked up. She had no idea whether she'd hit the window, but the light was now off.

She waited a few minutes, then moved back, away from the house. When she heard and saw nothing, she moved slowly around the house toward Dinh's two vehicles. If she could make

Dinh think she was disabling his vehicles, perhaps she could draw his men out of the house.

Eventually, Crys was behind a tree and had the two vehicles between her and the building. She assumed Dinh would have put a guard on them since he needed them to make his getaway. She watched carefully for several minutes and saw nobody. But since it was still pretty dark, she couldn't be sure she was right.

She picked up a stone and threw it as far as she could away from her. She heard it hit the ground. No response. But maybe they were getting smart and were waiting for her to show herself. She didn't like that thought one bit.

She waited a few more minutes, then put the assault rifle to her shoulder, braced herself, and pulled the trigger, spraying one of the vehicles with bullets and blowing out the tires. Immediately she ducked behind the tree, waiting for return fire. There was none. Perhaps Dinh wasn't as smart as she'd thought.

Crys waited a moment, then started moving to a position where she could give the second vehicle a going over. She could see no one and heard nothing.

She'd only taken a couple of steps, when a figure stepped out in front of her.

"Drop your gun." Crys could see the man's assault rifle pointed straight at her chest. She froze. She had no option. She dropped the rifle.

"Hands on head. Dinh looking forward to seeing you again."

He jabbed her in the back and started pushing her toward the front door.

"Dinh, I have her," the man shouted in Vietnamese. "Open the door."

Crys cursed herself for being so stupid.

"Move," the man said, pushing his gun hard into her back. There wasn't much she could do. She took a small step forward.

"Quick. Move."

Another push.

Crys thought what Dinh might do to her and stopped. She wasn't going to make this easy.

"Move," the man screamed. He jammed his rifle into her kidneys, making her gasp with pain.

"Walk." Another brutal jab.

She heard someone running toward them. The rifle left her back in the direction of the footsteps and let off a burst. Then, even through her partial deafness from the firing, she heard a crack followed by a cry of agony.

She turned around to see the figure drop what looked like a tire lever and jerk the rifle from the man's hand and put him in a headlock. The two fell to the ground, each trying to gain an edge. The Vietnamese man was pulling desperately at the arm around his neck; the figure was clinging on for dear life.

As Crys grabbed the man's rifle, she realized who the figure was. Bongani! He must have only been slightly injured when they shot him.

She pushed the rifle into the man's side. Hard. It was payback time.

"Stop!" she shouted. "Put your hands on your head."

The man continued to struggle. She jabbed the rifle even harder.

"Stop!"

He moaned and slowly did as she'd told him.

Bongani let go of the man's neck and tried to stand up, but groaned and collapsed.

"Where are you hurt?" Crys asked not taking her eyes off the other man.

He groaned and pointed to his left shoulder.

"I have to get you out of sight of the house," she said.

She jabbed the rifle into the Vietnamese man's neck. "If you move, I'll kill you," she told him in Vietnamese.

He looked startled.

"Understand?"

He nodded.

She tried to lift Bongani to his feet, but he was too heavy.

"Bongani, grab my hand and I'll pull. Try to stand. You need to get out of here."

Keeping her eye on the man on the ground, she stuck out a hand and Bongani grasped it. Crys pulled as hard as she could as he tried to stand. Not quite enough. She had to put down the gun and pull with both hands. This time they made it, and Bongani was on his feet.

He grunted something and pointed at the house.

The Vietnamese man was running toward the front door. "Open the door," he shouted.

Quickly Crys picked up the rifle, aimed, and fired a short burst, but missed. The recoil pushed her backwards. She pulled the trigger again. Nothing happened. She tried again. Still nothing. It was out of bullets.

"Come," she said, helping Bongani away from the house to safety behind the vehicles.

"Wait there." She ran to where she thought she'd dropped her rifle. Her instincts were good, and she found it quickly. Then she returned to Bongani.

"Can you walk by yourself?"

He nodded.

She walked a few yards away to recover the .303 and handed it to him. "Take this. I think there's only one bullet left. I hope you don't have to use it. Now walk as far as you can away from the house. Then lie down. Mabula will be here soon. Hopefully he can put an end to this quickly. Now go."

As soon as he was out of sight, Crys paid attention to the house again. The man she'd had on the ground was nowhere to be seen—Dinh must have let him in.

Then the front door opened and the porch lights came on. She dropped into a crouch. First out of the door was Søren. One of Dinh's men had an arm around his neck and what looked like a handgun pointed at his head. His rifle was slung over his shoulder.

Then came Johannes. This time it was Dinh himself, holding him in the same way.

"You try anything," Dinh shouted. "We kill your friends."

Crys hadn't banked on this.

Then the third man came out dragging something heavy. Crys looked carefully—it had to be Michael. A wave of relief washed over her—they wouldn't be taking him if he was dead. The man left the body next to the vehicle and ran back inside. A few moments later, he reappeared carrying something over his shoulder.

Was it Anton? No, it wasn't big enough for him. It had to be his stash of rhino horn.

A few moments later, she heard something being dumped into the first vehicle. It sounded hard. The man ran back inside the house again, only to reappear a few seconds later, again with something over his shoulder. He dropped the bag in the vehicle.

Two large bags. That was a lot of horns. Worth millions on the street.

The man went back a third time and repeated the process.

So much for Anton telling everyone that the horns were in a bank vault in Phalaborwa. They were in the house all along. But why?

Dinh's two men picked Michael up and dumped him in the back of the undamaged vehicle with the rhino horns. She stifled a cry as she saw his slack body. Then Søren and Johannes were pushed into the back seats of the vehicle. One of the men jumped in next to them, handgun at the ready. Dinh climbed into the passenger seat and called for the third man to get in and drive. The man jumped in, started the engine, and moved off in a sharp right turn to get back on the road that took them off the farm.

In the middle of the turn, one of the back doors opened, and Søren fell out.

There were a couple of shots from the car, and Crys let off a burst, aiming high. She didn't want to hit Michael or Johannes by mistake.

Dinh sprayed a burst in her direction, but nothing came close, and a few seconds later the vehicle was out of sight.

"Søren," she shouted. "Are you all right?"

"Yes," came the choked reply. "Had the wind knocked out of me."

"Get over here."

A few moments later, Søren limped into view.

Crys pulled her phone from her pocket, turned it on and handed it to Søren. "Mabula is the last person I called. See if you can reach him. Tell him that Dinh just left here in a vehicle with the rhino horn. Johannes and Michael are hostages, and they are heavily armed. Then see if you can find Bongani. Don't worry, he's on our side. I'll explain later. He headed off in that direction." She pointed. "He's armed, so make sure you identify yourself. He was shot earlier, but I don't think it's too serious."

"What are you going to do?" Søren didn't look too happy.

"See if Anton is still alive."

Without waiting for his reply, she headed for the house, rifle at the ready, just in case.

———

When Crys reached the front door, she hesitated, then ran in, checking left and right.

Nobody.

She dashed into the living room and then took the stairs to the second floor. She moved quickly and quietly, her mind completely focused.

She heard no sound. Not knowing where Anton would be, she ran into the first room she came to. The light was on. That's where he was, lying on the floor facedown, oozing blood onto the floor from a nasty head wound. One hand was tucked under him; the other hand was missing all of its fingers. She gasped and took a small step back.

Dinh had been determined to find the horns.

She knelt next to Anton and felt for a pulse. There was a very weak one. She pulled a handkerchief from her pocket and tied it tightly around his forearm, hoping to stem the flow of blood from his hand. Then she ran out of the room to find a blanket and grabbed one from the bed next door. She came back and covered him with it. If he wasn't in shock already, he soon would be.

Crys took a quick look around and saw a desk pushed aside and an open safe behind. It was large, certainly big enough to store three bags of horns.

She sped down the stairs. Søren was on the front porch. He was still on the phone.

"Is that Mabula?" she asked.

He nodded.

"Tell him we need medical help urgently. Anton is still alive, but only just. All I can do is keep him warm and try to stop the bleeding."

Søren relayed the message, then hung up.

"He's only a few miles from here. They've set up a roadblock for Dinh, if he goes that way."

"I think there's only one way out of here, so they should be in the right place. Did you tell him they were heavily armed?"

"I did. Twice."

"Okay. Let's find Bongani and get him inside and see what we can do for him."

Crys was sure there were no other men here now, so the two of them headed off in the direction Bongani had gone.

"Bongani, where are you?" she shouted.

No reply.

"He's probably passed out, but we should be able to see him soon. The sky is getting lighter." She pointed upwards.

"Bongani, where are you?" she called again.

This time they heard a weak response. "Over here…"

They followed the sound and soon found him lying on the ground, clutching his shoulder. His shirt was drenched in blood.

They slowly headed back to the house with Søren supporting Bongani. When they reached the living room, he helped Bongani onto a sofa and made him lie down. Crys fetched a glass of water and another blanket.

"Take it easy, Bongani," she said. "A doctor is on the way."

Finally, she went for two more glasses of water, and handed one to Søren.

Crys sat down, took a deep drink, and started shaking uncontrollably.

Chapter 37

"Crys, I can hear automatic weapon fire," Søren called out. He'd gone out onto the porch.

Crys checked on Bongani and then joined him there. She also heard distant gunfire. She very much hoped it was Mabula taking down Dinh and his men and prayed that Michael was safe. And Johannes.

As if on cue, her phone rang. It was the colonel.

"Crys?" he said, surprising her by using her first name. "Are you all right?"

"Yes," she gasped. "What's happening? Have you got Michael?"

"We've stopped them at the road block," Mabula continued, "but it's a standoff. I don't want to risk Malan or Davidson. Update me on what's happening there."

"Anton Malan's in trouble. I don't think he'll last long without medical attention. Bongani Chikosi has also been shot, but is not as bad. He has a bullet in his shoulder. I think he's lost a lot of blood. Søren and I are okay."

"Are you certain that there's no threat there? That they didn't leave anyone behind?"

"Just the man I shot, but he's probably dead by now. I'm sure there's no one else."

Mabula was silent for a moment. "You shot someone? How did you do that? No, never mind, I'll find out later. There's a civilian medivac helicopter nearly there. But I can't let them land if there's any danger."

"It's fine. No danger. We've everything under control."

"Okay. I hope you're right. I'll call you back when they get there."

Crys and Søren stood on the porch and watched the dawn spread over the sky. They didn't say a word to each other. What was there to say?

About ten minutes later, they heard a chopper approaching. At the same moment, Crys's phone rang.

It was Mabula again. "Crys. All clear?"

"Yes. And there's a helicopter pad here. It's on the north side of the house."

"I'll let them know."

When she heard the chopper coming in to land, Crys realized with a shock that it'd been less than a month since she had flown in one from there into the Kruger Park. It seemed like a lifetime, so much had happened.

The chopper touched down, and two men jumped out and ran toward the house, looking from side to side. Mabula had clearly warned them to be careful.

Had they been there an hour ago, she thought, there would have been more casualties.

"Where's the injured man?" one called as they approached.

"There are two. In the house. You'll need a stretcher for one. I think the other can walk, if you help him."

They followed her into the house, and they went straight upstairs to Anton. The men gasped when they saw him.

"What happened here? Who did this to him?"

"The men Colonel Mabula is fighting right now. Is he still alive?"

"He is right now. But we need to check him."

They applied a soft tourniquet above the wrist of his mutilated hand. Then checked his neck and other limbs. "He's badly bruised, and he's lost some teeth, but I think we can move him safely," one paramedic said. "But I don't know about internal injuries. With bruising like that, it could be bad."

The other nodded. "Let's get him out of here. He needs to be in hospital."

They started strapping him onto a stretcher.

"Can you take all four of us?" Crys asked.

He shook his head. "Not more than two. You'll have to wait for the police."

She followed them as they carefully maneuvered the stretcher down the stairs, then went to look for Bongani. He wasn't in the living room, where she'd left him.

"Where's Bongani?" she asked.

"He's in the kitchen," Søren said. "He refuses to go with them."

She found Bongani slumped on the kitchen chair. They'd tried to bandage his shoulder with a torn-up sheet, but now it was dripping blood again.

"I can't go with them, Crys," he said. "They'll say I helped the attackers. And I did. I thought they were just here for the horn. That Mr. Malan would give it to them, and then they'd go. But they're not the ones who work with my people...the poachers..." He gasped, and his breath rasped. Maybe his injury was worse than she'd thought.

"I couldn't stop working for them, Crys. If I did, they'd kill my family."

"And if you die, your family will have nothing."

He shook his head. "The head man will look after them. That's the way it works."

"Bongani, you saved my life and everyone's here. We'll make a plan."

He shook his head again. "No, Crys. This is how it is. Will you please help me? I'll hide in the bush until I'm stronger."

"Don't be an idiot, Bongani. You won't survive without medical attention."

"If that is what God wills..." He collapsed forward in the chair; Crys had to grab him to prevent him from falling.

"Bring another stretcher," she screamed. "Hurry."

A few moments later the medivac men ran in. They lifted Bongani onto the stretcher and strapped him down.

"Quick," she cried. "He's been shot. It's worse than I thought..."

They hurried to the helicopter and secured the stretcher next to Anton's. They put an oxygen mask over Bongani's face. Then they put him on a drip.

"Will they live?" Crys asked.

"Not if we waste time here," the one paramedic snapped. "Let's go," he said to the pilot.

A few seconds later, they were airborne. She just had to hope they would both make it.

———

Once the helicopter left, she called Mabula.

"They're on their way to the hospital in Giyani," she said. "What's happening there?" And she held her breath, he pulse racing even though she was sitting down.

"We've pinned them down and disabled their vehicle, but we can't rush them or they'll kill Malan and Davidson. We've got one of our choppers on the way, and more vehicles. Once they get here, it'll all be over. It's light now; they won't be able to hide in the bush. We'll pick them off. I have to go. Just wait there."

As though we have any choice, she thought.

She wondered how far away Dinh's men were, and whether they might try to get back to the house. Turning to Søren, she said, "Mabula says he has them pinned down, but I think they might double back. We should keep a lookout. Take one of the rifles and watch for anyone coming from the front gate."

"But I've never fired a gun," Søren said, nervously. "And I don't think I could shoot anyone."

"If someone's going to shoot you, make sure you shoot first."

"But—"

"Just do it, dammit. I'm going upstairs. The safe is open there, and I want to take a look before the police get here. Shout if you see anything."

Crys headed back upstairs to the room where she'd found Anton and the safe. There was no money or horn left in it, just stacks of papers and documents. She knew she shouldn't be going through his personal stuff, but she was past caring. She was sure Anton was to blame for this mess, and now she wanted some answers.

She pulled out the folders and flipped through them. Accounts, letters, title documents. Nothing of interest. Then she found a diary. She flipped through it. It seemed mainly blank with a few appointments filled in. She tossed it back into the safe.

Then it occurred to her that keeping a diary in a safe was very strange—very inconvenient. Quickly she retrieved it and started looking through it more carefully. Most days were blank, but she found a couple of entries that just said "D'Oliviera." Below them were two numbers. One was around twenty, the other much higher—over a million. Crys started to understand. She smoothed her hair as she thought about weight in kilograms and money in South African rands. Anton was getting nothing like the street price of rhino horn, but it was a lot of money all the same.

She flipped to the current date. There was nothing, but as she looked back over the previous week, she discovered the biggest entry so far, with a huge question mark drawn at the side of it. The transaction hadn't taken place, but the horns had been in the safe, waiting. Somehow Dinh must have known about that.

That has to be Michael's "something big," she thought.

Søren yelled from downstairs. "It's Colonel Mabula on the phone. He wants to speak to you."

"Okay, tell him to hold on a second."

She quickly shoved everything back in the safe. Then she hurried down the stairs and took the phone.

"It's okay," Mabula said. "They scattered into the bush, but we'll find them once the helicopter arrives. We've moved their vehicle off the road, and we're on our way. Don't shoot at us!"

"What about Johannes and Michael?"

"Both are with us. Badly beaten up. I don't think either is in any danger. Malan probably has some broken bones and maybe some internal injuries, but he's walking. I don't know about Davidson. He's conscious, but very groggy. Malan says he was out for a long time. I hope it's no worse than concussion."

"Michael's tough. He'll pull through," Crys said. But it sounded like someone else saying the words. Her head swam. She felt weak with relief.

It was over.

Chapter 38

Two police vehicles arrived, and men in body armor spread out to check the house and grounds.

Trembling, Crys focused on the vehicles.

And then, there he was—Michael, staggering out of one of the vehicles.

His battered face broke into a grin when he saw Crys.

She flew to him and hugged him, tears mixing with the dirt and sweat on her face.

They held each other without saying a word. Crys felt a warmth and happiness that required no questions or answers.

At last she let him go, stepped back, and looked him over.

"I thought you were dead." She choked back a sob.

The side of his head was a mess of caked blood, and his face was so bruised and swollen that his left eye was invisible. His clothes hung on him as though they'd been bought for a much bigger man, and his skin was pale, almost gray. He was stooped and his usual glow of energy was gone. Crys was at a loss for words.

"It's so wonderful to see you…" she said at last. "Let's go inside, I'll help you get cleaned up before the medics arrive."

Next Mabula and Johannes climbed out of the vehicle, also looking the worse for wear. Mabula was exhausted and walked with a slight limp, and Johannes looked nearly as bad as Michael. His face was bruised, and he had a black eye that was badly swollen. He shuffled as he walked, half bent over, clutching his stomach—the result of Dinh's vicious kicks. All three were covered with dust and scraps of vegetation.

"We have to get a doctor for you all," Crys said, still holding Michael's arm tightly.

Mabula nodded. "It's arranged. Once the chopper has refueled it'll come back and pick up these two. We have to wait. Everything else is tied up in Kruger."

He herded them onto the porch, instructing them to stay there until he'd checked the crime scene. When his men gave the all-clear, he went into the house.

Johannes collapsed in a chair. "How's my father? Is he going to be okay?" It was painful for him to talk.

"He was alive when he left, but I'm afraid he's in bad shape," Crys replied, helping Michael sit down next to him. "He's on his way to hospital now. How did you get away from Dinh?"

"Dinh? That was his name?" Johannes paused, wincing with each breath. Crys guessed Dinh may have broken some of his ribs. "When Mabula's team started closing in, his men ran away. He yelled at them, but they paid no attention. He shoved me into a knob-thorn bush and ran off himself. I'm lucky he didn't shoot me. Bastard."

"They thought I was still unconscious," Michael said, "so they just left me in the back of the pickup." He looked at the ground. His voice was weak. "I've spent six weeks trying to talk Dinh's men out of shooting me. I made up stories about knowing this house and its security. And I told them I knew how to open the safe. That's the only reason they didn't kill me right away."

So that was the reason, Crys thought. She couldn't speak.

In fact, no one said anything for a few moments.

Then Johannes said, almost in a whisper, "He tortured my father. I hope they shoot the bastard." He leaned back and closed his eyes.

Crys had a million questions, but the two men needed to rest. She could wait.

"I was sure you were dead," she said quietly to Michael after a moment. "Even after they found your note. And when I saw you lying on the floor in there…" Her eyes burned with fresh tears.

"Could we get some water?" Michael asked. "I'm so nauseous. And dizzy." Crys filled a coffee cup from an outside tap for him. He drained it, and she filled it again.

Mabula joined them a few minutes later. A few of the Tshukudu staff had arrived, and Mabula asked for coffee, water, and cereal to be brought out. And any fruit.

"But please don't go into the living room or upstairs," he ordered.

Then he turned to the group. "Good news. They've got Dinh and one of his men. The other one tried to take out the helicopter with his AK-47, and they flattened him. Good riddance."

Mabula turned to Crys. "I also got an update from Kruger. What you deduced was correct, Crys. All three rhino-horn stores in Kruger were attacked last night. Even though our people were ready for them, there were casualties on both sides. But there was no attempt to hold tourists hostage or to harm them. In any case, all the attackers are dead—including your Portuguese friends, we think—or in custody. But it will take quite a while to sort it all out."

Crys was pleased to hear that. She could write her story now, but somehow that didn't seem important anymore.

One of the policemen came up. "I found a body lying under a tree near the chalets," he said. "He's been shot in the chest."

Mabula looked at Crys, and she nodded.

"Let's get some drinks and something to eat. Then you'd better tell me your stories," he said.

———

They went through to the dining room and settled down with coffee, fruit, and cereal, and then Johannes began the story of what had happened that night.

"My father woke me about four. He said he'd heard something downstairs and was going to the gun safe to get weapons. But then an Asian man appeared with an automatic rifle and he forced us downstairs. There were three more men in the living room. One of them was Michael"—Johannes nodded in Michael's direction— "but I didn't know who he was. I've no idea how they got past the entrance gate or into the house without waking us." He winced and took a few moments to catch his breath. "My father shouted something about Chu Nhan saying the deal was off, so why were they there. I didn't have the faintest idea what he meant, but one of the men—who seemed to be the leader—just laughed and said the delivery had been moved forward, and then, for no reason, bashed my father with his rifle. Bastard!"

"That was Dinh," Crys put in. "They're from Vietnam. He's with the government...but he obviously uses that as a cover for his other activities."

"I told him we had nothing here," Johannes went on, haltingly, "but he told me to lie on the floor facedown and shut up unless I wanted the same treatment as my father. Then he told him to open the safe." He pointed at Michael and glared at him. "God knows how you knew about it."

Crys reached under the table for Michael's hand. He grasped it.

"Your father showed me around when I was here," Michael said, "and I spotted it hidden behind the desk. I had no idea how to open it, but I had to tell them something to make them keep me alive. So, I pretended I knew the combination. I went upstairs and moved the desk and fiddled with the handle and the combination dial a bit, but of course I couldn't open it."

"So, he came downstairs," Johannes continued, "and told this Dinh character that my father must have changed the combination. The man went ballistic. I thought he'd shoot Michael on the spot, but instead he turned his AK-47 around and slammed the butt into his face. He dropped like he was a sack of mealies. I thought Dinh had probably killed him."

"I only came to when the pickup started bouncing around," Michael added, "but I just lay there. Seemed best to play dead."

Johannes picked up the story. "Just after that there was a commotion, and a fourth man came into the room with Søren at gunpoint. And Bongani was behind him, also with a gun. I was shocked. First Michael and then Bongani—both apparently working with them."

Crys then related how she and Bongani had tried to join forces, and how Bongani had been shot in the process.

"After that, the Vietnamese were nervous," Søren said. "They turned out the lights and demanded to know who was outside. I said it must be the farm's security guards, and Johannes backed me up, but Dinh didn't buy it. He threatened to shoot me if Johannes didn't tell him the truth, so Johannes told him it was just a woman reporter. Dinh laughed and said he knew her and that she wasn't going to be good security. He sent one of the men out to find her and bring her back alive. He said it would be very easy."

"That was a mistake," Crys said. Michael squeezed her hand.

Mabula smiled slightly. "It was," he said. "I could've told him that."

"Then the bastard started torturing my father," Johannes said, his eyes tearing up. "He demanded the combination of the safe. Dad kept telling him there was nothing in the house, that everything was at the bank, but he wouldn't believe it. But Dad refused to open the safe. They started hacking off his fingers, one at a time! Even when Dad said he'd open it, Dinh kept on. It was so awful. I could do nothing."

Johannes put his head in his hands and sobbed. None of them said anything. Crys stood and put her arm around his shoulders.

When he'd recovered, he took a deep breath and continued.

"Eventually they dragged him upstairs, and I guess he opened the safe."

"And he did have horn up there," Søren said.

"No doubt about that," Mabula said. "A lot of horn. Worth millions of dollars on the street. We found it in their vehicle, as well as—"

He was interrupted by his phone ringing. He answered it and listened for a few moments without speaking, and then passed the phone to Johannes. "It's the Giyani hospital. They need to talk to you."

Johannes must have known what was coming, because he struggled to his feet and shuffled into the garden, his shoulders slumped.

"Mr. Malan died in the helicopter. They didn't even manage to get him to the hospital," Mabula said quietly.

Crys sat back down and took Michael's hand again. They all remained silent.

After a couple of minutes, Johannes came back and returned the phone. "My father didn't make it." Before any of them could say anything, he continued: "I just want to be on my own for a bit. To try to understand all this." He turned away and started walking into the grounds. Crys thought Mabula would stop him, but he let him go.

"I think I know what happened after they got the horn," he said. "The details can wait." He turned to Michael. "However, it's your story I really want to hear."

Chapter 39

Michael shifted in his seat. "I don't really know where to start."

"The beginning is a good place," Mabula commented.

"Well, the beginning is *National Geographic* commissioning me to write a story on the rhino-horn trade. But the start of all this was meeting Dinh in Ho Chi Minh City. I went to ask him questions about what Vietnam was doing to meet the CITES ban on trade. He was very friendly, and told me a story about how they were trying to track the trade from South Africa through Mozambique. We got on well, and he took me out for dinner. Maybe we drank a bit—that Mekong Whiskey. It's firewater." He paused. "It was then that he persuaded me to help them, to get information on the trade route under the cover of being a journalist. I agreed. It was stupid. I didn't know him from a bar of soap. I guess I never thought I'd really accomplish anything in any case." He stopped and finished his glass of water.

"But I did," he went on. "I was lucky, and Bongani made some contacts for me. Money talks loudly in this part of the world. It started right here. Anton was selling the horn to a Portuguese gang who smuggled it into Mozambique. I followed them and documented it all—even got great pictures. Dinh's men took all that, of course. Actually, I nearly got caught at the house where the Portuguese transferred the horn. They were scanning with binoculars, but they went right past me. I was so relieved, but I ended up with something worse. It was out of the frying pan into the fire…" He sighed. "When I phoned Dinh and told him what I'd found out, he was so courteous and grateful. The next thing his men grabbed me with orders to kill me, but I managed to talk them into letting me live. For a while."

He took a deep breath and had to grab the side of his chair to prevent himself falling. "Crys, could you get me some more water?" he asked in a weak voice.

Crys went to the buffet, frowning. She'd seen Mabula's face. It was the way he looked at her when she said she didn't know about the money.

"Was Nigel Wood involved in all this?" Søren asked.

"Wood?" said Michael. "No. Why?"

Søren just shook his head.

Crys gave Michael the full glass and he drained it.

Then Mabula asked, "What about the emails?"

Michael frowned. "What emails?"

Crys borrowed Mabula's pen and pad and wrote down the email address and passed it to Michael. He looked up at her, surprised.

"The emails about the twenty thousand dollars, Michael," she said.

He shifted uncomfortably, biting his lip. "Oh, that was Dinh. It's his private email. He offered me money. I played along, but I never meant to take it…"

Mabula was still staring at Michael. "I have the other emails, Mr. Davidson," he said, his voice hard now. "The ones from your personal address. I know the whole story. And you took the ten thousand dollars paid to you in advance. I think you knew what you were doing all along."

Michael suddenly slumped down in the chair, his eyes closed. Crys jumped up and grabbed his hand. It was ice cold even though the day was already starting to warm up. "He's passed out," she said. "We have to get him out of here. You can't ask him any more questions now!"

Mabula said nothing.

After a moment, Crys asked quietly, "Did he really take the ten thousand dollars?"

Mabula nodded. Søren was shaking his head.

"He was playing along with them! It's not what it seems!" Crys exclaimed. "Can't you see that?"

But she was trying to convince herself—to deny the truth. To quell the anguish that had gripped her.

By this time Michael was coming around. He looked about, obviously disoriented.

She looked into his unfocused eyes, and it came to her what Michael's father had told her when she'd spoken to him back in the States—that he needed that money for his daughter's surgery. Much the same as Bongani had needed money. Both knew what they were doing.

Crys's heart sank. She felt as if all the strength had left her body.

Well, I found him, and he's alive, she thought. But I want something more than that.

Hiding her pain, she helped Michael into the living room to lie down on the couch.

She left him without a word and returned to Søren and Mabula.

"I'm going to give you some background," Mabula said as she sat back down. "Both of you know some of it, but maybe between us we can put it all together. For the last couple of years, I've been working on smashing a rhino-poaching ring in this part of the world—"

"Dammit, you could have told me that right at the beginning! Just think of the problems you could have avoided!" Crys was almost shouting. Why had no one been honest with her?

"I understand your anger, Crys, but look at it from my side. We've had a few successes, more failures. But we were getting closer.

We knew that the man Ho, who was on that plane that crash-landed, was a money courier for a cartel in Vietnam, bringing it in through Maputo in Mozambique. It seems customs there was paid to look the other way. Then you appeared out of nowhere, Crys, right where Ho's plane crashed. And you were also Vietnamese. What was I to think? The obvious answer was that you were involved too. Maybe a honey pot for all I knew. I had to treat you as one of them. I had no choice."

Crys looked at him in astonishment. It had never occurred to her that he'd seen her as anything but an American journalist—an obstacle between him and half a million dollars.

"Around the time the plane crash-landed," he continued, "we'd heard rumors of something major being planned with a lot of money involved. Our guess is that Ho was carrying that money. Maybe he saw an opportunity to keep it for himself, or maybe the plan was always to get rid of the pilot and so cover his tracks. We'll never know. But obviously Mr. Chikosi was supposed to meet him and drive him to a rendezvous somewhere. He was lucky about the plane crash. If he'd met Ho, he would now be as dead as the pilot."

"And what was the money for?" Søren asked.

"We think it was headed here to Tshukudu. It was payment for all that horn that's sitting in our vehicles right now."

"No!" Crys exclaimed. "You mean that Bongani was supposed to bring him here to Tshukudu with the money?"

Mabula shook his head. "I doubt that. He was supposed to get back to you at the camp. He was just a link in the chain. But once the money went missing, that must have disrupted their plans. Especially as they were organizing the big attack on Kruger at the same time. That's why I was so desperate to trace that money." He glared at her. "You didn't help much."

Crys didn't know what to say, so she kept her mouth shut.

"And it fits with what Johannes heard Anton say," Mabula continued. "That Chu Nhan said the deal was off. Chu Nhan's not his real name, but we believe it's the nickname of the boss of the cartel in Vietnam."

"So, Anton was selling horn illegally to the Vietnamese, who were smuggling it out through their usual routes," Søren said. "What made you suspect Tshukudu in the first place?"

"Just bits and pieces we picked up from informers. But we had no real evidence. We have now, but it's rather late in the day…"

"End Extinction also had information that some horn was leaking from South Africa—not poached, but smuggled from the farmers," Søren said. "We had no information pointing here specifically, but this is the biggest farm, and there were rumors it was in financial trouble. So, we had our suspicions."

Crys remembered that her bungalow had been searched after she'd asked Anton about Michael. Afterwards, she'd found Anton standing outside the house smoking and making up stories about fireflies. Now Crys thought she knew the answer. He had to know if she was who she said she was, or if she was investigating the rhino-horn smuggling in some way.

"There's a diary upstairs that I found in the safe. It documents the money Anton took from Pockface and his gang," Crys said.

"So, you went through the safe too," Mabula growled. "I'm not sure why we bother to have police at all." He couldn't keep a straight face, however.

The three of them sat in silence for a few minutes. Eventually Crys asked, "But how does Dinh fit in? And Nigel Wood?"

It was Søren who answered her. "I told you we believed that there was something very strange about Rhino International. And I've been puzzled about why Wood would go to such lengths to find out about what Chu Nhan's group was up to. I started thinking he and Dinh might be connected somehow to a smuggling mafia different from this Chu Nhan. After you and I spoke the other night, I warned Colonel Mabula that if I was right, Wood might have an ulterior motive. Obviously, he'd be happy about Chu Nhan losing men and money and face, but there was another possibility. If he somehow knew about the deal with Anton, and could get his hands on that horn, it would be a huge coup for him. Millions of dollars of horn for hardly any money." He looked around. "I must say that, after Michael's story, it doesn't seem as likely that Wood is involved. Maybe he was also duped by Dinh. As Michael was."

"Where is Wood now?" Crys asked.

"We're holding him," Mabula replied. "If he had contact with Dinh last night, and we can prove that through cell-phone records, we'll be able to arrest him. And, of course, we have Dinh. He's facing a murder charge now. I'm sure we can persuade him to cooperate. We'll find out the truth about Nigel Wood. And about Michael Davidson."

They heard another helicopter approaching.

"That's the medivac chopper back," Mabula said. "It can take Davidson and Malan. I have a transport chopper coming for the rest of us from Phalaborwa. It should be here in about an hour."

Crys just nodded, lost in her own thoughts.

She'd probably never know whether Nigel was completely aboveboard. And now she knew that Michael was willing to compromise the principles he was always so strong on, and maybe discard them altogether.

She stood up and went to the window.

How can I judge him, she thought, when I've also done things I'm not proud of?

She turned back to face the others. "What will happen to him?" she asked.

"Davidson?" Mabula said. He shrugged. "Depends. We don't really have much, and Dinh's word will be worth nothing. If he has a good lawyer and sticks to his story, maybe he goes home. Maybe he even gets to keep the ten thousand dollars. I don't think he gets to keep his reputation though."

She nodded and went to tell Michael that the medivac had arrived.

And to say goodbye.

Chapter 40

After she'd seen Michael to the helicopter, Crys needed a little time to herself to come to grips with everything that had happened during the night. The adrenalin had faded, but she could still feel the tension gripping her mind and body. Her hand was aching, and her shoulder still very paiinful. And worst of all, her head was spinning with Mabula's revelations. And with the pain of Michael's betrayal.

But was it really that? He never asked anything of her. She'd taken it upon herself to find him.

Had all this been for nothing?

No, she thought. I've helped do a lot more than simply save one man.

When she got back to her bungalow, she closed the door and spread some towels on the floor. She twisted into a half lotus and began to chant quietly.

Úm ma ni bát ni hông. Úm ma ni bát ni hông. Úm ma ni bát ni hông. Úm ma ni bát ni hông.

After a while, her heart slowed, and she felt calmer and more relaxed. She stayed in that position a little longer, emptying her head of thoughts. Eventually, she was ready to move on. She returned the towels to the bathroom and started to pack. She didn't have much.

As long as she had her laptop and her camera, she'd be okay. She'd proved that.

Crys started thinking of the future. Michael, Johannes, and Bongani—none had a smooth road ahead. Michael and Johannes would manage. However, in Bongani's case, maybe there was no road at all.

"Crys. Are you there?" It was Johannes calling from the porch. She was surprised, and went out to see him. He still looked terrible, although he was walking more easily.

"I thought they were taking you to Giyani," she said.

He shook his head. "I told them I was okay, and didn't go," he said. "I've too much to sort out here: paperwork for my father's death and arrangements for his funeral. He had a lot of friends and business acquaintances. And I've got to put the house back together and go through all his papers. He could be quite secretive. So, I wanted to say goodbye before you head off."

"You need to see a doctor, Johannes. You may have broken ribs and maybe internal injuries…"

"Some friends are coming over. One is a doctor. He can drive me to Giyani, if necessary. I don't want to be stuck there."

Crys nodded. "I understand. Johannes, I'm so sorry about your father. I think he tried to do something very special here and for the right reasons. But sometimes these things go wrong."

He nodded. "I've suspected something for a while now. He changed. He became bitter and always worried about money. And we didn't get on as well as we used to when we started out. It was a shared dream then."

"What will you do? Can you save the farm?"

"I hope so. I can sell that horn on the legal market, but I won't get much. And raise what I can from selling my father's businesses. Also, he had a lot of key-man insurance for them. He always used to joke that he was worth more dead than alive. Maybe with all that, I can pay off the debts and keep Tshukudu going for a while.

But in the longer term, if we can't sell horn for a reasonable price, I just don't know. But I'll try." He paused, and Crys saw a man who was beaten down, but full of pride and determination.

"How do you feel about your father?" she asked, putting her hand on his shoulder.

"I've always been so proud of him." He swallowed a sob. "He was very private, very proud, very stubborn. And saving the rhino was the most important thing in the world for him. Had he told me how serious his financial difficulties were…"

He stopped and took a few deep breaths. "Maybe he wouldn't have gone over to the dark side. Maybe we could have found an honorable solution."

He stood there, looking embarrassed.

"Anyway, thanks for everything, Crys. I'm sure Dinh wasn't intending to leave any of us alive. The only reason he did was that you forced him to take us as hostages."

"Bongani helped," she said. "He thought it was your father's people he allowed in last night. Without him, I couldn't have done anything."

Johannes nodded. "It was thanks to both of you."

She stepped forward and gently wrapped her arms around him. They hung onto each other for a long time, rocking slightly, rubbing each other's backs. They both needed it.

When they let go, she said, "You're a good man, Johannes. I think you'll make Tshukudu thrive."

He nodded, gave a half-smile, turned and left.

She went back into her chalet to finish her packing, her mind whirling.

Then, she spent a few minutes on the internet finding the telephone number of the hospital in Giyani. She phoned and asked about Bongani, saying she was calling for Colonel Mabula. They told her the bullet had been removed, and that he was now in intensive care, but stable.

Well, that's good news, she thought.

Crys grabbed her bag and headed for the helicopter. There was one more thing she needed to do before they left.

———

Crys found Mabula talking to the pilot. He looked cheerful. Things had worked out pretty well from his point of view. She asked to speak to him alone.

"Colonel, I think you know more about Bongani than you've let on."

He nodded. "He's been tipping off the poachers and doing errands for them. Like picking up Ho that night."

"Yes, he admitted that to me. He says he's tried to stop, but he's terrified for his family's safety. He really is between a rock and a hard place."

Mabula didn't respond.

"And he saved everyone here last night," she continued. "Without him, we'd all be dead."

"What are you suggesting?" he asked.

"If he came clean and helped you round up the rest of Chu Nhan's people here, you could forget about what he's done in the past."

Mabula nodded. "And? There's more, isn't there?"

"He can't live here anymore. He'll have to move his family away, otherwise they'll get to him somehow. He'll need help getting a job somewhere else. And he'll need money."

"I suppose that's true." He wasn't going to help her get to the point.

"That money from the plane," Crys said. "Suppose he had information that would allow you to recover it. Would there be a reward? You suggested that once."

"That was just to see if you were dishonest or stupid. You weren't either."

This time, she waited.

"Well, if we recovered that money, I could recommend a reward for him. Maybe five percent. I can't promise."

"But you *will* make something happen, right?"

He laughed. "Are they all like you in Minnesota?"

Again, she waited.

"All right. Yes, he'll get a reward."

Crys was sure he had no idea how much money was involved, but that was fine. If the reward was five percent, twenty-five thousand dollars would set up Bongani very well indeed.

"I'll include the reward in my story then."

He laughed again. "You still don't trust me!"

She took out her cell phone and found her fake phone numbers, which were actually the latitude and longitude of where the money was buried, and then shared them with his phone. "I just forwarded Bongani's information."

He glanced at his phone and nodded. "You know I could charge you with lying to the police, withholding evidence, assaulting a police officer, leaving the country without permission, and a lot more if I thought about it."

She smiled. "I suppose you could."

Crys saw Søren walking up from his chalet, and he joined them a few moments later.

"You two look pleased with yourselves," he said.

Neither of them commented. This was between the two of them.

———

With all the adrenalin drained from her system, Crys felt a void inside. Apathy had replaced energy; melancholy had pushed aside optimism.

The short flight cut over the expanse of the southern African bushveld. Crys saw little of it, her mind turned inward. She felt a pang of loss as she realized this would probably be her last look at wild Africa for a long time. But deep down, she knew she'd come back one day. She'd caught the Africa disease.

National Geographic had sent her to Africa to write about the plight of the rhinos. She arrived with a clear vision of what should be done—stop poaching and ban the trade in rhino horns. And of course she'd had her personal goal too. The thought was like a stab in her heart.

She turned her mind to how Mabula had smashed the ring of poachers and smugglers. He was pleased about it—and had a right to be—but he knew another gang would take over, another smuggling route would be opened. Rhino horn was just worth too much money. And in the short term, the price of horn would probably go up because of the temporary shortage.

Stopping poaching was like digging a hole in a swamp. No matter how hard you bailed, you just couldn't stop the water seeping back and filling the hole again. It was depressing to realize that rhinos still died, despite all the efforts of the anti-poaching teams, the conservationists, the police, and dedicated organizations like CITES.

Would people eventually become discouraged and give up, leaving rhinos completely vulnerable?

As Crys watched a herd of elephants moving away from the noise of the chopper, everything cried out that there must be a way—a way to leave the rhinos in peace, undisturbed, completely wild. But nothing she'd discovered in South Africa, or in Geneva, or in Vietnam over the last month suggested that was possible. As long as the rhinos had their horns, they'd be killed for them. So, the horns had to be removed. Should you then sell them to produce an industry to support people like Bongani's cousin? Or should you destroy every scrap of horn until you'd starved the horrible trade to death?

To that, she didn't have an answer.

And of course, there was Michael, the real reason for her trip.

She was overcome with sadness, not of the loss of what was, but of the loss of what could have been.

Her eyes stung with unshed tears. She'd had such high hopes for a future together, of shared passions, shared laughter.

And shared values.

Then he'd made a deal with the devil—a contract signed in money instead of blood. He'd insisted that he was only trying to trace the smuggling route to help stop it, but in her heart she knew that wasn't true. Even if he was going to use the money for a good reason, the deal was purely selfish, and others had been hurt. Certainly, he'd ended up paying a high price, but his soul had been exposed. And she didn't like what she saw.

For a few minutes she let herself wallow in regret, in the pain of what they could have had together.

Then she shook herself and sat up in her seat.

It was time to move on.

Below her the area's wildlife preserves spread out with their endless rolling plains of acacia trees, thorn bushes, and scrub, where the world's greatest animal kingdom thrived.

There were stories to be told.

Attack On Kruger

Crystal Nguyen, South Africa

Late Sunday night, gangs armed with assault rifles and stun grenades attacked three separate sites in South Africa's iconic Kruger National Park. Their target: Kruger's store of rhino horn.

"We were ready for them," Deputy Minister Tolo told this reporter. "We'd been tracking their plans for months. I personally coordinated the resources of the anti-poaching teams, the police, and the South African Defense Force to produce a trap that totally crushed these gangsters." When I asked him how they had discovered the timing of the attack so accurately, he said that his "sources in Ho Chi Minh City had helped them close the noose."

Rumors that the attack was carried out by Islamic terrorists were "absolute nonsense," he added. "They were nothing more than desperate, heavily armed poachers. Our guests in Kruger were never in the slightest danger. We would have evacuated the park had there been any possibility of that."

Colonel Mabula of the Giyani police near Kruger has been focusing on the rhino-poaching syndicates for several years. He was the overall coordinator of the operation. In an exclusive interview, he told me, "We did have some casualties. On the other hand, not a single attacker escaped. Five were killed and the rest are in custody facing a variety of charges including murder. Our operation was one hundred percent successful." When I asked about the long-term impact, he said: "This gang has been totally destroyed. We arrested its senior members, and the Mozambique government has promised to cooperate in closing the smuggling route through their country for good. This could turn the tide for the rhinos."

In a related development, the South African government is fighting an extradition request from Vietnam for Dinh Van Duong who has been charged with the murder of Mr. Anton Malan during an attack on the Tshukudu Game Reserve for its stock of rhino horn. Dinh is also alleged to be behind the poaching gang which held well-known *New York Times* environmental reporter Michael Davidson for nearly two months. Davidson, who was injured in the attack, has been released from hospital and will be returning home later this week.

The rhino-conservation world has expressed shock at Dinh's involvement in the illegal trade. He is an official of the Vietnamese government, representing the country at meetings of CITES and has close links with rhino-conservation NGOs. The director of Rhino International, Mr. Nigel Wood, today announced his resignation over the scandal. In a statement, he said he would use his private means to work *pro bono* for the conservation of endangered species.

Acknowledgments

We have many people to thank for their help and encouragement with this book.

We thank our agent, Jacques de Spoelberch of J de S Associates for his continued support.

We are delighted to be published by Sourcebooks through its imprint Poisoned Pen Press, and thank Barbara Peters and her team for their input and enthusiasm for our stories. We'd also like to thank Karen Sullivan and West Camel of Orenda Books, which published this novel as Dead of Night in the UK, for all their input and suggestions.

We benefited greatly from the valuable input of Steve Alessi and Steve Robinson, as well as the Minneapolis writing group— Gary Bush, Barbara Deese, and Heidi Skarie. Linda Bowles and Caro Ramsey read the completed novel and gave us important feedback that we used for this edition of the book. With all their comments, it's hard to believe that the book still has mistakes, but it probably does, and we take responsibility for any that remain.

Many people have generously given us their time to make this book as authentic as possible and to help us understand the complicated issues around rhino management, trade in horn, and poaching prevention. Michael 't Sas-Rolfes, an international expert on trade of protected species, explained the mechanics of a possible legal trade in rhino horn, and how that might affect the balance between supply and increased demand. Mario Cesare, who manages the Olifants River Game Reserve and is heavily involved with rhino protection in the region, not only gave us his perspective "from the front," but also the benefit of his broad knowledge on the subject.

Finally, we thank everyone working to preserve the rhino from extinction for their tireless efforts. Without them, the species will inevitably disappear.

About the Authors

Michael Stanley is the writing team of Michael Sears and Stanley Trollip. Both were born in South Africa and have worked in academia and business. Stanley was an educational psychologist, specializing in the application of computers to teaching and learning, and is a pilot. Michael specializes in image processing and remote sensing and teaches at the University of the Witwatersrand.

On a flying trip to Botswana, they watched a pack of hyenas hunt, kill, and devour a wildebeest, eating both flesh and bones. That gave them the premise for their first mystery, *A Carrion Death*, which introduced Detective "Kubu" Bengu of the Botswana Criminal Investigation Department. It was a finalist for five awards, including the Crime Writers Association Debut Dagger. The series has been critically acclaimed, and their third book, *Death of the Mantis*, won the Barry Award for Best Paperback Original mystery and was a finalist for an Edgar award. *Deadly Harvest* was a finalist for an International Thriller Writers" award.

Visit Michael and Stanley's website, michaelstanleybooks.com and follow them on Twitter at @detectivekubu and on Facebook at facebook.com/MichaelStanleyBooks.